Friends TO Lovers

Christi Barth

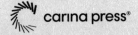
carına press®

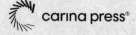

ISBN-13: 978-0-373-00263-4

Friends to Lovers

Copyright © 2013 by Christi Barth

www.ChristiBarth.com

Dear Reader,

I'm thrilled to welcome you back to the Aisle Bound series. Here's a big confession: I've written fourteen books (including five since I finished this one) and Gibson Moore in *Friends to Lovers* is *still* my favorite hero ever. He's so handsome I get a little breathless just picturing him. Drop-dead charming. Titled and with a knee-melting British accent, every woman wants to turn this serial dater into a boyfriend. Except for his best friend, Daphne, who secretly wants him but knows him too well to expect an ounce of commitment. But once they accidentally kiss, there's no going back to being just friends...

Since this is book three in the series, I'll assure you it has everything you've come to love: a handful of quirky, funny friends, reality television shenanigans, wedding hoopla and oodles of romance. Warning—this one's got a three-hanky (happy) ending!

My hope is that you'll adore book three, *Friends to Lovers*, as much as I do. I had such a good time researching the language of flowers and coming up with spectacular centerpieces for you. And don't miss not one, but two, weddings in the conclusion to the series, book four, *A Matchless Romance*. In it, a matchmaker transforms an awkward nerd into a sexy stud and is sorely tempted to keep him for herself! But first, enjoy *Friends to Lovers*. And if you do, please let me know at christibarth.com—I'd love to hear from you!

Christi

For my husband, who started out as just a friend,
and then transformed into so much more.

Acknowledgments

Hugs to the MRW Scribblers for their invaluable help. Don't forget to notice that Gib's slippers made it to publication!

Gratitude to my beta readers: Eliza Knight, Lea Nolan, Joya Fields and Stephanie Dray, who heroically carved out the time to read this during the holidays. And thanks to my wonderful editor Angela James. She not only squelched my addiction to similes, but helped me turn this from a two-tissue ending to a pass-the-whole-box ending!

ONE

*In the hope of reaching the moon men fail to see
the flowers that blossom at their feet*
                                ~ *Albert Schweitzer*

DAPHNE LOVELL LOATHED working on New Year's Eve.
Other days certainly vied for a spot near the top of her
craptastic workday list. The day after a bout of food poisoning. Birthdays (which everyone ought to get off as
a personal, government-sanctioned holiday). Any day
when the coffeemaker malfunctioned. As a wedding
florist, she worked most holidays. Just gritted her teeth
and focused on the hefty surcharge they levied on all
Aisle Bound clients who scheduled events on holidays.

But New Year's Eve trumped them all. Most of the
time she could handle standing on the edges of a wedding, watching everyone party like crazy around her.
Party jealousy never bit her in the ass, because she
rarely knew any of the wedding guests. Far better to
collect her vases, head home and stretch out on the
couch with a pint of chocolate peanut butter ice cream.

Except that the whole world—literally—partied on
New Year's Eve. Working this night felt like a punish-
ment. Like Fate had grounded her for bad behavior.
Daphne believed there was something magical about

midnight on New Year's Eve. Her father always said you should start the year the way you meant to continue. So most people did it right. Eating fabulous party food, drinking like crazy, spending the entire night with their favorite people and then kissing a loved one at the stroke of midnight.

Tonight Daphne was managing two out of four and last time she checked, fifty percent wasn't considered a passing grade. She looked around the crowded ballroom of the Cavendish Grand hotel at the drinking, laughing, thoroughly happy people and bit her lip to keep it from unfurling into a full-on pout. The DJ pounded a fun dance beat that had half the guests on their feet, and the delicious scent of spicy food hung in the air.

Her best friend and business partner, Ivy Rhodes, swished up next to her in a silver taffeta dress with a cap-sleeved lace jacket. "I can't thank you enough for working this wedding with me."

Daphne shrugged, making the ruffles on her gauzy white shirt flutter. "It didn't feel right to ruin anyone else's New Year's Eve. We own Aisle Bound, so we should have to do the dirty work. And to be clear, this does qualify as dirty work. You owe me for this one. Big. You know how epically big the final battle scene was in *Return of the King?* Think twice as big."

"What if I promise you don't have to dance with my handsy cousin Lewis at my wedding?"

"Please—that's a given. You love me too much to subject me to him. I'm going to have to mull the possibilities for a while." Daphne drummed her fingers along her cheek. "There is a good chance it will involve you letting me choose all your songs the next time we do karaoke." Ooh, that was good. Ivy loved to watch karaoke. She hated to sing, and did a side-splittingly bad job when shoved in front of a mic. Just worrying about the possibility would keep Ivy on edge for weeks.

Ivy wrinkled her nose, then laughed. "I get it. Trust me, I knew before I begged you to help that there'd be a price to pay. But because this is a traditional Filipino wedding, there are just too many people for me to handle by myself."

No kidding. The elegant, gray, silk-covered walls of the ballroom were bursting at the seams with hundreds of guests. "I wanted to ask you about that. Why the heck are there forty-five people in the wedding party? That's bigger than the last three royal weddings put together. I just about crippled myself wiring the boutonnieres for this one." She flexed her hand, remembering the claw shape it had cramped into by day two of prep.

"In addition to the usual bridesmaids and grooms-men, there are principal sponsors, coin sponsors, veil sponsors, candle—"

Daphne cut her off with a flick of the wrist. "You've lost me already. I take it back. I don't want to know. Esoteric details like that are why *you're* the wedding planner and *I'm* not."

"True. But I am officially grateful you're spending your New Year's Eve here with me. And it isn't so dire. Look at how sweet Gib was to throw us a party."

Gibson Moore was far from sweet. Polished, elegant, refined and swoon-worthily sexy, yes. A wicked lust-'em-and-leave-'em ladies' man. He snared them without even trying. The combination of his upper-crust British accent, wavy brown hair and eyes the color of a tropical sea pulled women to him with the strength of a tractor beam. Gib lived in the moment, and when that moment was gone, so was whatever woman had been lucky enough to share a few hours, or at most, a few days with him.

Because he happened to be one of her closest friends, Daphne saw past the womanizing exterior. She saw a man who embraced life. Unfortunately, no matter how many times she fantasized about him, that carpe diem spirit of his never led Gib to embrace her. Not as anything more than a fellow soccer fan, someone to drink beer with and laugh at cheesy action movies. Certainly not as a woman. Which frustrated her to no end.

"Gib didn't throw us a party," Daphne clarified. "Don't make him out to be all selfless. As hotel manager, he's stuck overseeing this shindig well into the new year. I wouldn't call opening up a conference room for us to hang out in as throwing a party."

More likely he recognized he wouldn't be able to go to a party, so he brought the party to him. With Ivy and Daphne here already, it was easy for him to lure Ivy's fiancé, Ben, into kicking back in front of a plasma screen with an unlimited supply of beer. As producer for a reality television series, Ben traveled so much that he jumped at any opportunity to spend time with Ivy. Even if that time turned out to be in ten-minute increments once every hour.

"He did stock it with appetizers. You know how much you love those Brie puffs."

True. Daphne couldn't cram the oozy, creamy nuggets of deliciousness into her mouth fast enough. The chef at the Cavendish used to work at the White House. Daphne could hardly wait for her next chance to nip into their room and try whatever fresh delicacies he'd made for them. So far she'd also sampled crab claws, caviar-topped deviled eggs, two kinds of pâté and cherry peppers stuffed with prosciutto and provolone. "I appreciate the snacks. I definitely appreciate them being there for me a mere ten steps away from this wedding."

Ivy waggled her finger. Light from the multitiered crystal chandeliers ricocheted off the two-carat sparkler Ben had placed there to warn off all other men. "Plus, Gib has champagne for us to toast with at midnight."

Great. Ivy and Ben would be wrapped around each other tighter than moss on stone. Their friend Sam had promised to stop by for the big toast. He'd spent all day moving his fiancée, Mira, out of Daphne's apartment and into his. So the two of them would be all lovey-dovey and in a lip-lock that lasted longer than it would take Daphne to drain her glass, refill it and guzzle another. All the while wondering why she didn't have anyone to kiss at midnight. Gib would undoubtedly have a lineup of at least five beautiful and eager contenders from tonight's wedding. Heck, he'd probably find a way to kiss all five of them in the time it took the twinkly ball to drop in Times Square.

With a swift inhale, Daphne pulled herself out of her pity party. Forced herself to look around the room a second time. Smiling, happy people in snazzy suits and colorful dresses surrounded them on all sides. The

DJ spun toe-tapping music. Her centerpieces of lemon and peach roses mixed with two-toned orange-and-red lilies perfumed the air. Someone got hugged about every eight seconds under the glittering crystal chandeliers. How many people could say that about their working conditions?

"You're right. I'm glad the six of us found a way to start the new year together. That's what counts, right? We all work with people we adore and respect. I get to spend my days playing with flowers, and even manage to get paid for it. We're in pretty good shape, overall."

The bride and groom swirled by in an impromptu waltz. They both grinned from ear to ear and waved at the women. "Benjie and Diwata look so happy."

"They'd better. We're throwing them one hell of a party." Ivy checked her watch, then checked the official itinerary for the night. When Aisle Bound planned a wedding, everything ran like clockwork. No matter what, thanks to the perfectionist/slightly anal retentive streak deeply ingrained in her friend. To forestall any raised eyebrows (like the time a few years ago when she'd lingered in the bathroom a whopping thirty seconds past the scheduled first toast), Daphne had made a point of synchronizing her watch with Ivy's. And remembered the shrieking chaos of the bouquet toss was scheduled to happen in ten minutes.

"I noticed. It's crazy loud in here."

"There are a ton of Filipino superstitions about New Year's Eve. We incorporated most of them. For example, they make as much noise as possible to scare away evil spirits. That's why they keep banging on the gong." Ivy pointed to the bowls of shiny purple grapes on every table. "You're supposed to have a grape in your mouth at the stroke of midnight."

"Doesn't that make it hard to kiss?"

"Smart-aleck." A vertical worry line creased Ivy's brows and she stared into the distance as she pondered. "You've got a point. I didn't check to see if a kiss at midnight is part of Filipino custom."

"Don't beat yourself up. Nobody expects you to orchestrate or skip a kiss. Kissing is organic. It either happens or doesn't."

"Are you trying to make me feel worse? You know nothing at one of my weddings is organic. Every moment, every eventuality is ruthlessly planned in order to appear natural and fun."

Daphne patted the bulge in the hip pocket of her satiny black pants, a bulge created by Ivy's three-page, detailed itinerary for tonight's event. "I'm well aware."

Ivy set off in the direction of the cake table. "See the tablecloths?"

Trying not to wince from her already-aching feet, Daphne followed. "How could I not?" Tangerine polka dots practically leaped off the white tablecloths.

"Anything round signifies prosperity. That's why the bridesmaid dresses are covered in polka dots, too." Ivy picked up the toss bouquet, a miniature of the giant calla lily and rose version the bride had carried down the aisle.

"Thanks for the trivia. I'll file it under *things I might need to know if Ivy gets hit by a bus the day before our next Filipino New Year's Eve wedding.* However, right now the only round thing that interests me is popping another crab puff. Are you ready for the next set of tag-team breaks?"

"It's a hell of a wedding, ladies." Gibson Moore, the handsomest man in the room, threw an arm around each of them. "Why on earth would you want to take a break from all this merriment?"

The scent of cypress, cedar and vetiver (and a few other things she couldn't remember) tantalized her nostrils. As though on a zip line, it went straight from her olfactory nerve down to the place between her legs that tingled every time she smelled Gib and his damn enticing cologne. She'd asked him a few years ago what it was, and just what the heck was in it. Had to be some magical concoction of pheromones a mad scientist whipped up to drive women into a frenzy. After making a fool of herself at a department store, insisting on reading the ingredients and sniffing five different bottles, Daphne gave up. He wore the same cologne every day. It always engendered the same Pavlovian reaction—an urge to lick him up one side and down the other. But the cologne itself wasn't special. Only when it met Gib's skin did it weaken her knees. Not that she'd ever let him know.

"Great wedding, isn't it?" Ivy beamed with pride. No matter how many weddings she planned at Aisle Bound, each one was her favorite on that special day. After almost seven years in the business, she still teared up every time she sent a bride down the aisle with a final fluff.

"You outdid yourself. Both of you," he said, giving Daphne a quick squeeze at her waist. The heat of his hand burned through her thin blouse. Maybe he hadn't actually seared a handprint into her skin. But tonight, alone in bed, when she looked down at her stomach, she'd see the spot he touched. She'd know. "The flowers are spectacular, as usual."

As usual. The business side of Daphne's brain knew it to be a compliment. But the emotional swamp of her heart didn't agree. *As usual*, Gib had a way of raising her hackles almost as fast as he spiked her libido. Newspapers got delivered, as usual. Every July here in Chicago was humid as hell, as usual. Her centerpieces, however, were artistic masterpieces. Each one the result of weeks of planning, sketching, tweaking, ordering and painstaking arranging. Absolutely nothing usual about them. Gib made it sound as simple as filling an ice cube tray with that offhand compliment.

"Somebody's got to do the grunt work." She steeled herself before sneaking a peek at him. Yup. James Bond suave, Gib wore a tuxedo as though born in it. He'd gelled his hair into a Superman swoop in the front. Hard to tell if she'd rather stroke her fingers through that, or through the light mat of hair she'd seen on his chest the last time they all went sailing together on Lake Michigan. Lighting cast shadows beneath his high cheekbones. It just made her focus more on those kissable lips. Maybe kept her from glancing at the way the jacket hung off his lean frame. Kept her from wondering if he'd take it off at some point in the night so she could stare at his squeezably tight ass. Then Daphne realized she'd been so busy ogling him—really, the man was a vortex, a black hole of gorgeousness that sucked her mind right out—she'd forgotten to finish her pointed rant. Which she'd scale back to a teasing Gibe. Because that was what best friends did. They teased and poked each other. Just not the kind of sexy poking at each other that she craved.

"Seems like the only contribution you made, Gib, was to unlock the front door. Nice going on that, by the way. Oh, but wait—the Cavendish has a doorman. Well, way to go on signing the contract for this shindig without getting a paper cut."

"Thanks for the compliment. I pride myself on how little actual work I do here. A good manager delegates, you see, and I'm very, very good." His voice dropped to a caress on the last three words. She'd pulled the sides of her long blond hair into a barrette to keep it out of the way. What should've been a simple hairstyle choice turned into a gigantic mistake. Leaning in, his final breath tickled the side of her exposed neck. It set off a chain reaction of shivers from head to toe.

Daphne gulped. "I guess we should be honored you chose to go vertical for the night and join us. Must be a big sacrifice, getting out of that comfy leather chair in your office."

"You couldn't keep me away. All the pretty women are down here. A wedding this big is like chumming the water for a shark." He bared his perfect teeth in a menacing grin.

Ivy pinched her lips together. She always hated it when they bickered. Daphne couldn't get her to understand that volleying the snark back and forth was a game to them. One they both enjoyed tremendously.

"Remember, there are clients present," Ivy hissed. "Best behavior. Save the sniping for our party room. Or someplace more appropriate, like a cage match."

"No worries. I just popped by to check on you. Be sure everything was running like clockwork. As usual," he said, raising one eyebrow at Daphne in an *I'm pushing your buttons and what are you going to do about it* way.

"Since you're here, we could use your help." Ivy checked her watch for possibly the five hundredth time tonight.

"We could?" No. What Daphne needed was for Gib to disappear for half an hour while she recovered from the whole neck-chill thing. It would probably take at least that long for her heart rate to drop back into double digits.

"It's time for the bouquet toss. I'll be with Diwata. You two need to herd the single ladies toward the center of the dance floor."

Gib rubbed his hands together with the untempered glee of Scrooge McDuck contemplating a pile of gold doubloons. "My pleasure. Nice of you to put all the available eye candy together for me. As a man, I appreciate one-stop shopping."

Daphne reminded herself that the inner Gib was far different from the playboy exterior he so meticulously maintained. The real Gib rarely worked less than a sixty-hour week. Loyal beyond measure to his friends, he also bent over backward to help his staff with any personal crises. He did play fast and loose with women, but exercised great caution doing so at any Cavendish events. Daphne reminded herself of these things to keep from kneeing him in the 'nads when he made such idiotic comments.

"Go on. Take care of the bride. We'll do the rest." She shooed Ivy away. The DJ, a friend who'd worked with Aisle Bound enough to know Ivy's predilection for timeliness, made the announcement at almost the same moment. Good. No time alone with Gib. Laughing, shrieking girls launched themselves onto the dance floor. Right on the edge, Daphne and Gib were caught up in it, unable to do more than be pushed into the center.

"God, it's like a rugby scrum," Gib shouted.

"Except that I imagine girls smell much better."

"You forget, I went to a private boarding school deep in the English countryside. The only things we smelled of were old money and dry rot." That broke the snarling tension between them, and they both laughed.

See? Gib was funny. So much fun to hang with, and tease. Why couldn't they just be good friends? Why did she have this stupid crush, as impossible to remove as her own shadow? Life would be so much easier if she wasn't always on guard, always braced against the onslaught of his charm and good looks. If only her hormones didn't go into overdrive every time their thighs brushed when they sat on a couch. If she didn't discard men faster than a losing hand at a poker table because none of them were Gibson Moore.

She reached for him, almost caught the crisp edge of his French cuff to pull him out of the throng. Then all the lights went off. Oddly enough, the noise stopped, too. As if everyone held their breath, waiting to see what would happen next. Having studied the schedule, Daphne knew the lights shouldn't be off. No weather to speak of outside, unless you wanted to cuss a blue streak at the temperature hovering right above zero. Something had probably gone wrong at the breaker box. Any minute now a waiter would backtrack through the darkness into the bowels of the building to get a message to a custodian. Meanwhile, other waiters would break out emergency light sticks and pass them out to the guests. The glowing green-and-purple tubes would only add to the festive mood.

The professional part of Daphne knew all this. Aisle Bound planned for every eventuality, and had contingency upon contingency in place. She also knew she had at least two solid minutes of pure blackout. Two minutes, in the dark, with Gibson Moore. This could be her only shot. Who needed the magic of midnight? She'd steal her New Year's kiss right now.

Daphne pushed her way closer as her hand moved up his arm. Light wasn't necessary. She'd stared at Gib for endless hours, memorizing the contours of his face, the shape of his body. Once everything lined up, she framed his face in her palms. On tiptoe, she closed her eyes. And dove in.

The first brush of her lips against his was light, questioning. Oh so soft. Timid. As if with the mere touch, she'd open her eyes to discover it was all a dream. But why waste the moment with hesitancy? He feathered back a kiss, as delicate as the breath he'd blown on her neck earlier. It was all the green light she needed.

To brace herself, she slid her hands down, digging her fingers around his broad shoulders. Daphne slid her tongue along the crease of his lips. They opened, eagerly, she'd like to think. Gib's hands came up, fingers thrusting into her hair, thumbs caressing her cheeks. She'd begun the kiss, but he owned it. He learned the shape of her mouth, tasting, then plundering the inside. Each sweep of his tongue pushed a sweep of warmth deeper into her body. Every nip, every deep, wet incursion that stood every nerve ending in her mouth up at attention led her to surge closer. To press against his rock-hard muscles, and something even harder which pressed back against her stomach in obvious appreciation.

Bodies still crowded around them. A buzz of worry spread through the room. Daphne focused solely on the sound of a low moan rumbling in Gib's throat. At twenty-nine, she didn't dispute she'd not only had sex before, but had her fair share of great sex before. But she'd never been turned inside out into a puddle of sensation with only a kiss. Lost herself to the intricate mating of two mouths, joining. Stirring and pulling sensations from all her senses to create a giant pool of hot, raw lust.

Without conscious thought, Daphne lifted her right leg to wrap around his calf, twining them closer. God, she wanted to cover him like a vine, leaving no inch untouched. And then, she knew without a doubt, Gib would make her unfurl like a blossom opening to the brilliance of the sun. She would open to his heat and—

"Ladies and gentlemen, please stay where you are. Cavendish staff members will bring out emergency lights momentarily while they work to resolve the problem." The DJ's calm announcement quieted the crowd. His microphone and sound system were working. Hotel power must be on, which meant some idiot had managed to hit the kill switch for the entire light panel. They'd come back on any second. With a last, lingering pull on his lower lip, Daphne disentangled herself from Gib. And nearly keeled right over. Thank goodness for the crush of women around her, jostling forward and holding her up.

Being on the receiving end of a kiss by Gibson Moore was a powerful thing, indeed. The end result? Not much different from running a marathon (or so she imagined, because really, she saw no reason to run that many miles. Unless she was being chased by pitchfork-wielding villagers, or to nab the last doughnut in a fifty-mile radius.). Knees buckled, heart both racing and palpitating, breathing heavily, Daphne could barely think for the sheer joy of it.

In a harsh barrage, every bank of lights came back on at once. Blinking, Daphne locked her gaze on to Gib. Mouth open, eyes glazed, he looked as dazed as she felt. Not bad. She'd happily take credit for rocking his world. Gib spun in a circle, arms outstretched. Then, in a move completely out of his fastidious character, he spiked his fingers through his hair. He tugged at it manically while he spun around again the other way, head swiveling back and forth. Finally, he spotted Daphne. A smile burst across his face. Brusquely, with the barest minimum of civility, he pushed aside the two women between them.

"Daphne, oh my God. It was wonderful. No, she was

wonderful. Simply enchanting. The best kiss I've ever had." His blue eyes burned, slightly unfocused and wild. "You've got to help me find her."

The compliments were nice. A huge relief, actually. Thank goodness the earth had moved for him, too. Finally, after all these years, now he'd see her as more than a pal. Now Daphne could safely admit her true feelings, how much she adored him. As soon as Gib stopped swiveling his head like an owl, frantically sweeping the room with that blue-flame stare of his. "Who are you looking for?"

"The woman who just kissed me. I swear, if it takes kissing every woman in this room, including the bride's ninety-year-old grandmother, I will. I've got to find her." Gib dug his fingers into her arm. "You were next to me, right? Did you see who it was? Will you help me find her?"

Her heart dropped, shattering into a million pieces. Crap. In Gib's mind, it was more likely that a ninety-year-old seated clear across the room kissed him into oblivion, than one of his closest friends standing right next to him? She'd just kissed him inside freaking out, and he still couldn't imagine for a single instant that *she* might've been the one to do it? Couldn't think of her as anything more than a sister? Forget making the short list. He hadn't even bothered to put her on the list of possible kissers?

Daphne wanted to scream. Well, she really wanted to grab him by the collar and kiss him again. This time with his eyes open, so there'd be no doubt who had stirred him up. Then pour a pitcher of ice cubes down his pants for insulting her. For not including her. For not thinking she was woman enough.

Yup, working on New Year's Eve sucked. And that naked, fat-ass Cupid would probably still be laughing at the epic backfire of her stupid, reckless stunt in six weeks on Valentine's Day. Daphne glanced at her watch. In half an hour, she'd face down midnight alone, not kissing anyone, and feeling less desirable, twice as foolish and more alone than when the night started. Happy New Year? Not even close.

TWO

All the flowers of all the tomorrows are in the seeds of today

~ *Indian proverb*

NOSE BURIED DEEP in the bag of cinnamon hazelnut coffee beans, Daphne inhaled. Usually the sweet, rich scent perked her up with a single whiff. Or at least enough to fill the carafe with water and jab at the on button. Not today, though. Not on freaking New Year's Day—the day when you were supposed to do everything the way you wanted it to go the rest of the year. The trouble with working until the ass crack of night was that morning still came, just as early as ever. Lack of sleep, even a desperate need for sleep, never postponed the unrelenting dawn. Guess this meant three hundred and sixty-five days of unrelenting exhaustion lay ahead of her. Or that coffee's magical rejuvenating powers wouldn't have an effect on her this year. Woo hoo.

Going back to bed wasn't an option. Her guests could knock at her apartment door any second. Using the microwave as a makeshift mirror, Daphne contemplated her reflection. She'd twirled her hair into a messy top-knot to keep it out of the way. Two layers of concealer didn't begin to disguise the dark circles under her eyes, big enough to deserve their own zip code. On the plus side, hitting the after-Christmas sales had netted her the snazzy, deep apricot warm-up suit. Paired with a push-up bra with the jacket zipped to just below her breasts, it showed off her assets in a way guaranteed to jump-start a man faster than a triple shot of espresso. The fuzzy Tigger slippers that completed her ensemble? Well, they *were* orange. Not sexy, but they matched, and more importantly, put a smile on her face with every step.

To heck with Gibson Moore. If he couldn't see her as a viable possibility for last night's kiss of the century, well…the lips reflected in the microwave door pushed down and out into a pout. Who was she kidding? Putting herself on display for Ben and Sam to politely ogle this morning wouldn't change anything. Their friendly, respectful appreciation wouldn't take the blinders off his eyes.

Sure, it'd put a bandage on her bruised ego. But when she finally ripped off that bandage, Daphne would still be the woman who'd tossed and turned all night. Who couldn't sleep a wink after participating in the best kiss of her life. Okay, maybe the element of reckless naughtiness amped it up a little, but Daphne knew most of the credit belonged to Gib. For years, she'd secretly imagined how epically wonderful a kisser Gib would be. This was one case of ignorance truly being bliss. Because now that she'd experienced firsthand the leading edge of his bedroom talent—well—he'd laid on her the kind of kiss that ruined a girl for anyone else. Ever. When your dreams simultaneously came true and went horribly askew, what could be next?

Ben burst through the front door without bothering to knock. "Is there coffee?" He brushed back his sexily-too-long blond hair. In jeans and a Cubs sweatshirt Sam had given him for Christmas, he looked as grouchy as a bear awakened halfway through hibernating season. "Because Ivy only dragged me out of bed with the understanding there would be vats of coffee here. And something to hop me up on sugar, too."

Ivy bit her lip. "Sorry. Lack of sleep apparently wipes out all of Ben's memory where manners are stored." Still, she ran a loving hand over his back. "I don't live here anymore, remember? You can't still barge in without knocking. What if Daphne was in here, strutting around half-naked with a guy?"

"You really think mentioning the possibility of seeing a gorgeous girl half-naked is an incentive to *start* knocking?" Ben lurched forward to swing Daphne in a circle, ending with a dip that had her bent backward over his leg. "What man wouldn't want to catch a glimpse of this knockout pulling a Lady Godiva impersonation? After all, what's a little nudity between friends?"

Daphne clutched tightly at his neck. Ben sported impressive biceps from his years spent hauling around video cameras. Still, she did have an unholy addiction to sweets that might push him past his limit. Flattening her ass by landing on it didn't sound like any fun. "Please. You're so besotted with Ivy, you wouldn't notice if I stripped naked and did a hula dance with flaming batons in both hands."

On the heels of her teasing words, the rest of her friends tumbled through the open door. They promptly stopped at the sight of Daphne in Ben's arms. To cap it off, his movement was enough to loose her hair from its topknot. It swung down to brush the floor. Daphne's eyes skittered to Gib. He wore, what was for him, supremely casual attire of a cashmere sweater over an oxford shirt, slacks and a thoroughly bemused expression.

"Maybe I misunderstood the American take on this holiday. I thought that last night was supposed to be the debauched party. Free rein to drink to excess, grope at will and kiss anyone at the stroke of midnight? But then New Year's Day was merely about recovery and football. Did I get the order wrong?"

Five seconds in the door and he'd mentioned kissing already. How was she supposed to not think about those sensational seconds of lip-lock if he kept bringing it up? And it would've been nice for an iota of jealousy to darken his eyes at seeing her in Ben's arms. So what if that would've only happened on the unlikely chance he'd had a revelation that Daphne was his mystery kisser? It was unlikely, not impossible. A girl could dream, right? Or was she just steeping herself deeper in misery by continuing to hope?

Ben popped her back to vertical. "Nah, you can still keep your green card. You got it right. But it does sort of make me wonder how you Brits celebrate."

"Mostly the same, although we do open the door at the stroke of midnight to let the old year out. And don't think you can distract me from the burning question of why you and Daphne were embracing. I think this is a story we'd all like to hear."

"Question for the men." He beckoned Sam and Gib

forward with a crook of his finger. "All things being equal, if you knew you had a shot at catching Daphne without any clothes on, would that make you more or less inclined to knock before entering?"

Sam ran a hand through his thick, dark hair with a sheepish look back at his fiancée. Mira laughed. Uncrossing her arms from the front of her blue cashmere sweater, she gestured for him to go ahead. "I can't wait to hear your answer."

"As a card-carrying, red-blooded man, I appreciate any chance to observe a beautiful woman. Especially when naked. And every woman in this apartment is beautiful."

Gib clapped slowly, with overly big waves of his arms. "Oh, well done. You skirted the minefield and dropped a compliment. Have you been going to charm school in your spare time, Sam?"

"Just inspired, I guess." He shot Mira a look so drenched in love that it took Daphne's breath away. The hollow feeling left behind in her diaphragm reminded her of the brunch items cooling by the minute on the counter.

"Grab a seat anywhere," she ordered. Was it silly and schoolgirlish to hope that there'd be room for her to sit down next to Gib? Stupid. Their kiss hadn't changed anything. He'd made that very clear. She'd grab a pillow and sit on the floor. And be happy about it, damn it. "There's coffee and hot cocoa, both spiked and non, since most of us were too busy working last night to get our drink on."

Ben licked his lips. "I'm a big fan of cocoa, and the

peppermint schnapps is inspired. But Ivy mentioned there was more to this than just a recovery breakfast?"

Oh, yes. The memory was like a cloud darkening her normally sunny heart. Daphne shifted from one foot to the other. She hated being the focus of attention, even amid friends. Caught an encouraging smile from Ivy and launched forward with the recitation that never grew less painful, no matter how many times she gave it.

"Let me catch the new people up to speed. In exactly fifteen minutes, the Rose Parade will start."

Mira wrinkled her brow, thought for a moment. "Floats, flowers and marching bands, right?"

Plucking the drawstring at her waist, Daphne nodded. No matter how many years passed, this story would never be an easy one to tell. "That's the one. My mother adored flowers, and helped decorate the floats when she was in high school. It was always a crazy week, sticking petals and seeds on for twelve hours a day or more. But she said it was a week spent in heaven, because she ate, breathed and slept flowers. So once she moved out here to go to Northwestern, she still watched the parade every year."

"You can take the girl out of California, but not the California out of the girl," mused Gib. He tossed his parka onto the growing pile on the coat tree.

"Exactly." She smiled, remembering her mother diligently squirting lemon juice over her blond hair on May 1, no matter how cold, and sitting in the sun to "rinse out winter." "But not everyone in the Midwest thought it was as big a deal. So to talk my dad into three hours of watching flowers roll by at five miles an hour, she always bribed him with a big brunch."

"With the legendary cranberry cinnamon rolls." Gib patted his stomach and sighed. Daphne tried not to wonder if he made that same sigh when being licked like a man-sicle. "I swear, no disrespect, mate, but they're better than the ones at Lyons."

Sam feinted a right hook. "I'd punch you in the arm for that insult, if it wasn't so true. Ben, I know you've got a dedicated sweet tooth. These cinnamon rolls will make your eyes roll back in your head."

"It grew into a big family tradition. All four of my brothers would sit, trying to pretend they weren't spellbound, as long as they could shovel more rolls in their mouths. And when she died—" Her voice caught, just for a second. Years had passed, but the pain somehow could still spike as fresh as the day it happened.

Ivy put an arm around her waist, then leaned her head over to rest on Daphne's. "Do you need a tissue?"

"Tissues only treat the symptom. A shot of vodka, now that would cure the problem," Ben suggested with a nod of sage wisdom.

Daphne sniffed. No crying allowed. This was supposed to be a happy morning. Bad enough she'd moistened her pillow over Gib already today. "It wasn't my idea, that first year. Dad disappeared into the kitchen on New Year's Eve. After about an hour he came out and begged me to help. Tears in his eyes, covered in flour from head to toe. He'd wanted to surprise all of us with the rolls, as a way to keep the memory of Mom with us. Cooking wasn't really his strong suit, though.

We'd been living on takeout and spaghetti in the four months since she'd died."

She and her brothers had ranged in age from twelve to eighteen. None of them had believed they'd miss having Mom insist on a salad with their meat loaf, or get tired of eating burgers and fries. But even teenagers had limits. The older boys started eating at their girlfriends' houses most nights, and the family van slowly grew a carpet of wrappers and unused ketchup packets.

"Dad remembered that I'd always helped Mom roll them out the night before, and hoped I could figure out where he'd gone wrong. I've made them every year since. And it did help. We cried a bit that first year—all of us—but as the years went by, even after my brothers went off to college, they made sure to be home to watch the parade. It's harder now that they have families. Dad started spending New Year's in Minneapolis with Nick and his first set of grandbabies. So I keep the tradition going, with my extended family—all of you."

Dampness sparkled in Mira's eyes. "Well, that's a thoroughly beautiful story. I think I'm too choked up to be able to swallow."

"Then you're missing out. Dry up the waterworks by the time the parade starts, or I'm eating your share," Gib threatened.

His lighthearted tone erased Daphne's own melancholy. "Don't worry. I expanded the menu a bit this year. Nobody's going hungry." She carried the last tray over from the kitchen counter to the oval coffee table.

"There's an egg and ham casserole, brown-sugar bacon, sausages, fruit salad with a lime and yogurt sauce, ginger-carrot muffins, and, of course, the famous cranberry cinnamon rolls. Oh, and a pitcher of Bloody Marys, along with the coffee and hot chocolate."

After gaping at her for a second, Gib bowed with a dramatic flourish. "You are a kitchen goddess."

Daphne wanted to stomp her foot at the nice compliment. She'd far prefer to hold out for a compliment on her bedroom skills. Would rather make him drool with lust than with actual hunger.

Ben hustled into the living room to peruse the heaping platters. Sam followed him like a hound dog flushing prey. "Yeah, this is a fantastic spread. You really hit it out of the park this time, Daph."

Ivy, on the other hand, didn't budge. Instead, she fisted her hands on her hips and scowled. Her stern demeanor was at odds with the festive look of her pink-and-white polka-dot sweater topping fuchsia skinny jeans. "What's wrong?"

"Nothing."

"Most of the time you subsist on pizza and pb&js. Trust me, I paid close attention while I was your roommate. Your indomitable metabolism freaks me out and infuriates me."

Mira nodded. "Every time you eat cookies all day long and not gain a pound? It's like you're giving women everywhere the middle finger. So not fair."

Ivy held her ground. "You only cook this much when you're stressed out. There's enough food here for at least a dozen people. Come on, you know I'm just going to pester you until you tell me."

Nope. No reason to share last night's humiliation

with her friends. Their sympathy would only get her all churned up again. Daphne needed to *not* think about Gib and his lips. They were friends. Best friends. As close as siblings. And it was eight kinds of ooky to think about craving the lips of an almost-brother. Or so she kept telling herself. "Pester away. But you'll waste your breath. I'm fine. We're a bigger crowd this year now that Ben and Mira are part of our circle. Just thought I'd throw a real brunch like a grown-up. You know, start the year off right."

"Uh-huh." Clearly unconvinced, Ivy gave her the stink eye for another moment, then moved into the living room.

Interrogation averted, Daphne grabbed her mug of minty cocoa. She posed in front of the holly-and-pine-framed fireplace, arm raised. "I'd like to make a toast. To my mother, Shelly Lovell, who I miss every day. And to all of you, for making the supreme sacrifice of crawling out of bed before noon to share my little tradition. Happy New Year."

They all echoed her toast, clinking ceramic mugs. But when Daphne tried to sit down, Ivy held up a restraining hand.

"You're not finished yet. Before we start in on this orgy of food, you have to explain the centerpiece."

Could she blame the crackling fire for her suddenly flushed cheeks? Daphne didn't mind her flowers being in the spotlight. But she never liked that light shining on her. Discussing her geeky obsession with the Victorian floriography would be sure to bore her friends to tears. "Nobody cares about that."

"They will once you explain it. Daphne's big on the language of flowers." Ivy pointed to the low glass bowl, full of shiny greenery and spiky blue flowers. "If she took the time to make a special centerpiece for today, it means something."

Mira bent over to sniff the display. "Ooh, lovers used to send secret messages through nosegays and bouton-nieres, right? That might be fun to highlight at A Fine Romance. Maybe highlight a flower of the month and its meaning."

"If she starts brainstorming for the store, we'll lose her for at least an hour. Especially if Ivy joins in." Sam pressed a tender kiss to Mira's forehead. "Reel her back on topic, Daphne."

"Well, there's rosemary, for remembrance. For my mom."

"Nice," Gib said as he scooped a spoonful of eggs onto his plate.

Daphne ran her fingers through the fluffy greens. "Parsley, for festivity."

"Great." Ben plucked off a leaf and popped it in his mouth. "When brunch is over, you can dump it into a pot and make stew. And when you do, count me in for a bowl."

"Very funny. After the workout I gave my pots and pans this morning, I probably won't be cooking again until the spring thaw."

Gib used the tongs holding a fat sausage link to point at the cluster of tiny white berries. "Isn't that mistle-toe? I've seen a bunch of it over the past month. Our head housekeeper, Letitia, keeps hanging it over the time-card punch station. I've tried explaining to her that it's inappropriate, but she's got her eye on one of the maître d's. She thinks trapping him under mistletoe is the only way to get him to notice her."

"Might work," said Sam.

"True," Gib conceded.

Ben loaded two cinnamon rolls onto his plate, leaving a drizzle of thick icing across the table. "You of all people should be in her corner."

"Not in the least. I've never dipped into the company well. Too dangerous. Rife with complication to get involved in the workplace, and twice as bad since I'm the manager. Regardless, a built-in kissing station is a bad idea with three hundred employees of both genders."

A kissing station at Gib's work. Daphne was sure the maître d' wasn't the only man that housekeeper hoped to trap into a secret smooch. "Mistletoe means *I surmount all difficulties*. I thought it would be a positive affirmation to start the year."

Gib barked out a laugh. "What's the flower to avoid all difficulties? Seems easier."

Men. Always wanting a shortcut. "The language of flowers is rather limited. It's not like that full Klingon dictionary you bought last Halloween."

"I wanted to be able to converse with all women, no matter their nationality. And trust me, those *Star Trek* nuts are quite keen to show their appreciation if you go the extra mile."

"Gib, you're incorrigible," Mira laughed. "What's the tall flower?"

Daphne appreciated being pulled off the detour her mind took in picturing Gib rolling around in bed with a lusty, green-skinned Trekkie. "As my former room-mate, I'm sure you'll appreciate that one. It's hyssop, for cleanliness. You know, that thing I'm woefully lacking? Sort of my New Year's resolution. To de-clutter and re-member to clean before it gets so bad I can write my name in the dust on the mantel."

"This is the year you're going to land a man," Gib declared.

Was it upside-down-backward day? Had he figured out his best kiss ever came from his best friend? Was he about to offer himself up to her, and maybe carry her off to the bedroom to finish what they'd barely begun? "What do you mean?"

"Surmounting difficulties? Keeping the place tidy so it's always prepared for an unexpected visitor? Ob-viously you're on the prowl." He leaned back, crossing one ankle over his knee. "Now that Mira and Ivy are cozily hooked up, you've decided that it's your turn to bag a trophy."

"Better than your catch-and-release habit." Her re-tort tumbled out automatically, the way they always yanked each other's chain. It was the most normal she'd felt conversing with him since the kiss. Maybe Daphne could recalibrate her emotions. Go back to their stan-dard friendship, unimpeded by her unrelenting lust.

"Hey, nobody gets hurt my way."

And normalcy disappeared just that fast, pinched off like a dead flower. "Want to bet?"

Ben sank cross-legged onto the pale purple throw rug in front of the fireplace. "I know somebody Gib wants to catch—and keep."

Ivy pounced on his announcement. "Who?"

"The mysterious Cinderella from last night's wedding."

Freezing in place, Daphne tried not to react. Nobody needed to know that her heart had just sped up in an almost opposite amount that time had suddenly slowed down.

Sam shook his head. "You've really gone round the bend on this girl. You talked me deaf in one ear about it last night."

"We don't have to talk about it now." Gib stood abruptly, heading to the kitchen to top off a mug that looked suspiciously still full of coffee.

"Oh, I think we do," said Ivy. She perched on the purple sofa arm next to Sam. "Gibson texted me three times last night, begging for the guest list to the wedding. He has some ridiculous notion that I'd violate the privacy of my bride and let him phone up every single female guest."

Sam scratched his head. "What's your game plan? Just burst out with, hey, did ya happen to kiss a random stranger during the blackout?"

"Seems like a straightforward question." Gib sat back down, irritation obvious in his stiff spine and clenched jaw. It made Daphne want to stroke a soothing hand from those chiseled cheekbones down to his lickable lips. God, why couldn't she stop looking at him like a playground of passion? That kiss unlocked a door she'd dead-bolted shut for years, and now she couldn't find a mental crowbar to slam it back into lockdown.

Ivy pursed her lips. "It seems like a way to piss off about—what—a hundred or so women?"

"Why—did you change your mind? Will you give me the list?" Hope bubbled off his voice.

"Of course not. But if your kisses are as spectacular as you claim, maybe your Cinderella will come looking for you."

Mira waved her napkin in the air to interrupt. "Speaking of dating, I need a favor."

Sam raised an eyebrow. "Tired of me already?"

"Not for at least another eighty years." She nuzzled his cheek, then continued. "With Valentine's Day right around the corner, I want to spotlight an aphrodisiac-based picnic in A Fine Romance."

Whip-smart idea. Ivy might've come up with the idea—and the capital—for a romance store, but Mira had put her personal stamp on it from her first day as manager.

Sam rolled his eyes. "Come on, do you really believe in that stuff?"

"I really believe it will sell like crazy, and make the store tons of money. If nothing else, there's probably a placebo effect. Two people who like each other enough to share a picnic will undoubtedly begin to feel amorous as they feed each other finger food. The point is, I need to do a trial run."

Sam shoved Mira's sleeve up and trailed a string of kisses up her arm. "Sweets, lima beans and day-old crusts are aphrodisiacs as long as I'm with you."

"Exactly the problem. Ivy and I can't test these, because we're already putty in the hands of our fiancés. What I need are unattached, objective volunteers. Daphne, are you in?"

Anything to help a friend. Not to mention that as a silent partner with Ivy, anything that helped the store profit would get Daphne's accountant off her back about how fast she'd recoup her investment. And nibbling tasty gourmet treats was far from a hardship. "Sure. I love to eat."

"And, Gib, I want you to do this, too."

What? Had Mira lost her mind? No. No freaking way. Not in a million years. Daphne could not, would not sit across a table playing sexily with food and Gibson Moore. A woman could only bear so much disappointment, and last night she'd taken her share of it for the entire year.

"No," he said.

Whew. Crisis averted.

"Stop scavenging the town for fresh meat for one lousy night. Help a girl out. It'll be fun."

Gib sighed. "This is almost insulting. Or at the very least, overkill. My charm, my accent and crystal-blue eyes are all the aphrodisiac any woman needs."

Truer words were never spoken. As far as Daphne was concerned, Gibson Moore could talk her into bed any night of the week with the accent alone. She couldn't begin to count the nights they'd sat on this very sofa, watching a game or a movie—and she'd had to move to the chair in order to resist the urge to touch him.

"Be that as it may, I can't sell you in my store." Mira gave him an unabashed once-over, from the forehead wave of his thick brown hair down to his polished loafers. "Although I think you'd fetch top dollar."

"Kind of you to say. In point of fact, at a charity auction last year, I was sold for the whopping sum of three thousand dollars. Highest bid of the night."

Ben nipped a piece of bacon off Gib's plate. "Dinner with you can't be worth a quarter of that. Not even if you treated them to steaks and a bottle of Dom at Gibsons."

"Who said I stopped at dinner?" Gib waggled his eyebrows and smirked with a full dose of male smugness. The intimation sent Daphne's R-rated imagination down the wrong and very dangerous road yet again. The one where she pictured his hair tousled, and a sleepy morning smile as the only thing he wore... It helped distract her from the sharp ping of jealousy that hit every single time he talked about his many, many conquests. The jealousy she could never let him see, or their friendship would be horribly damaged.

"Look, you don't have to believe that what you're eating is an aphrodisiac. You just need to let me know if everything tastes good and works well together."

"Very well. For the lovely Mira, I will do it."

The room closed in around Daphne. This must be what it felt like inside bubble gum when it popped. The air vanished, and the walls almost folded in on her. In a panic, she backed through the doorway into the kitchen. It didn't help. Her apartment had an open floor plan, so there wasn't a comforting wall hiding Gib from her view. Backing away even more, she circled past the refrigerator to land in the hallway. Pressing both palms against the wall, Daphne concentrated on breathing.

"What is going on with you?" Mira poked her head around the corner.

Ivy put a hand on Daphne's forehead. "You're acting wacky. First you stress-cooked, and now you're as white as a wedding gown."

"Don't make me do it, Mira," she begged in a shaky whisper.

"Do what?"

To prevent the slightest chance of being overheard, Daphne hustled them all into the bathroom. With the door firmly shut, she used the cool white tiles for support, as though facing a firing squad. "Have dinner with Gib."

"I don't get it," Mira said. "He's one of your best friends in the world. You guys have dinner together all the time."

"That was—before."

"Before what?"

God. She wouldn't be able to talk Mira out of this horrible idea without revealing her secret. Daphne's knees bent of their own accord, and she slid down the wall to the bare wood. "Before last night."

"Sounds like a bad movie title from the eighties," Mira snickered.

Ivy just looked confused. "What are you talking about? We were together all last night. I didn't see you and Gib get into a fight."

"We didn't. We went the other way." Daphne sucked in a deep breath. "I'm his mystery kiss."

"Really?" Two sets of eyes, one hazel and one blue, goggled at her. Both women sank to the floor, hands loosely hugging bent knees.

"Trust me. I wouldn't kid about something this cataclysmic."

"How was he? Gib's got such a reputation as a ladies' man. He's super hot, and an amazing flirt, so I've always wondered if, well, he could possibly live up to the hype."

"This is a crisis, Mira. You really want to start by me grading his kiss?"

"Well, yeah."

Ivy chimed in with a, "Me, too."

Now that the secret was out, she wanted to tell them everything. Except the more she talked about it, the more she'd sink into her own personal emotional quicksand of wanting Gib, who she absolutely, one hundred percent could not have. "He's spectacular. He's everything you expect him to be. He knows my lips better, more intimately from that two-minute kiss than any man I've ever dated."

They all took a moment to let it sink in.

"Okay, but *why* did you kiss him?" Mira asked. "Because the way he tells the story, you made the move in the dark."

Daphne could still hardly believe she'd gathered a blend of stupidity and courage to seize the moment. "I did. I kissed him because I've wanted to for years."

Ivy's jaw dropped. "Seriously? You've had a crush on Gib all this time?"

"Yes."

"And you never told me? Even though I helped you put together outfits for dates with other men, and told you tons of details when Ben and I started dating? You kept this huge a scoop from me?"

"How is this suddenly about you? Look, there wasn't any point in mentioning it. Gib and I are friends. A quick slide between the sheets with a man who goes through women faster than I go through a pint of chocolate chip mint would ruin that friendship irrevocably. He's like a movie-star crush—someone you like to imagine getting naked with, but are perfectly fine never actually pursuing. I mean, would you ever try to kiss Brad Pitt?"

"Maybe. If the lights went out and he was standing next to me."

Mira poked Daphne in the thigh. "So why are you torturing the poor man? He's going out of his mind trying to figure out who Cinderella is. Just tell him."

"I can't." Daphne realized her hands that she didn't remember balling into fists were cramping.

Mira tossed the curtain of long, dark hair over her shoulder with a quick twitch. "For God's sake, it was one kiss. It won't burn the friendship bridge to the ground. Tell him, and we'll all have a good laugh about how he never guessed you were Cinderella."

"Exactly."

Ivy tapped her first finger against the floor. "Explain."

"When the lights went out, and when they came back up, I was standing right next to him. Sure, fifteen other women were within arm's reach, but I was literally a foot away. And it never even occurred to Gib that it was me. That I was the one who rocked his world. Because he doesn't see me in that way. He sees me as a buddy, a sounding board, somebody to hang with when he doesn't have a date. It's beyond humiliating that he couldn't even for a moment imagine I could be the woman who kissed him." Since when was airing deep humiliation a sanctioned New Year's event? This party had definitely gotten off to a rocky start.

"Maybe you're taking this too seriously," Ivy suggested. "Just because he's never thought about you in that way—which we don't actually know to be true—doesn't mean he couldn't."

"I can't risk it. First of all, my pride still smarts. Gib is on the cover of *Windy City* magazine this month as one of Chicago's top bachelors. He could have any woman in the city. He's so far out of my league there are entire galaxies between us."

"Not true. You've landed several yummy men."

"Yummy enough for me," Daphne clarified. "Nowhere near as yummy as Gib. I accept it. And I don't want to jeopardize our friendship. So I'll chalk it up to the craziness of New Year's and move on. But I need the cushion of time before any more cozy dinners with Gib. He's like a giant hot fudge sundae in front of me, and I've had one taste." God, how she wanted to keep on licking! "I've got to have a little distance until the temptation fizzles."

"That's one way to look at it." Mira leaned forward, scrunching up her nose. "If you want to be a chicken. You've got more backbone than that. Especially if you've been keeping your hand off the spoon for years. Ever hear the cliché about getting right back on the horse?"

"Thinking about mounting and riding is giving me unhelpful visuals."

"Two minutes to parade," Ben hollered from the living room.

Mira stood, then grabbed Daphne's hand to pull her up, too. "You're going to do this aphrodisiac dinner. None of us believe food has magical properties to strip away your inhibitions. So confront your British sex demon, and prove to yourself that you and Gib still have the same relationship as before the kiss so great it stopped time."

Daphne only had one rebuttal left in her arsenal. "I don't want to."

"Think of the mistletoe you put in the centerpiece," Ivy suggested. "You're sure to surmount all difficulties this year. But you've got to start by getting over this first one."

All this considered, she'd rather deal with a bridezilla who hated her carefully handcrafted wedding bouquet. Or have an entire week's shipment of roses go missing. Or even swim a mile in the frigid waters of Lake Michigan during today's Polar Bear Plunge. Who was she kidding? Giving up on men entirely sounded easier than forgetting the eye-popping, panty-drenching goodness of a Gibson Moore lip-lock.

THREE

It is at the edge of a petal that love waits
                              ~ William Carlos Williams

A HARD KNOCK rattled the glass door to Gib's office. "I need ten more minutes," he said, without tearing his eyes from the computer screen. Everyone knew the rules. When his door was open, he'd talk to anyone. No problem too small, from a dispute between sous chefs about garlic scapes versus scallions to garnish the bisque, to moderating a discussion between the day and evening concierges about how to fairly split their substantial tips. But on the rare occasions Gib closed his door, it signaled he needed absolute silence and zero distractions.

"Fat chance." Ben barged in, shut the door behind him and then leaned against it with his arms crossed. Body language put him at relaxed and slouchy, but the cold glint in his blue eyes tipped the true scale toward pissed off. "You're already ten minutes late. After I busted my ass to get here on time, I might add. We're supposed to be working out, remember?"

"Clearly not." Bloody hell. He could've waved an employee out of his office without a problem. Ben, however, proved much more immovable. Flat-out stubborn, most days.

"I watched you tuck away four of those cinnamon rolls at Daphne's brunch. Plus, you stole the last strip of bacon right out from under my fork. I'm not the only one who needs to sweat off a few pounds. Aren't all your precious suits hand-tailored? I wouldn't want you to pop a button. Unless, of course, that's your plan to score women even faster. Just walk around town with your pants already halfway open."

"I like the ease of accessibility, but as it's hovering just south of zero outside, I see a gaping hole in your strategy. So I'll join you in the gym. I just need a few more minutes." Gib tapped his pen against the blotter on his desk. Nowadays, a blotter was more of a nod to style than a practical office accessory. But he liked the old-school look. It reminded him of his father's desk, the one he'd played at as a child. Dark, carved wood that looked very much like his own desk here, thousands of miles and an ocean away from the original. Just the way he liked it. Because truly, Gib couldn't get far enough away from his father.

Ben plopped down in a chair. "Geez, you run a hotel. Guests check in, guests check out."

"Thank you for reducing my career to the easy life of a library book." Gib pressed Print. Maybe putting pen to paper would help him fix the weak spots in his document. And provide a visual hint to propel Ben back out the door.

Elbow on the desk, Ben propped his head on his fist. "Isn't that the whole point of being the big-cheese manager? You know, that you delegate everything? I'm supposed to meet Ivy for dinner in exactly two hours. If I'm late, she'll read me the riot act."

"Some things are too important to hand off." If Ben wouldn't leave, ignoring him was the next best plan. So Gib turned to the printer and drummed his fingers while waiting for the paper to spit out. No matter how annoying Ben became, this project needed to be finished. And it needed his full concentration to be not just finished, but perfect. He had twelve separate attempts at a personal plea for Cinderella to step forward. A carefully worded ad for three papers, different-length notices to fit all forms of social media, and a flyer. So far, none of them had the right tone. Or a way to make *come kiss me again* sound anything more than skeezy.

"What's this?" Ben scanned the sheaf of papers Gib had spent much of the day actively avoiding.

Gib sighed. He'd have better luck ignoring a squalling toddler kicking the back of his seat on a transcontinental flight. "I don't come to your office and mess up your desk."

"My desk is my couch. One of the perks of working from home. But you're welcome to fly out with me to RealTV headquarters next week and shuffle around the DVDs in our video library."

"Thanks."

Ben continued to paw through the stack of printouts. "Organic alfalfa farming? Since when do you care about alfalfa?"

Funny. After skimming all twelve articles last night, Gib still knew only one thing about the topic. "Believe me when I say that I truly do not care one iota about alfalfa. And I'm quite convinced the word *organic* is a way to charge someone twice as much because you were too cheap to fertilize properly and spray for bugs."

"So what's with the articles?"

To generally annoy the crap out of him? To ruthlessly exhume his carefully buried guilt over leaving England? "My caretaker sent them to me. Hickson's constantly trying to keep me involved with the operation. He wants to make some rather pricey changes. Becoming an all-organic operation carries a hefty enough price tag that he requires my buy-in."

"You have a caretaker?" Ben dropped the papers. His gaze skewered Gib faster than a puppy distracted with a new chew toy. "Does this have to do with that mysterious royal title of yours I just found out about?"

"I'm a member of the nobility. Not a royal." And he thanked God every day for that distinction. "Not unless seventy-five other people in the line of succession drop dead first."

"It still fascinates me." Ben pushed to his feet and executed a sloppy bow. "The Honourable Viscount Moore. Do you have a castle?"

Why were Americans so gobsmacked by titles? Gib enjoyed using that peculiarity to his advantage with long-legged brunettes. But from his friends, this line of questioning became tiresome and borderline embarrassing all too quickly.

"The castle belongs to my father, the Earl of Ashburnham. It's always cold, and doesn't have satellite television."

"Boo hoo. The castle can't rock a single movie channel? Hard life, man," Ben mocked.

Gib knew how to wring out some sympathy. "None of the sports channels, either."

"Now that's a deal breaker." Ben sat back down, topping off his hoodie-and-sweats ensemble with a look of outrage.

"Which is why I stay far away." Absolutely true. Of course, the lack of cable channels ranked about eight hundredth place below the more substantial reasons why he eschewed the family holdings. But Gib saw no reason to air all his dirty knickers.

"So how do you explain the alfalfa?"

As an unending punishment inherited from his mother's side of the family? "My father is busy with the Ashburnham castle holdings. So as his heir, I manage my own separate, smaller estate. Or rather, I pay a caretaker to do it for me."

"You really are the king of delegating. But no castle on your land?"

"Merely a manor house." He held up a hand, anticipating Ben's next question. "Fully wired for sound and cable, which I'm sure my staff appreciates. The estate primarily deals in alfalfa, sheep and a few other odds and ends. As the revenue from it helps keep me in my hand-tailored suits, I try to pay it minimal attention once a quarter. Now, may we please move on to a more interesting topic? Say, for instance, the fact that an overly entitled group of twentysomethings stoned out of their minds caused the toilets to overflow in half the suites on the eighteenth floor?"

Ben snickered. "Sheep, huh?" He rolled into a belly laugh.

If Gib wasn't the one stuck managing hundreds of acres from afar, responsible for the livelihood of all the people who worked his farm, he'd probably laugh, too. "It is every bit as uninteresting as it sounds, I promise."

"Sorry—I'm picturing you in overalls with a pitchfork over one shoulder. Does Armani make overalls? I can't wait to tell Sam that you're a farmer."

Gib jerked a thumb at the door to shoo him away. "Go now, why don't you? I'm very busy."

Ben slapped the edge of the flat-screen monitor to skew it toward him. "You're on Twitter. You're not busy. Twitter's no excuse for skipping a workout."

"It is today."

"Didn't even know you had an account." He peered intently at the screen. "What's your handle?"

"I don't have one. I'm on the hotel's account." Gib returned the monitor to its proper position. He didn't need Ben sticking his nose into this particular project.

"Checking for gripes from your staff?"

"No. What? My staff are still reveling in the glory of the Christmas bonuses signed by yours truly." Now that Gib thought more about it, Ben might be able to help. As long as he could put up with the unavoidable mocking. "I needed a way to contact the public, and this seemed easy. That is, until I realized I'd have to constrain my considerable thoughts into such a tiny space."

"What the hell are you tweeting about?"

Gib leaned back in his ergonomic miracle of a chair and steepled his fingers. "I'm trying to find Cinderella. Your stubborn fiancée refuses to give me access to the guest lists from the New Year's Eve wedding."

"Her answer's not going to change. So stop asking her to abandon all professional integrity."

"It's just so damned frustrating. The identity to my mystery kisser is locked up in one of Ivy's spreadsheets."

Ben crossed his arms over the black and gold logo on his hoodie. "Would you hand out info on one of the Cavendish's guests?"

Not unless he wanted the two-fer of getting a pink slip *and* a lawsuit. "No. Of course not. I just hoped that Ivy had more elastic morals than I do. But I understand her reticence. So I'm coming at this from another angle."

"What are you going to do? Stake out the bride's house when she gets back from her honeymoon and ask for the names and numbers of all her friends?"

"I can't wait that long."

A low whistle split the air, as sharp as the crease on a really good paper airplane. "You've got it bad for Cinderella."

Pushing off the edge of his desk, Gib stood. Paced from one file cabinet, past the broad width of his desk to a display case filled with a smattering of the hotel's awards and trophies, then back again. It bothered him that the pale gray carpet muffled his footsteps. He wanted to hear each deliberate stomp of frustration. "I must find her."

"Gibson Moore. Man about town. Lusty Lothario."

Those words red-lighted his pacing. He'd narrowly avoided a spit take the first time he read them. "The intro from the piece about me in *Windy City* magazine. I'm touched that you took the time to memorize it."

"Can't make fun of you at our next poker night unless I get all the labels right." Ben twisted around to face him, making the black leather cushion squeak. "The point is, you've made a name for yourself sliding out of beds as fast as you slide into them. To you, the city of Chicago is a giant smorgasbord of available females."

"Well, it is a city of eight million people. Seems pointless to ignore that sort of babe buffet."

"Exactly. And women line up six-deep to spend a night with you. Miraculously, whether you're with them for an hour, a day or a month, they all walk away with a smile on their face and nothing but praise for you on their lips."

Dealing with female tears and temper ranked right up there with root canals and missing the annual suit sale at Armani. He'd wasted enough emotional currency with that on his mother through the years. Keep it light, keep it sexy, keep it drama-free. If Gib were to redesign his family's coat of arms, that would be the new motto scrolling across the bottom. And not in Latin. In plain English, so nobody missed the importance of it.

"If I do something, I like to do it right. And I like to satisfy women."

Ben scratched his head. "With none of that breakup awkwardness, though? If you could bottle and sell that trick, you'd be a millionaire. I mean, on top of whatever you rake in off of your alfalfa fields." He snickered at his own weak pun.

"Trust me, having a wide network of happy women at my disposal is a useful thing."

"Exactly!" Thoroughly at home in Gib's office, Ben

opened the tiny closet and pulled out a gym bag. To hammer home his readiness to leave, he then stood with one hand on the chrome door pull. "You're not a one-woman guy. You like your women like your satellite television—hundreds of options on any given day."

Giving in to the inevitable, Gib turned off his monitor. Maybe they could brainstorm a compelling tweet in the gym. Pounding one foot in front of the other on the treadmill always cleared the debris from his mind. "Variety is the spice of life."

"My point is that you don't just have notches on your bedpost. You've probably got enough notches to crimp the frame of every bed on the fourth floor of this hotel. So why are you so focused on this one woman? You didn't see her, you didn't talk to her, and I've seen you literally crook your finger at women and have them fall into your arms. What makes Cinderella so special?"

Good question. One that had kept him nearly sleepless for two nights straight. "I don't know."

"You might want to figure that out before you find her."

Gib waved at the middle-aged woman with a teased crown of brown hair at her command post just outside his office. "Agatha, I'll be at the gym for a couple of hours."

"Too many Christmas cookies?" She gave a pointed glare at his midsection over the top of her cat's-eye glasses. He'd inherited her awesome traffic-controller-like skill set wrapped in rayon from the previous Cavendish manager. Running the hotel without Agatha would be as scary a prospect as—hell, being forced to return to his homeland. Their first two weeks together had been dicey. Learning to listen past her thick Polish accent was a full-time job in and of itself. Determined to hate him on sight for having the gall to replace her retiring boss, she hadn't cut him an inch of slack. And at the end of those two weeks, as a reward for surviving without burning the place down (and remembering to keep the Frango mint jar on her desk filled), she all but adopted him. Sunday dinner at her house once a month was nonnegotiable. She only excused with serious proof of bodily harm, like a cast, or a minimum of ten stitches. Still didn't cut him much slack, though.

"Miss Lovell's cinnamon rolls, if you must know. Their sweet goodness called to me."

"And you answered their call for two hours straight." Ben puffed out his cheeks in mock distress. "Our man's going to pot, Agatha. You might want to reinforce his chair legs while we're gone."

"I did that after his date with the tennis player," she deadpanned.

Ah yes, the lovely Selena with thighs that could latch on to a man with the tensile strength of rebar. Energetic, too. Come to think of it, he'd ended up replacing a splintered coffee table that hadn't survived their weekend together. Good times. And good to know Agatha kept his office, well, ready for anything.

"Call if there's an emergency." Remembering his promise to Mira, he shook his head. Being available to his staff at a moment's notice came with the position, but tonight he needed to focus all his attention on Daphne and their picnic. "Nothing less than a disgrun-

tled multimillionaire, if you don't mind. I've got a dinner appointment I can't miss."

Ben opened the outer glass door, the one with Gib's
name arched in gold letters, and they headed down the
hallway, papered in subdued gray stripes. "Come on,
tell me what makes Cinderella worth pursuing."

Why was Cinderella so special? The question niggled
at his brain like a fire ant's bite. One reason surfaced,
but sounded inane. In his own head it sounded stupid, so
saying it out loud was bound to exponentially increase
its lack of sensibility. Gib stabbed at the elevator button.
When the car didn't instantly appear, he straight-armed
the door to the stairs. Maybe jogging up two floors to
the gym would limit conversation. "We fit."

"If this is a height/weight thing, might I remind
you of that week you dated half of a soccer team? Or
the touring cast of the Rockettes in December? Eight
women, all with the identical height and build…and
legs that wouldn't quit." In a burst of speed, Ben edged
ahead of him. Legs widespread, he blocked Gib's access to the sixth-floor landing with his arms crossed
like a pissed-off genie. "There's got to be more about
this one woman besides compatible anatomy tying you
up in knots."

The more Gib tried to put it into words, the more ridiculous he felt. All he had was a bone-deep feeling of
rightness. "Maybe it's because I've been with so many
women that I can recognize when something different
comes along. Almost, I don't know, familiar in some
strange way? Her kiss, her touch…I sound completely
barmy, I know."

"You sound like a teenage girl crushing hard. I should check your binders." Ben let him pass, and they took the last set of stairs two at a time. The door led them directly into the large fitness complex attached to the spa. The ever-present faint smell of chlorine tickled Gib's nose.

"What binders?" Gib asked as he slipped out of his suit coat, despite the fat snowflakes drifting past the wall of windows. Rows of potted palms and bright pink hibiscuses encircling the room required it be kept at jungle-like conditions. At least once a quarter Gib had to resist a strong temptation to smuggle in a couple of lizards. Just to add to the atmosphere.

"That's right—you wouldn't know because you went to some fancy all-boys school. Talk about a prison for your raging teenage hormones."

"Eton? Yes, generally considered fancy. But not exactly an institution with bars on the windows. They did let us see girls. By the time I graduated, I'd dated girls at every school within three counties." Sure, Eton bussed them in once a month for dances. Ben, however, didn't need to know all the particulars of *how* it happened; merely that it *did*.

Ben unzipped his jacket as they walked the length of the Olympic-size pool. "Teenage girls in school, over here at least, draw all over their binders when they're in the throes of puppy love. Hearts, flowers, their initials, smiley faces. And now you're up to speed on your American trivia for the day."

"Is that like word-a-day toilet paper? Am I supposed

to find a way to work binder doodling into a conversation later?"

"Nah. You're a smart guy. I know you'll remember." Ben swiped a bottle of water from a well-stocked shelf by the door. "So since it's too late to recapture your lost youth, what's your big plan to find this girl that's turned you monogamous?"

"Take that back," Gib growled, throwing Ben into a semi-playful head lock. Monogamy carried with it all sorts of implications, the chief being a serious relationship. Gib didn't have a problem with the idea of only sleeping with one woman for the rest of his life. He did have a problem with contemplating an emotional connection strong enough that any woman could have the power to screw him over. No, he wanted to find his Cinderella to work her out of his system. Like the way he sweated alcohol out with a long run after an epic night of drinking.

Ben struggled for a few seconds, then raised his arms in surrender. "Sorry. I don't know what I was thinking. You'll never lock your dick up and hand the key to a single woman. In fact, I think the entire female population of Chicago would stage an intervention if you even considered it."

Gib let him go, hiding his grin of triumph. Even after six months of putting Ben through his paces in the gym, he could still take him down. "Damn straight."

"But do you have a plan? Aside from nagging my fiancée to death?"

As they finally hit the locker room, Gib tugged off his tie. "Social media. I can't find her by myself, but in today's world, I don't have to. I can put out a plea on every single social media site—" A truly inspired thought pinged into his brain. "Why don't we fire up that camera of yours? Tape my plea for help finding this wondrous woman. It could go viral by tonight. Someone out there must know who she is, have heard about the magical kiss she shared with a stranger on New Year's Eve." Because it *had* to have been as world-tippingly special for her, too. On his worst days, Gib could kiss a girl senseless. Not bragging, but mere fact. He liked to think it helped make up for his inability to make a commitment to a woman.

Ben tossed his jacket into a locker and began to stretch his quads. "You keep acting crazy like this, and we're going to slap you silly. Or stick ice cubes down your shorts to snap you out of it."

Why wouldn't Ben help him? Since he'd locked Ivy's heart up tight with a diamond ring, Gib had assumed Ben would be sympathetic to his quest, at the very least. "You don't understand."

"Really? I didn't have any contact with Ivy after our first date for six weeks. I'd pretty well burned that bridge, of my volition. But I still thought about her, day and night. Wondered about her. Replayed the slide of her skin against mine, the sound of her laugh. Did I abandon all pride, cut off my balls and appeal to a world-wide audience to get her back? Hell, no."

Gib twirled the dial on his teak locker. "My therapist would undoubtedly be proud enough to throw me a parade for—how did she put it? Treating women like disposable napkins. Why can't you be?"

"Because, even though you don't pay me by the hour, I'm more invested in your long-term happiness than some shrink. When this goes south—and it will, believe me—I'll be here to pick up the pieces. You know, get you shit-faced at a strip joint."

"No pieces," Gib scoffed. "You pointed out that every time I walk away from a girl, she's still smiling. And I never get seriously attached." Or even semiseriously attached. It would be like eating lobster ravioli every night. Delicious, but so boring after a week he'd want to claw his own tongue out. "There's simply no downside to finding her."

"Wrong. Have you thought about how this would reflect on you professionally? If you go viral with this plea, a news source will pick it up. You're already this month's cover of *Windy City* magazine. People know who you are. Dig a little deeper, and someone's going to pop the lid on your title. The headline would be something like British Noble Crazy for Chicago's Cinderella—Or Just Crazy? It'll go more than viral. This story will be carried by the national press, and then British rags will get their hands on it."

Christ. Wouldn't that be a living nightmare. The negative publicity would undoubtedly make some women think twice about dating him. Gib had no desire for any obstacles that might inhibit his choice of bed partners. "I hadn't thought about it that way."

"Which is also totally out of character for you. You've got this cool, slick exterior, but on top of those designer duds, your mind ticks with the precision of a

Swiss clock. Chalk this one up as a holiday to remember, and move on."

Probably quite sound advice. Gib hated advice. He far preferred to make up his own mind. Another reason he avoided the albatross of a serious relationship around his neck. But he still couldn't ignore the need to find her, and kiss her again. Over and over and over. "It's not that easy."

"Why not? You don't need her. You've got Milo, the best roommate in the known universe, doing your laundry and keeping the house tidy—"

Gib cut him off as he neatly creased his trousers before draping them over the hanger. "Hey, Milo swears that he enjoys cleaning. He likes to play with the feather duster. And as a trade-off, I set him up with fantastic orchestra seats at the Goodman and Ford Oriental for every show that comes through town."

"Let me finish." Ben let go of his ankle and began ticking points off on his fingers. "You've got most of the eligible hotties in town ready to roll into your bed at the blink of an eye, and you've got Daphne to watch soccer with and share those nuclear hot wings you love."

They were both addicted to the sweet heat that blistered their lips when they ate enough. Once she introduced wings to his bland English palate, there was no turning back. Their fingers and lips were usually stained bright orange during their wing nights. He'd never let any woman in the world but Daphne see him like that. Around her, Gib could let down his guard. Being in her company was like slipping into a pair of often-washed flannel pajamas. Soft, easy, comfortable.

Gib kept talking while he swapped his French cuffed shirt for his favorite red Under Armour compression tee. He liked the way it shortened his recovery time after an extensive circuit of the weight room. "Another useful thing about Daphne is that she's always ready to impart the female perspective on life. I find having a conduit to that information quite valuable when chatting up women."

"Oh yeah—Daphne's never afraid to tell you what she thinks. She's the whole package, no question. Which brings me full circle to my point. You don't have any holes in your life. There's nothing this mystery woman could give you that you don't already get from someone else. Except for a whole world of trouble. And possible arrest as a stalker. So let her go."

Ben made sense. Gib couldn't dispute a single point he'd made. Chasing this woman over the internet could easily cause embarrassment both personally and professionally. No woman was worth that. He had a great life. Why do anything to change it?

He sat on the bench to put on his running trainers. "You're right. And you've stopped me from making a total cock-up."

"What the hell?" Ben's startled gaze swung straight to Gib's groin. "Since when is your cock up, and why are we talking about it?"

Barking out a laugh, Gib fig-leafed his hands. "Sorry. Don't wig out on me. It's slang. The British version, at any rate. A cock-up is a big mess."

"Huh. I'd recommend you never, ever use that phrase in a locker room again."

Gib pointed at the door, and waited for Ben to exit into the weight room. "You're chock-full of good advice today. It's kind of like hanging out with a spot-on fortune cookie." He could joke with Ben, and resolve not to waste any more time looking for the girl with the luscious lips. He could put New Year's Eve in his rearview mirror, and concentrate on the actual new year in front of him. But Gib knew that deep down, he'd never be able to forget exactly how she felt, how she tasted and how perfectly they meshed. Bloody hell.

FOUR

Hopes are planted in friendship's garden where
dreams blossom into priceless treasures

~ Anonymous

DAPHNE PULLED OFF her beloved Bears jersey, balled it
up and tossed it in the corner. Comfortably ancient,
she'd worn it in front of Gib a hundred times. Which
was why she should wear it tonight. Make it just another ordinary night of them hanging out. Nothing special whatsoever. Two friends, no agendas, no tension,
no unfulfilled sexual longings…damn it. She couldn't
fool herself. So how was she supposed to fool Gib into
not noticing everything was different between them?

Part of her wanted to crawl into yoga pants and a
fleece. Play it cooler than cool. Another part of her
wanted to slip on that aqua cashmere sweater Ivy had
given her for Christmas. Low-cut and tight-fitting, it
screamed date night. The last part of her brain wanted
to strip completely down, lay herself out on the coffee
table like an offering to the gods and hope like hell Gib
took the bait. Obviously, her brain hadn't really worked
right since their kiss.

Because she knew Gib wouldn't take the bait. He'd
probably ask her if all her clothes were in the laundry,
then sit down in his usual spot on the couch and ig-

nore her. The events of New Year's Eve proved that he couldn't begin to see her as anything but a buddy, a pal who just happened to have much longer hair than him. His indirect rejection that night had hurt worse than the two broken ribs she suffered during her days as captain of the high school field hockey team. She imagined that a direct, purposeful rejection by Gib would be somewhat on the level of being flayed alive.

"Daph, he'll be here any minute. Hurry up," Mira yelled from the dining room.

Right. Wouldn't want to be caught fussing for the benefit of her sexy dinner partner for the sexiest dinner ever. To split the difference between loungewear and fit-to-be-seen-in-public wear, Daphne topped off her jeans with an oversize flannel shirt she'd borrowed from her brother Michael at Christmas. The garish red-and-green plaid screamed lumberjack, not sex kitten, even if it did occasionally slip off one shoulder.

"How are you doing?" Mira hovered at her bedroom door.

"Fine." A strong slam of her sock drawer emphasized her calm, collected fine-ness. "At least I will be, after tonight. Gib and I are alone all the time. Once I get that behind me—without caving to more than five years of suppressed lust and sucking his lips right off his face—I'll know that the weirdness of New Year's Eve can be relegated to history." Then she twitched at one set of the pale green sheers hanging from her canopy bed. "You making us do this ridiculous dinner together is good. I think. It'll be totally normal."

Mira just stared at her for a minute while Daphne yanked on a pair of green socks so thick and fuzzy they could masquerade as slippers. Once she moved on to tugging her hair into two low pigtails, Mira crept forward to perch on the end of the bed. "Right now, it's like you took normal and overdosed it on speed. Luckily, there are cocktails with dinner. Get a shot or two in you, and I bet you simmer down."

"Seriously? It's not bad enough you're making me eat food that's supposed to stimulate naughty thoughts? You're liquoring me up and loosening my inhibitions, too? Do you want me to utterly humiliate myself tonight?"

"Don't be silly. I'm on *your* team. If Gib can't recognize what an awesome woman you are, he doesn't deserve you. Therefore, there shall be *no* throwing yourself at him. No matter what. And I'm sorry about the drinks, but we're including the recipes in the aphrodisiac picnic pack. This is business. I asked for your help before I knew anything about the whole kissing fiasco, remember?"

"Business. That's good. I can come at tonight in full-on business mode. Ivy's clients dither about their wedding menus and ask my opinion all the time."

"There you go. Now, I go." Mira stood. "Don't forget to take notes. And I left you guys some fun facts about aphrodisiacs that we want to add. Let me know if they're informative, or just too much. Oh, and if by some miracle they actually work, I want to know that, too."

A loud hammering on the front door signaled Gib's arrival. Daphne had left the door unlocked for him (as usual), and he hollered a hello (as usual). So far, a whopping five seconds in, everything was going great. "You and Sam have fun tonight." She gave Mira a one-armed hug as they wandered down the hall.

"Oh, we will. We're doing our own food sampling tonight. A white-chocolate and raspberry truffle for Valentine's Day, and a chocolate cherry bread pudding for the bakery."

"Want to trade?"

"Nope. My tasting comes with the one thing you'll be lacking—a serious serving of sex on the side."

"Wow. Does Sam know he's marrying a woman with such a sadistic streak?" Daphne teased as she opened the door. And then she froze, watching Mira give Gib a peck on the cheek and hurry down the stairs. Mira leaving hammered home that she was about to spend the entire night with the man with movie-star good looks hanging his overcoat in the closet. Just the two of them. In that moment, Daphne realized that she'd done more than merely kiss Gib on New Year's Eve. She'd opened a veritable Pandora's box of emotions and longing. No force in the universe could tamp them back down. While she might talk a good game about keeping their friendship unchanged, it simply wouldn't work.

"You ready to get sexed up?" Gib growled in her ear as he grabbed her from behind. Both arms around her waist, he rocked her sideways playfully. Daphne barely felt the motion.

She *did* feel the spread of his chest across her back, the way his lips brushed the crook of her neck. How his strong legs anchored on either side of hers, and how if she let herself droop, just a little, his fingers splayed across her midsection just might brush the bottom of her right breast. Oh, she was ready all right. Good thing the oversize shirt hid how blatantly her nipples had sprung to attention, craving *his* attention.

"I'm game if you are," Daphne said, in a rush.

"Then we'd better get a move on. Snow's starting to fall. I'm sure you don't want me snowed in with you once this dinner gets me all worked up." With one quick shake, he released her. From the sharp clip of his Italian loafers against the hardwood, Daphne could tell he'd headed into the dining room. Good thing he hadn't stuck around. The image of being snowbound with an aroused Gib melted her knees to the consistency of slush. Daphne grabbed the end table for support.

Ivy constantly begged her to come along to yoga class, and Daphne caved about once a month. Felt like a whole lot of standing around instead of exercise. If she wanted to stretch for an hour, she'd rather do it in front of a game on her plasma TV. The one thing she did like, though, was the nifty breathing technique hammered into her in the first class. When clients were stressful, or her weekly flower order arrived with ranunculus instead of roses, she'd push aside the stress with deep breathing.

Unless a space pod full of slimy green aliens carrying ray guns materialized in her living room, she couldn't imagine a more stressful situation than ignoring her body's response to Gib. So Daphne slumped even lower and began the cycle. First, a deep, four-second breath in, then hold for seven seconds. But before she could release it, a sharp, masculine bark of laughter echoed down the hall.

God, was he laughing at her? Had he seen her wobble? Humiliation hardened her knees and back until she was as straight as the Sears Tower. Turning around, she hurried the few steps into the dining room to brave whatever ridicule Gib heaped upon her.

"Holy crap."

Gib laughed once more. "I agree. Our Mira really pulled out all the stops."

A row of votive candles flickered down the center of the dining table. Two multiarmed candelabras on the buffet reflected twice their light off of the mirror framed in white, wrought-iron curlicues across the room. Each pair of petaled place mats held a different course, on gilt chargers and glass plates, and a different set of drinks. In the background, the mellow sound of a saxophone wailed a melody over the rest of a jazz quartet. The only things missing were a velvet-covered round bed and a box of condoms.

"I didn't expect this. I thought she'd set out a plate with a couple of appetizers and some chocolate. This… this is too much. I'm going to kill her. In fact, I'll call her right now and make her come back." Daphne knew she was babbling. That her words were bulleting out so fast and so high she probably sounded like a squealing mouse. How could Mira have gone to these lengths? Was this some kind of cruel joke?

"Calm down." Gib laid a hand on her arm, which produced exactly the opposite reaction he'd requested. "She just set the stage for us. We're actors tonight, remember? Two people using food to romance each other."

"No. Not something I would've agreed to in a million years. I hate acting. In the third grade I was a tooth-

brush in our hygiene play. Not only did I forget all my
lines, but I tripped over the floss and fell into the kid-
die pool we used for saliva. The only thing I agreed to
do was eat."

Gib gave her that look down his nose that said she'd
flipped her lid. The one he'd given her when she claimed
that Italy's team would beat Spain in the Euro Cup. Or
when she'd tried to convince him that he wouldn't regret watching the fifth *Pirates of the Caribbean* movie.

"Where's your sense of fun?" Taking her hand, he
bowed slightly as he brushed his lips across her knuckles.

"What are you doing, Gib?" she asked warily.

Instead of answering, he said, "Hit me with some
soap-opera-type names."

Where was he going with this? And why was he still
holding her hand? "I don't watch soap operas."

"Right. You're not the girly type to get sucked in to
daytime drama."

Not the girly type? Why not just hit her over the head
with a brick stamped *I don't find you at all attractive?*
Oh yes, Daphne had definitely made the right decision
in not telling him they'd kissed. He'd probably laugh
in her face.

Unaware of her inner turmoil, Gib barreled on. "I
don't remember the convoluted rules Ben taught me
about bowling names. So we'll go with posh, silly
names from my homeland."

"Why do we need fake names at all?"

"Because we can't be Gibson and Daphne. We'd
laugh ourselves silly. And we've got to take this challenge seriously to help Mira. So for tonight, we'll be

Daisy and Graham." He took her other hand as well, and stared deep into her eyes. God, he had beautiful eyes. The same icy turquoise as Iceland's famous Blue Lagoon geothermal pool. Yeah, she had a slight addiction to the Globetrotting Network.

"Daisy and Graham," she echoed, nodding. Why not? Let herself spend one perfect night as Gib's dream date? Nothing more than a fantasy, so nobody would get hurt. She'd get to keep holding his hand, drinking in the melodious accent that made flutters deep in her belly with every word. One night for her mental scrapbook, to go with the one kiss they'd shared.

"We're two lovers on the brink, wooing each other. Waiting for the perfect moment, the right excuse to take that next step toward bliss."

"Is this really the kind of nonsense you spew at the legions of women you bed?"

"Yes. With a very high success rate, I might add." He scowled. "Now stop being Daphne, the constant mocker of my sexual conquests. You're mucking up the mood."

"Sorry."

A heart-melting smile was her reward for compliance. "Be Daisy, the lovely and willing, who wants nothing more than to fall into my arms by the end of the evening."

She might have sucked at playing a toothbrush, but Daphne would have no trouble finding the motivation for this role. "Okay."

Gib pulled out a chair for her. "Your seat awaits, milady. Prepare to be undone by this feast for the senses."

Oh. Oh God. Oh my.

THIS WAS GOING to be fun. Looked like Mira hadn't skimped on the snacks. Gib was fairly certain that he recognized the magical combination of John Coltrane and Miles Davis on the stereo. Not to mention that, given a choice of anyone to relax with, he'd always choose Daphne's easy company.

"Dessert's at the opposite end of the table, so this must be where we start." He sat down next to Daphne, close enough to brush her shoulder with his arm. Bubbles the color of cherry blossoms flitted in sparkling rows to the top of the champagne flutes. "I'd say going with pink champagne is overkill. But if we're stuck drinking any rosé, then Veuve Clicquot is the way to go."

"You're such a snob."

"Discriminating," he corrected. His favorite comfort food was the ubiquitous fish and chips, with a couple of pints of Boddingtons to wash it down. Obviously not the profile of a snob. But bad wine could be like drinking turpentine. Life was too short to torture his taste buds.

"I'll drink anything with bubbles in it. Pour club soda into fruit punch and I'd be happy." Daphne lifted her glass to take a sip. Gib barely snatched her wrist in time to stop her.

"What do you think you're doing?"

"Letting the bubbles tickle my nose while they've still got some oomph."

"We need to toast. A romantic dinner always begins with a toast." He raised his glass. "To my beautiful companion, whose laugh is as effervescent as our drinks." Cheesily romantic to play to the night's theme, but also true. Once they clinked, he took a sip, noticing that Daphne's cheeks had flushed to match the champagne. "Are you too warm? Should I go adjust the radiator?"

She jerked her head to the side, staring down at the heart-shaped printed card next to the plate. "I'm fine."

"Then here we go." Gib picked up the card and read aloud. "'Figs stuffed with blue cheese. An open fig emulates the female sex organs and is a sexual stimulant.' Well, she's not pulling any punches, is she?"

"Why be subtle? I mean, if two people truly want each other, and hope that sharing a meal will bring them closer, why not just go for it?"

A viewpoint he'd never, in all his experience, heard uttered from a female's lips. If it was anyone but Daphne, he'd call it the verbal equivalent of a land mine. "Hmm. I thought women didn't like the wham, bam, thank you, ma'am, approach."

"Don't get me wrong." Daphne guzzled half her glass in a single swallow. "Foreplay's great. Love it." Her gaze skittered around the room, looking everywhere but at him. Had she drank too much coffee this afternoon? She seemed all hopped up. "What I don't like is all the gamesmanship leading up to a lip-lock."

"I prefer to think of it as a dance." He picked up the deep-purple fruit, feeling the contrast between the slightly sticky skin and its moist flesh. Slowly he lifted it, waiting until Daphne's eyes latched on before bringing it to hover even with her lips. She'd swiped red gloss across them, and they looked as full and plump as the fig.

More often than he liked, Gib caught himself thinking wholly inappropriate thoughts about Daphne's lips. As a friend, he respected her too much to consciously crave a taste of her luscious mouth. Sexy, smart-aleck Daphne. The only woman he'd ever encountered seemingly immune to his quick charm and quicker smile. But the lust snuck up on him unannounced, like fog stealing through the night. He'd have to be three days in his grave not to notice her earthy, sensuous beauty. So tonight he could partially give in to the simmering curiosity he'd ignored over the years, and have a little otherwise-forbidden fun with her.

Her lips parted, and he rubbed the fig along the bee-stung bottom lip until she opened enough for him to pop it in. "Well? Does it work for you? Are you ready to straddle me and go at it like a pair of minx?"

She finished chewing, eyes hooded. "Not quite yet."

"Ah, well. My turn, then." Gib nudged the plate toward her.

"What?" With the precision of a laser sight on a rifle, her gaze whipped back up to his face.

"You have to feed me. This is finger food. Be Daisy, a woman on the cusp of possessing the man she so greatly desires. Touch the food, all the while pretending that you're touching me. Use the food to seduce me." Knowing she'd never back down from a challenge, Gib leaned back in his chair with a smirk. "If you can, that is."

The determined jut of Daphne's chin told him she'd rise to his teasing bait. "Not a problem, Graham." She lingered over his fake name, dropping to almost a whisper. Then she reached across him for the next card by two wine goblets. "'Red Burgundy mixed with ginger, cloves, vanilla and sugar is known as the potent Hippocras aphrodisiac. Vanilla in particular is believed to increase lust.'"

"I am partial to vanilla pudding." Gib swallowed a laugh. He could practically see the cogs turning in her head, trying to figure out how to make him crack. This felt more like a strategic chess match than a seduction. Either way, he was having scads of fun.

Daphne shifted until she knelt on her chair. She squinted for a second, as though trying to get a read on a wary target. After hitching in a quick breath, she picked up the goblet. "Tip your head back and close your eyes."

"Why?" Last summer, after working nine days straight during the political convention, he'd fallen asleep on her couch during an *Iron Man* marathon. Her soft heart allowed him to nap there for four hours, undisturbed. Her wicked streak, however, woke him up by pouring a tumbler of ice water over his head. Gib was no fool, about to fall for the same trick twice. "Play nice, Daph."

"It's Daisy," she corrected. Her shirt slid off one shoulder as she raised her arm to bring the goblet nearer. Suddenly there was a whole lot of creamy skin a breath away from his face. The long, perfect line of her neck, the hollow of her collarbone—on any other woman, he'd be unable to resist the urge to map a trail of kisses along it. Gib gripped the edges of his chair. Hard. And thanked God he'd spread a napkin over his lap. Otherwise she'd see about eight rock-solid inches of wholly unsuitable reaction to her proximity tenting his trousers.

Now that he'd acknowledged—just for tonight—his attraction to her, the intensity of it overwhelmed him.

"Now close your eyes, or the dance is over."

What did she have planned? Closing his eyes, he tipped his head against the high, tufted chair back and waited. A droplet of liquid hit the seam of his lips, and Gib flicked out his tongue to catch it. The rich darkness of wine swirled with spices warmed his taste buds. The feel of her finger grazing the tip of his tongue shot heat straight to his cock. Gib's eyes flew open.

"Tastes good," he said.

Daphne smiled, a Mona Lisa smile, both innocent and mysterious. Then she dipped her finger back in the wineglass and rubbed it against his lips once more. "Does it taste like lust?"

It tasted like eight kinds of trouble. Like there should be sirens blaring and red lights flashing. "Tastes more like Christmas, I'd say." He sat up straight again, and she slid back onto her chair. Now he had space to breathe without inhaling the citrus scent of her. The scent as bright as her hair, and as cheerful as her smile. She so rarely wore perfume, not wanting to conflict with the aromas of all her flowers at work. Gib always noticed when she spritzed herself with the sunny scent. "But I wouldn't want to pass judgment without its proper food pairing."

"Good point. Let's try everything once, make our notes for Mira and then we can go back to our favorites."

"Did you pre-snack or something? This is dinner. I'm eating everything in sight, favorite or not." He grabbed the nearest plate. Pushing Daphne to pretend-seduce

him might have been a bit wrongheaded. This evening
was supposed to be nothing more than a bit of playact-
ing. There'd been no way to anticipate Daphne actually turning him on. Whatever she set her mind to, she
accomplished. He'd always admired that mix of bull-
headedness and perseverance in her.

"Here we've got goat cheese drizzled with honey on
a baguette. 'Honey was used by the Egyptians as a cure
for impotence. Medieval honeymooners drank honeyed
wine to sweeten their marriage.'"

"I don't care how good it tastes. Mira can't use this."

"Why not?"

"Being forced to think about impotence and marriage
in the middle of foreplay demolishes a man's amorous
intentions. You might as well stick his dick into a bucket
of ice." He jammed a piece of bread into his mouth.
Once you overlooked the description, the flavors melted
together into an amalgam of sweet, creamy tanginess.

"Why are men so allergic to the slightest mention
of marriage?"

"Why are women so single-minded about the topic?"

Daphne popped a piece of bread into her mouth and
chewed slowly. "Mmm, that's good." It almost came out
a purr. Did she do that on purpose? Make sexy noises
over a simple, three-bloody-ingredient hors d'oeuvre?
Was her end goal now to drive him stark-raving mad
with desire? Damned if he'd let her take the upper hand.

Picking up the goblet, Gib drank deeply, taking a moment to switch gears. He'd ease off the sexual throttle
for now, let her get comfortable with him again, and
then he'd go in for the kill. What topic could clear the

tension from the room? Ah, nothing would relax her more than talking about her great passion in life.

"I see you've got a new arrangement on the table." Gib took another sip, then waved his hand at the low centerpiece. "Tell me about these flowers. Do they have a hidden meaning?"

"Yes. Not that all my arrangements do. The language of flowers isn't that vast."

"There's no flower that says *I had a crappy day and really need a glass of wine?*"

"Much like Latin, I'm afraid it's a dead language."

"You should think about changing that. Imagine how much extra you could charge for carnations if you convinced people they were the official *sorry you lost your cell phone for the fifth time* flower."

Daphne chortled and popped another fig. "Gibson Moore, you are a marketing genius. I swear, your talents are wasted at that hotel."

"As long as they pay me well enough, I'm good with the status quo. So, these flowers?" he prompted.

"I had some orange lilies in the shop left over from the wedding at the Cavendish. And orange lilies just happen to signify desire and passion. With our plans to attack romance head-on tonight, I was compelled to bring them home. But lilies stuffed all alone in a vase either look like a funeral or Easter. So I made a nest for them out of balsam pine boughs, signifying ardent love. The frilly green stuffed in between the blossoms is coriander, for lust. I know it's silly. But I have fun with it."

"How'd you even find out about such a dead language?"

"My mother."

"Was she a florist, too?"

"No, just desperate to find a way to cheer me up."

"I don't understand."

"School didn't go so well for me at first. My teachers, and my parents, swore I was smart, but I couldn't do the simplest things. Luckily, it didn't take too many years for them to figure out I had dyslexia."

He couldn't believe she hadn't revealed that in all the years they'd known each other. Gib never would've guessed. His respect for her as a businesswoman, already sky-high, shot up into the stratosphere. "Wow, I had no idea."

"Good. That means that years of practice and frustration paid off. There's no cure, but if you work hard enough, you can figure out ways around it. Tough going at the start, though. Just because you're diagnosed doesn't mean there's a magic pill to fix it. I still felt like the stupidest person in the room most of the time. I was angry, and I was a handful. My mom talked to my tutor, my teacher, my therapist, but they all just said everything would work out in time. That's when Mom remembered hearing about a flower language. We learned it together. I was so thrilled there was an entire vocabulary without words. Within days I memorized it by rote. And got the self-confidence boost I needed to start to make real progress."

"Quite a story."

"Yeah. I had a great mom." Turning to skewer him with that laserlike gaze, she said, "You never mention your mother."

"That's right. Very observant of you. And you know

what I observe? There's one more appetizer that goes with this wine."

"Can't we skip right to the main course? It looks like lobster salad. I love lobster."

"Lobster and fennel salad, to be precise. But no, we can't skip ahead. There's a different drink for that course. Pink, again, I see."

"What, you'd prefer a Blue Hawaiian, so you can feel masculine?"

"That drink comes with a half-pound of fruit as a garnish. There's nothing masculine about it."

"Fine. Asparagus wrapped in prosciutto. 'Three courses of asparagus were served to nineteenth-century bridegrooms due to its reputed aphrodisiac powers, most likely because of its phallic shape.'"

"There she goes, hinting at marriage again. If I didn't know better, I'd swear Mira was trying to sell engagement rings along with this picnic."

"Hush."

"I'm sorry, but it's off-putting. When I see something described as a miniature penis, I'm not going to be in the mood to stick it in my mouth."

"Fine. I'll do it myself." Daphne picked up the asparagus spear and held it between her fingers like a cigarette. "Whoops! I almost forgot about my character. Daisy will now commence to feed herself, as Graham's apparently not feeling up to the task."

Once again, she pursed those red lips into a tight circle. Gib's heart lurched. That must be what happened when all the blood drained out of it in a single pump and relocated south of his belt. She bit off the tip, staring at him like a master hypnotist. "Salty. Delicious. Sure you don't want a bite?"

Christ, he wanted more than a bite. Gib yanked the asparagus out of her hand and dropped it back on the plate. Then, his own glass already drained, he reached for Daphne's wine and finished it off.

"What's wrong? Gib, you can't stop now. You have to sample everything."

"You're right. I do." He didn't care that it was stupid, and idiotic, and inappropriate and complicated. All he cared about at that moment was tasting her. So he did.

Gib pushed out of his chair and kicked it behind him, out of the way. Then he sank to his knees and framed Daphne's face with his hands. The face he'd stared into a million times. He knew the glacier-blue tint to her eyes. He knew intimately each one of her smiles, and the different degrees of each. He knew the pert tilt to her nose. But tonight he looked at the amalgam of all those parts, and saw a deeply beautiful woman who'd completely entranced him.

Where to begin? In the normal course of a seduction, he'd go slow, to tease both of them. A few light butterfly kisses just below her eyes, following the slash of her cheekbone, now as red as the spiced wine. Or maybe a nuzzle at the sensitive curve where her graceful neck connected to her smooth shoulders. If they were both in a playful mood, he'd rip that ugly flannel shirt apart right down the front, and bury himself in the valley between her breasts. Not tonight, though. They'd teased each other enough. So he dipped his head and took her glossy lips.

Daphne opened for him eagerly, as though they'd kissed a hundred times already. They latched on to each other hungrily. Gib couldn't believe he'd thought the champagne sweet, and the honey even sweeter. Nothing they'd tasted tonight compared to the singular sweetness of her kiss. And yet, even as he thought that, as she fell forward into his arms and straddled him, the sweetness disappeared.

Passion, raw and demanding, replaced it. Gib tried to take in the exquisite feeling of her thighs across his. The way the notch between her legs rubbed against him as her firm, wondrous breasts rubbed against his chest. But really, all he could concentrate on was the dark heat of her mouth. The slickness as her tongue twined with his as he explored her mouth. Finding just where to lick and nip to make her breath catch.

Driven by the need to make her purr again, he shifted his hands down to hold her close in a proper embrace. As he settled them loosely at her waist, a memory settled in place as well. Déjà vu, but a hundred times more real. He'd held her body like this before. Well, without the straddling. Just the embrace and the kiss. Gib would swear to it on every designer suit in his closet. He'd kissed this woman, held this body not two nights ago, in a pitch-dark ballroom.

The memory cemented itself on top of the reality, like placing a negative on top of a printed photo. The match was seamless. Daphne Lovell, his Daphne, was his Cinderella. Gib pushed her back to stare at her in shock.

"Why didn't you tell me?"

"What?" Her eyes slowly fluttered open.

"You're her. You're my mystery New Year's Eve kiss. Don't even try to deny it."

Daphne slid backward off his thighs onto the floor. "Yes. I am."

"Why didn't you tell me?"

Her expression turned defiant, with pursed lips and glowering eyes. "I didn't think you'd want to know."

"Are you insane? I spent the entire Rose Parade going on about how much I wanted to find that woman." He thought of how close he'd come to embarrassing himself all over the internet looking for the woman right in front of him.

"I mean, I didn't think you'd want to know it was me." She turned her head, dropped her gaze to the floor.

Gib stood, held out a hand and pulled Daphne to her feet as well. Then he surveyed the room; the chair he'd pushed onto the floor in his haste, the untouched lobster and a plate of chocolate-covered strawberries for dessert. And then he looked back at Daphne's face, now as white as the snow falling in clumps and sticking to the dark windows.

"I have to leave," said Gib.

FIVE

He who wants a rose must respect the thorn
                                        ~ Persian proverb

GIB SLAMMED THE door of his town house and shook himself like a dog. A thick coating of snowflakes flew onto the floor, the end table, the drapes and the damn white armchair that Milo adored and Gib detested. What good was furniture that you couldn't sit in to eat? He dropped his briefcase and a white paper sack onto the floor to shrug out of his overcoat.

"You're home early." Milo took in the dusting of snow on the green velvet drapes covering the bay window and rushed into action. With the speed of a fireman wielding a hose, Milo whipped the satin sash off of his kimono and used it to brush off each flake. Gib averted his eyes. He didn't know what his flamboyant roommate wore under the ankle-length blue robe, and he wanted to keep it that way.

Gib let his coat puddle onto the arm of the tufted, burgundy leather sofa. "Taking sex out of the equation makes for a shorter night."

With a disapproving tsk, Milo picked up the heavy coat and hung it in the closet. "That would be true, if you were with any woman but Daphne. I've seen you wander home from her place, bleary-eyed, in the middle of the night after watching a string of horror movies."

"Movies weren't on the agenda tonight." Of course, kissing hadn't been either. Still shell-shocked, Gib picked up his takeaway bag and walked down the hall to the kitchen.

"I thought dinner was, though. Why do I smell Indian food?"

What would it take to shake his bloodhound of a roommate with a nose for gossip? If he wanted to talk about the implosion of his night, Gib would've stayed with Daphne. "I fancied a curry." He kicked out a white, wooden stool at the breakfast counter to make room. After rolling up his sleeves, Gib pulled out the carton of curry. Then the bag of garlic naan, and cartons of samosas, rice and dal.

"Is Daphne coming over here now?" Milo asked. "There's certainly enough food for two of you. Probably for all three of us, if you were willing to let me stick my spoon in, too."

"Get your own damn dinner," Gib growled.

"Crankypants. You've had a burr under your saddle since you walked in the door." Milo perched on the stool and gasped. "What is that?" He pointed at Gib's trouser pocket with a shaky finger and a look of terror widening his brown eyes. Saying that Milo had a tendency to overdramatize situations was akin to saying the Pope liked to pray. Or that lingerie models looked good in their underwear.

"Just my tie."

"But it's crumpled up, hanging out of your pocket."

"I shoved it in there earlier." The moment he'd fled Daphne's apartment, it got hard to breathe. And his head began to pound so hard he swore he could hear his own blood pressure rising. "Christ, what do you care?"

Milo started to answer. His mouth opened, but then he shut it again. Then he got up and retrieved plates and silverware. Silently, he opened each carton, set two places on the counter and ripped off two paper towels for napkins.

"Thanks." Gib dug a spoon into the curry. He'd ordered it extra hot, hoping the spices would sear away the lingering sweet flavor of Daphne from his mouth.

"My wonderful roommate, Viscount Gibson Moore, loves clothes almost as much as he loves romancing the ladies. We first bonded over a Ralph Lauren gray cashmere sport coat. Of course, he wanted to wear it over a dress shirt, and I wanted to pair it with a Douglas tartan kilt. Made more of a statement."

Gib remembered that day. He remembered wondering how crazy you'd have to be to wear a kilt on the streets of Chicago. The two of them had gone out drinking that night, trading the jacket back and forth every time they changed bars. Milo might be a fashion lunatic, but he was also a hell of a lot of fun. Except for when he got on a soapbox, like this.

Working up a good head of steam, Milo came back around and braced one hand on the stool, and the other on the counter. "My roommate has more ties than most women have earrings. He treats his suits with the amount of devotion other men show their dogs."

Gib heaped rice and dal onto his plate, then mixed

everything together. He shoveled in a few bites. At least he didn't have to worry about being called upon to speak with his mouth full. Though Milo seemed disinclined to let him get a word in edgewise. Not that Gib wanted to talk. The big plan for the rest of the evening was to achieve a food coma as fast as humanly possible, then go to bed.

Milo leaned forward, a hard glint in his flat, brown gaze. "I care when my roommate appears to have undergone a psychotic break. This erratic behavior indicates one of two things. Either the Gib I know has been bodysnatched by an invisible alien, or something is very wrong." Whipping a cleaver out from behind his back, he brandished it at Gib. "If you are an alien, I'm prepared to defend myself."

"God, man, put that down." Despite his foul, mixed-up mood, Gib had to laugh.

"Not until you tell me what's going on. Did you and Daphne have a fight?"

If only. A fight would've cleared the air. A fight would've been easy. "Quite the opposite."

"I don't understand." Milo lowered the cleaver and hitched himself onto the stool.

"I kissed her. No," he caught himself. The order mattered. It made all the difference, in fact. "She bloody well kissed me first. On New Year's Eve." His fork fell from suddenly numb fingers, clattered against the china plate. "She's the one."

"Our Daphne?" Milo hopped off the stool. He paced the length of the kitchen in quick, jerky steps. "Daphne

Lovell? My boss? Co-owner of Aisle Bound and florist extraordinaire? Your best pal?"

"Yes to all but the last thing. Since I don't go around kissing my pals. Christ on a crumpet, now I don't even know what to call her anymore."

Milo tugged with both hands at his spiky blond hair, arms akimbo. "I can't believe she's your Cinderella. You really had no idea?"

"Of course not." Never in a million years would he have guessed Daphne would plant one on him in the dark. Why? Did this mean she wanted to screw him? Why now, after all these years as friends? Why then, at the wedding? Anonymously, in the dark? If she wanted to change the status quo, why not own it? "The point is that she didn't tell me. And then tonight, at the stupid aphrodisiac dinner, one thing led to another."

Milo froze, hands in hair, mouth working into surprised Os. "You mean the aphrodisiacs actually worked?"

He hesitated, then went with the expected answer. "How could they?" Except, was there any other smoking gun? "I don't know. I doubt it." Was it the food, or the game he made out of it? Gib couldn't entirely say what flicked the switch on his libido. It sure as hell hadn't been a conscious decision. "I can't explain it. All I can say is that I kissed her. Once we got into it, I knew."

"Got into it?" Trust Milo to latch on to the least important piece of information. He jumped back onto his stool with a lascivious grin. "More than a peck, then? A full-blown...what's that word you tea-and-scone types like to use? Snog?"

Americans. Fought for their independence, and yet

more than two hundred years later, were still titillated by all things British. "Yes. We snogged."

"And then what?"

Gib pushed his plate away. He'd been kidding himself to entertain the notion of eating. The knotted sea serpent of emotion lurching around his stomach left no room for food. "I left."

"No, before the leaving and after the snogging. What was her reaction?"

Probably would've been a good idea to stick around and catalogue it. "You don't understand. I just up and left. With almost no conversation. It was hideous."

"Makes sense. Must've been a lot to take in." The empathy and warmth coloring Milo's voice vanished with a naughty wink. "Realizing that Daphne has girl parts, I mean."

"She's not an androgynous robot. I'm quite aware of her womanly aspects." Now. Now, he was aware of her firm breasts and petal-soft lips and the way the flare of her hips gave him the perfect handhold to steady her on his lap. He'd spent years studiously ignoring all her curves. Some days it had been harder than others, but he'd made a go of it. Never again, though. Gib couldn't un-see, un-feel her body squirming closer to his, setting off a chain reaction between his heart, his dick and all the nerve endings in between.

"This isn't a forgettable bad grope in a bar. What's next?"

"Well, you can have all the curry, for starters." Gib got up to rummage in the refrigerator for a ginger ale. Wondered when Milo would stop channeling his feminine side and quit talking this thing to death.

"Be serious. Because the situation certainly is."

Gib walked down the hallway lined with art deco prints, shedding his shirt along the way. Oh, and desperately resisting the urge to sniff the collar and see if any of Daphne's scent still lingered. To his dismay, Milo didn't take the hint. Instead, he followed Gib into his bedroom, badgering all the way.

"You and Daphne talk to each other almost every day. You spend oodles of time together. What do you think will happen the next time you see each other? Which, if I remember right, will probably be tomorrow?"

The monthly National Association of Catering Executives meeting. The gathering place for everyone in the wedding industry. With a vicious wrench of each ankle, Gib sent his loafers flying into the corner. He and Daphne always went to the NACE meetings together. They liked to sit in the back and whisper to each other. This month's speaker was on events. He couldn't miss it. More to the point, he couldn't—wouldn't—hide like a scared schoolboy. "Tomorrow night, yes," he muttered.

"It'll be weird." Milo sat on the black down comforter.

"Undoubtedly."

"You need a plan."

"I don't have one." How could he come up with a plan when he could barely think? When he did think about the kiss, his dick surged in his shorts. That sort of reaction usually short-circuited thinking. Gib dropped his shirt on the bed. "How about giving me some space?"

He glared at Milo, then jerked his head toward the door. It didn't budge his roommate.

"What would Doc Debra tell you to do?"

Really? Like he didn't have enough to worry about tonight? Milo might as well ask him to come up with a solution to fossil fuel dependence while he was at it. "Why would you bring her up?"

"She was your shrink for almost six months. Didn't you go to her to figure out how to deal with your commitment issues?"

If he'd been a vampire, Gib would've hissed and bared his fangs. Or as a werewolf he could've growled. Hell, even kittens could make their fur stand on end as warning. But the most Gib could do was slam the closet door once he retrieved his slippers shaped like soccer balls. Daphne had given them to him as a joke last Christmas. However, Chicago winters were no joke, and as ridiculous as they looked, he appreciated the warmth.

He spat out the psychobabble line Doc Debra had drummed into him at every appointment. "I don't have commitment issues. I incurred an emotional trauma in my formative years and am still dealing with the fall-out."

"Potato, potahtoh," Milo said in a singsong voice. "My way is shorter than saying 'my family treated me like crap but nobody else can hurt me if I don't let them get close to me.' Didn't the good doctor tell you to start engaging in deeper relationships?"

"Yes." Over and over and over again. "But I already have a deep relationship with Daphne."

"That gives you a leg up, doesn't it?" Milo bounced

on the bed with the energy of a toddler. Gib wished he'd bounce right down the hall to his own room. "You need to ask her out on a date."

"What would we do on a date?"

That stilled his bouncing. "You're kidding, right? How often do you two go to the movies, or watch sports together, or grab dinner? Aside from missing out on the nervousness, perfume and enough hickeys to turn into a connect-the-dots anatomy lesson, you guys have essentially gone on hundreds of dates already."

"I'm not sure dating one of my best friends is a good idea." In fact, it sounded just about as dangerous as juggling running chain saws, or flaming swords. Or both, at the same time.

"You promised Doc Debra you'd try. Before she agreed to cut you loose, you promised to make a stab at a healthy, normal relationship."

"I obviously tell you too much. Either that, or I talk in my sleep and you listen at the door." Gib pulled out his pajamas, and then slammed the drawer. And yet again, Milo didn't take it as an invitation to drop the subject and walk away. The problem with having a really close circle of friends was that as the years slipped by, it became harder to hide any deep, dark secrets. Which meant truths that hit uncomfortably close to home could be lobbed when they were least expected—or wanted.

"Do you ever wonder why I don't have a serious boyfriend?"

Now that was an easy one. "Because you flit through the clubs like a bee with ADD in a rose garden?"

An uncharacteristically still, expressionless Milo

stared back at him. "Don't be glib. We're having a sharing moment."

To his great dismay. "Must we?"

"I'm not like Ivy. I don't think every man I meet could be 'The One.'" Milo made air quotes with his fingers. "But I'm constantly looking. I want to find my soul mate. The person who makes me happy, day or night, just by being in my life. The olive in my martini. The guacamole to my tortilla chip. The bun to my—"

Gib held up his hand. "Stop. I get it. You want to find true love. Good for you. Doesn't mean I feel the same way."

"I think you do, deep down. You're just scared. Otherwise you wouldn't be fighting it so hard. Don't treat Daphne like a disposable toy. You both deserve better. Ask the girl on a date. If it all goes south and you laugh your way through it, no harm done. But don't squander this chance. Not everybody gets one."

Too bad he hadn't known Milo could be so insightful. Gib wouldn't have wasted two hours a week for six months with a shrink.

THE DINING ROOM at Gulliver's Pizza and Pub wasn't very crowded. The ceiling, on the other hand, didn't have an inch of spare room. Ornate chandeliers, Tiffany-style lamps and gilt sconces vied for space. Marble busts sat atop the end cap of each booth. Daphne had no trouble finding her father at a table in the center of the restaurant, holding court.

Decades ago, Stuart Lovell began the weekly tradition of a night of beer and pizza at Gulliver's with his buddies. Once his wife died, it morphed into a safe haven. Someplace he could go to escape the drama of four teenagers. As his children left the nest, Gulliver's became a haven from his empty, lonely house. Daphne knew he came here often. The staff treated him as a regular. The owner, Marge, treated him like a potential third husband. All in all, Gulliver's was a good stand-in for when his children weren't around. Which was most of the time. Daphne tried to meet him for dinner a couple of times a month.

"There's my favorite daughter."

"Bar's pretty low, Dad, seeing as how I'm your only child that wears a bra." She kissed his cheek and took a seat.

"Don't sass me. After spending a week with your brother and his brood, I've earned a healthy share of peace and quiet."

"Oh." Maybe she should go. Save the soul-baring for another night. Or maybe order a couple of boilermakers to loosen him up?

"I missed you. Did you have a good New Year's Eve?"

Whoa. Dad had no way of knowing he'd just picked the scab off her still-raw heart. But she wasn't ready to spill it all yet. Maybe she was the one who needed liquid courage. Daphne knew she should've tried that last pink cocktail Mira had set out. "I was working, remember?"

"Doesn't mean a handsome groomsman didn't charm you out of a kiss or two at midnight." A bushy, salt-and-pepper eyebrow dipped in the middle as he winked at her. "No man in his right mind could resist those blue-bells you've got for eyes."

They might not be at all objective, but her father's compliments always felt good. Warm and comforting, like a towel straight from the dryer. "Thanks, Dad."

"What brings you out in the middle of a snowstorm? I didn't expect to see you tonight."

As a Chicago native, it was easy for Daphne to ignore anything less than a full-blown blizzard. "It's just a few flurries. And I wanted to talk to you. I made Mom's cinnamon rolls yesterday. Everybody came over to watch the Rose Parade. I guess it made me want to reminisce."

His big, meaty paw, the one that could still throw a tight spiral when they played flag football on Thanksgiving, came to rest on top of her arm. "Let me ask you an important question."

"Okay." Geez, what could it be? They'd just seen each other a week ago. Why'd he look so serious?

"Did you save a few of those rolls for your dear old dad?"

"Of course." Daphne dug into her bag for the foil packet she'd prepared before leaving home.

He lurched out of his seat to plant a smacking kiss on her cheek. "Then you really are my favorite child."

"They're a day old now, so they might need a little extra butter." The waitress dropped off a foam-topped, frosty mug. Eagle-eyed Marge must've seen Daphne come in. She lifted the beer in a salute of thanks toward the bar. "Is Marge taking good care of you?"

"She always does. But don't think you can change topics on me. You've got something on your mind. And it's not a certain restaurant owner who brings your dad lasagna when he's sick."

Interesting. Dad had turned a polite but blind eye to Marge's blatant advances for years. As far as Daphne knew, he hadn't seriously dated anyone since her mother died. There'd been several four-day weekends away. He usually came home from those rumpled and smelling of perfume. Never once, though, had he brought a woman home to dinner with his kids. She wondered what finally tipped the scales. Daphne also vowed to order this magical lasagna next time around.

"Does she really?"

He pinked up to the color of the baby carnations she used on pomander balls for flower girls. "Promise me you won't mention it to your brothers."

She pantomimed zipping her lips and throwing away the key. Not ratting him out wasn't a big deal. Not when she could still razz him about it. And maybe invite Marge out to drinks and pump her for details soon, too. "So here's the thing, Dad." Daphne placed her palms flat on the table. "I kissed a boy."

"Not for the first time. I know that for certain." He returned to his plate of cannoli as though they were still discussing the weather.

"Do you?"

"God help me, I'll never forget it. You kissed Rory St. Cloud on the couch when you were fourteen. You two were supposed to be watching the Cubs on TV. I'd gone down to the basement to start a load of laundry. Never occurred to me you were old enough yet to be having shenanigans with a boy during a ball game."

Good thing she was sitting down, or Daphne would've hit the floor. Guess Dad still had a few surprises tucked up his sleeve. "I didn't realize you knew about that. How come you didn't barge in and break us up?"

"Fathers—especially single fathers—know how important it is to maintain boundaries. If you recall, your brothers ended up watching the rest of that game with you. Let's just say it wasn't entirely their idea."

Stunned yet again, she sat for a minute. Only the clink of glassware and the comfortable hum of satisfied customers broke the silence. Finally she took a pull of her beer. "Sneaky. Brilliant, but sneaky."

"Grasping at straws is a better description. I was not ready to deal with my daughter turning boy-crazy." He ground the heels of his hands over his eyes, as though trying to rub out the memory. "Caveman instincts kicked in as soon as I saw that little slug mashing his face into yours."

"What sort of instinct? Because I think I'd remember you dragging me by my ponytail up to my room and throwing away the key."

"I wanted to let your brothers beat up any guy who looked at you twice. About the only thing I knew for certain, though, was that I'd have to ignore my instincts. I drove out to the cemetery that afternoon and railed at your mother. Not one of my finer moments. Sat on her grave and asked her how I was supposed to raise a daughter all by myself."

Daphne shrugged, with a cocky grin. "I'm still here, aren't I? Guess you didn't screw it up too badly." It shook her, though. That her dad had struggled to finish raising five kids by himself was obvious. What she'd never taken into account, though, was that handling a female in the midst of very testosterone-scented territory must've been a whole different kind of torture.

"What I'm guessing is that I'm not finished yet. Otherwise why would you hike out here to tell me you kissed someone?" His blue eyes narrowed. "What's really eating at my girl?"

"I think I should've kept my lips to myself. Now everything's messy and complicated. I don't see how to go back to the way things were."

"Why bother? Don't waste your time pining for the past. The only way to deal with whatever life throws at you is to move forward."

Her father was supposed to be a master plumber, not a philosopher. "Did you steal that from the back of a self-help book?"

"I'm serious. Maybe it was time for things to change."

"No. Gib and I were fine."

"Gibson, eh? He's got quite the roving eye for the ladies. Why don't you want it turning on you for once?"

"He's the one with the problem. He's the one who's not interested. Who never bothered to notice that I was right under his nose the whole time."

"Ah, so you threw a Hail Mary. Took your one shot at scoring."

"Dad!"

"Did he not, uh, catch the ball? If so, the man's blind as a bat and dumb as a box of hammers. You're everything a man could want, sweetheart."

"He wanted to make a first down—geez, can we stop the sports metaphors? Gib didn't know it was me." She squirmed. Her regrettable cannonball into spontaneity didn't hold up well under scrutiny. Best to gloss over the details. "Long story. But then, tonight, *he* kissed *me*."

"Did he now? Then why aren't you spending this snowy night cuddled up with him, instead of keeping me company?"

God. Talking to her father about boys was just as uncomfortable now as when he first attempted it after her mom died. And yet no matter how Daphne protested, he continued to insist on trying to be both parents to her, no matter what the subject. Although always awkward as hell, she did have to admit he was really good at it. "Gib left. Once he realized that I was the one who kissed him on New Year's Eve, he just got up and left."

"Unusual reaction." The words slipped out fast, and her father looked like he regretted them instantly.

This was why she'd come here tonight. To beg Dad for insight. Unfortunately, doing so opened up a cache of insecurities bigger than Soldier Field. "Mom was supposed to teach me how to be a woman. She had it all mapped out. On my thirteenth birthday she'd let me read a racy romance novel. On my fourteenth birthday she'd teach me all about makeup. And on my fifteenth birthday, she'd teach me how to flirt."

"I wish you'd told me there was a road map for all these milestones," he said, pushing away his empty plate.

"It was a mother-daughter secret. Our special plan. Except she never got to do any of those things. Those were the big ones, but I bet there were a hundred tiny things she never got to teach me, too."

Daphne plunked her elbows on the table, sighed and sank her chin on top of her hands. She'd always been able to tell her dad anything. But this was laying out on a silver platter her biggest fear. Trotting out her emotional Achilles' heel. Daphne hadn't felt this exposed since her last trip to the gynecologist.

"What if I missed something? Some intrinsic life lesson? Something major, that would make all the difference in dealing with the opposite sex? What if that's why Gib is so horrified at the thought of kissing me that he'd leave without a word?"

Her father scooted his chair closer. Then he put his arm around her shoulders. The heavy wool of his fisherman's sweater scratched her neck. "Don't think for a minute that you're lacking in any way. You're an amazing woman. The proof is in your circle of good friends, the two businesses you co-own, and that you're the apple of your father's eye." A pinch on the cheek punctuated his listing of her attributes.

"I'm telling you, there's got to be something I'm missing. Gibson Moore would flirt with a tree frog if it was female. Yet he can't stand the thought of doing it with me, one of his closest friends. What was the big secret to being a woman that Mom never told me?"

"If I could help you, I would. I'm afraid I'm not part of that club. But I think if you were putting your lipstick on wrong, Ivy wouldn't hesitate to step up and tell you."

Sitting here in the familiar antique-filled chaos of Gulliver's in her dad's embrace, Daphne felt herself slipping back through time. He hadn't always had the answers when she sought his advice, but he'd always had a warm hug, and the patience to listen. Of course, now Daphne was older. Savvy enough to realize that no matter how good the hug felt, it didn't sweep away any of her problems with Gib. Just getting it all off her chest didn't actually solve anything.

Marge bustled over, hair teased as impossibly high as it was impossibly scarlet. "You two doing good? Daphne, do you want some dinner to wash down that beer?"

"No, thanks. I ate already." Sort of. Once Gib left, she'd been too churned up to eat another bite. Before going to bed, she'd have to try at least one bite of everything. Then write up her thoughts on the menu for Mira. What the heck would she say? *Surprise—aphrodisiacs apparently really do work?* Maybe the whole picnic should come with a label. *Warning—these products are more effective than you may believe.*

"You look down in the dumps. Did you lose a chunk of money betting on all the bowl games over the holiday?"

"Marge, I don't bet on sports." Daphne shook her hands in the air, as if wafting away the very idea of it. "Watching's enough excitement for me."

"Really? Your dad sure lost a bundle. He sulked all the way through his dinner about it, until you showed up." She ruffled his salt-and-pepper hair. "I thought you two were peas in a pod."

After all these years, how did her father still have any secrets stashed up his sleeve? Placing sports bets *and* romancing Marge? Daphne couldn't wait to get home and email all her brothers with the latest. "Dad, you gambled? Do you have a bookie that you meet in a dark alley? It sounds dangerous. I don't want you getting kneecapped."

"Thanks for winding her up, Marge." He scowled and batted her hand away. "Nobody's coming after me with a crowbar. I never bet more than I know I won't mind losing. Well, I mind, but you know what I mean."

This coming from the man who never let her spend a cent of birthday money from the grandparents. He insisted it all go straight into Daphne's college account. "I had no idea you were such a risk taker."

"Sounds like you just took a pretty big gamble of your own."

Good point. And look where it had gotten her so far—confused, upset and alone. It'd be a cold day in the Congo before she took a risk like that again. "Well, I do feel like Gib sort of kneecapped me when he walked out tonight."

"Don't be so sure. I don't think either one of you is ready to call it yet. You changed the rules of the game. Give him a chance to familiarize himself with the new playbook."

Marge toed out a chair and sat down. "For goodness' sake, Stu, are you coaching the Super Bowl or your daughter? Stop beating around the bush. You'll both be uncomfortable for less time if you just spit out whatever you're trying to say."

The tips of his ears turned red. Just like when he'd wordlessly dropped her off at the gynecologist for the first time. "A kiss can change everything. If you let it. If you want it to. Do you?"

Good question. But the good questions were rarely the easy ones. To answer something this tough, Daphne needed much, much more sugar to boost her brain cells. Like an entire cheesecake's worth, covered in chocolate and caramel sauce. "I don't know."

"Gib probably doesn't either. Why not sleep on it and see how you feel in the morning?" Finally. Her dad's go-to solution for everything: a good night's sleep. With the same frequency other parents pulled aspirin and antibiotics from their arsenal of cures, her dad wielded the mighty power of shut-eye. He claimed it could mend friendships, heal wounds and guarantee good test scores. All Daphne thought it did was prevent her eyes from looking like she'd gone ten rounds in a mixed martial arts cage match.

"Just because it can change everything, doesn't mean it has to." Marge squeezed her hand. "Men move slowly." She shot a poison dart of a look at Stuart. "It takes them time to wrap their heads around something new. So give the boy a little time to adjust. Just go about your business like normal, and wait for him to catch up."

Daphne could do normal. For years, her normal had meant hiding her true feelings from Gib. She could pull that off even without a caffeine jolt. But how long would he make her wait? And if nothing changed, how would she know if he'd decided to ignore the whole thing, or if he was still adjusting to their new normal?

SIX

*If seeds in the black earth can turn into such
beautiful roses, what might not the heart of man
become in its long journey toward the stars?*

~ *G. K. Chesterton*

DAPHNE LOOKED AT the bucket full to the brim with pine
boughs and sighed. They smelled good. In fact, the
whole shop smelled good. But her hands would be sticky
for the rest of the day from the sap, poked by sharp
needles and grooves worn into her fingers from wiring
each piece of pine to a lisianthus blossom.

This week's Aisle Bound bride—the difficult one,
anyway—wanted every chair at dinner to have its own
swag draped across the back. Even though there were
only fifty guests, this single piece of her order would
take Daphne an entire afternoon. Without allowing her
to make any headway on the centerpieces, bouquets,
corsages or ceremony arrangements. Maybe she should
skip the NACE meeting tonight. Turn on some Weezer
and work till her fingers bled or the music ran out. It
wouldn't be the first time she'd pulled an all-nighter.
Flowers were delicate, and short-lived. This wasn't the
kind of job where you could work very far ahead on a
project.

Except she absolutely could not, would not, skip the NACE meeting. These meetings were vitally important to her business. The networking couldn't be matched for any price. Much of the wedding industry worked by word of mouth. One night of chatting over acidic wine and cubed cheese on toothpicks could net her five or ten referrals. Clients didn't want to do the work themselves. And Daphne didn't blame them one bit. There were over two hundred reception sites to choose from in Chicagoland. After wading through all of those, who had the energy to call fifty different florists?

NACE meetings were also a long-standing tradition between she and Gib. The two of them wisecracking from the back row was the only way to survive the tedium of the official program. Gib always brought a handpicked bag of classic candy like Curly Wurlys and Flakes for them to split. Or, in reality, for her to hog while Gib fought her for a scant third of the pieces.

He'd be there, no doubt. If she didn't show, he'd interpret it the wrong way. What was she supposed to do, send a note? *Please excuse Daphne, she has work to do and swears it has nothing to do with what happened last night.* Whether everything changed or nothing changed, they were still friends. That alone wouldn't change. Gib ran last night. Daphne refused to let him think she'd run away, too.

"It smells good in here." Ivy joined her in the back of their shop. Her rose-colored, midcalf tight skirt with a ruffle at the bottom and fitted jacket pointed to a day packed with client meetings. Daphne hoped they all not only signed up for Ivy's services, but desperately needed a florist, too. The Aisle Bound summer schedule was pretty much finalized, but there were still a few fall weekends clamoring to be penciled in as profit makers. "I brought you a snack. It's National Chocolate-Covered Cherry Day, so here's a chocolate cherry scone from Lyons Bakery."

Daphne wiped clammy palms on her lavender apron before snapping up the sugary goodness. Finally, someone to be the whipping boy for her frazzled nerves. "Did Lisbet forget to turn over the calendar page? Shouldn't we remind her that Christmas is over?" Daphne shook the nearest branch. Its needles flared like a Victorian debutante's fan. "I had more than my fill of dealing with all things pine-related last month. As did all of her expected guests, I'm sure. Why on earth didn't you talk her out of this?"

"Me? I only mediate between the bride and whoever she brings along to the appointment. From day one, you told me, and I quote, to 'keep my big, loud mouth shut during any and all floral consultations.'" Ivy made air quotes with her fingers to drive home her complete lack of responsibility in the matter.

"Still holds true, by the way. That particular clause in our partnership contract will never expire. But the next time you see me letting a bride do something this stupid, at least kick me under the table." Shin splints would be far preferable to another Christmas in January snafu. Daphne scarfed down the scone in three bites. It didn't soothe her much. It did make her crave a white-chocolate mocha. With whipped cream and chocolate jimmies.

"It will be my pleasure." Hitching up her skirt, Ivy

shimmied onto the white iron stool with a lavender cushion at the counter. It looked like a salvage from a turn-of-the-century ice cream parlor. "I agree that the pseudo-Christmas decorations are a big mistake. Lisbet is one of our more—how do I put this—artistically challenged clients."

"Stop sugarcoating it. She's got crappy taste."

Ivy wrinkled her nose. "I'd never say such a thing. You know the rule. Whatever makes the bride happy is the right choice for them."

Uh-huh. Sure. Just as believable as oh, say, all the dirty magazine centerfolds having natural breasts. Or that an aging movie star's trophy wife hadn't demanded a prenup. Daphne grabbed another pine branch. Shook the water off the ends. "You've got that super-saccharine tone in your voice. Like a pixie stick took over your vocal cords. Lisbet must be a hot mess. Come on, where else has she gone wrong?"

"Daphne, we don't talk badly about clients. Ever. Not even the ones who believe their dachshund will successfully pull a wagon carrying the six-month-old ring bearer down the aisle. And especially not the ones who invited all the groom's ex-girlfriends as a surprise."

Daphne pitied her friend for the wedding day fraught with guaranteed trouble. On the other hand, Daphne couldn't wait to hear all the gritty and entertaining details. Too bad it wasn't a week when the reality show *Planning for Love* followed Ivy around with cameras rolling. "You are going to earn your keep this weekend. Sounds like it has the potential to turn messy. Need any help?"

Ivy shook her head. "All in a day's work. Ultimately, I'm sure that Lisbet and Brett will have a wonderful day. And by that, I mean I'll *make* sure."

She didn't doubt her partner's abilities for a second. "Can you hang out back here and keep me company while I get started on these swags?"

"Sure. Julianna's doing a client walk-through of the Field Museum for the rest of the morning. We're pretty quiet. Are we having an impromptu partner meeting?"

"God, no." Daphne shuddered. Numbers gave her mental hives. "You know I require a pitcher of margaritas when we start discussing profit margins and all things accounting."

"Then are we finishing the blow-by-blow description of last night's smooch fest? Because I'm still not clear on whether or not I'm supposed to be mad at Gib." Ivy waved her hand back and forth like a teeter-totter. "Right now, I'm leaning heavily toward being both insulted on your behalf and ready to seek revenge. Maybe we could do something to his beloved car. Shaving cream the windows? Fill it with packing peanuts?"

Daphne's mood immediately lifted. Best friends were waaaaay better medicine than a stupid good night's sleep. Not that she'd done more than catnap all night. "Good brainstorming, but I don't want you to be mad at Gib. You're sworn to secrecy. I want the status quo of our happy little group to remain unchanged. This kiss thing is just between him and me."

Milo poked his head around the door. The frosted blond tips spiked skyward. A vintage mustard tie wider than his hand fluttered from his neck. "Hardly."

Like a gossip grenade, the presence of their office manager splintered any hopes of this remaining a secret into infinitesimal fragments. "Were you eavesdropping?" Daphne demanded.

"Just a little." He edged into the room. High-waisted pants that would've looked right on Jimmy Stewart—in his heyday—skimmed across shiny brown wing tips. "Purely out of male solidarity." Milo wagged a finger at Daphne. "You broke my roommate last night, you know. He came home completely shattered. A mere shadow of his former self."

Daphne bit her lip to keep from smiling. "Really?" Unexpected, but welcome news. An upset Gib meant that he hadn't just taken their kiss in stride. It affected him. Exactly how, she didn't know. But any reaction was better than none. "Tell me more."

Slowly, Milo swung his head back and forth like a pendulum. "Sorry. It would be a breach of the roommate code."

Ivy harrumphed. "What about the you-work-for-us code?"

He struck a thinking pose, stroking a wholly imaginary beard. "Good point. As long as it's on the record that I'm not recklessly spilling secrets."

Right. As if he didn't share every single secret he learned with everyone from the shoe-shine guy to his parents back in Iowa. "Of course. You're the soul of discretion," Daphne muttered, not bothering to coat her sarcasm in even a thin layer of legitimacy.

"What do you want to know? You kissed him—"

"He kissed me," she corrected hotly. Bad enough

that she'd leaped off that particular cliff on New Year's Eve. Daphne refused to take the blame for this latest episode. "Gib started it."

"Whatever." Milo swished away her objection with nails that shone from a fresh buff. "He might've started it, but you finished him. Gib's not moody. He's either working hard or playing harder. Last night, though, he was wallowing. The man couldn't eat. He could barely string two sentences together. He looked like the big, scary monster from inside his childhood closet had just leaped out from behind the tapestries and scared twenty years off of him."

With pursed lips, Ivy gave a tight nod. "Good. He shouldn't be able to walk out on Daphne without feeling shaken."

"But Daphne looks fine," Milo protested. He waved an arm up and down at her. "Why are you so worried about her when Gib is a wreck of a man?"

Good to know she'd camouflaged the worst of her emotional crisis. Better to know that the forty-five dollars she so reluctantly spent on concealer was actually worth it. "The whole storming out with no explanation thing stung, I'll admit." Stung? It was the worst rejection of her life. Gib piloting a riding mower across her heart would've hurt less. "But I'm definitely not a wreck." In fact, hearing that Gib hadn't shrugged off their kiss as one among millions cheered her more than a triple-chocolate brownie.

"Glad to hear it," trumpeted an unfamiliar voice from the hallway.

All three of them swung around to gawk at the woman framed in the door. She stood with her feet braced wide to counterbalance the matching briefcase, laptop case and purse that could double as an overnight bag. A no-nonsense brown bob was tucked behind both ears. Short and wide, she wore a blue suit that made her look like a postal box.

"Ruth?" Ivy hustled forward first, arms spread for a hug. "It's so good to see you."

Ruth dropped the bags in a pile. "Thought I'd come accept your wedding invite in person."

Hardly. Wiping her hands on her apron, Daphne bit back a suspicious grunt. Ruth Moder blasted through cities faster than Godzilla. If she fell asleep in the same time zone she'd woken up in eighteen hours earlier, she considered it a lazy day. RealTV kept her hopping. The network produced all its own programming, and promised no repeats before midnight or after dawn. That left a lot of hours of reality television to fill. Ruth was their closer, contracting people, companies, pets, whatever had a chance at keeping America's eyelids in the vertical and locked position. Her appearance here at Aisle Bound could be nothing less than wholly job-related.

Daphne followed them down the hall to the front seating area where they did most of the bridal consultations. Watched Milo clatter into a frenzy of preparing a tray of coffee cups, spoons, hastily plated cinnamon chocolate cookies and a bud vase sporting a single deep-purple tulip. Her overdeveloped sweet tooth instantly begrudged their visitor each of those cookies she had yet to even taste. Daphne had harbored private afternoon plans for them, involving a quiet, dark place and a noble drowning in a glass of chocolate milk.

Ruth splayed her hands wide on the armrests of what

Daphne called their throne chair. Like something out of
Alice in Wonderland, the seat back rose to almost five
feet. Covered in white brocade, it enveloped a bride,
putting distance between her and the matching sofa
where Ivy relegated however many well-meaning but
overbearing relatives accompanied her.

"Thank God you have coffee. I left Vermont at dawn.
This adorable cheese and sheep commune, filled with
lesbians. Mark my words, the ratings for that will be off
the charts. Every red-blooded eighteen-to-thirty-five-
year-old man will watch, convinced *he'll* be the one
who could turn them." Ruth shook her head. Her hair
flew in a nimbus, revealing streaks of gray. "Egotisti-
cal idiots." But she smiled as she said it.

Daphne figured she must be picturing the waist-high
stacks of cash a show like that would generate. Probably heard a dinging in her ears akin to a slot machine
paying out.

"People will watch anything." Ivy settled onto the
long white sofa.

"And thank God for it!"

With the solemnity of the waiters at any of Chicago's
venerable steak houses, Milo poured for all of them.
He must've remembered Ruth was left-handed. The
delicate white mug was handed to her with handle facing left. While he might look like nothing more than
a flighty trend-chaser, Milo's attention to detail made
him an invaluable member of the Aisle Bound team.
He retrieved Ivy's notepad from her office and placed
it on the glass coffee table.

Daphne understood why he fussed. Milo loved any
excuse to play host on top of his office manager duties.

And she definitely understood why Ivy would now and forevermore at least listen to any pitch from Ruth. The two contracts Ruth had hand-delivered to Ivy were the foundation of one heck of a nest egg. Ivy had used it to open A Fine Romance. Ruth had earned the place of honor by giving Ivy a chance to make her dreams come true.

What Daphne didn't understand was what on earth Ruth could want from Ivy. The contract to film Ivy and Ben's wedding was already signed. They'd told her, in no uncertain terms, it would be the last thing Ivy filmed for RealTV. Daphne hovered by the front door. Not sitting allowed her to watch everyone's body language and expressions. She liked Ruth well enough. Just didn't trust that the woman had any motivation or ethical stance that wasn't rooted in money.

"I'd love the chance to catch up, but that will have to wait for your wedding day," said Ruth, with an apologetic twist of her lips.

Riiiight. Because a bride and groom had nothing better to do than shoot the breeze while they and their hundred closest friends were being filmed for live television. Daphne darted her hand in for a cookie. An objective observer still needed fuel. Then she faded back to hang by the display window. Mostly because she thought it rocked.

To wipe the visual red-and-green slate of Christmas away, she'd gone with an elegant, winter-white theme. Daphne had covered two Styrofoam snowmen with leftover Christmas tree flocking for texture. One wore a shiny black top hat and a duo of white ranunculus. The stems were wrapped in glossy black ribbon. The snow-bride's twig arm ended in a bouquet of white sweet peas and narcissus, interspersed with black privet berries. Black satin cinched it all together in a tight braid. Branches of white snowberries lay crisscrossed in between the bride and groom. No doubt she'd get ten calls before the week ended asking about the sophisticated bouquet.

Draining her coffee in one big gulp, Ruth dropped her hands to her lap. Her gaze followed, a split second later. "I'm here to beg a favor."

No. Whatever it was, the answer had to be no. Ivy had sacrificed enough of her private life to this network of vampires, who profited by sucking everyday life out of their reality "stars." Daphne wolfed down her cookie, ready to back up her friend when Ivy tossed the intractable Ruth out on her ear.

"We've got a show finale coming up in just over two weeks. This one is big. Has a huge following. You wouldn't believe the number of tweets it gets every week. But one of our participants had to back out." Ruth leaned forward and dropped her voice to a whisper. "I can't tell you why, but if you guessed botched plastic surgery, I'd give you a knowing nod."

Ivy tucked the toe of one beige platform pump behind the heel of the other. After watching Ivy drool over the Duchess of Cambridge's most-buzzed-about shoes, Daphne had bought her a pair as an engagement present. Ben, however, didn't get a present. She adored him, and truly believed he'd be a wonderful husband. But he'd snatched Daphne's best friend—and best roommate—away from her. She considered Ivy to be gift enough for him.

"I'm grateful that you gave me the means to kick-start A Fine Romance. Grateful beyond words that you brought Ben and me together." A conciliatory smile belied the ice hardening Ivy's green eyes, as delicately hard as hoarfrost on pine. "But I won't be on another show for you."

"Yeah, I got that the first twenty times. You don't have to hit me over the head with a rock." Ruth lifted her head to stare straight at Daphne. "I want your partner."

Good thing she'd finished that cookie, or the breath she sucked in would've vacuumed the crumbs straight to her lungs. Daphne flattened her palms against the glass door. Amazing how such a ridiculous notion tripped her heart into triple time. All she had to do to quell the panic was spit out one simple, unequivocal word. "No."

As sinuous as the serpent who tempted Eve in the garden, Ruth arched her body forward. A smile flirted at the corners of her unpainted mouth. "You haven't heard my proposition yet."

Mouth dry, blood pounding in her ears, Daphne reminded herself of the obvious. Ruth had no angle here, no leverage to convince Daphne to do the impossible. The reason Ivy agreed to let RealTV's cameras follow her for months on end was to bring a long-held dream to life. But Daphne didn't have any unfulfilled dreams left. Owning the floral shop, partnering with Ivy in Aisle Bound was everything she'd ever hoped for.

Almost. One pipe dream still flitted through her consciousness. Now, more than ever, she'd barter away her

Catholic soul for the chance to sleep with Gib. But even Ruth Moder wasn't wily enough to make that happen. Daphne pushed off the door. "You want me to be on television, right? The answer is no."

"Daphne doesn't like being the center of attention," Milo explained. He patted Daphne's arm. It made her feel a bit like a skittish colt being settled. But he was right. Her four brothers were so big, so loud, that they'd taken up most of the space in her life for a good many years. Daphne found it easy to fade into the background at home. She had no idea how to compete with the status—and makeup-obsessed girls in high school, so the background comforted her there, too. Attention made her self-conscious. It fit about as well as a wet suit three sizes too small.

"You think I don't know that? Hours upon hours of good footage, left on the cutting room floor because this one's," Ruth hooked her thumb at Ivy, "love-drunk fiancé insisted on keeping you out of the shot."

Awww. Maybe she'd get Ben a present after all. Right after shooing Ruth and her crazy-ass offer out the door. "Ben knew I didn't want to be on camera. I'm sorry if his respecting my wishes complicated your production schedule. But *Planning for Love* signed a contract with Ivy, not with me."

"Millions of people would kill to accidentally be captured on film." Ruth shook her head. "You're one of a kind, Lovell."

"Maybe so. Nevertheless, I'm afraid you've wasted a trip." Standing her ground got easier each time. After all, Ruth didn't scare her. The clammy skin and near need for a paper bag washing over her right now was only about Daphne's camera phobia.

Ruth combed stubby fingers through her hair. "Will you at least hear me out? I did fly all the way to this ice-pit of a city to pitch you."

Why not? Ivy had drummed into her that it cost them nothing to be nice, no matter how crazy a client might be. A little courteous listening might dial back the concern she saw reinforcing the titanium-like tightness of Ivy's posture. Now that she'd made her stance clear, Daphne could relax. Nothing Ruth said would make her change her mind. "Let me pour you a second cup of coffee. I know you'll need to race out the door after that."

"We've got a flower competition show—*Flower Power*." Ruth slitted her eyes. "Surely you watch it."

Slowly, Daphne shook her head. "I watch lots of movies. And *The Bachelorette*."

"We both do," said Ivy. "Frankly, it's because we like to stare at hot guys who take their shirts off ten times an episode."

"Who doesn't?" Milo winked.

"Wish we'd thought of that show. Brilliant concept. Constantly reinvents itself, so it'll never die. God, the money that show's brought in could buy a small European principality." Ruth shook her head, clearing the regret from her eyes. "Well, think of a chef competition, where they all try to make dishes off the same theme in an hour." She waited until they all nodded. "Now do it with flowers. Monkey-themed baby shower. Orange-and-purple wedding. Funky birthday bouquet."

As much as Daphne hated to admit it, the show

sounded like fun. Maybe she'd try to catch up on a few episodes online during the next blizzard. She handed Ruth a brimming mug, and snagged another cookie. "Is this where I say no again, or is there more?"

"Ha! You've got a zingy edge. Like a kumquat. Our viewers will eat you up."

Ewww. "And yet still I say, no."

Ruth barreled ahead as if Daphne hadn't said anything. "We've had weeks of preliminary competitions, semifinals, quarterfinals, etcetera. Now we're finally down to the big finish. We're taping it right here in Chicago."

Huh. Maybe she'd misjudged Ruth. Watching the live competition could be a heck of a lot of fun. "Oh, well, if you're offering free tickets, that's a different story. Sure, I'd be happy to come sit in the audience. I'll even bring my big foam finger from the last Bears game."

"The woman didn't fly all the way out here to offer you tickets." Milo pursed his lips, staring at Ruth. "My guess is color commentary. She wants you to narrate all the technical stuff. So they aren't limited to talking about pretty orange flowers and even prettier pink flowers over and over."

"And, that would be a no as well. No talking to the camera." God, her skin crawled just thinking about it.

Ruth shook her finger. "You said you'd hear me out."

True. But the thought of all that awaited her back in her workroom made Daphne want to hurry this along. "Sorry."

"No need for you to do color commentary. We have a host and a judging panel already. Did you not hear me say this has been running for a whole season?" The look of exasperation she shot Milo sent him into a full retreat back to his desk. "What we're missing is one of our four finalists. Maria Carmelo. She's pregnant, which isn't a problem, but her mandatory bed rest for the next four months *is* a huge problem."

Ivy's tongue pushed out the side of her cheek. "I'd say it's a bigger problem for her."

"You'd be wrong," Ruth snapped. "The doctors assure her that both she and her baby will be fine if she stays horizontal. RealTV, however, has sponsors and advertisers and a devotedly rabid fan base. We can't bring back a former contestant. Not once they've been judged as unworthy of being in the finals. The viewers wouldn't stand for it. So we've got to come up with a fourth finalist, out of the blue. Someone whose floral creations are out of this world. Someone who could easily hold their own against the three best florists in the country."

Blah, blah, blah. Ruth could pour the sugar on all day. Daphne knew a snow job when she heard one. "Correction—someone who is desperately seeking either fame or money." Belatedly, she remembered to add, "No offense, Ivy."

"None taken. When I agreed to do *Planning for Love*, it was to raise the money to open my romance store. I've never hidden that fact. In fact, you're the one who talked me into doing it."

Ooh, it was a low blow for Ivy to bring that up. "True. Because it was a brilliant solution to a tough problem. For you. For me, who neither wants fame nor particularly needs a windfall, it would only cause ulcers and unhappiness." Daphne dusted the cookie crumbs off her fingers. "So my answer remains unchanged."

Ruth leaned back, both hands cradled around the mug. "Why don't I tell you about the other contestants? There's Luther McGraw from Southern Gardens, Maude Henderson from The Bloom Box and Sheila Irwin from, well, I believe you know Sheila?"

Ohhhhh. Now it all made sense. This was, indeed, no random visit. No scroll-through the contact list, turning over every possible stone. Ruth's diabolical plan deserved its own soundtrack: a screeching, evil cackle. The word *no* didn't form so easily all of a sudden. Too shocked to spit out an automatic rejection, Daphne stalled. "Should I bother to pretend otherwise?"

"No. We thoroughly vet all our stars. Can't have a closet nutcase lose their minds in front of the cameras. There are a lot of weirdos out there."

"Auditioning for reality television?" Milo piped up. "Imagine that."

The look Ruth shot him this time promised that she'd never ask *him* to be in one of her shows, no matter what. "When we checked Ivy's background, naturally, as her partner, we ran you through the same screening process. I could tell you the name of your elementary school, your gynecologist and the size shoe you wear."

Daphne had never experienced firsthand the clichéd nightmare of walking naked into a crowded room. But she certainly felt stripped bare now. "Aren't you supposed to buy me dinner before we get all intimate?"

"Honey, the money we'll pay you will buy dinner every day for a year."

"Wait, you're considering doing this?" Milo ratcheted his neck, turning from Ivy to Daphne and then back again. "What did I miss? Who is this Sheila Irwin?"

Where to begin? Daphne could describe her in three words, three sentences or a three-hour diatribe. "My first boss. My mentor. Oh, and also the first person to can my ass."

Milo drummed his fingers against the white frame encasing the banner-size Aisle Bound logo on the wall. "More, please."

Saying Sheila's name still roiled her digestive juices as badly as the iffy fried cheese curds Daphne had on a memorable-for-all-the-wrong-reasons trip to Milwaukee. Maybe eating them after two rounds of jalapeño poppers, baked beans and a burger had been a bad idea. She'd just been trying to eat a balanced meal. Dairy had to squeeze in there somewhere, right? To strike against osteoporosis? Her misguided attempt at nutrition had landed Daphne on the bathroom floor, curled around the toilet. Which is where she wanted to be anytime the memory of Sheila Irwin sludged into her brain. Daphne lowered herself onto the couch.

Ivy took pity on her. She crossed to Julianna's empty desk and perched on the edge of it. "Sheila took Daphne under her wing, let her intern summers during college. Taught her everything about the flower business. Like Julia Child teaching someone how to cook. Daphne adored her, and Sheila, well, she loved being adored. Two weeks after graduation—"

Daphne cut her off. "—because you made me traipse around Niagara Falls with you." Not Disneyland, not

Manhattan, not even Miami. Nope, Ivy had dragged them to Podunk, New York, for their big graduation trip.

"It is a breathtaking natural wonder of the modern world." Ivy firmed her lips. It was only about the five thousandth time they'd had this argument.

"It is a giant faucet."

Ignoring her, Ivy turned back to Milo. "—Daphne joined the team at Lakeside Flowers as a full staff member. Sheila worked her hard. Our Daph soaked it all up like a sponge. Almost too well. Clients started asking for Daphne. Requesting that she be the only one to do their flowers."

"Uh-oh." Milo wrinkled his nose as if he caught a whiff of the stench of Sheila's rottenness across the years.

"Yeah. Jealousy fits Sheila like a well-tailored glove. She couldn't take being upstaged, even though Daphne was making money for her hand over fist. So she fired her. At the top of her lungs. Claimed it was because she was 'too innovative.' No severance, no recommendation. Worse than that, she blackballed Daphne. Told every florist in town that she'd let her fingers linger too long and too often in the till."

Outrage jack-in-the-boxed Milo out of his chair. "She accused you of stealing?"

"Yeah." Daphne tried to shrug it off. But even after all these years, it still put a stake of humiliation and hurt straight into her chest.

"Daphne couldn't get a job. Anywhere," Ivy said with grim finality. "When I came to her a month later with the idea for this partnership, she was waiting tables at Gulliver's."

Thank God Marge took pity on her. "Made good tips. I've got awesome legs, and I'm not afraid to show them off."

Ivy stared for a moment, then hauled Daphne up by the arm. "You'll have to excuse us, Ruth. I need to consult with my partner."

"Just like last time." Ruth rested her sensible low wedges on the edge of the table. "Do you two have to take each other's temperature on everything?"

Milo rolled his eyes. "The big stuff. All the time. But they usually do it over margaritas and chips."

Daphne let Ivy trundle her down the hall. In her flower prep room, the spicy scent of pine slapped at her nose. "What? Why are we pretending to have a confab?"

"We're not pretending." Ivy crossed her arms over her chest. She looked one head bob and a pair of harem pants away from being a genie. "I'm telling you to do this."

"Very funny."

"I saw you just now. How many years later is it, and your face still droops when we talk about Sheila. She castrated your career. Attempted to, anyway."

Daphne picked up the wire and a pine bough. Might as well be productive while Ivy wasted her breath on stupid suggestions. "That's right. She didn't succeed. You and me, we're an unstoppable team."

"Thanks for making my point for me. Don't hide behind the safety of our team. Go out there and show her that you can floralize her skinny ass into next week."

"Floralize? Not even a word." She nipped off the end with wire cutters, and wrapped it with floral tape. God forbid the tiny, barely sharp edge snag someone's dress.

Ivy planted her hands on the worktable and leaned forward. "You need this boost to your confidence. And you need to publicly punish Sheila, the same way that she publicly punished you. She treated you like crap. Left you a pathetic shell of yourself."

The reminder was utterly unnecessary. "Only for a little while. You picked me up and dusted me off."

"Exactly. This is your chance to pick yourself up. To serve up her revenge. Sheila could've made you a partner, could be garnering all the acclaim that we are. Instead, she was a shortsighted, self-centered bitch. She didn't deserve you. Go out there and prove it to her."

Ivy painted a tempting picture. Since Daphne and Sheila worked in the same town, with all the same vendors, revenge had never been a possibility. She couldn't afford to be petty. Wouldn't risk losing a single referral just for the sake of revenge. But this competition might be the one and only way to grind the spiteful hag's nose into the dirt. On the other hand, it could be a second helping of humiliation for Daphne. If karma kicked her in the ass again and she lost. Why take that risk?

"She might not be as cutting edge as we are, but Sheila still knows her way around a dozen roses. What if I don't beat her?"

"Are you kidding?" Ivy tossed her ponytail. "You are the most competitive person I know. Wait, I take it back. You and Gib probably share that title. Every time we play a game, you treat it like a third world war. You're cutthroat. You're resourceful. And you are one hell of a florist. Don't for a second think you'll do anything but wipe the floor with her. Along with those other two florists."

Excellent points. Ivy was one heck of a salesperson. But she'd only chipped away at one layer of worry. Daphne's anxieties around doing this show had as many strata as the Grand Canyon. She picked another handful of boughs out of the bucket. "I've never competed, not in a flower show, and definitely not on television. There are a lot of unknowns to worry about."

"I'm sure you'll worry about all of them sufficiently. We'll probably triple our cookie and candy budget for the month to keep you in a good mental place." Ivy reached across, grabbing both of Daphne's hands. "But you need this, sweetie. Your self-esteem has never been overflowing. Which is ridiculous, because you are a whole package of goodness. Creative, talented, funny, beautiful—everyone sees it but you. This is your time to shine. It'll be sooo good for you."

"Do I even get a say in this decision?" She'd never been steamrolled by compliments before. But Daphne trusted her best friend. In business and in the messiness of her personal life, Ivy had never steered her wrong. New year, new start. Time to face down old fears. Maybe use the windfall to vacation someplace with a sexy, shirtless masseuse. Daphne took a second to think about being oiled down on a sandy beach by—damn it, why were the talented hands in her vision attached to Gib's body?

"No, you don't." Ivy smiled. "It's a one-off. No cameras trailing you twenty-four/seven. Three other contestants, so the spotlight will be diffused. Just a single day of doing nothing but making bouquets. You can do that. You can do that with both eyes shut."

"I might have to, so I don't see the cameras," Daphne joked. And just like that, the decision was made.

"So you'll do it?"

As if she'd had any choice once Ivy started in on her. "I kicked off the year by bungee jumping off an emotional cliff. If I could screw up the courage to kiss Gib, I can do anything, right?"

SEVEN

*True friendship is like a rose: we don't realize its
beauty until it fades*

~ *Evelyn Loeb*

GIB TIGHTENED THE already-perfect Windsor knot at his
throat. The tie boasted wide diagonal black-and-light-
gray stripes. It echoed the narrow pinstripe in his suit.
He tugged infinitesimally at the silver pocket square.
Then he patted a hand along the hair he'd gelled upright at his forehead. A little wavy, because he knew
the ladies liked it. He'd kept his five o'clock scruff for
the same reason, instead of going home to scrape it off
before the NACE meeting.

Then he banged the top of his head against the mirror. What kind of a man hid in a hotel bathroom? From
his best friend, no less? Clearly, a spineless one. And
Gib had never thought of himself that way.

He'd dislocated a shoulder on the soccer pitch at age
nine, and hadn't shed a tear when the coach yanked it
back into place. At no less than three garden parties,
a polo match and one interminable interval during *La
Bohème*, he'd made small talk with Her Majesty the
Queen. Not to mention the inner fortitude it took to all

but renounce his family and create a new life in a foreign country at the tender age of twenty-two.

"Stop being a ponce," he muttered. A tug at the bottom of his jacket. What would he do next to postpone the inevitable? Unlace and relace his shoes? Disgusted with himself, Gib slammed his shoulder against the door and stepped into the hallway.

"Hey there," said Daphne. She gave him a casual finger waggle of greeting.

Unbelievable. At least fifty people clogged the fourth-floor hallway of Chicago's historic Palmer House Hotel. Another twenty-five were probably already in the room, waiting for the monthly NACE meeting to begin. Or, more likely, trying to see how many glasses of wine they could toss back before the meeting started. The chances of him stepping out of the blasted bathroom directly into Daphne's path should've been slim. Gib never took statistics at university, but he still knew it shouldn't have happened.

"Uh, hello." He gave her a swift once-over. Gib had teased her plenty over the years about her utter lack of fashion sense. She was too pretty to hide behind bad clothing. Now that he knew—intimately—the tightly lush curves of her body, it physically pained him to see her fading into the background.

The black skirt hung on her like a bag. Daphne always tried to dress professionally for these events. She just didn't try very hard. A rust cable-knit sweater also hung on her shapelessly. Gib did approve of the black boots that probably hit just below her knee. He'd approve a lot more if he could see her in just the boots and her knickers...

No! No stray sexy thoughts. They'd tormented him for an entire night and day already. The memory of her bowing under his hands, moaning under his mouth ran through his head with the unflagging sharpness of an alarm clock with no off switch. Milo had only said what Gib knew in his heart. Daphne was special. She didn't deserve to be laid and left. Kissed and kicked out. He'd bloody well ask her out on a proper date. Not a preamble to sex. Not a drink to loosen her up. A right, proper date, with dinner and absolutely no funny business. No matter how boring it sounded. He'd keep his lips to himself all night.

"Good crowd tonight." Daphne pivoted around, taking in the crush of people rushing down the hall. For the most part, men and women alike wore dark business suits. The only difference to be seen was the sky-high heels on the women. "The pot for the fifty/fifty raffle should be worthwhile. I might spring for more than one ticket."

"You've got to play to win," he agreed. Was this what the portent of a proper date reduced him to? Stilted conversation and clichés? Taking sex out of the equation evidently muffled his mojo.

Daphne rubbed her upper arm with her hand. "I had a weird day."

"Me, too," Gib confessed. Good to know their kiss had equally unsettled her. But he didn't want to talk about it right now. Not in the middle of the rapidly emptying hallway. There had to be a better place to admit that he'd doodled her in no less than seven different sexual positions before running the paper through his shredder. Maybe she'd made a mock-up of him out of flower petals?

She stared up at him with those big, delphinium-blue eyes. The ones he'd forevermore remember glazed with passion. "Talking to you about it would really help settle my mind."

Bollocks. Couldn't that wait for the date? The one he still had to summon the courage to ask her on? "Right. We'll get it all sorted. But not now. Don't want to miss the start of the meeting. Roll call's the only way to find out if there's a new member in the room."

She rolled her eyes. "Network the newbies, I know. Gotta lock them down before any other florist sweeps them off their feet."

"It's the only reason to choke down the plonk they're pouring at the bar," he agreed. There. Back to their normal banter. As easy as slipping into a comfortable sweatshirt. He could contemplate dating Daphne and still treat her like a real person. Instead of just another in an innumerable line of mattress squeakers. Gib gestured with his arm toward the meeting room. "Shall we?" But she didn't budge. Just stared at him, an expectant look on her face. "Go on, then," he urged.

"How long are you going to make me wait?" Daphne asked, her voice low and breathy.

Gib gave a swift glance up and down the hallway. Had anyone else heard her plea? She couldn't be asking what he thought. Could she? He tried to back away, but his heel barely moved before hitting the kick guard on the bathroom door. "Pardon me?"

Closing the already-narrow gap between them,

Daphne put both hands on his lapels. Then she stroked around in a tight circle. "Come on, Gib. Are you really going to make me beg for it?" Her right hand dropped to his hip. It slid down his thigh, moved inward just enough that in another second she'd feel his cock twitch at the unexpected visit.

Enough was enough. Daphne was his best friend. Of course he wouldn't make her beg—unless she was naked. Different rules applied in bed. Now that she'd opened this particular Pandora's box, the possibilities raced into his brain. In fact, he'd like nothing more than to lick her all over until she begged him to crawl on top of her. Crawl into her.

But for right now, he'd settle for a taste of her. Enough to take the edge off the lust rampant enough to drive Daphne to feel him up in the hallway. Gib grabbed her neck with one hand, her waist with the other, and reversed their positions. He drove her against the wall. Tried not to notice how well he fit into the notch between her thighs. And then he kissed her. Just like she wanted.

Gib unzipped her lips with a single swipe of his tongue. She opened to him, giving access to the hot silk of her mouth. The firm grip he had at her neck allowed him to angle her head up to meet him. Fingers thrust deep into the dandelion-soft glory of her hair. He heard the soft, mewling noise coming from the back of her throat, the rasp of her god-awful skirt against his trousers, the muted buzz of the meeting trickling into the hallway.

But mostly, Gib felt. Felt his cock swell. Her pulse

galloping beneath his thumb. The slick mating dance of tongue against tongue a tease for what he now knew to be inevitable. Every stroke a fiery arrow straight to his crotch. Every new inch of her flesh he tasted thickening him, exciting him. Her arms cinched tight around his back, pulling him impossibly closer. This wasn't a *hi, how's your day* kiss. This was a *launch sequence countdown begun* kiss. Neither of them held back anything.

If Gib didn't stop right now, he'd push her through that bathroom door. Hitch up that oh-so-handy skirt. Hike her legs around his waist. Take her in a stall until she screamed so loud the front desk would have to come investigate. And Gib was fairly certain that didn't fall under the parameters Milo had laid out for treating Daphne to a real date.

So he backed off. Reluctantly. With a final, bruising brush of lips. Enough to swell her mouth so she'd run her finger over it in an hour, and think of him. Gib planted one hand on the wall, boxing her in to keep Daphne right where he wanted her. With his other, he stroked the edge of her cheekbone, following the path of summer freckles that refused to fade. "Is that what you wanted?"

She blinked a couple of times. Fast. "No."

The woman was insatiable! Just the way he liked it. "I can't give you any more, pet, unless we blow off this meeting. There are about five hundred hotel rooms on top of us. Not as good as mine, naturally. But they've all got locks on the doors, which is all we'll need." Gib regretted the offer immediately. Now it hung out there, like an X-rated thought balloon over a cartoon character.

The agenda for tonight, for once in his life, did not

contain sex. He and Milo had laid out a painstaking plan. A decent amount of flattery as a base. A tip of the hat to their close friendship. Cap it off with the dazzling offer to wine and dine her. No mention of the kiss they'd shared. Milo predicted his roommate to be incapable of physical restraint if it came up. After all, an old dog can't learn new tricks in a day. Gib had tried to resist. But when a woman rubbed herself on him, why wouldn't he kiss her?

"Whoa. Did you just offer to do me? And in a rival hotel, of all places?" She cocked her head to the side. Wrinkled her nose. "I'm not sure which I find more insulting."

Maybe they were on opposite sides of a time vortex. Or an alternate reality. Everything Daphne said now directly contradicted her words, and the blatant come-on, prior to this kiss. Or maybe he'd watched too many hours of the New Year's Day marathon of *Dr. Who*. "Isn't that what you wanted from me?"

"No." She shook her head so hard that her hair whipped his cheek. "No. I wanted the candy."

"Well, I haven't got any." Why were they arguing about candy when he'd bet half his paycheck that her nipples were currently every bit as hard as his cock?

This time, her hands on his chest pushed him backward. Hard. Enough so that he stumbled to catch his footing. "You always bring candy to the NACE meetings for me. Since I got slammed at work, I came straight here without grabbing dinner. I'm so hungry right now, I could eat your tie. I just wanted to know where you were hiding the candy bars."

Fuck. How had he managed to ruin the plan before he'd even gotten to step one? If he still had weekly appointments with Doc Debra, she'd give him one of her squelching looks. The ones that said he could be such a better man if he bothered to try. Even once. Those looks always sent his balls scrabbling to climb back up inside his body. And Milo would kill him. Would probably open the apartment door to deliver a scathing lecture, and then slam it in his face. Gib let his chin fall to his chest. "I thought—"

"Trust me. It's crystal clear what you thought, you horn dog." Shoulders squared, chest heaving, Daphne looked ready to slap him.

"No, you've got it all wrong." Ready to launch into a florid apology, Gib opened his mouth. And then promptly shut it. She'd raised a single finger to trace her pink, puffy lips. Oh, she might talk a good game about how he'd so wrongly jumped to conclusions. Throw a bit of a tantrum. But no matter how much Daphne protested that she'd only wanted chocolate, he was staring at the face of a woman who thoroughly enjoyed the sweetness he'd lavished on her instead.

So he'd be damned if he'd apologize. Committed dating might not be his thing, but Gibson Moore was bloody well an expert on kissing. "You needed a good snog more than you needed a Mallow Melt. And I'd wager you're ready for another go-round." His statement colored up her cheeks to the same bright shade as her lips. Gib walked her back until she was against the wall again, and caged her in with his arms.

"Daphne, there you are. I knew I saw you earlier."

Maria Ortiz, their Chapter president, appeared at their sides from out of nowhere. With an attempt at casual swiftness, Gib dropped his arms. He knew she must've come down the hall from the meeting room. But his focus on Daphne obviated everything else. Two seconds later and Maria would've gotten a real eyeful.

Luckily, she didn't appear to notice the waves of sexual tension rippling through the air. She grabbed Daphne by the elbow. "Everyone's waiting." They hustled along the burgundy-and-gold carpet toward the double doors into the meeting room.

Gib trailed behind. No reason not to enjoy the view. "The whole membership is waiting on us? Since when do we have to punch a clock?"

"Not you, Gibson. Your soon-to-be-famous friend."

This might be an interesting meeting after all. "Who?" he asked, with the eagerness of...well, Daphne looking for chocolate in his jacket.

"Daphne, of course. I want to kick off the meeting with her big announcement."

Weird. Had Daphne scored a celebrity client? Even so, she wouldn't brag about it. Aisle Bound took great store in their client confidentiality. Moreover, his best friend would've told him any big news. Maria had to be confused.

The Red Lacquer Room of the Palmer House Hilton was a jewel box of a room. Ornate gilt molding topped walls of shiny red lacquer. Gold velvet curtains swagged tall, paneled windows. Ornate crystalline and ruby chandeliers swung from wide, gold starbursts on the white ceiling. It made Gib think of a room in Versailles, or Russia. His own hotel radiated modern, sleek elegance. But he loved the over-the-top abundance of the historic Palmer House.

Automatically leaving the aisle seat for Daphne, he slid into an empty row about halfway back. But she didn't sit. Instead, Maria propelled her straight to the podium centered in front of a gold satin panel. Between the grimace on her lips and the bloodless cast to her cheeks, Daphne looked like she'd eaten bad oysters. And like she'd make a break for it if Maria loosened her grip at all. What the devil was going on?

Maria gaveled the room into silence. "Welcome to the January meeting of the National Association of Catering Executives, Chicago chapter. Before we do the usual round of member introductions, there's some late-breaking news I'd like to share. News that will shine a national spotlight on the preeminence of Chicago event professionals."

A round of applause halted her speech. Gib straightened in his chair, gaze locked on to Daphne gnawing on her bottom lip. Her discomfort was palpable. No surprise. She loathed being the center of attention. Avoided it like the plague. Years ago, before they knew better, a group of them had gotten waiters to sing "Happy Birthday" to her when they delivered a candle-bedecked crème brûlée. The whole restaurant clapped for her. Daphne had practically burst into tears and fled the table. Held captive in front of seventy of her peers? Gib knew how miserable she must be.

"The hit reality competition show *Flower Power* has kept us on the edge of our seats all season. We're honored they decided to film the finals here in Chicago at the Millennium Knickerbocker Hotel. Let's give a round of applause to Michael DeWitt for an outstanding job landing that event!" When Maria let go to clap, Daphne shrank back three steps. "We all know that Sheila Irwin's eye-catching floral designs have propelled her easily to this final stage of competition. Sheila, you're officially one of the four best florists in the country, and we're so proud of you." More clapping. More of Daphne inching backward.

God, he was so nervous for her. In a habitual gesture, Gib shot his cuffs. It always soothed him to rub his thumb along the engraving of his family crest. Grandpapa Moore had bestowed them on him for the occasion of his eighteenth birthday. Right before the charming old bugger died at the ripe age of ninety-four. His heart gave out after a wild night of whiskey—and cigar-fueled debauchery. Grandpapa had always stood by him. Taught him how to ride a horse, tell a dirty joke and tie a bow tie. Good thing he'd passed on before Gib's cataclysmic split with the family. It would've broken his heart.

Sheila stood and nodded regally to the room. She must've gotten another in a series of face-lifts to prepare for her time on television. Her cheeks and forehead were tighter than a bass drum. Jet-black hair edged her face in a fringe, and was shorter than his in the back. Rail-thin, with what Gib's keen eye declared to be surgically enhanced breasts rounding out the top of her designer suit.

"Having Sheila as a finalist is truly an achievement. But having two Chicago florists battling for the trophy is even better." A low buzz of anticipation rolled through the rows. "One of *Flower Power's* finalists has dropped out unexpectedly. I'm thrilled to announce that our own Daphne Lovell was chosen, after an intensive nationwide search, as the worthy replacement. Let's hear it for Daphne!"

Gib sagged back into his seat. How could a woman so palpably nervous in a room full of general support-ive colleagues choose to be on live television? Under-going the scrutiny of millions of strangers? The minute the applause died down, Daphne mustered a sickly grin and sped down the aisle. She dropped into the seat next to Gib. Her hands trembled slightly. Gib reached over and cupped his own around them. She sucked in a deep breath and stilled beneath his touch. He stroked his thumb along the sensitive inner flesh of Daphne's wrist. To calm her ruffled nerves or calm his urgent need to feel her?

Crooking his neck, Gib pressed his lips right against her ear. Her thick hair provided a mattress for his cheek. Too bad the silken strands weren't draped over other parts of his body. God, they'd unlocked the flood-gates with just a few kisses. Sexual, sensual thoughts of Daphne bombarded him now on a constant basis. Could they ever go back to their comfortable friendship?

"So, any other gigantic bomb you want to drop?" he whispered. "Did you win the lottery last night? Discover a long-lost secret sister? Start up an email friendship with a billionaire sheikh?"

"I tried to tell you. Earlier. Remember? You cut me off."

True. Gib regretted that blip in their safe-to-share-any-and-everything relationship. Cowardice had won the day, since he hadn't mentally suited up to discuss their second in a line of epic kisses. Now he and his supposedly platonic best friend had somehow totted up three in less than a week. How'd things gotten out of hand so fast?

"You could've given me a hint." Gib caught a whiff of balsam and rosemary clinging to her hair.

"I said it's been a weird day." A hiss of frustration ran through her stage whisper. Loud enough to swivel two heads disapprovingly toward them.

Gib didn't care. "A weird day means your supplier sent hollyhocks instead of tulips. Or Lyons Bakery was out of all three of your favorite doughnuts this morning. Agreeing to go on television? You, of all people? That's about ten light-years past weird."

She tugged on his lapel. "You really don't have any candy?"

Her sweet tooth had an unfortunate tendency to stage a coup on the rest of her brain. "No. I forgot. Didn't realize you'd planned your daily consumption around my bulging pockets. Or lack thereof." Gib had second thoughts about that statement. "I am, however, willing to entertain you with other, non-pocket bulges."

Daphne gave him a look that could easily restore all the melted polar ice caps to their solid, frozen glory. "I'm hitting the bar." With a swift yank, she freed her hands.

It took a second to weigh the options. Play professional, sit on his ass and listen to the interminable roll call? Or follow the saucy minx? Gib enjoyed chasing tail. Excelled at it, in fact. But never at the expense of

his career. The only way he'd risen so quickly to manager of one of the finest hotels in the country was by
putting work first.

On the other hand, the deep relationships with his
closest friends came first. Gib's family treated him like
something they'd scraped off the bottom of their shoes.
So he'd forged a new family here in the New World. And
they were all the more precious to him because they
chose to care about him. Daphne upset? Acting out of
character? Definitely a top priority. He caught up with
her at the hors d'oeuvres table at the back of the room.

"Sorry I didn't hear you out earlier. Want to talk
through it now?"

"Here? In the middle of the meeting?" Daphne stuck
a toothpick in each of the six different cubed cheeses
and piled them onto her plate. In the few seconds before he joined her, she'd already managed to slather two
pieces of baguette with hot artichoke dip.

"Don't pretend that either of us will be able to pay
attention until you get sorted."

With the smooth speed of an owl, Daphne swiveled
her head around to him. "Oh, I'm nowhere close to
sorted. I won't feel normal again until January twentieth is behind me."

"What's special about that day?"

She jammed three pieces of cheese in her mouth,
then went back to reload. "Competition day."

"So soon?" Talk about last-minute. Daphne would
barely have enough time to fully work herself into a
state before the competition was past.

"You see why I'm nervous. No time to prepare. Oh,

and the little matter of having six cameras recording my every movement. Just like Ivy, I'm petrified my ass will show every cookie I've eaten in the last year as an individual lump. Ten, twelve million people will watch this." She closed her eyes, her voice low with abject horror. "They'll all judge me."

"Stop." Gib cracked out the word like a verbal whip. It worked. Her eyes flew open.

"What?"

"Dial back the self-indulgent crazy talk. Nobody is holding a gun to your head."

"You've never met Ruth Moder," she muttered. "I'd rather face off to a double-barreled shotgun than Ruth."

Gib knew Daphne. Knew her moods, her strengths and weaknesses. So he knew that mollycoddling wouldn't do her any good. "Be that as it may, you made this choice. No one else. Which means the pity party ends right now."

"You're right." She crammed in two stuffed mushroom caps at once. With her other hand she made a five-high tower of mini quiches. Daphne elevated stress-eating to a competitive level. After a disagreement with a client's unhappy mother, he'd once seen her put away an entire Giordano's deep-dish pizza. The kind it usually took four of them to polish off. Then she'd cleansed her palate with a whole order of parmesan garlic fries.

"I'm assuming this isn't about the free publicity, or the win. This is about Sheila. The way she smeared your name. This is personal."

She shook her head, sending her hair tumbling across her back. "This is payback," she corrected. "At least, it will be if I win. Not even win. As long as I place higher than she does."

"You will."

"Mayyyybe." Her whole body slumped in on itself, like a Boston cream doughnut with the filling sucked out.

Gib grabbed her arms. "Look at me, Daphne." Chin still down, she gazed up at him through the curtain of her lashes. "You will beat her for three reasons. Because you are genuinely more talented. Because that pilot light of revenge will fuel you to work harder. And because, quite simply, you must."

A smile the width of the sunrise broke across her face. "Would you be willing to write down those talking points for me?"

"If necessary." The urge to pull her into an embrace tilted him forward from the waist. Gib forced himself to let go. Still not the time or place. Not with the low drone of scattered applause every thirty seconds. Roll call would go a lot bloody faster if they didn't have to clap after each name. There were only a handful of newcomers at each meeting. Why bother to clap for someone you'd seen every month for five years? Perhaps all this restraint toward Daphne had turned him cranky.

"Thanks, Gib. I guess you managed to sort me out after all."

"Not entirely." If Daphne could face her fear, by God, so could he. "I'd like to discuss one more item."

She swiped a chip into enough guacamole to fill a piñata. "Sure."

Gib shot his cuffs again. Put a hand to the knot in

his tie. And rued the day he'd ever darkened Doc Debra's door. The rumor that therapy should make you feel better? Utter rubbish. The rock of Gibraltar had lodged in his throat. Someone had vacuum-sealed all the air out of the room. An invisible elephant balanced on his diaphragm. He was a citizen of the British Empire. The urge to suppress emotions had to be encoded in his DNA.

"Daphne, I'd like to take you to dinner."

"Sure," she repeated without looking up from loading her plate. "A couple of handfuls of cheese won't begin to fill me up. Were you thinking pizza? Or I could go for a pad thai. We could take it back to my place and watch the new Bond flick. I just got it on DVD, so I can hit pause and stare at Daniel Craig till my eyes cross with sheer delight."

If anyone made her eyes cross, it would bloody well be him. Not some poncy actor. Gib spoke through gritted teeth. "No, not tonight."

"Well, I've got a lot of prep left for the DeWitt wedding on Saturday, so that'll probably keep me at the shop pretty late tomorrow night. But if you want to swing by and split a pizza, that's okay."

Was she being deliberately obtuse? He'd never imagined Daphne to be a game player. "You don't understand. I'd like to take you out on a proper date. Milo checked your schedule for me. No events on Sunday at all. Let's go out on Sunday evening."

Her mouth dropped open wide enough to take on a candied apple in one bite. Just for a heartbeat. When Daphne closed it, her eyes shuttered as well. "A date? A real date? You pick me up, I shave my legs even though it's January, candles-and-wine-type date?"

"Yes."

She cocked her head to the right. Abandoned her plate on the table to fist her hands at her waist. "Is this because I'm about to be famous? Now that I'm on television, I'm good enough to add to your rotating roster of arm candy?"

"Hardly."

"Thanks a lot."

Under normal circumstances, Daphne was the one person to whom he could say anything. Talk with utter ease. Now he'd dropped the dreaded four-letter word into the conversation. Gib had apparently also dropped all ability to string together a coherent thought. Immediate backpedaling was in order.

"No, I meant that you've always been immeasurably better than all the women with whom I've dallied."

"Oh." She waited a beat, then scooted to her right a few steps. "I need a drink for this conversation." A few pre-filled champagne flutes were left on the end of the table. Daphne drained one, set it down, then picked up a second.

"Really?" Gib plucked the glass out of her hand and set it back down. "If you need alcohol to consider the mere idea, what sort of pharmaceutical cocktail will it require to get you through the actual date?"

"I haven't agreed to it yet, have I?" With a jerk of her chin, she led him out the door. Gib followed her to a gold-and-crimson brocade divan recessed in an alcove. Instead of sitting, she paced in front of it.

"Why?" he asked.

"That's my question. Why? Why now, after all this time?" She stabbed her fingers at her sternum. "Why me, after all those women?"

"Do you need a recounting of your finer points? How many compliments will it take to shake a 'yes' out of you?" Flowery compliments were the currency he used to bribe pretty strangers into dinner and drinks. Gib had thought that with Daphne he could be direct. Tell her that he wanted to spend time with her, without having to go through the whole song and dance as to why.

"I'm serious, Gib." Daphne sat down, hands on her knees. She had to crane her head to look up at him. "You can't just crook your finger and expect me to come running. Or, for that matter, potentially jeopardize a friendship that means the world to me. We can ignore one aphrodisiac-fueled night of flirting. A real date changes everything."

"Quite right." This entire ordeal brought to mind the memory of his first date ever, with Pippa Jones-Smythe. Her father, the Duke of Savoy, grilled him for a quarter of an hour. Gib was forced to stand an inch from the roaring fireplace the entire time. Sweat poured off his body. He'd locked his knees to keep them from shaking. And remembered thinking Pippa had damn well let him get to second base to justify all the trouble.

"So explain to me why I should date you."

Gib pressed his fingers to his suddenly throbbing temples. She already knew him, liked him. Even loved him, as a friend. Why put him through this ringer? "I might remind you that I'm the number one bachelor in the city, according to *Windy City* magazine. They did put me on their cover this month. Apparently, I'm quite a catch. I promise I know how to show a girl a good time."

"Bully for you. I already know how fun you are, Gib. We do stuff together all the time. That doesn't explain why we should upgrade to the deluxe package." The impassive mask finally lifted. Like a storm rolling in off the ocean, her eyes darkened. "What happens when the next B-list starlet checks in to your hotel? Or a leggy chorus girl doing eight shows a week at the Ford Oriental? You always go for a splash with your choice of date. I'm more of a puddle."

Never would he have guessed insecurity loomed behind her relentless grilling. Or her reluctance to give him—them—a try. Gib sank down next to her, capturing her chin between his thumb and first finger. "First of all, I don't date. I dally."

"Really? You're going to argue semantics with me?"

"Pay attention. I have assignations. Dinners, trysts. One, two, three nights at most. I don't engage in meaningful emotional relationships."

"Sounds like something your therapist would say."

"She did. On multiple occasions." The Suzuki method of learning violin—by repeating everything so many times a student had no choice but to learn? Doc Debra applied that to therapy.

Daphne jerked her chin out of his grasp. "Don't try to psychobabble your way out of this."

"But Doc Debra was right. I enjoy the company of women. The way they laugh, the way they smell like a summer day. The slow build-up to a seduction. From a shared smile on the street to tangling fingers over wine to—"

She leaned away from him, like a clothespin popping open. "Stop right there. I don't want the X-rated version."

"I don't connect with any of those women. We flirt, we spend some mutually agreeable time together, and we fall into bed. That's where it ends." Gib racked his brain for how to explain the difference to her. "I might mention the name of my first horse—"

"Archibald," she said with a nod.

"—but none of them know that he died after missing a jump with a trainer. Or that when I heard the news, I hid in the tack room at Eton for twelve hours, remembering him. None of them know that I refuse to check my mailbox alone on my birthday. But you do."

"Because you need someone to hold your hand when you realize your family didn't send so much as a card. Again."

"Right." Gib took her hand. Brushed the back of it against his cheek. Now that he'd begun, it turned out to be simple sharing how he felt. Because Daphne was the one person he could tell anything.

"You're the one who holds my hand. You're the one who knows my secrets. You're the one I can relax with, let down my guard. You're the only one who knows the real me, not just the affable bachelor out for a good time. That's why I want to date you. Because I think we've spent years already doing so, without realizing it. And without the kissing. Which is first-rate, might I add."

Heat pinkened her cheeks. "You may."

"As to your second point, I'll overlook it. Chalk it up to your extreme hunger." He frowned down his nose at her. "I'll assume you didn't mean to insult me by suggesting I'd be so disrespectful as to drop you for the next pair of stilettos that walks by. And you certainly didn't mean to insult yourself by inferring you are anything less than gorgeous."

Then Gib leaned into her, reaching around to stroke his fingers through the golden strands across her back. "Hair like silken sunshine. Breasts I've never been able to resist looking at. A smile that warms all the dark places in my heart."

"See?" The sass he knew he could always count on from Daphne twinkled in her eyes. "If you'd started with that, I would've said yes right away. You shouldn't make a girl wait, Gib."

"You'll change your tune." Bringing his other arm around her waist in a loose embrace, he stared into eyes darkening from an entirely different sort of storm. "I'll show you just how good it is when you wait. If you wait for the right person. Or the right thing." Gib rimmed the edge of her ear with his tongue. A sharp nip to her earlobe made her quiver in his arms.

"So what you're saying is that you're Mr. Right?"

His usual involuntary reaction to that title would be a full-body shudder of horror. Gib tensed every muscle to prevent just that. Certainly, he wanted to take a big step here. But no reason to leap forward a mile. "No reason to throw around labels. I don't want to—how did you put it? To simply forget our aphrodisiac-fueled night of flirting. A real date changes everything. And that's what I'm hoping to do. To change from a friendship to a relationship. Or at least give it a go."

"All right." She scooted to the far end of the divan. The rolled arm was all that kept her from falling off. "But no sex."

Gib scratched the back of his head. "You and I have very different definitions of the word *relationship*."

Laughter pealed through the hall. "No. Trust me, if we do this, sex is definitely on the table."

"You want to start on the table? Kinda kinky. Hard on the knees, but okay."

The blush that had barely begun to fade reddened her cheeks once more. "The when and where can be up for discussion. No sex on our first real date. That's the line in the sand. That way, if it doesn't go well, it'll be easier to go back to being friends."

Reasonable. More than that—quite smart. He didn't want to fuck up their friendship, either. "And if it does go well?"

"Make sure it does—" Daphne cast him a sidelong glance full of promise, "—and you'll find out."

EIGHT

Where flowers bloom so does hope
                                        ~ Lady Bird Johnson

GIB SHIFTED THE grocery bag higher against his shoulder.
It kept slipping off of his thick gloves. With his other
hand, he opened the door to Aisle Bound. It shone like
an oasis of light in the dismal January morning. Three
gray days in a row should hardly rate a complaint. Back
home in London, three solid weeks of January could
pass without the sun making more than a sporadic appearance. He'd gotten soft living here. Well, if one could
describe walking through gale-force winds off the lake
and surviving blizzards that drove the city to a stand-
still every year as soft.

"Shut the door. Or pay half our next heating bill,"
Daphne threatened. "Your choice." With sneakered feet
propped up on the coffee table, Daphne sprawled bone-
lessly across the couch. She already wore her wedding-
day uniform. A white shirt and jeans poked out from
behind the full-length lavender apron. The same color
bow wrapped her hair in a high ponytail. He'd seen her
in these same clothes a hundred times. Daphne looked
utterly normal. Sensible. Ready to walk innumerable
laps through a church and reception site.

But today, his mind used a different filter to see his friend. And through that blue-balled lens, she looked adorable. Her position put thoughts into his mind. Thoughts of locking the door, peeling off her clothes and pressing her deeper into that couch. Maybe leaving her in just the apron? Gib blinked away the vision. Of course, the couch being white, Ivy would kill him if that ever happened.

"Ignore her mood. She's been here since dawn." Ivy took the bag from him and set it on Milo's spotless desk. Her wedding-ready green taffeta skirt swished like leaves crackling underfoot. "Lisbet, our difficult bride du jour, called at midnight requesting three extra boutonnieres, a pomander ball instead of petals for the flower girl, and a bathroom arrangement."

"I can top that." Gib tugged off his gloves. "The prince of a tiny but wealthy country—"

Daphne popped upright. She adored his stories of esoteric guest demands. "Which one?"

"That would be telling. The Cavendish Grand is known for complete confidentiality." Which he'd never violate. Dropping a hint, however, put all the legwork on Daphne. And made it fun. He unwound his cashmere scarf. "As he's official visiting royalty, we *are* flying his flag. In case you find yourself driving past later."

"Oh, I'll find a reason. Go on."

Gib forced himself to slowly undo his coat. Remembering the string of idiotic, destructive things the prince did? It tensed his fingers enough to snap off the buttons like a stripper pulling off his breakaway pants. "The royal jackass proceeded to draw a dartboard on a six-hundred-thread-count pillowcase. He hung it over an antique wall mirror and was shocked to discover that chucking steak knives at it caused it to shatter."

"Drunk?" Sam ambled into the room. Both hands supported a napkin-draped tray. With the caution of a bomb demolition expert, he placed it in the middle of the coffee table.

"After five bottles of Cristal? I imagine so." Gib hung up his coat on the tree near the door while he watched a standoff between Sam and Daphne. Hands laced on top of his head, Sam stared at Daphne. Actually, he glared at her hard enough to melt glass back down into sand. Huffing, she took her feet off the table.

Amused by the ferocity of their nonverbal squabbling, Gib continued. "Not so drunk he couldn't feel the subzero cold when he walked out onto the penthouse balcony. I had to wake up my head maintenance tech at two in the morning to get heat out there for him."

"That must've cost you." Sam nudged the tray an extra millimeter toward the center. What the hell did he have hiding under that napkin? Gold-plated truffles?

"Tony hijacked me for courtside Bulls tickets the next time the Pistons are in town. We piled into his truck, woke up Rob over at Everything Events and got four patio heaters."

Ivy crossed her arms over her lace top. Funny how formal wear took the sting out of her outraged expression. "You got Rob—cranky Rob who barely grunts unless I flirt outrageously with him—to answer his business line at two a.m.?"

"This isn't the first time—or even the twentieth

time—he's had to help us out. Rob's cell is on my speed dial." That privilege cost Gib a hundred dollars a month retainer. And every month, somebody like the prince ended up more than covering it for him. "Once the heaters were running, His Highness still wasn't warm enough. This time I hightailed it over to Macy's State Street, to pick up a full-length sable coat from Kathy DeWitt."

"You have the cell number to the manager of the Fur Vault, too?" She sank onto the sofa, shaking her head in disbelief.

That one didn't cost him a monthly retainer. It came as a perk of a hot weekend that consisted of box seats at the Goodman, dinner at Charlie Trotter's and breakfast served naked the next morning. Better for Daphne not to know the specifics. "Being hooked in and hooked up is a big part of managing a hotel. There isn't anyone in this city I can't reach at a moment's notice. I could get the mayor over here with a five-minute head start."

Daphne threw her hands in the air. "What would the mayor do here?"

Gib dropped his voice to a growl. "Anything you want. Just say the word." While she giggled, he poured a cup of coffee. See? Nothing had changed. Their dynamic as friends remained as easy and comfortable as ever. They'd stay best friends, with the added potential bonus of hopefully frequent sex. What could be better?

"Can you finish the story of your problematic prince later?" asked Ivy. She popped off the couch and crossed to tug at the sleeve of his gray sweater. "I'm too excited to wait any longer."

"What about Ben? Shouldn't he be here for this?" A glance at his watch told Gib they didn't have more than an hour before the Aisle Bound crew would have to leave for their wedding.

"I dropped him at the airport already. RealTV needs him to run cameras at a wedding in Minneapolis today. The real cameraman got food poisoning at the rehearsal dinner. As well as half the bridal party. Anyway, he already knows."

"Knows what? I smell a secret." Daphne bounced around to face Sam, who'd settled in the big chair. Anticipation sparkled the exhaustion right out of her eyes. "Do you know?"

"Mira told me to bring over my latest batch of test chocolates for you guys to taste. She'll be here soon." He spread his hands wide, palms up. "That's it."

"Damn it." Daphne pulled her ponytail over her shoulder, twirling the ends around her finger. "Now I don't know which I'd rather do first. Try your chocolate or learn the secret." Gib knew which way he'd vote. First, he'd rub the chocolate along the edge of her lips. When they opened, and her tongue peeked out, he'd tease a little more. Pull the chocolate away. Replace it with his own lips, tasting the cocoa sweetness on her.

Sam cracked a smile. He used to dole them out with the frequency and solemnity of communion wafers. But since falling ass over teakettle for Mira, he wasn't nearly so stingy with his grins. "They're dark chocolate filled with goat cheese steeped in a pear liquor."

"Sold." She leaned forward to whip off the napkin. A glistening row of ridged chocolates sat on a doily-covered silver tray. "Geez, Sam, lose the doily. Unless you're marketing to nursing homes."

"Not so fast." From the other side of the table, Ivy lifted the tray out of reach. "You'll be lost in a flavor orgasm if I let you try those. Hear me out, first. I want to talk about my honeymoon."

"Really? Right now?"

Sam, as protective as a mother grizzly, took the tray from Ivy. He re-centered it on the table. "I thought Ben insisted on planning the honeymoon."

"Actually, I need to go first." Too bad Ivy was so dead set on making whatever her big announcement was today. Ben had emailed him at dawn, begging Gib to share his secret first, even though he couldn't be here. Gib rummaged in his grocery bag. He couldn't wait to see Ivy's reaction to his surprise. No doubt she'd be gobsmacked. "Ben got a little help."

Ivy executed a full-body shudder. "Don't tell me that you helped him pick out lingerie for me to wear. I know you probably see more lingerie in a month than the buyers for Victoria's Secret do in a year. But still, that would just be weird."

"Sadly, despite my expertise, Ben hasn't asked for help in that matter. He required my professional expertise." Gib handed Ivy a croissant. "Here you go."

"No, thanks." She pushed it back at him. "I had breakfast three hours ago."

Women could be so literal. And so frustrating. "This would've gone much more smoothly if Ben were here. Sure we shouldn't wait to do this when he's here?"

Daphne wadded up the napkin and threw it at Gib.

"You all have about a minute left before I tackle someone to get at those truffles. So start talking."

Bossy. Gib wondered if she gave orders in bed, too. Wondered how many dates it would take to find out. Wondered why he suddenly couldn't be in Daphne's presence without constantly thinking of sex. "Ivy, you've given the man an identity crisis. Ben's still convinced you don't think he believes in romance."

"He doesn't." Ivy shrugged. Her eyebrows lifted into *what can I do about it* arches. "The closest he'll come is admitting that he believes in our love. Which is good enough. For now."

"Maybe so." Gib pushed the croissant back at her, curling her fingers around it this time. "But he's taking you to the most romantic city in the world for your honeymoon. Thanks to yours truly pulling in a few favors, you'll be staying at the Cavendish Grand Paris for a week. Free of charge. In the honeymoon suite."

Her fingers clenched. Flaky crumbs fluttered to the floor. "You were right. We should've waited for Ben. Because I really, really want to kiss someone right now."

"Well, I did make all the arrangements. I think that makes me a worthy substitute."

"Good point." Uncharacteristically heedless of the mess, she dropped the croissant and launched herself at Gib. He caught her in midair. Ivy planted a smacking kiss right on his lips. "I'm sure you had to promise your firstborn to swing this. We can't thank you enough."

"True. But I'm open to any appreciative gifts you might send my way. Especially if you happen upon any haute couture store on the Rue du Faubourg Saint-Honoré."

"Don't downplay your generosity, Gib. This is an incredibly thoughtful gesture." As usual, Daphne jumped at any opportunity to shower him with praise. And, as usual, it made him feel both simultaneously uncomfortable and hugged from the inside out.

Sam nodded his agreement. "Nicely done. Guess I'd better start planning my own honeymoon. Don't suppose the Cavendish has a property in Bora Bora? I'm pretty sure I'll have to go that far to take Mira anyplace she hasn't already been with her parents."

"I haven't been anyplace with *you* yet. That's all that matters." The bitter cold of January in Chicago followed Mira through the front door. She dropped a kiss on the top of Sam's head.

"You're just in time." Ivy practically ripped Mira's puffy parka from her back. "I have an announcement. A big one."

Mira fluffed her long, black hair as she settled onto Sam's lap. "Let me guess. You managed to sign the president's daughter as a client."

"That wouldn't be a secret. I think the Secret Service would spend weeks vetting all of us before she even picked up the phone to call me. I also think every event planner in D.C. would come gunning for me if that happened. A little more trouble than it's worth."

"Okay, the governor's daughter?" Daphne guessed. Gib hoped she was wrong. He'd spent a few days with said daughter. Well, more to the point, a few nights holed up in a hotel room so the paparazzi wouldn't catch wind of it. She was…exuberant and bendy. And probably not someone who should be spending time with the woman he was now trying to date.

Ivy bounced on the balls of her feet. "You're getting colder. Think the opposite of weddings."

"Oh, no. Are your parents getting a divorce?"

"God, of course not, Daph. Why would I be excited about that?" She pointed at Sam. "You want to take a shot?"

He shook his head. Both hands cinched Mira tight around the waist, as though making sure she wouldn't fly away. "I'm a bad guesser."

Time to play a belated Saint Nick. Gib emptied his bag onto the table. "Let me put you out of your misery." He couldn't wait to see Daphne's expression. When she smiled, *really* smiled, her eyes sparkled like a mid-July sky. One by one, he handed out thick envelopes and stoppered plastic tubes.

Daphne waved her envelope in the air. "What's this?"

Ivy clasped her hands. Cleared her throat. "We've had a crazy, terrific year here at Aisle Bound. The uptick in our client load since *Planning for Love* started airing is huge. Daphne, you've been working yourself ragged. And, Mira, what you've done with A Fine Romance is far beyond my original vision. I can't believe you already have it turning a profit. We all deserve a vacation. So I'm closing both businesses while Ben and I honeymoon."

"You're kidding. Turning off the lights and letting all the calls go to voice mail?"

"Only at Aisle Bound. The store will remain open, but with shorter hours. Helen and Hays have agreed to shoulder the load. I think we've got a potential new team member who will help as well, but I don't want to rain on Mira's parade."

Mira nodded. "Hold that thought."

Daphne pulled out the cork stopper from the tube. Sniffed. "I'm confused. Are these bath salts? A hint that we should relax during that week?"

Now he pictured Daphne in a tub. Gib would sit at the opposite end, watching her nipples play hide-and-seek through a cloud of bubbles. He couldn't wait to discover what color tipped those nipples. Blush pink? Rosy? Apricot? God. Less than two minutes had elapsed since the last time he thought about sex and Daphne. The obvious tightness in his trousers sent him to hide behind the bulk of Milo's desk. "Pink sand straight from Bermuda's famous beaches. It just arrived this morning."

"Which makes these—"

"Airline tickets. To Bermuda," Ivy shouted. She threw her hands in the air and jumped a few times. "For all of you—Mira, Sam, Daphne and Gib."

Mira and Daphne rushed forward to hug her. Sam looked at Gib and mouthed *wow*. Screeches of happiness filled the room. It gave Gib a deep sense of fulfillment to know he was part of it. That this close-knit group, in each other's pockets on a daily basis, loved each other enough to spend their vacation time together as well? To him, that signified they were a family far more than blood ties ever could.

As everyone settled down, Ivy continued. "The trip is my thanks for your support and friendship. With a special thanks to Gib for yet another amazing hookup. You'll be staying at a beachfront condo he's arranged."

Damn. Did she really have to tell them? This was Ivy's idea, her big surprise. He didn't want any credit for the small part he'd played in helping her.

"Not a Cavendish property. So it must belong to one of your fellow peers of the realm? The Earl of Whosit? The Duke of Whatsit?" Mira teased.

If only his friends knew the misery his title brought him. Would it break their obsession with all things related to the British peerage? Not that he planned to tell them. When Gib had come to America, he'd broken with his past, with the pain, and severed ties—almost irrevocably—with his family. He did his best not to ever dredge up those memories.

"The Viscount Eversley owns it. He uses it exactly once every year for a three-day fishing trip. Which is actually more of an all-the-beer-you-can-drink stint. Don't even think he bothers to load fishing poles onto the boat. Instead of letting it sit musty and unused, he opens it up to his friends. Really, it isn't any bother at all."

Daphne raised her hand. She wiggled her fingers to get his attention. "Um, big question over here. How many bedrooms?"

Aha. Hard to tell from her tone if the thought of sharing a room with him landed in the pro or con column. They'd done it when they were merely best friends on a camping trip to Michigan. Had fallen asleep on each other's laps during movie night countless times. Now that they were on the brink of adding sex to their friendship, she suddenly needed her own space? That sat about as well with Gib as an order of onion rings would after his third Italian sausage at a Chicago Fire game.

"Worried I'll mount an assault on your chastity?"

"No."

"Worried that I won't?" Gib leaned forward, burning his eyes into Daphne's as though they were inches apart, and not the width of the room.

"Just answer the question," she snapped with enough heat to whip every head in the room toward her.

"What's going on?" Ivy looked back and forth between the two of them. "This news was supposed to put smiles on your faces, not bring out the claws."

Now he felt lower than a grass snake. Ivy had presented this amazing, thoughtful opportunity, and Daphne forced him into a childish squabble. "Sorry. We're all good here." He jerked his chin toward the sullen blonde. "Someone's just overtired."

"I'm not a child," Daphne retorted. "And we're far from good. Answer the question. The longer you dance around it, the more I worry. Are there only two bedrooms?"

"Yes." One of them with two beds. Not that he'd tell Daphne that anytime soon. She'd officially pushed him past annoyed into pissed off.

Until four days ago, they'd never exchanged so much as an improper brush of their hands. Gib's prowess in the bedroom catapulted him to minor legend status in Chicago. It was an image he enjoyed cultivating, and didn't mind using it to his advantage. But he only ever engaged with willing, enthusiastic partners. How could Daphne think otherwise? How dare she? Daphne,

who knew him better than anyone. Daphne, one of the
very few who saw past his playboy facade. Who measured his worth as a man, not as a bed-hopping bachelor. "Worried they'll both have mirrors on the ceiling?
Handcuffs on the bedposts?"

"Huh. Do they?" Sam asked.

"Knock it off." Ivy pointed her finger at Gib, then
Daphne. "Didn't you two ask to share a bedroom at the
cabin in Michigan last summer?"

"Yes." Daphne had offered to share so Gib wouldn't
be stuck sleeping on a couch six inches too short and
full of thirty years of lumps.

"Platonically? Without any hanky-panky?"

"I didn't so much as smooth the covers on her bunk.
We kept to our own sides of the room, like grown-ups."
What he didn't admit was that night was one of the times
when his imagination broke free of its lockdown. Lying
five feet away from Daphne all night hardened his cock
to an uncomfortable level. Over the entire weekend, Gib
hadn't clocked more than about five hours of sleep.

"Yeah, well, that was then. Now I'm concerned about
other, more intimate activities that grown-ups do."

Gib crossed the room in three fast strides to glare
down at her. "Why?"

He bent, bracing his hands on either side of her head.
It positioned his lips to within a breath of hers. Given
his druthers, he'd rather be kissing them. Rather than
waiting to hear why his closest friend wanted to be
able to lock him out of her bedroom. Not a propitious
step in anticipation of their big date. Did she expect it
to go so badly they wouldn't still be together in April?

For that matter, did she not expect it to last beyond tomorrow night?

They'd only kissed so far. No betrayal of friendship there. Hell, she'd stayed fully clothed. Gib hadn't even unclasped her bra. It all came down to one question. "Don't you trust me anymore?"

Before Daphne could answer, Ivy tugged him away. She sat on the couch, and pulled Gib down on her other side. Then she took his hand, and Daphne's, and held them on her lap.

"This is about your date tomorrow night, isn't it?"

"Maybe." Daphne shifted, tucking her legs up beneath her. "It's awkward."

Since when did the thought of spending time with him make her so uncomfortable? Gib's temper ratcheted back up a notch. Last he checked, there wasn't a gun to Daphne's head. "We've been to dinner hundreds of times. We've already kissed. Nothing scary there. In fact, you seemed to enjoy it quite a bit. All three times."

Sam shifted Mira in his lap. "Are you wondering if he can seal the deal? 'Cause I can get you a signed affidavit from about eight dozen women attesting to it. Probably without walking more than ten blocks."

"Not helping, Lyons," Gib snarled.

Ivy banged their hands against her thighs. "Enough. I won't let you two go out at all. Not if it causes this much tension."

"There's no dating by committee. You don't get a vote."

The look she gave him was the same his Latin teacher gave him the first time Gib conjugated a verb wrong.

Condescending pity. "Evidently there's still a few things you don't know about women. Of course I get a vote."

"We're a pretty tight-knit group, Gib." Mira leaned forward to pat him on the knee. "All we're saying is that you and Daphne better not screw it up."

"Swear to it," Ivy demanded.

"What? That I'll show her a good time?" Gib knew how to wine and dine a woman. Nobody did it better. If charming a woman into bed was an Olympic event, Gib wouldn't just have the gold—he'd hold all the medals.

"No. Promise that nothing will change, no matter what happens on your date. Gib, you'll still go running with Mira and Ben. Daphne, you'll still have Gib over every Halloween for that horrible marathon of monster movies you both like. The inevitable sex—no matter how good, bad or indifferent—won't change our group dynamic."

"Did you just accuse me of performing indifferent sex?" That stung more than the fear of Daphne not trusting him. Engaged to Ben or not, he'd offer Ivy a go-round in her office right now. See if she didn't melt into a smiling, satisfied puddle after less than fifteen minutes with him.

"I'm pretty sure that was aimed at me." Pulling a throw pillow into her lap, Daphne huddled even deeper into the corner of the couch. "I'm not the one featured on the cover of a magazine this month for my dating acumen."

Ivy waved her hands as if erasing a chalkboard. "You're both focusing on the wrong thing. Forget about the date until you're on it. And don't worry about the sleeping arrangements for the trip. A lot can happen between now and April. As long as you promise to stay best friends, it'll all work out. Promise."

Gib had to hand it to Ivy. Her expertise in handling difficult people, difficult situations, was unmatched. And she was right. Their years of deep friendship were the only reason he'd taken this step toward a different sort of relationship with Daphne. It was the basis of everything. The foundation of the community he'd so carefully cobbled together here in his adopted city. The very bedrock of his happiness. From the sheepish look on her face, Daphne had come to the same conclusion.

"You and Ben, Daphne, Milo, Sam and now Mira—all of you—are, quite simply, my home. Nothing will change that." He kissed Ivy on the forehead. "Sorry if I did anything to make you think otherwise."

"I'm sorry, too," Daphne piped up. "Sorry I got all in my head. Then blurted it out like an idiot." She leaned across Ivy, golden ponytail slipping down till the tips of it caressed her breast. Right where he wanted to be. Lucky ponytail. "Of course I trust you, Gib. I'll dish out another heaping scoop of apology. I love hanging out with you. Putting on a dress? Letting you pay for dinner? It shouldn't change anything."

"You let me pay for dinner all the time," he groused. At least they were back on a solid footing. And speaking of solid, the prospect of seeing her in a dress hardened his cock to pure steel. He rested an ankle on his knee. It lessened the obvious tenting in his trousers, but not by much. Gib had to get off the couch before anyone noticed. If this kept up, he'd have to start carrying a portfolio in front of him at all times. Or start wearing a jock strap. Even if he double cupped it, though, the thought of Daphne's legs bare beneath a swirly skirt would probably still ramrod him straight through his zipper.

Daphne toyed with the ends of her hair. "The prospect of going on a date with Chicago's most eligible bachelor scared the pants right off of me."

"Then this will be a very good date. My work's half done."

"Ha. I just need to get my head in the game."

"Precisely why I'm here." Gib stood, relieved for an excuse to get up. He crossed the room and hefted the grocery bag. "Have I ever mentioned I captained the debate team at Eton?"

Daphne rolled her eyes. "Only about a million times."

"And when you do, your accent gets even more butlerlike," Mira added. "I expect you to pull a tray of tea and crumpets out of that bag."

"No such luck. But if Daphne does well enough, there might be a gingerbread scone hiding at the bottom of this bag as a reward." Gib knew how to motivate Daphne. Sure, she'd accepted the stint on *Flower Power* out of equal parts pride and revenge. But that only propelled her so far. Bribing her infamous sweet tooth might get her the rest of the way.

"You had me at gingerbread." Daphne bounded off the couch. "What do I need to do?"

"My legendary experience at Eton—we beat Harrow four years running—means I can whip you into shape. You're a domineering smart-ass to your friends. But you morph into a shy wallflower in the spotlight. At the NACE meeting, I thought you were going to either puke or pass out. And you were only up at that podium for less than a minute. Let me help you get past that fear."

"How?"

Gib pulled out a tiny piñata. Red, white and green ruffles covered the papier-mâché elephant. "We're going to practice. I watched every episode of *Flower Power* last night."

"You're kidding." Daphne's jaw dropped. "You did that for me?"

"Of course. Your competitors had to be studied. To find their Achilles' heels. I fast-forwarded through the commercials. It only took six hours." Six hours he'd never get back. Six hours of inane commentary and ridiculously dramatic music. He'd wanted to claw his eyes out for about five hours and fifty minutes of it. But the research had paid off. Gib now knew their weak spots. A little coaching, a lot of Daphne's amazing talent, and she'd be untouchable in this competition.

"After all that reality television, are you brain-dead yet?" Sam asked.

Ivy tapped the very pointy toe of her shoe into his shin. "Hey, don't bite the hand that pays for your trip to Bermuda. If it wasn't for reality television, I wouldn't have opened my store, and you wouldn't have met the love of your life."

"True. But it doesn't make it good TV. Or any less mind-numbing."

"Maybe when you're in the audience at a live taping, you'll see it differently." Gib reached into the bag once more to produce a shiny sheaf of papers covered in flowers. "I got tickets for all of us to Daphne's show. Already sold out, by the way. I had to pull out all the stops with my ticket broker to nab these. He was fuzzy on the terms, but I think I owe him both my firstborn son and my ancestral home. Possibly one of my kidneys."

"Can't wait." Sam trotted out another of those increasingly common smiles. "Honest, Daph, I'll be in the front row clapping for you until my palms blister."

"The piñata is the starting point. Head into the back, and make a centerpiece around the piñata, using whatever you've got on hand. Sometimes the trick to the show is the lack of flowers, sometimes it's an almost impossible theme. We'll practice under both conditions. Every day. With me throwing questions at you and generally trying to be as distracting as the two-hundred-person audience and announcer will be."

Daphne ran her fingers down the elephant's trunk. The motion was so evocative of what he wanted her to do to him that Gib almost dropped the piñata. "But wedding setup starts in less than an hour," she said.

"Exactly. Right now you're tired and in a hurry. Just like you will be on competition night."

"Thanks." Her voice as soft as six-hundred-thread-count sheets, she looked up at him with eyes that shimmered. A man would do just about anything to earn a look like that. "You've thought of everything, haven't you?"

No. Not yet. Gib hadn't figured out—entirely—what it would take to get her into bed. He'd run through a bunch of tried-and-true scenarios. None seemed right for Daphne. But he'd damn well try them all until he found one that worked. Because the next time he saw that look of gratitude on her face, he wanted her to be naked. And underneath him.

NINE

A rose is a rose is a rose

~ *Gertrude Stein*

"DAPHNE, YOU SPENT all of breakfast yammering on about last night's wedding." Her dad ran a hand through his thick salt-and-pepper hair.

"A lot happened. Besides, we were only in there for fifteen minutes. We had doughnuts and coffee, not an all-you-can-eat brunch." Daphne gripped her dad's arm as she skated across a patch of black ice on the sidewalk. Chicago's skyscrapers provided all-day shade in some areas. Walking downtown could be dangerous in winter, when the temperature rarely rose above freezing. It made his request to "stretch their legs" for a few blocks less than appealing. But walking off those doughnuts was probably a smart idea.

He ticked points off on his fingers. "I know about the crazy number of bridesmaids. I know exactly where you stand on using pine for decoration after Christmas."

"So you're going to throw out the wreath on your front door as soon as you get home?"

Stuart sighed. "Yes."

"Good. I'll make you one of eucalyptus instead."

"That should keep the neighbors from complaining."

He scooped a handful of snow off the top of a newspaper box. Being a man, and stubborn, Stuart refused to wear gloves. Calloused hands molded it into a hard-packed ball. "I also know the bride cried when she saw the bouquet you made for her."

Such a great feeling. Well, not the tears. The makeup artist had shot her a look of pure venom when that happened. But knowing she'd contributed to the bride's happiness on such a special day softened Daphne's heart to near marshmallow levels. What a great perk of her job. "Made it worth every sore finger and scratch I accumulated this week."

He lobbed the snowball at the apex of the stone archway over the doors to Holy Name Cathedral. Perfect hit. With his arm, her dad probably could've hit the top of the 210-foot-high steeple. No wonder all her brothers had gone to college on athletic scholarships. "What I don't know is anything about your date with Gibson Moore."

Blindsided. Had the doughnuts been a ploy just to soften her up so he could get some dirt? He could be sneaky that way. "How did you find out?" Daphne asked. She tried to sound casual. She probably sounded guilty and accusatory. Just like when he'd caught her sneaking back in long past midnight after going to the Justin Timberlake/Christina Aguilera concert at the United Center.

"I'm your father. I've got my ear to the ground where you're concerned." He wiped his hands on faded jeans. "Why didn't you tell me?"

Because she'd already exposed a boatload of insecurities to him once this week. Because she didn't want to come across as an emotional wreck. As the problem child. Worse, as a total *girl*. "You stopped vetting my dates when I graduated from high school."

"And yet four days ago you blurted out that Gib kissed you. Little late to put that cat back in the bag."

When he dug his heels in, her dad had the tenacity of a puppy gnawing on a slobbery piece of rope. Might as well give him the basic deets and get past it. "Fine. We're going out tonight. On a real date. Are you happy now?"

"Are you?"

Damn it. Perceptive fathers were an anomaly. Why'd she get stuck with one? "Yes. No. Mostly." Daphne kicked at a snow drift. "Maybe more nauseous than happy."

"Probably just that third jelly-filled not sitting right."

"Actually, it's the combination both of the prospect of going out with Chicago's hottest bachelor, and being on television in fourteen days. I'm not sure which one scares me more." The practice with Gib yesterday went well. Eventually. After she broke the heads off three gerbera daisies and let not one but two vases slip right out of her hands to shatter in the sink. Daphne hoped another few sessions would spank her nerves into at least a sham of calmness.

"You've never backed down from a challenge. Except for letting that Sheila woman sweep you out like garbage."

"I didn't have a choice, Dad. She fired me. There's no hanging around to plead your case when that happens." Instead, it had been an immediate bolt for the door before tears started to fall. Pride kept her eyes dry through the whole El ride home. Right up until

Daphne collapsed, sobbing, into her dad's arms. Not her finest moment.

Her brother Nick had been fired from his first job flipping burgers. His plans to save up for a car evaporated after he gave a guy a hundred-dollar bill for change instead of a single. But he didn't cry. Michael hadn't shed a single tear when he dislocated his knee sledding—or when the doctor popped it back into place. Whereas Daphne seemed to be in possession of more than her fair share of the family tear ducts.

"Hmph. Glad you're getting the chance to show her what's what. It's about time you put that skinny-ass bitch in her place."

"Dad!" Stuart Lovell could let fly a blue streak when the Cubs lost. Happened every season. But he rarely weighed in on his children's lives so...*vehemently.*

"Call a spade a spade, I say. Point being, you'll beat her. You're better, you're younger, you're more motivated and you're a damn sight prettier."

Unknowingly, he'd poked at a very tender spot. Daphne sucked in a deep breath of air that burned her lungs with its cold. "Honestly, that's what worries me the most. Even more than freezing up in front of four cameras and hundreds of people."

"What?"

"The whole the-camera-adds-ten-pounds thing. And that high-def will show the entire country the crow's-feet I didn't even know I had." She yanked her ponytail over her shoulder. "I pull my hair up because it's easy. No need to look in a mirror. I'm not a six-foot-tall model. I'm certainly no skinny, big-boobed actress. When I'm not working, I spend most of my time in sweats and sports jerseys." A quick tug at the bottom of her Bears parka illustrated her point. "You raised a tomboy, Dad. So yeah, I'm afraid I'm not pretty enough to be on television. And I'm certainly not pretty enough to go out with the legendary Gibson Moore." Daphne looked both ways to check the always heavily trafficked Wabash Avenue. But fingertips digging into her arm prevented her from crossing.

"Stop it. Right now."

"The light's green, Dad."

"I don't care. Stop demeaning yourself." He pulled out his wallet. Flipped to the well-thumbed wedding portrait that had ridden his hip for the past thirty-nine years. "Look at this."

"I've seen that picture a million times." Still, Daphne brushed her mitten around the rounded corner, craving even that small a connection with the mother she missed so very much.

"But have you really looked at it? Since you left home? You are the spitting image of your mother. On her worst day, she was a knockout. Beautiful inside and out. The pert little nose, your smile, those big eyes wide enough to take in the whole world—they're hers. Mixed in with my eyes and your grandmother Irene's hair. You, my baby girl, are even more beautiful. I'm sorry if I didn't tell you that enough."

Stupid cold spell. It froze the stupid, unstoppable tears balanced on the edge of Daphne's lashes. Every blink felt like she lifted tiny barbells. But there wasn't a woman alive who could stop her emotions from trickling straight down her cheeks after hearing a speech like that. "Thanks, Dad."

He steered her across the street while she sopped up the tears with her mittens. "As for Gib, he's been an idiot for years. There you were, right under his nose the whole time."

"Don't blame Gib. We're perfectly happy as friends." Or at least they had been. Now they'd tasted something… more. Daphne had—just barely—kept her physical longing for Gib under control until that kiss. Didn't drug dealers give the first hit for free, knowing their clients would do anything, pay any amount to recapture that bliss? Yup, that's pretty much where Daphne sat after three mind-blowing kisses with Gib. Willing to risk a perfectly terrific friendship. Willing to let Ivy fuss with her hair and asphyxiate her with sprays and mousses. Willing to do just about anything to get his lips south of her collar.

"Okay, I'll spread the blame around." A swift shoulder squeeze, fast and hard. The kind that said he loved her, but was about to lower the boom. "You should've kissed him sooner."

"Dad!" They were crossing into uncomfortable territory. Mostly uncomfortable because Daphne had been thinking the same thing for all six days of this new year.

"I like Gib. He's polite, but not stuffy like you'd expect from a hoity-toity Brit. Somehow gets me into a box at Wrigley at least once a season. And he hangs on your every word."

"Tell me, how much are the dues to be a member of the Gibson Moore fan club? Is there a T-shirt?"

"Remember, he's damn lucky to have a shot at you. That's all I've got to say." Her father wrapped his arms around her for a strong hug. "Have a good time."

Daphne held on a few extra seconds, so grateful for the way he could restore her solid footing with a couple of sentences. "I think I will."

"Call me when you get home."

"You're reinstating my curfew?"

"I like Gib. But I'm not wild about his reputation. I want to know you're home by midnight." Stuart shifted from foot to foot. "Not, you know, doing things I don't want to picture my little girl doing behind closed doors."

"God, I don't want you picturing anything, either. I promise I'll call."

"Love you." He started to walk away.

"Wait. Where are you going?"

"I delivered you here. My job's done." With a wave, Stuart continued down the slushy sidewalk. It made no sense. Daphne turned around to stare at the three-story glass facade of the Cavendish Grand. Was this a joke? Had she gotten confused, and her sexy dinner date was really a run-of-the-mill lunch date?

"Surprise!" Mira and Ivy pushed through the doors, almost bowling over the top-hatted bellman. Both coatless on this freezing day, they wore yoga pants and hoodies. Ivy, of course, in pink and Mira in blue. Very Stepford Wives-ish of them. Plus, it made Daphne super aware she wore sweatpants with a large sap stain at the knee from her late-night adventure with pine boughs earlier in the week.

"What's going on?"

Ivy tucked her hands beneath her arms. "Your father was our decoy. Because we knew you'd say no if we gave you any possible out."

"Say no to what?" What could be so horrible at the

Cavendish, of all places, that they'd need to trick her into showing up?

"We're treating you to a spa day." Mira threw up her arms into a ta-da pose. Daphne's instinct was to blow a raspberry in response, but she held her tongue.

They each grabbed an arm and led her into the refined gray-and-black elegance of the Cavendish Grand lobby. A soaring atrium rose three stories, with one entire wall of windows overlooking the hustle and bustle of Michigan Avenue. The walls were covered in dove-gray satin echoed in the chairs and sofas grouped around a cascade of water streaming from the ceiling into a mound of shiny black river stones. Sheets of glass formed the check-in desk, supported by columns of dark granite.

"Wait a minute." Daphne dug in her heels to halt their march toward the elevators. "Christmas is over. My birthday isn't for months. What gives?"

Mira and Ivy exchanged a look. A let's-flip-a-mental-coin-to-see-who-deals-with-this look. Mira apparently lost. "You've been on edge since kissing Gib."

"Totally freaked," corrected Ivy.

Daphne wasn't thrilled about the assessment. But they weren't in any way wrong. Self-conscious, she unzipped her coat. Then continued to run the zipper up and down, just to give her hands something to do.

"So the spa day has two objectives." Mira spoke slowly. Like a teacher trying to explain long division for the first time. "To calm you down, and to buff and polish you to within an inch of your life."

"You'll be so bright and shiny, Gib might have to avert his eyes."

"Kind of defeats the purpose," Daphne muttered.

Ivy took her hand off the zipper. "You've looked in the mirror in the past three days more than you have in the last month. And every time you do, you frown. Scowl. Sometimes look like you're sniffing curdled milk. Milo said he noticed you staring at your reflection in the floral cooler, and, I quote, framing your ass with your hands."

Also true. Daphne knew her diet of pizza and cookies and ice cream to be far from balanced. Her dentist made that abundantly clear with every new filling. Ironic. You'd think Dr. Meyers would be a little more grateful that she was helping put his kids through college one cavity at a time. Still, her addiction to sugar didn't just affect her teeth. Daphne's ass had definitely grown. On her feet most days, and always up for a game of pickup basketball or tennis, she didn't worry about it. Much. Except when a guy who usually dated models and stewardesses and actresses suddenly started running his hands all over her body. Now she couldn't stop worrying about the size of her ass. And only hoped her breasts would distract him from it.

"We know you're beautiful." Mira linked her arm through Daphne's. "The mailman leaves a little trail of drool behind every time he looks at you. Gib obviously thinks you're hot. The only thing left is to get you to believe it. This is the Day of Daphne."

Ivy had tried to talk her into a spa day several times. The thought of someone covering her in goop and poking at her never sounded remotely appealing to Daphne. But this gesture from her friends was too thoughtful to refuse. "Does this get me off the hook from you messing with my hair?"

"Not at all." Ivy walked backward, facing Mira and Daphne as they walked past the check-in desk. "I've got plans for your hair. Hot rollers and hair spray. Trust me, it'll drive Gib wild."

She'd sit through any torture that guaranteed Gib's hands on her faster. In fact, skipping dinner and going straight to the smooches sounded great to Daphne. "Okay."

"You won't regret it," Ivy promised. Daphne wondered if she could demand that in writing.

Mira tugged off Daphne's coat. "Plus, we've got a plan to make the whole day painless."

Yup. She'd heard that one from Dr. Meyers, too. And had learned the hard way that his definition of *painless* differed from the dictionary's version. His version meant "once a couple days go by and you pop lots of ibuprofen, there won't be any more pain." Daphne hoped that Mira's definition ran to the more traditional. "So I won't have to get naked in front of some hulking woman named Ilke who doesn't speak English grinding her elbow into me?"

"God, stereotype much? Where do you get these ideas?"

"Seventies B movies that I watch with Gib." Their favorite was *Sorority Babes in the Slimeball Bowl-O-Rama.*

Ivy huffed out a breath. "It figures. Since this is your first time, I made sure to put you with a woman. Beth's wonderful. Magic fingers. We've already checked in."

"They're letting us use the couple's massage room." Mira winked. "I might have dropped the manager's name to make it happen. Don't tell Gib. It'll be a tight squeeze for all three of us, but more fun that way."

Daphne pulled off her mittens. Hopefully they were the cause of her sweaty palms. But with each sweep of the second hand, she got more and more nervous about the night ahead. The spa would have to pump Valium through the air vents to calm her down. "I'm still not hearing the painless part."

"Bellinis, to take the edge off. Thought they'd appeal to you more than cucumber water. And then I'm going to tell you all about the woman I hired this week. She's going to be the matchmaker at A Fine Romance."

This was news. Daphne goggled at Ivy. "I thought you hated the idea of running a dating service out of the store."

"I did. But Mira wore me down."

Mira cleared her throat. Loudly.

Ivy caught the hint. "That is, Mira's keen business acumen and well-thought-out proposal convinced me. The first few Match-n-Mingle events are already sold out. If this is how Chicago wants to find love, who am I to stand in the way?"

If this was their monthly partner's meeting, Daphne would suck it up and pay attention. Would even happily debate the pros, cons and possible profit margin. But a recounting of the strengths and weaknesses of candidates today? After a week of long hours topped off by a very, very long wedding? It would only make her nod off. No matter how hard Beth-of-the-magic-fingers dug into her back muscles.

"Here's a little tip. I don't find blow-by-blows of job interviews entertaining. No matter how many Bellinis you pour down me."

Undaunted, Mira just smiled. Like she knew a delicious secret. "That's because you've never interviewed Tabitha Bell. Here's a teaser—she claims she knows everything there is to know about men because she was raised in a brothel."

Okay, that was a new angle. "So she's a time traveler from Regency England?"

"Nope, this is real. Nevada still has legal brothels. Piqued your curiosity yet?"

"Obviously." This story had scooted to the top of her need-to-know list. Right up there with wanting to see a picture of Prince Harry's latest unclothed and unauthorized photo shoot. "Who wouldn't want to hear the inside scoop on a brothel?"

"Anyone with a modicum of civility and couth." Sheila Irwin glared down her surgically narrowed nose at them. She looked annoyingly perfect, from her highlighted hair to her vacationing-at-the-Cape preppy combo of turtleneck and sweater. Topped off with the cliché of a string of pearls. And, because she never did anything halfway, a matching pearl bracelet. No bags under her eyes. Even though Daphne knew Sheila probably did two events this weekend. No Sunday sweats that verged on jammies for her. The only jarring note to Sheila's appearance was the attitude coating her from head to toe. Similar to the slime that grew in flower vases when the water didn't get changed after four days.

"Or anyone with a stick up their ass." Ivy delivered the inflammatory words with a smile as sweet as Sam's famous marshmallow frosted s'mores cake. It warmed Daphne to the core that Ivy stuck up for her. She just hadn't expected it to escalate to a mud-slinging battle in the hushed and sophisticated lobby of the Cavendish.

"It's not surprising you have such a gutter mouth, considering the company you keep." Sheila sniffed. "It is, however, amazing they let you on television."

Ivy's face held on to a pleasant mask with the determination of a local affiliate's weather girl. "RealTV *courted* me. They kept throwing money at me, begging me to do their show until I finally agreed. Not like you, having to claw your way through round after round of competition."

Wow. Ivy's usual sweetness-and-light personality had morphed into a leather-studded warrior princess. She was in it to win it. Daphne couldn't help but enjoy watching.

"Your attempt to gloss over the facts is the funniest thing I've heard all week." Sheila stroked the pearls at her neck. "Everyone in the industry knows RealTV only chose you because you slept with that videographer."

Ivy widened her stance. Jammed her fists onto her hips. "Take that back."

"Certainly. I misspoke. It was because you fucked that videographer."

A mother exiting the elevator gasped. She grabbed the hands of her two toddlers and hustled away with a ferocious frown. Round-eyed, Mira clutched Daphne's hand. Daphne kind of wanted to dive behind the nearest chair. But she couldn't let Ivy take any more of Sheila's vitriol. The snarky catfight had just turned much too bloody. "Whoa. Sheila, you're way out of line. And we both know your grudge isn't with Ivy. If you have to let off some steam, aim it at me, where it belongs."

"Gladly."

Daphne held up her hand. Not done yet. They'd need to reach some sort of a peace—even if only temporary—before RealTV turned on their cameras. Both their businesses would suffer if this nasty sniping hit the air. But she'd have to finish her thought before Sheila said something else inflammatory that might derail her.

"Don't forget that we're going to share a very small television screen in two weeks. It's no secret here in Chicago that we don't like each other. But do we really need to broadcast our problems nationwide? Can't we call a truce? Agree to act professional while we're on *Flower Power?*"

Sheila resettled the strap of her Coach purse a little higher on her bony shoulder. "That's really up to you. I am a consummate professional. The reputation of Lakeside Florist is unsurpassed."

Okay. Agreeing wouldn't kill her. Lakeside Florist did routinely handle some of the biggest and best events in the city. They did the symphony gala every year, and for the past fifteen years had sold more Valentine's Day bouquets than any other vendor. All reasons why Daphne had interned there in the first place. "Sheila, you are absolutely right. Your shop is top-notch."

"You, on the other hand, work at an upstart patchwork of a business."

Too bad Daphne's blatant attempt at ass-kissing didn't halt Sheila's tirade at all. In fact, she'd raised her voice. Enough to make the concierge look over with a raised eyebrow. Daphne was a fixture at the hotel, so she gave a silent shrug of apology to Monique. But better to let Sheila get it all out of her system now than in front of an audience of hundreds.

"Flowers are obviously not the priority at Aisle Bound, and it shows in your work. Your slapdash designs will make a mockery of the final round of competition. On the bright side, you'll be exposed as a laughingstock. As someone who chases trends," she spit out the words as if they tasted fouler than burned coffee, "and doesn't respect the art and classic beauty of flowers. Maybe this will be enough to erase you from the NACE vendor list once and for all. And then I won't have to risk having my name sullied by anyone remembering you used to sweep the floors of my shop."

"Get out." Gib clipped the words, his cool ire made all the more effective by his British accent. Daphne had no idea how much he'd heard. Equal portions of relief and embarrassment flooded through her. She looked down at her raggedy clothing, remembered she wore no makeup and had just cinched her hair into a ponytail. To look like this, on the day of their first real date—*this* was what Gib wanted to buy dinner for? Nope, embarrassment won out by a mile.

"Gibson, this doesn't concern you." Sheila shooed

him away with both hands and a tight-lipped smile. Or at least, she tried to. Gib didn't budge.

"This is my hotel. Everything that happens here concerns me."

Sheila blinked a few times, then folded her hands at her waist. "Yes, of course."

"I'm concerned that my guests—" he lifted a hand to indicate the rest of the lobby, "—have been disrupted by your verbal accosting of Miss Lovell."

Her simpering smile grew wider. Faker. Sheila leaned in to bestow a reassuring pat on Gib's arm. "Whoever called you down here clearly overstated the incident. I never raised my voice. Didn't cause a scene. Trust me, your guests are undisturbed."

A single step away dislodged her hand. "I'm more concerned with the unprofessional, shrewish way you attacked Miss Lovell. I won't stand for any of my friends or colleagues being treated with such disrespect. So you will leave. Immediately."

Screw shining armor. Her knight wore a gray wool suit. With onyx-and-silver cuff links. Daphne tore her eyes away to check on Ivy and Mira. They, too, were riveted by Gib's polite but irrefutable smackdown.

Sheila looked, one by one, at all four of them. Cranked out one more halfhearted smile. "Well, despite your questionable choice in friends, Lakeside Florist maintains very cordial relations with the Cavendish Grand. I'm sure you don't mean to do anything rash. Nothing, for example, that would impact any brides we might have in common on the books."

"I'm sure I was quite clear when I told you to leave."

He crooked a finger, summoning Anthony from across the room. Anthony, who used to work as a bouncer at a strip club before Gib hired him to provide extra protection for the Cavendish's celebrity guests. Anthony, who weighed probably more than every employee of Aisle Bound put together. The well-cut suit Gib provided as a uniform couldn't disguise his muscle-upon-muscle bulk. You expected the floor to shake as he approached. Daphne wanted to do a little dance of glee to see him towering—and glowering—over Sheila.

"There's no point demanding the apology Miss Lovell deserves. We all know you wouldn't mean it. So Agatha will call your office tomorrow to work out details with your assistant. None of our current brides will be inconvenienced. But you will *never* set foot on this property again. Should you do so, security will toss you immediately." Gib crossed his arms. "If I recall, brides always book a reception site first. Deciding on the florist happens later. As of today, you're scratched from our approved vendor list."

A hiss of outrage escaped Sheila's lips.

"I've no doubt it'll cost you clients. Every time it does, remember why. Remember that you brought this on yourself." He turned his back to her. Anthony took it as his cue to cup Sheila's elbow and lead her across the lobby.

Daphne gave in to the urge to dance. Jumping from foot to foot and shaking her butt kept her from going with her first instinct: sticking her tongue down Gib's throat in gratitude. Because that would look silly. "Oh. My. God. You were tremendous."

Gib brushed at the coat sleeve where Sheila had touched him. "She had it coming."

"You crushed her like a bug," Ivy said approvingly.

Mira jabbed her finger repeatedly into Gib's diamond-patterned black tie. "You honed that rapier-sharp British accent into a freaking verbal bayonet and impaled her."

"She's a snide little shit. Needed to be taken down a peg."

No. No false modesty allowed. Daphne put her cheek on his lapel and hugged him tight. "You're my hero."

"Nonsense."

But he hugged her back. Rested his cheek on the top of her head. And they took a moment. Until a horrible thought slithered into her brain. Daphne pulled away so she could gauge his reaction. Watch to be sure he told the truth, and didn't sugarcoat.

"Will you get in trouble? Could you really lose business, just because you stuck up for me?"

"Not a dime." Gib shot his cuffs and smiled. The familiar gesture reassured Daphne. When he did it with a smile, it meant he felt cocky. When he did it with no expression, that's when she worried. "Ivy, you know what I said is true. All wedding planning trickles down from choosing the site. She can't touch me, or the hotel."

Ivy nodded her agreement. "Sheila's got a few diehard fans at NACE. People who kissed up to her back when she was president ten years ago. But a few whispered comments at the next meeting should be the sum of the fallout."

"This was just a warm-up round." Gib feinted a slow

swing at Daphne's jaw. "It's up to you to knock her out in the competition."

"She almost ruined me, you know. Almost ended my career before it barely began. Shattered my self-confidence." Daphne grabbed Ivy's hand. Squeezed it with two, happy pumps. "I clawed my way back up, thanks to Ivy. But until today, I never got retribution. I don't know how to thank you."

"We can discuss that when I pick you up. Better yet, we'll discuss possible ideas over dinner. Work on implementing them…" Gib dropped a kiss on the inside of her wrist, letting the pilot light of his passion flare brightly behind his eyes, "…after."

Daphne knew she looked like she'd rolled right out of bed. Mostly because that's exactly what she'd done. Who dressed up to eat doughnuts with their dad? So she wasn't too embarrassed to be in the Cavendish lobby as a total mess. Especially since she'd be bundled into a spa bathrobe in a matter of minutes. Mortification, however, heated her cheeks hotter than the lavalike cheese on a Pizzeria Uno's deep dish. All because Gib Moore had made her panties damp with a single brush of his lips. And it felt like there was a big, cartoon thought bubble over her head, proclaiming it to the world.

Ivy cleared her throat. "If you're done saving the day, Gib, we're on our way to a day of pampering in your amazing spa."

"Don't let them go overboard," he cautioned Mira with a stern glare. "I'm quite partial to Daphne as she is right now." Gib tangled his fingers through her ponytail. Pulled her closer. Close enough the heat of his body radiated past his shirt, through her sweatshirt. At least, she imagined that it did. "Most of all, don't let them cut a single strand off of this loveliness."

Daphne never appreciated it when guys ordered for her at dinner. Or picked a movie without consultation. An overbearing, alpha male didn't appeal to her. Until today. Until Gib's voice darkened with need as he spoke of her hair. Even though on the surface it sounded like he'd issued an order, Daphne knew differently. Knew that she held all the power. But she couldn't let him *know* that she knew. "Uh, I'm right here. Or have I turned invisible?"

Brushing his lips along the rim of her ear, Gib whispered, "You're the only thing I see." Then he walked away, into an open elevator that appeared as if he'd flicked a remote in his pocket.

Holy knee-wobbliness, Batman! Gib as a friend had kept her twisted up with longing for years. With his dating persona turned on, however, Gib blew her away. No wonder the man was a legendary lothario. He had the goods, and knew how to use them to melt a woman into a giant, satisfied smile.

"I'm all in," she said to Ivy and Mira. "Do whatever it takes to turn me into a knockout for him."

"Oh, Daphne," sighed Mira as she took her arm, "it won't take anything at all. Except for you to believe it."

TEN

I'd rather have roses on my table than diamonds around my neck

~ Emma Goldman

DAPHNE HESITATED FOR the third time on the threshold, hand on the doorknob. Then she looked down the hall from the front door. It was a straight shot to her bedroom. The blue border of her mother's snowflake quilt draped over the bed was visible through the doorway. Nope. No way could she risk letting Gib into the apartment. Because the fact they had reservations didn't matter. Neither did the half day she'd spent at the spa, followed by another hour at the salon.

One touch is all it would take. One oh-so-sexy raised eyebrow in invitation. Who was she kidding? It wouldn't even take that much. Especially not after the heroic way he'd rushed to her defense earlier today. The moment Daphne opened the door, all her pent-up longing would take control of her limbs. Kind of like a poltergeist. A lust poltergeist. She'd rip his clothes off halfway down the hall. Maybe they wouldn't even make it to the bedroom. Chances were good she'd straddle him on the floor, push up her skirt and go for it. Which absolutely, positively could not happen.

They'd had no trouble generating sparks each time they kissed. Tonight's test wasn't about physical attraction. She and Gib would have to see if they could build an emotional bridge across the yawning cavern of awkwardness between friendship and a relationship. Redefine their roles. Therefore the bridge had to be a no-nooky zone.

So Daphne shut the apartment door behind her. Buttoned her coat all the way to the top and tied her scarf in a knot. She carried her black patent leather pumps down the stairs. Pacing barefoot, Daphne waited until she saw a car double park and throw on its hazards. Time to go. Shoes on, she hurried outside. According to the WGN weather guy the thermometer hovered just above zero. The cold air took her breath away. Tamped down a bit of her white-hot need, too. The snow that wedged into her shoe? Total overkill.

"Daphne, what are you doing?" Gib stood, one hand on the passenger door of his sporty silver convertible, looking at her as if she'd lost her mind.

"Brutally cold tonight. Didn't want you to bother getting out." She slid into a soft leather seat. And moaned. They were heated. Did she even need sex with Gib after the bliss of a heated car seat? The answer came to her before the door shut. Two seconds of being that close to him flared her lust back to full flame.

"Damn it, Daphne, this is supposed to be a date. A first date. You have to let me treat you as such. That means I knock on your door, I pull out your chair and I help you off with your coat." He sounded grumpy. Put out.

Attempting an air of solemnity to pacify him, she said, "Duly noted."

"Are we bloody well doing this for real or aren't we?"

She looked around at the inside of a car in which she'd never sat before. It was Gib's dating Excalibur. He refused to use his car except when pursuing a woman. Never used it to bring home bags of groceries, or to drive to the movies when the thermometer dipped below freezing, or even to pick up friends from O'Hare on their rare visits. He swore he only used it on dates, and *only* when close to sealing the deal.

Just to be sure, she asked, "Is this a rental?"

"Of course not." Gib smoothly manipulated the gear shift and they sped down the street. God. It had been ages since she'd been in a stick-shift car. Watching his big hands caress the padded knob made her press her legs together in anticipation. Far safer to look out the window. Most homes still had candles in the windows left over from the holidays. A few bare-limbed trees sported strings of white lights.

"Then I guess we really are doing this, if you're finally letting me in your famous bootymobile."

He sighed, as if insulted. "She has a name. This is Moll Davis."

Daphne bit back a giggle. He named his car. Did he name other, more intimate things? "Seriously? Wasn't she one of the most famous mistresses in history?"

"Maybe not in all of history. Certainly in England's history. Good old King Charles II warmed her sheets for years. Beneath her flashy exterior, that woman not-so-secretly held all the power in the land. Just like my baby here." He stroked the steering wheel with both hands.

God, would he touch her like that? A bolt of desire shot through her. And was she actually jealous of a car? "I'm beginning to feel like I should get out and leave you two alone."

He whisked his head sideways to smile at her. Quick and fast like a flashbulb going off, it blinded her with its brightness. "She's game for a threesome."

Gib excelled at sexual repartee. A few times she'd even been his wingman, and watched him toss it out with the ease of a fly fisherman casting in a deep river. Having it wholly focused on her, though, took her breath away. But Daphne reminded herself that tonight was her one shot. She needed to go for it. Commit one hundred and ten percent to the idea that she actually belonged next to the handsomest man in the city.

Laying her hand on top of his, she channeled her inner Marilyn Monroe and purred, "Maybe I want you all to myself."

Once more, Gib turned to look at her. This time he flat-out stared, mouth slightly open, lips curling up. Then he swore and jerked the car to the right. He'd almost missed making the turn onto Michigan Avenue. "You're right. We really are doing this. Daphne Lovell, welcome to your date. It is on."

About time. "Like I said, the car alone made that clear. But as I understand your parameters of use, warming my seat on her cushions goes hand in hand with an expectation that you'll be warming my seat tonight."

"Generally, yes. If a woman gets in Moll Davis, she ends up in my bed. Simple as that."

"Not so simple. We agreed tonight would be a test. To see if we can really morph from friends to—"

Gib cut her off. "Lovers?"

She bit her tongue. Counted to ten before answering so the word *yes* didn't fall off her tongue. "No. There's no question we could do that. The burning question is whether or not we should. If our friendship would survive. So we give dating a try tonight. But without any sex to complicate the equation." Although she was hoping for more kisses. Whatever groping he could accomplish without removing any of her clothes. And knowing Gib, that could be quite a bit.

"I took calculus. I can handle complicated equations."

"Be serious."

Another, more labored sigh. "Of course I don't expect you to fall into bed with me tonight. We're starting a relationship, not a one-night stand. But you're a beautiful woman. Which means I will flirt with you relentlessly. Take it as a compliment. And I'll take your ban on the bedroom as a challenge."

A challenge, huh? Daphne honestly couldn't say who she wanted to win that one. Gib cut the engine as the valet opened Daphne's door. A chill ran through her that had nothing to do with the icy wind whipping off the lake. This was it. The moment she'd dreamed of for years. Gib would be suave and charming and sexy. And hers.

With a hand at the small of her back, Gib ushered her forward. She stopped after two steps. Looked up. And up and up at the iconic black Xs that crisscrossed their way up one hundred floors. "We're at the John Hancock Center?"

He pushed her back into motion. "Nothing but the best for you, and the Signature Room on the ninety-fifth floor has the best view in the city."

Even though she'd lived in Chicago her whole life, Daphne had never been to the famous restaurant. Her mom promised they'd celebrate her high school graduation there. By the time it rolled around four years after her death, Daphne didn't have the heart to remind her father. But she had told Gib the story in December, when they'd strolled past while Christmas shopping. It touched her deeply that he remembered. That he'd try to fix that unfulfilled promise.

While they waited for the elevator, Daphne unwound her scarf. Gib stopped her. "Let me." He gathered it, hand over hand, oh so slowly. The periwinkle mohair tickled the back of her neck. She shivered. Gib stuffed the scarf in her pocket. Then he unbuttoned her full-length coat. As the elevator doors opened, she turned away to let him slide it off her shoulders. Daphne leaned against the rail at the back of the car, legs crossed at the ankle. Gib gaped.

As well he should. Sex might be currently off the table, but she still wanted him thinking about it the whole time. A black lace dress hugged tight to her curves. The sheer lining kept her decent, but barely. It gave the illusion of lots of bare skin. Aided by the plunging V-neck that hid almost nothing. Thanks to the patient ministrations of Adele and Wendy at the salon, her hair hung in loose curls over one shoulder.

Finally, he said, "I don't know what to say. The elevator ride is only thirty-nine seconds long—"

"Thanks for the trivia."

"—and I don't think I could come up with the words to describe how beautiful you are if I had thirty-nine hours."

Just that quickly, the lingering chill from outside vanished. His words warmed her from the inside out. Still, she tried to play it cool. So he wouldn't realize she was ready to throw caution to the wind and do him between floors thirty and sixty. "And thanks for the compliment."

He shrugged out of his coat. This time it was Daphne's tongue that almost rolled out of her mouth. Gib wore suits like a uniform. They were also a particular obsession of his. So six out of every seven times she saw him, Gib wore a suit. But tonight, he'd kicked it up a notch.

The black wool had obviously been tailored specifically to draw attention to the breadth of his chest, the width of this shoulders, the long line of his legs. Even in her four-inch-high platform pumps, Gib still topped her by at least four inches. Black tie with some sort of matte shine to it. Contrasting white pocket square. Onyx-and-silver cuff links glinting at his wrists. He was the living embodiment of the word *debonair*.

A high-pitched ping announced their arrival. Gib gestured for her to go ahead. Thanks to her day of pampering and primping, she already felt like Cinderella. Entering the restaurant was akin to entering the ball. The rows of tables were lined with snazzily dressed couples. Black-rimmed chargers popped against the white linens. But what really popped was the view. On three sides, the bright lights of skyscraper upon sky-scraper reflected the grandeur of the city. Straight out sat the dark lake, like a black sheet beyond the floor-to-ceiling windows.

"Good to see you as always, your lordship." The maître d' slid his hand into Gib's, smooth as an eel. A waif of a girl whisked away both coats.

Gib held a finger up to his lips. "Frank, I told you to quit calling me that."

"Ah, but the ladies like it. Am I right?" He nodded at Daphne with a smarmy grin.

"Not so much." She knew that Gib never talked about his title. Or his family, or how he felt about being nobil-ity. It didn't matter to her if he was seventy-sixth in line to the throne of England or the illegitimate son of a... prostitute. Blood didn't matter. Character did. Although if she did ever think about his title and baronial hold-ings or whatever they were, the only way it made her feel was nervous. And she was nervous enough tonight.

"Your usual table's ready, *Mister* Moore." A wink indicating Frank would humor Gib, just this once, with dropping his title. Pretentious jerk. "Best seat in the house."

Daphne would've stuttered to a stop without Gib's hand at her back, guiding her to the wall of windows. The usual table? Gib came here often enough to have a regular table? Had to be with his ever-changing stream of women. This wasn't a business lunch type of restau-rant. So he hadn't remembered her mother's promise. Hadn't put special thought into choosing a restaurant that would have special meaning just for her. Daphne felt as though she'd just been dropped onto an assembly line. Would the entire date be formulaic?

Wait. Better talk herself off the corner of Crazy Street and Jealous Avenue. The Signature Room, no matter how often he came, was nevertheless one of the most romantic restaurants in the city. Gib ran through women the way a frat house ran through kegs of beer at homecoming. It'd be hard to find a restaurant in all of Chicagoland where he *hadn't* taken another woman.

So she sat down without comment after he pulled out her chair. A stunning bouquet of a dozen roses caught her eye. One side of the petals were snow-white, and the other…well…rose-red. A quick glance confirmed that their table was the only one so decorated. "Fire and ice roses?" she murmured.

The right corner of his lips curved up. "A mere token in honor of your beauty. Despite the frost outside, I'm afire inside every time I look at you."

Another twinge of disappointment. Sure, fire and ice roses were a step up from the unexceptional red. But his delivery sounded as well-rehearsed as a third-grade class reciting the pledge of allegiance. "That is one of the worst lines I've ever heard. In the summer, do you switch to circus roses? You know, the ones that are yellow like the sun on the outside?"

If she didn't know Gib so well, Daphne would've missed the minuscule twitch in his eyelid. The same tell that gave him away whenever he tried to bluster his way through a fake word in Scrabble.

"No." He captured her hand, stroking his thumb slowly over the side of it with a touch that raised a solid layer of goose bumps over her entire body. "Not everyone has your vast knowledge of flowers. Roses might not be original, but they are romantic. And I aim to romance you tonight."

For every ten yards he lost, he managed to regain enough ground for her to grant another first down. Who was she kidding? If he kept touching her like that for another five minutes, she'd clamp one of the damn roses between her teeth and dance a strip-tease tango on the table for him. "Sorry. But come on, Gib, give me a little credit. I won't fall for your lines. Don't bother trying to snow me."

"Fair enough." A waiter set down a waist-high silver bucket on a footed stand. The ice in it crunched as he swirled the champagne bottle up and out. Then another flourish with a whisk of the napkin across the cork.

"Dom Pérignon. Your favorite 1996 vintage, sir."

Huh. Gib's favorite. Not something he picked out especially for her. Another automatic—and therefore meaningless—gesture. For a man with such a reputation of smoothness with the ladies, it surprised her. Given how their date was going so far, she'd categorize Gib as knowing very little about women and how to please them.

"Alain. You remembered." Gib flashed a warm smile. "Daphne, this man's the best waiter in town. A year from now he'll remember what you wore tonight."

A bob of his shiny, bald head. "If you'll permit me, miss, I'll remember the way you look tonight for the rest of my life."

"Thank you," she said.

Gib's smile morphed into outrage. "That's obviously a line. You're not going to call him out on it?"

"The man's pouring me champagne. Why would I do anything to make him stop?"

"So you can be bribed?"

"By the right man. For the right reasons."

"I'll keep that in mind." He lifted his glass as Alain stepped back soundlessly. "To the breathtaking Daphne—" Gib paused and arched one jet-black brow, "—and the hope I'll get the chance to steal your breath away later."

Daphne's back teeth ground together. Another line. She'd bet a week's worth of profit on it. "One step at a time." A quick sip of the champagne sent her spinning into doubt again. Dom Pérignon came by its prestigious reputation honestly. It tasted like golden fairy dust dancing across her taste buds. Maybe Gib really had ordered it for them because it was quite simply the best. Oh, and maybe she should stop analyzing every second of this date and just enjoy it.

"What do you think of the view?" Gib twisted in his chair to point at the spectacular cityscape. "We're facing south, which I think is the best at night. North's a bunch of condos, and east is the lake, but with a south view, we can see most of the city."

Like he was reading from a freaking script. "Mmm-hmm. Nice." Daphne dutifully stared out the window while she took another slow sip. Listened to something with strings piped over the sound system. The couple behind her murmuring in Italian to each other. And wondered how much of this dinner she and her best friend would spend in awkward silence.

Gib slammed his glass onto the table. Or tried to.

It landed on top of his silverware with a sharp clank. "Look, I'll be honest. I'm not entirely sure what to say to you."

So she hadn't been the only one to notice the utter weirdness. "About what?"

"Exactly." He trailed his fingers down the back of her hand. Chills skated up Daphne's arm, then tingled down her torso to the vee between her legs.

"Is that code? 'Cause I don't have a clue as to where you're going with this."

"We already know each other inside and out." Gib drilled his index finger against the table. "I know what you had for lunch three days ago."

They shared a weakness for sandwiches. The bigger and messier, the better. "I had to let you know about that new deli. You love a well-made Reuben as much as I do."

"Quite so. But we already share the little stuff—and the big stuff. To my point, you know I fired one of the fourth-floor housekeepers yesterday."

Finally. A real conversation. "Because you called me all worked up. In a lather. Spouting the same did-I-just-consign-her-to-a-life-of-homelessness-and-prostitution crap you do every time you fire someone. As though you're a superhero. As if you're single-handedly responsible for keeping all of Chicago gainfully employed. If I recall, once I talked you off that ledge, you promised you wouldn't feel guilty anymore."

"You actually said I could mope through the weekend, but would have to shake it off by Monday. Don't rush me."

Awww, his big marshmallow of a heart was showing.

She turned her hand over to interlace their fingers. "Gib, a guest walked into her room to discover the maid taking a bubble bath. You had no choice but to fire Elena. As I've already told you at least twenty times."

"Exactly my point. We've already shared all the big stuff. Yet this is supposed to be a new beginning."

"I get it." Daphne flip-flopped for the umpteenth time. Sounded like he wanted to make an effort with her. Plus, they were back to talking normally, with the added bonus of full-body goose bumps every time he touched her. "If we can't start from the beginning, where do we start?"

"I suppose we could try to follow a standard date outline."

"Your inner anal corporate executive is showing. A date outline? Do you even have one, or do you just count to ten and then unclasp their bra?"

He tsked. "Don't be insulting. I count to twenty. I like to take my time. Touch and taste and explore until talking's no longer an option. Until the need to be naked is as powerful as the need to breathe. Until the anticipation spreads across you in an undulating wave of heat."

Glass halfway to her lips, Daphne paused. Swallowed hard. Found it amazing her bra hadn't unclasped itself at his words. "Duly noted."

Their waiter came by with menus. While he recited the specials, Daphne drained her glass. Then drained her water glass. A man who used the word *undulate* to describe sex had to be really, really good at it. If practice truly made perfect, Gib should be a freaking black belt in sex. She couldn't wait to put him through his paces.

Once the waiter left, Gib cleared his throat. "Let's see—usual topics for a first date. You're from Chicago, I'm from England. Moving on."

"How about college? I mean, I know you went to Cambridge, and I've heard some of your stories about your cricket team, but there must be more."

"All right. Saying you went to Cambridge is too broad, like if you're from the United States, instead of Illinois. I went to King's College. Founded in 1441. Boasting such famous alumni as Salman Rushdie, the economist John Maynard Keynes, Robert Walpole, the first Prime Minister of Great Britain, and yours truly."

Daphne mimed an exaggerated yawn. "Welcome to Snoozeville. I could pull all that up on my phone in three seconds."

"I don't think I ever told you I was in the choir there."

She pounced on that tidbit. Normally Gib stayed as closemouthed as an oyster about his college days. On the rare occasion he did speak of it, a priceless pearl was revealed. "You can sing? How could you have kept something that juicy to yourself?"

"Because I didn't want to be trotted out like a trick pony every time a birthday cake appears. But I've sung my whole life. Papa said it was a waste of time. God, how he hated it." A rueful, hollow laugh accompanied the downward slash of his brows. "Which is probably the main reason why I kept it up all the way through school."

"We're going to karaoke. I won't take no for an answer. We'll do a duet. Something cheese-a-licious. 'You're the One that I Want' from *Grease*. Or 'Promiscuous.' I'll be Nelly Furtado and you can be Timbaland."

"I'd be more likely to do the famous Act II duet from *Tristan und Isolde*."

"So you don't just listen to opera to annoy me. You really like it?"

"Love it. Dabbled with the notion of doing it professionally, before my father made his displeasure with the idea known. So I contented myself with singing at university. The King's College Choir is quite famous."

A jagged gash in her heart opened every time Gib let slip the depth of the pain his father caused him. She still didn't know why, what caused the great schism in his family. It didn't matter. If his father ever came to America, she'd kick him in the balls for putting that dark shadow behind Gib's eyes. So she countered with levity. "For what? Those dopey-looking Peter Pan collars on top of your choir robes?"

"A woman who wears an apron at work has no room to criticize." He refilled her glass. "The choir's made too many recordings to count. Every year they do a Festival of Nine Lessons and Carols that's broadcast worldwide on Christmas Eve. I never miss it. Well, thanks to TiVo."

Daphne made a mental note to check YouTube as soon as she got home. An angelic-looking Gib in a choir robe was a vision she did not want to miss out on. "I never asked. What did you end up doing on Christmas Day?"

"Doc Debra."

Good thing she'd put her champagne down, or Daphne would've done a spit take. "Come again?"

He looked about one percent sheepish, four percent complacent and ninety-five percent cocky as hell. "All of you did the family thing. I was lonely. Doc Debra was, well, Jewish and looking for a way to make the day go by faster. So we made merry. I gave her a reason to be jolly. Instead of Jack Frost nipping at her nose, I nipped at her—"

Hands waving, she cut him off. "Enough! Here's the deal. You can brag about your success in the sack to your *friend* Daphne. You can't do it to your *date* Daphne." She usually laughed at his sexual shenanigans. But not tonight. Not after shaving above the knee for him.

"Sorry. I forgot that we've drawn a new line in the sand."

Where to begin? With the fact he thought it was okay to talk about banging other women while on a date? Which led her to believe he still didn't truly see her as a desirable woman. Gib still looked across the table and saw the best friend that ate wings with him in her sweats. She'd been kidding herself to think otherwise. How many chances should she give him? Daphne didn't have Mira or Ivy around to consult, but it felt like one more would be her limit. On the off chance she'd yet again blown something he said out of proportion, Daphne led with the legally reprehensible issue.

"Isn't Doc Debra your therapist?"

A one-shoulder shrug. When her finger drumming finally clued Gib in that Daphne expected more, he said, "She was. Until about a month ago."

"Isn't that wildly unethical? Yank-her-license un-ethical?"

He leaned forward. Crossed his heart and said, "Nothing happened while I laid on her couch twice a week."

"Wow. Bet that's the first time you've ever uttered those words."

"Cut me some slack. Do you want to know what happened, or do we lower the cone of silence?"

Daphne rolled her hands in a *go on* gesture. Dating etiquette probably said he shouldn't tell her. But he'd already said too much. Not spilling the whole story now would be like using a condom during sex with a pregnant woman.

Leaning back in his chair, Gib extended his legs to poke out from beneath the tablecloth on her side. "A few weeks after the doc cut me loose, I ran into her at a holiday party. Bad party and even worse booze. We left to find better drinks." Gib paused, finally choosing his words carefully. "We had fun. So when I felt glum on Christmas, I called her. No big deal."

"Really?"

"She's a good doctor. Ask Sam. I hooked him up with her practice. Says it's going great. If it wasn't for her, I never would've pulled myself together enough to give this whole relationship thing a go. Doc Debra puts her patients first. No way would she risk her license just to screw me."

Gib probably believed that to be true. Having spent years lusting after him, however, she also believed that a woman would do just about anything for the chance

at a few hours of bliss in his arms. Was that the champagne talking? Maybe. Jealousy that another—in an
extremely long line of women—had beaten her to the
punch? Definitely.

Their waiter dropped by again. This time he depos-
ited a basket of rolls. Hovered a bit, waiting for their
order.

The butter pats were cut into tiny hearts. So adorable. "Is that brioche heart-shaped?"

"Of course," said the waiter. And if Daphne had been
even a second slower, she would've missed his sideways
wink at Gib. But she saw it. More to the point, she knew
what it meant. These weren't special gestures he'd gone
out of his way to arrange for her. They were part of his
usual modus operandi.

"If I go check the other tables, will their brioche be
heart-shaped?"

After glancing at Gib, the waiter muttered, "No."

Daphne meticulously folded the napkin back over the
rolls and pushed the basket to the center of the table.
They were lovely rolls. Maybe some other lucky table
would enjoy them. "This is like the roses and the champagne, isn't it? You order these stupid romantic rolls
every time you're here. Hell, you probably don't even
have to ask for it anymore. The hostess probably alerts
the kitchen to start rolling out the Gibson Moore special date package as soon as you book your reservation.
Every time. Every woman."

He put his elbows on the table, steepled his fingers
and rested his forehead on them. Even closed his eyes.
Very similar to a yoga breathing pose. Did the man have

to freaking meditate to summon up a response? Finally, he laced his fingers into a fist and looked over at her.

"Daphne, you're hardly the first woman I've ever dated. A fact of which you are well aware."

"I don't care. I don't care that you've slept with half the city. Your past isn't the issue. It's the present. All I care is that when you're out with me, well," her voice husked to a near whisper, "you're out with *me*. Not just the next in a string of sets of perky breasts and long legs. This whole night has been a checklist of lines and moves. I wanted it to be personal. You can date any random woman any night of the week. But tonight, I kidded myself that you wanted to be with me, not just any woman."

Gib shoved a hand through his hair. Swiped it down his jaw. "Daphne, it is personal."

"My last gynecologist visit was more personal than this date." Yeah, that sent the waiter scuttling away. "Oh, you do it up nicely. Your dates probably feel charmed. Looked after. I want to feel treasured, Gib. I want to be irreplaceable. I want to be different. I want to matter. And you've made it more than clear that I don't matter at all."

She finished her third glass of champagne. Hadn't even seen it get refilled. Then Daphne pushed up from her chair. "I thought we truly had a shot at growing from being friends to lovers. Maybe Doc Debra pushed you off the couch too soon. Taking that step toward commitment isn't about sex. It isn't about heat and stolen kisses. It's about letting a relationship blossom. Unfurling not just attraction, but respect and intimacy, to a whole new level. And now you've nipped us in the bud."

He reached his hand out. Stopped just short of actually touching her. "Don't leave."

"There's no point in me staying. I'll say mean things. You'll say things you don't mean. For the sake of our friendship, we should pretend tonight never happened."

The debonair mask slipped from his face. Blue eyes dulled to the color of faded denim drifted shut. After a deep breath, they popped open and he jammed a hand through his hair. "At least let me drive you home."

God, no. The thought of sinking into those heated leather seats while knowing it was the only warmth she'd feel from him tonight? "No. Stay and enjoy this—" she gestured to the roses, the champagne, the damn rolls, "—officially romantic meal." As she stalked to the exit, Daphne put an extra swish in her step, sure his eyes would be riveted to her ass. Might as well let him see what he'd be missing out on. Forever.

ELEVEN

When men and women are able to respect and accept their differences then love has a chance to blossom

~ John Gray

GIB HITCHED UP his sweatpants. The scent of something mouthwatering had broken through his haze of bone-deep exhaustion. As much as he didn't want to crawl out of bed, breakfast beckoned. The thick, dark roast of coffee in the air gave him the energy to get vertical. Overlaying that was caramelized sugar, seductive and beckoning. With an eye on the prize, he'd dragged on sweats and thick socks.

He opened his bedroom door. The puffy nylon of his parka smacked against his face.

"Put the coat on and grab your boots," barked Milo. At least, the voice belonged to Milo. A hunter's cap with fleece-lined ear flaps came down to his eyebrows, and a purple argyle scarf pulled up over his nose. The bulk of what had to be three pairs of sweats ballooned from beneath his snow-white parka.

One arm in his coat, Gib stepped into his black Sorels. In those boots, he could stand in a snowdrift in the Arctic for three days and not feel it. "Is this a fire drill?"

"Opposite. It's a blizzard."

"Really?" Disbelieving, Gib clunked across the room. One shove at the curtain revealed a gray sky. Below it, everything looked like it had been dipped in marshmallow fluff. Snow buried the line of parked cars up to their windshields. Bare, skeletal branches dipped low under the heavy wetness of it.

"Started about midnight. Looked bad right from the start, so I stayed up and threw together a strawberry-stuffed French toast. Should be ready by the time we finish our place." Milo handed over a blue knit cap.

"Did you call the guys? Are we starting here?" Gib, Milo and Sam usually pitched in to dig out the girls and the bakery. With Ben in the mix, it should go fast. Of course, now they had to shovel out Sam's bakery, Daphne's apartment, Ben and Ivy's new digs, and here. If anyone else joined their little group, Gib might have to break down and buy a snowblower.

"Ben and Sam swung by Daphne's already. Figured you wouldn't want to be seen over there this morning. Or more to the point," Milo said archly, "she wouldn't want to see you."

Here it comes, Gib thought. Although he'd spent several hours braced for a lecture, he hadn't heard Milo come in last night. Probably because he'd been busy cutting a bloody swath through a shoot 'em up car chase game. Gib had plugged into headphones as soon as he finished scarfing down a hamburger and cold fries. He cranked the volume way up. Every crash, every gunshot, every siren vibrated into his skull. It was fast and violent and the perfect match for his hideous mood.

He'd hammered at the joystick and buttons until his thumb gave out.

"You've got something to say? Spit it out, man," Gib ordered. Might as well get the ass-kicking over with.

Milo opened his mouth. Closed it. Walked to the front closet and pulled out their shovels. Handing one to Gib, he said, "You look like crap. Did you get any sleep?"

"Not really." He'd finally shut down the game after two. But lying in bed repeating every instant of his epic fail with Daphne wasn't the same as actual sleep. That didn't come till probably close to dawn.

"Do you feel as bad as you look?"

Doubtful. He'd have to be turned into pulverized raw meat to look as wrung out as he felt. "Yes."

"I'm sorry." Milo patted him on the back, then opened the front door. The good thing about snow was that it actually kept the temperature relatively warm. Well, above zero. But the shock of cold, especially so soon after crawling out of his warm bed, stole Gib's breath away. The heavy silence peculiar to a blizzard muted the usual white noise of the city. Then a sharp crunch drew his attention to Ben and Sam digging their shovels into the snow.

Behind them sat two snowmen. When nature dumped this much, they usually made snowmen that represented their friends. Always something pink on Ivy's, and a Bears hat on Daphne's. On today's version in front of his house, one wore Milo's favorite purple beret. The other had a licorice vine mouth turning down. In front of it, lying in the snow, were two meatballs and a sausage link. It looked…suggestive, to say the least.

"What's that supposed to be?" he asked.

Ben leaned on the handle of his shovel. "Well, the way we hear it, Daphne pretty much castrated you last night. Figured we'd make your snowman true to life."

Gib couldn't help but laugh. It was damn funny. "Well done." He tugged on his gloves.

"You okay?" Sam asked.

"Not even close." Gib started shoveling. Ideally, he'd shovel till he sweated through his many layers. He'd shovel a mile straight if it meant he'd be worn out enough to catch some sleep. Sam shoveled next to him. Milo started digging out the powdery lump of his Mini Cooper. Ben, however, still leaned on his shovel, just watching. And staring.

"You know, Daphne didn't rat you out," said Ben. "She texted Ivy and Mira when she left the restaurant. Just said she'd walked out on you and was headed home. Then radio silence for the rest of the night."

Which explained why the girls hadn't pounded down his door before midnight, intent on revenge. Nice to know she'd stuck by her promise to not let their relationship status affect the group as a whole. "Good."

"Remember, we did promise to tear you a new one if you hurt our girl," Sam added, in a calm, conversational tone. "So what happened?"

"I screwed up. I was a complete and utter pratt. A wanker." Gib buried his shovel too deep and couldn't lift it. In the process his feet slid out from under him. Ass first, he sank into the wet snow. Fuck. The rate he was going, soaked-through trousers would be the high point of his day. "I'm an idiot."

"Yup," Sam agreed. He tossed a shovelful of snow over Gib's head.

"In so damn many ways." Ben held up his hands and began to tick off points. "For not noticing the hotness of your best friend for how many years? For not asking her out the moment you kissed her. For whatever monumentally stupid thing you did that made her walk out on you at a restaurant that Ivy reminded me she's wanted to try since before her mom died."

"Christ." The memory zapped into his head with the stab of a red-hot barbecue fork. It shoveled a whole fresh layer of shit onto the already-steaming pile of mistakes he'd made with Daphne. "The promise her mom made about taking her there for graduation. I forgot."

That stopped Sam midthrow. "You *forgot?*" he growled.

"I've known her for less than a year, and even I knew the story." Ben shook his head in disgust. Gib didn't blame him. "So why did you take her there?"

"It's my go-to when I want to impress a woman. They all love it. The Signature Room pulls out all the stops for me. It's a no-brainer." Gib knew how bad that sounded. He'd known since Daphne hurled her spot-on accusations at him. Standing, he went back to shoveling without bothering to brush himself off. Frostbite would be his penance. It wouldn't be enough, but it'd be a start.

"Right place for the wrong reason." Ben shook his head. "Man, if Daphne figured out what you did—"

Gib cut him off. After the way she stormed out, it wasn't even a question. "I'm quite sure she did."

"Five minutes into this story, and you're already coming off as a royal douche bag. Is there more?"

So much more. Too much. "I did everything possible wrong last night, except call her by the wrong name. I made Daphne feel like *any* woman, instead of *the* woman. The worst part is that she had to point it out to me."

"You've been very, very bad, Gibson." Milo panted as he dug around the back wheels. "It goes without saying that you're on dish-washing duty in the apartment for at least a month. I think the moldings need to be dusted, too."

"Our housecleaners do that once a month."

"Not this month. Not once I tell them you've volunteered to get on your hands and knees and take care of it."

Gib preferred the idea of shoveling away his frustration and disappointment. But dusting still sounded better than Sam and Ben taking turns using him as a punching bag. "Fine. I'll take whatever punishment you all think I deserve. On one condition."

Sam pulled off his scarf and threw it toward the front door. Unzipped his coat. Resumed his steady shoveling. "What's that?"

This was what had kept him tossing and turning all night. "Tell me how to fix this. Tell me how to get a second chance with Daphne."

"Easy." Milo bounded forward. "You get on your flying carpet, swing past King Solomon's mine, pick up the magic brass lantern and rub it until a genie pops out."

Smart-ass. "I'm serious."

"You took a shot." Sam pretended to lob a basketball into the air. "You missed. End of story. Suck it up."

Gib got the impression that Sam's anger at him for hurting Daphne was about a millimeter away from breaking through. Still, he'd keep grasping at straws until they helped him. "America's the land of second chances. Of fresh starts."

"You're really going to play the immigrant card?" Ben laughed. And finally put his back into moving some snow. "Didn't Daphne talk you out of taking our citizenship test not too long ago?"

That memory stung. He'd stayed up way too late cramming. All about the Constitution, representatives, cabinet positions and an entirely different version of the American War of Independence (which he had to now remind himself to call the Revolutionary War) than he'd learned as a child. Then he wasted four hours waiting in line. When only two people were up before him, Daphne burst into the room. Wild-eyed and talking a mile a minute.

"Yes. She droned on forever about my responsibility to Queen and country. And something about the hotness of Prince William. I agreed not to become an American mostly to make her stop."

"An interesting basis for making your personal geopolitical decisions," smirked Milo.

"I fucked up." Gib tossed his shovel aside. Spread his arms wide in a mea culpa pose. "I know it, Daphne knows it and you all know it. I want a chance to clear the air."

Sam nodded slowly. "He's got a point. I scorched some chocolate yesterday. Stunk up the bakery. Melted down a fresh batch, and it covered up the stench."

"Hang on," said Milo. "Aren't you going to the Fancy Food Show this month? To hawk your amazing truffles to anyone who'll pay an arm and a leg for them?"

"That's the plan."

He stabbed with his shovel in Sam's direction. "Then shouldn't your days of burning chocolate be waaay behind you? Sounds like amateur hour to me."

"Tempering chocolate is an alchemical reaction. It can hinge on the slightest variable." Sam paused, pressing his fists into his lower back as he stretched. "Plus, Mira distracted me. There's nothing in the recipe books about taking a five-minute break to watch your fiancée show off her new bra."

"Niiiice," Ben drawled. "What flavor truffles did you end up making that day? And when can I try them?"

"White-chocolate passion fruit papaya with a lime glaze." Sam winked. "To match her new orange lace bra."

"Even nicer. Are you nervous about the show? Like a JV football team before their first big game? Or ready and steady—like LeBron at the free throw line?"

"I've got a plan. I've got an entire walk-in full of chocolate samples. Extra help lined up for that week. Mira helped me with some fancy cards. All I have to do is show up and wait for the seventeen thousand buyers to walk by." Sam tossed some snow from hand to hand, forming a perfect ball. "I'm more worried for Daphne. Her big competition is the weekend before. At least I know what I'm walking into—she's going into that blind."

Finally. A way to steer the conversation back to his

problem. Getting back into Daphne's good graces had to happen immediately. Before her anger cured, like wet cement. Sam's show wasn't for a few weeks. Gib cleared his throat. "Or she'll walk in on the arm of a supportive boyfriend. If you help me."

A triangulation of looks passed between his friends. Raised eyebrows. Waggled eyebrows. Shrugs. Sam stepped forward. "You gotta be sure. One hundred percent in it to win it. No more half-assing it."

"Right. Totally committed." In theory, at any rate. No guarantee he wouldn't muck it up. This being his first real go at it.

"You could be romancing three other woman with no more than a smile." Milo wagged a finger. "Daphne's going to take effort. Are you sure you want to work that hard?"

"Is there any chance you'll break her heart?" Ben asked.

"There's a much stronger chance she'll break mine." Gib figured his metaphorical cock and balls were already on display in the snow. Why not throw his raw, bleeding heart out there for them to stare at, too? "I didn't like watching Daphne walk out on me last night. The last time I felt that poleaxed was when I took a full-on kick to the solar plexus in soccer. Sidelined me for the rest of the game. Without Daphne, I'll be sidelined a lot longer. She's the first—and only—woman I've ever wanted to have stick. What if she's my only shot at true happiness?"

They were perfect together. All the time they'd spent as best friends proved it. Toss in their red-hot attraction for each other, and it was the perfect match. Well, as long as you disregarded the epic shit storm he'd created last night through his laziness. Stupidity. Blundering.

Ben gaped at him. "Did Ivy write you that speech? 'Cause I swear, pink cotton candy coated each word. Polka-dotted birds flew out your ass."

Milo squinched his face into the same death mask of pain he wore with a hangover. "Another sentence and you would've started growing breasts."

"Now I know why you Brits always bury your feelings. It's damn embarrassing when you air them out."

Gib could take the insults. Didn't disagree with any of them. "But will you help?"

"Of course. Or we wouldn't bother putting you through the wringer." Ben broke the twig arm off of Gib's snowman and started writing in the snow. "Here's where you start. Tell her something about yourself. Something scary real. Something deep. Something you'd never share with that endless string of perfect boobs and surgically perfect faces that parade through your bedroom."

This was going to be as bad as the Grail quest. Impossible from the first step. "Daphne's my best friend. She already knows everything about me."

"Does she?"

"I'M GLAD YOU came tonight." Mira reached to give Daphne a hug across a desk so clean it could be classified as surgically sterile.

Shelves filled with possible merchandise for A Fine Romance lined each brick wall in multiple rows. They made the closet-size space feel claustrophobic. Daphne wanted out. More specifically, she wanted to get upstairs and get her hands on a glass of wine. "Are you kidding? This is your first official Match-n-Mingle. I wouldn't miss it."

"I thought you might be too sad to do—you know—the whole thing."

"What? Shower and dress like a grown-up?" Daphne looked down at her outfit. Skinny jeans, knee-high black boots and a sweater she swore made her feel like Marilyn Monroe. Casual sexy. Exactly the right look for her cannonball into the dating pool.

"Well, yeah. Didn't you say you cried so much your eyelashes froze together on your walk yesterday?"

The problem with texting? Waaay too easy to overshare. Besides, the crying had stopped right about the time the snow tapered off. A little heavy breathing with her hands cupped over her face fixed the eyelash problem. The date was a blip. The worst error in judgment she'd ever made, but in the grand scheme of life, a mere blip. Time to shut the door on her foolish crush and move on.

"We had a blizzard yesterday. Conditions—all conditions—were extreme. Blizzard's over, and its back to business. I already spent an hour practicing for *Flower Power*. Now I'm ready to go out there and snag a man."

"Whoa." Mira stood, smoothing a dress the same deep red as her store's logo. "Men can smell desperation. Let's scale back that attitude a bit." She circled the desk, tablet in hand. "What if you go out there and just find someone to talk with? And remember the house rule."

"No sex in the bathroom?" Daphne knew Mira had already broken that one. Claimed it to be her right as store manager. Something about testing the soundproofing of the walls.

Sure enough, Mira's cheeks pinked up. Hmm. Maybe she and Sam had broken that rule again...and recently. "When you finish your drink, you have to move on to somebody else. Otherwise it strays away from a Match-n-Mingle and becomes a Match-n-Clump."

"I'm here as a favor, remember? To support you, and to make sure, as an objective observer, that the evening flows. If I want to clump on someone, you can't stop me."

"As long as you clump with Adam Miller, I can deal."

Daphne hoped it wasn't a friend of a friend of a friend. Or worse, Sam's second cousin twice removed. Or any sort of ostensibly related-to-their-group man who'd be impossible to shake. Probably with a receding hairline. Back hair. Unusually small...feet. "I'll bite. Who's Adam Miller?"

"Think about it. You know the name. I've heard you screech it at the television on Sundays more than once."

It couldn't be. Fate wasn't usually so evenhanded. "Adam Miller, the offensive coordinator for the Chicago Bears? The man with the tragic, career-ending crushed kneecap in his very first Super Bowl?"

"The man you drool over whenever the TV cameras pan to the sidelines?" Mira teased.

"Come on, Mira, be totally objective for a minute.

Forget you're living with your own personal sex god who rewards you by painting himself with chocolate in unmentionable places."

"Hard to forget, even for a second." A dreamy smile widened her red lips. "Sam's a talented man, in and out of the bedroom. I mean, in and out of the kitchen."

While she adored Sam, and admitted he was easy on the eyes, Daphne didn't like thinking about anything he and Mira did behind closed doors. It might affect her pure and unadulterated love for his pastries. Worse yet, make her wonder if he'd worn clothes while baking them. "Adam looks like all those brawny men in electric razor and shaving cream ads."

"Mmm. When you put it that way, now I wish I could see him shirtless and dripping."

Daphne did, too. But she was still waiting for the other shoe to drop. "You're telling me that karma ripped Gib away from me, yet has kindly replaced him in less than forty-eight hours? With a man whose biceps are bigger than my thigh?"

"Don't thank karma." Mira tapped the screen of her iPad. "All the credit goes to my new matchmaker, Tabitha Bell."

And there was the other shoe. "No way. I just lasted a whopping twenty-seven minutes on a first date—and that was with the man of my dreams. The last thing I need is a setup."

"It is exactly what you need. You're not mourning a lengthy relationship. Your big date fizzled in less time than it takes to get a manicure. Get right back on the horse. Ride 'em, cowgirl."

"I'm not against dating. I'm against being set up. It never works. So I'd be stuck on another date that wouldn't last any longer than your average salon service. I'm all in favor of a good date. What I can't handle is another debacle."

"Which is why I asked Tabitha to look through all the surveys of tonight's guests and choose the one man most suited for you. As a confidence booster." She turned the iPad to show Daphne a head shot of Adam in the corner of a spreadsheet. White teeth gleamed in a tan face. Strong cheekbones bracketed warm brown eyes. Not... blue. Not the color of a mountain lake, enticing you to slip into their depths and never come up for air. Not Gib.

But that had to be a good thing. Adam was the anti-Gib. As American as, well, football and apple pie. Big as a grizzly with the wide shoulders and thick muscles from his football days in contrast to Gib's lean, toned body, sleekly muscled like a jaguar. The body with such strength she'd yearned to have him unleash upon her. The body she'd surreptitiously drooled over when he'd come in from a run with Mira and Ben. The way he'd strip off his sopping-wet shirt and display a set of abs hard enough to polish diamonds.

With another glance at Adam's picture, Daphne said, "A purely selfless gesture, is it? This putting me on display for a total stranger?"

Mira looked down at her boots. "All right, it's a test. It's a test of how the event works, and a test of Tabitha's abilities as a matchmaker. I can't get this kind of information from a customer. You have to help me. Just like the aphrodisiac dinner."

Look how that turned out. "Tabitha's never met me."

"I might have filled out a survey in your name." Mira shut the cover quickly, and rushed ahead. "But it worked. You love sports, you're a lifelong Bears fan and you've crushed on this guy forever."

"I'm not good enough to be Adam Miller's date. He's gorgeous and works with people whose starting salaries are higher than the profit on all our businesses combined. What would we talk about?"

"Um, that you love sports, and you're a lifelong Bears fan?" Mira pushed her out the office door and up the stairs. "Oh, and Tabitha can't be here tonight. So I'll be nearby, watching and taking notes on her behalf."

Daphne halted in the doorway to the big, open room. Exposed brick gave it a casual vibe, along with the café tables and chairs in deep red. It was full of people already mingling and laughing. Probably because they were at least a drink ahead of her. "You're just going to stare at me all night? Like I'm a zoo animal?"

"More or less." Mira gave a not-so-subtle shove on her ass. Daphne stumbled across the threshold. A large, warm hand caught her elbow and steadied her.

"Daphne, right? I've been waiting for you." A blond giant of a man smiled down at her. The same smile she'd watched crease his face when the Bears won in overtime a few months ago.

She swallowed. Hard. Felt an idiotically big grin stretch across her face. "Hi."

"I've got a beer started at that table." He pointed with his chin. "Would you like one, or do you want some wine?"

"Beer's great."

Adam managed to snag another beer from a passing waiter while keeping hold of her arm to lead her to the table. Once she sat on the high stool, he slid his hand down to lightly rest on top of her wrist.

"I don't know if Tabitha sent you my info in time. I'm sort of a last-minute addition to the party tonight. My sister talked me into coming. Well, bribed me into coming. She promised to make me pot roast next weekend. Bread pudding for dessert."

"Just for going on a date? Your sister pimped you out?" Crap. First she couldn't string more than two words together. Then to rebound by insulting his sister? What was going on? Aside from the Gibson Moore disaster, Daphne was adept enough at dating. Flirty, fun, casual, not afraid to eat in front of a guy. No way would she let Gib undermine her mojo. Luckily, Adam laughed.

"I moped around for a while after we didn't make the playoffs. Jenny got ticked off. Claimed I ruined her New Year's Eve party with my pouting."

Daphne had sulked a bit herself after the debacle of his last game. "You deserve to be pissed off. The Bears were robbed. That final turnover against the Packers could've clinched you a spot in the playoffs. I think the ref was off his meds that day or something."

His eyebrows shot up. "You watched the game?"

"I watch every game. Go Bears." They clinked bottles. Daphne relaxed a bit. Adam was easy to talk to, and talking football made it even easier.

"That's a relief. A lot of pretty girls like you don't

like it when I talk football. I mean, we don't have to just talk about football. But it's my job, you know? Other guys talk spreadsheets and sales calls over a steak dinner. I talk about passing drives and wind sprints and spotting."

"Trust me, I get it. A lot of guys aren't wild about me complaining about the price of Dutch tulips going up, or that a shipment of hydrangeas is blue instead of pink."

His eyes crinkled adorably as he frowned. "Aw, you weren't supposed to tell me about flowers. I wanted to surprise you. I memorized your bio. All the fun facts about Daphne. That you're a florist, and that your favorite color is blue and you like horror movies."

"Don't worry. I'm impressed." Just like that, he'd pitched her back into the land of two-word responses. The handsome football hero called her pretty and memorized her stats. Kind of took her breath away.

"Good. 'Cause as soon as I saw your picture, I knew I wanted to meet you." His hand closed around hers in a firm squeeze. And God help her, a dimple appeared in his cheek. "You're even prettier in person."

"Thanks." Idiot. Say something else. Anything. Well, anything except that her favorite color actually used to be yellow. Until the day she met Gibson Moore, and saw the perfect, paint-palate cerulean-blue of his eyes. "I'm a big fan of yours. I've followed you since your last season with Notre Dame. Never thought I'd get a chance to meet you."

"Heck, I'm nothing special. The guys out on the field, they're the ones who put their heart and soul on the line every week. I just do what I can to help them."

Handsome. Sweet. Modest. Close to his sister. Daphne's eyes slid down to the way his biceps strained against the cotton button-down shirt. Not just handsome. Drool-worthy handsome. Unless this guy secretly snacked on puppies, he was darn near perfect. Definitely the perfect rebound guy. The perfect *hold me and lick me and make me come so many times I'll forget all about Gib* guy. If there was such a thing.

"That's how I feel about my brides. My job's to support her. I don't need a whole room of bridesmaids to ooh and aah over their bouquets. I want to know that I helped the bride feel her most beautiful when she walks down that aisle. That I helped her have the perfect day she's always dreamed of."

He sipped his beer, nodded. "But it's fun, right? I mean, I'm guessing you must like flowers. And your job is to play with them all day, so you have a good time? I love football. I get to think about it all day. So when I'm on a date, I can't help going on about it."

"Sounds good to me." She leaned across the table to whisper. And to brush her cheek against his, just to feel the scratch of five o'clock shadow rasp against her skin. "I have four brothers. I might even know more about football than you."

Adam let loose a big, booming laugh. He squeezed her hand again. "I can't wait to try you out. Damn it, I know that stupid bell's about to ring and make us switch people."

"Sorry. If I'd known you were waiting for me, I would've gotten here sooner." There. Flirting mojo absolutely reestablished.

"Good to know. So here goes. Let me take you to dinner. I promise to show you a good time. Smith & Wollensky? On the river? I'll even tell you my one and only flower story. It's about prom and a goat and a corsage emergency."

Why the hell not? Aside from the whole not-over-the-crush-of-her-life thing. Going out with Adam would probably be a really smart step toward not losing the best friend status quo with Gib. She'd do Adam, Gib would continue to do the entire female population of Chicago, and nothing would change. Nothing. Would. Change. It made her a little heartsick. But Gib clearly would not change. So Daphne would have to. With somebody. So why not with hot, hard-bodied Adam?

"I can't wait to hear it," she said.

Adam pulled a card out of his shirt pocket. "I don't want you to feel pressured. So take my card. Talk to the rest of the guys here tonight—" he dimpled again, "who won't be half as fun as me—then sleep on it. If you still want to go out, call me tomorrow."

A hand Daphne knew as well as her own grabbed the card in midair. "Daphne won't be ringing you up tomorrow." Those blue eyes she'd never stop wanting burned with an icy flame. Gib looked like he'd come straight from work. Or was on his way out to romance and bed a woman. Shiny matte green tie, darker green shirt beneath a black suit. Daphne would give anything, *anything* to grab that tie and use it to reel him in for a kiss.

"Gibson, you don't get a vote in this." Her brain hiccupped, trying to process he and Adam Miller sharing the same space. "What are you even doing here?"

"Sam called me." He ground out the words from be-tween clenched teeth. "Mira and I will have words later as to why she didn't tell me herself."

"Tell you what?"

"About her betrayal. About the way she auctioned you off in this dating circus."

Adam shook his head. "Dude, I didn't pay for Daphne. This isn't that kind of place. You owe her an apology for even thinking that."

Gib looked Adam up and down. She'd seen him give a week-old bagel a less dismissive look. Then some-thing changed. An abrupt dial-back of the dangerous vibe rattling off of Gib like a wind shear.

"Look, I get it. Daphne's amazing. Lovely. Of course you're keen to go out with her. I bet every guy in this room's pissed at you, wishing they'd gotten to her first. Except for the singular fact that you didn't." That dan-gerous edge crept back into his voice. "I did. I staked my claim. Did a piss-poor job of it, but did it nonetheless."

Had he lost his mind? Daphne couldn't help but thrill to his words. Still, she couldn't let him get away with them, either. "I'm not an unnamed mountain in the Himalayas. You can't claim me."

"Give me a chance to try." With a nudge of his legs to her knees, her chair swung around to face him. The move also pulled her hand away from Adam's. "I'm sorry. I'm sorrier than I can say. I'm a fool. I behaved like an utter ass."

"No argument here." Daphne hoped Mira really was nearby, taking notes. She wouldn't mind a word-for-word playback of this entire conversation once the shock wore off.

"I crapped all over our window of opportunity. And again, I'm sorry. I know you're mad. You should be. I'm furious at myself. All I ask is that you give me one more chance."

He had the appropriate hangdog expression of penitence. And was throwing himself on the altar of public humiliation for her. Daphne had to admit it bore all the signs of a genuine apology. But he couldn't snap his fingers and expect her to fall into line. Their friendship had survived one disastrous date. She couldn't guarantee it would survive a second.

"Why should I?"

Gib waggled Adam's card in the air. "You've got nothing to lose. All I ask is that you go out with me once. Tomorrow night. If you don't have a good time, a great time, I'll give you this card. You can ring Adam up and set up a date with him for next weekend." He edged closer. Daphne had to tilt her head up to look at him. A long, slow stroke down her arm ended with the familiar feel of his hand around hers. "But please, give me one more night. One night, just for you. The date you deserved from the start. One last shot to get you to change your mind."

The jazz piano piped through the sound system stopped abruptly, replaced by a tinkling bell. It was the signal to switch partners. A tall man with a shaved head and glasses elbowed between Adam and Gib.

"Time's up, guys. Move on," he said in a pleasant but firm voice.

Adam pushed back his chair. "Well, Daphne?"

Why did Adam have to be so perfect in every way—except that he simply wasn't Gib? The choice came down to the basic fact that she'd marinate in regret for the rest of her life if she didn't give Gib one more chance.

"Adam, it was fun talking with you. I promise I'll call you in two days and explain. One way or another." She hugged him, which was kind of like hugging a scantily upholstered building. Solid, immovable and big. Tempting, too. Daphne moved on to the new guy.

"Sorry, but I'm finished for the evening. These two wore me out." She winked at Adam. To her delight, he winked back. Tabitha the matchmaker really knew her stuff. "I'll make sure you get an extra drink or something." Then she turned to Gib. "Seven o'clock tomorrow. Don't fuck it up."

TWELVE

Life is the flower for which love is the honey
~ Victor Hugo

"Do I NEED to grovel some more?" Gib asked. His boots crunched against the fresh layer of snow on the sidewalk. "Because I'm willing. Seriously. You name the way you want it. Haiku. Shouted from the rooftop. Hell, I'll do a mea culpa with a bullhorn from the top of the Navy Pier Ferris wheel."

"I'm good for now. I'll let you know if the situation changes." It finally felt like Daphne had the upper hand. She liked it. Kind of wanted to keep making him work for it. Now that she knew he had it in him to grovel so thoroughly.

"Good. Because I'd like a fresh start. As if we've never done this before."

"Do you mean as if we'd never met? Pretend to be Daisy and Graham again?" Because that had worked very well. Anything that got her back in Gib's lap in under ten minutes was worth doing again.

"I'm all for role-playing in the bedroom." Gib stopped, looked down at her with a wicked smile. "Off the top of my head, I can picture you as a feisty pirate wench. One who needs to be subdued by an officer in the King's Navy."

Yes. She could see it, too. Michigan Avenue and the cars spraying slush disappeared. There was only Gib in knee-high black boots, a sword strapped to his hip. Pushing her back against the mast. Maybe tying her to it with a handy rope. Tightly. Daphne realized she was squeezing his hand like a tourniquet. And that she'd completely forgotten to take a breath.

"But I don't think we're quite there yet." Swinging their linked hands, he began to walk again. "I'd like to put my idiotic behavior of the other night behind us. You've every right to be mad at me. Which is why I'll continue to apologize as many times as you need to hear. My second attempt at a first date, however, won't be much fun at all if you're pissy."

"Righteously pissy," Daphne corrected.

He nodded briskly. "Of course. So are you willing to shelve your utterly righteous anger for about twelve hours? Let us have a clear shot as though it were our *first* first date?"

Funny. She'd already had this identical conversation with Ivy. Although Ivy had been a bit more direct, insisting that sulking wasn't sexy. "You don't have to keep apologizing. As long as you promise not to treat me like a one-night hookup, we're a clean slate."

"Brilliant."

A clean slate didn't mean she wouldn't still hassle him. "So far you've run me through an hour of drills to prep for the *Flower Power* competition. Driven us to the Cavendish and parked in your spot. Nothing special going on there. Now you've walked us out of the garage in what feels like an aimless ramble. Gotta ask, Gib. Do you actually have a plan for tonight?"

"Ouch." He pulled back with an exaggerated wince. "Your lack of faith is, well, warranted, I suppose. I parked at the Cavendish because the rates at other downtown garages are highway robbery."

"True." Daphne flipped through a mental map of the nearby options. Lookingglass Theatre might be fun, but he'd told her to dress casually, which scratched it off the list. "If we're going to Tiffany's, which would be a great way to show me how sorry you are, then you've overshot by about two blocks."

"Tiffany's. Really? That's cheeky." Gib chuffed out a laugh. "You and me, we're not quite *there* yet, either. This is only our first official date, remember?"

"Rats." Worth a shot. At least it felt familiar and fun to tease him.

"Didn't know your taste ran to shiny rocks. You rarely wear jewelry."

"Because I work with my hands in water and stems all day. My work uniform is an apron over jeans. A beautiful, two-carat, square-cut emerald pendant might look as if I were trying too hard."

"Interesting." Gib looked at her, *really* looked at her as if seeing her for the first time. "Why don't I know this about you? Your secret love for posh jewelry?"

"Never came up. Not really something pals discuss. Unless one of them is in the market to shop for a present. Face it, you've never stayed with a woman long enough to buy her a sparkly present in a little blue box."

"True. You can wipe that hopeful look off your face. We're not going to Tiffany's."

"The food court at Water Tower Place?" They did an amazing pad thai. A little buffet of add-ons, so she could overload on cilantro and limes.

"Daphne, there's casual, and then there's insulting. I'm not taking you to a mall food court on our first date."

"I give up."

They turned at the iconic Chicago Water Tower. One of the only buildings to survive the Great Chicago Fire, its limestone castle facade symbolized the resilience of Chicago. Daphne liked it because it reminded her of a fairy-tale castle. No one in particular. But being able to walk past a building that looked like it housed swaggering heroes ready to battle dragons and vanquish foes tickled her imagination. Not that she'd ever admit as much out loud.

"Tonight is about you. Not any other woman. A date made specifically for Daphne." They passed the park with trees still wrapped in lights from the holidays. "One of the most basic truths about you is that you've an enormous sweet tooth. So I'm taking you for a predinner drink." Gib pointed at, hands down, one of her favorite places in the city. The Ghirardelli store.

She couldn't help it. Daphne clapped her hands together in glee. "I never would've expected this. Ever." She raced ahead of him, but Gib's long legs still got him to the door fast enough to open it for her. Stepping onto the brown-and-white checkerboard floor was like coming home. Daphne found an excuse to swing by this store at least once a week. The clerks knew her name, knew her favorite orders. Gib really delivered. This time.

Sandy, a middle-aged woman with a magical touch on the espresso machine, waved. "You don't usually visit us this late."

"First time for everything," Daphne said with a smile. Then she turned to beam at Gib. "Do you trust me to order for you?"

"Seems only fair."

"Two salted caramel hot chocolates, please." The urge to smother him in kisses for being so thoughtful was strong. But Gib needed to make any and all moves. Daphne refused to put her heart visibly on the line again unless he did it first. "I'd be perfectly happy if we stayed here all night. Thank you."

"We aren't even staying five minutes." Gib leaned over the counter to Sandy. "Put those in to-go cups, please."

"But I'm just starting to thaw." The short walk from the parking garage, in addition to wedging a chunk of snow between her boot and shin, had chilled her feet and her ears to almost numb. Daphne had unfortunately decided against a hat. Neither frizzy static-hair or flattened hat-hair were looks she thought would put Gib in a sexy mood.

His lips tickled the top of her ear. It sent a different kind of chill straight down her spine. "I promise to keep you warm."

Okay, that sent a tingle down the front of her body. And it boded well. Flirty Gib had returned, and yet not overly obvious and practiced. His promise sounded as genuine as his earlier apology.

"Sure you don't want a brownie to go with these?" Sandy's hand hovered over the solid, gooey bar of choc-olaty goodness. "I could dip it in hot fudge for you."

Gib slid a ten-dollar bill onto the counter. "Tempt-ing. But I've got plans to keep her lips busy." He picked up the cups and headed for the door. Sandy gave a big thumbs-up. Biting her lip, Daphne waved goodbye and hurried after him.

"Come on, we don't want to keep him waiting." He set a brisk pace across the street.

Daphne wound her hand around his elbow. It kept him close, and it put her in position to grab for her hot cocoa. "Who?"

"Al Capone."

"He's dead. Are you taking me to a séance? Or a ghost tour? Because Halloween was months ago."

Gib stopped in front of a huge chestnut horse tethered to an old-fashioned burgundy carriage. He ran a hand over the white stripe on its nose. "Meet Al Capone."

The horse whinnied at its name, and tossed its mane. "He's very…big."

"Gotta be, to pull one of these." A man in a big fur hat stood by the open door. "Al's a workhorse. You could load this rig up with four chunksters and he wouldn't complain. Two skinny things like you won't be any problem at all."

"Good to hear." Fighting back laughter, Gib boosted Daphne inside. He did it so well that she bounced on the gray upholstered seat.

"We're really doing this?"

Gib latched the door. Then he grabbed a blanket and tucked it around their legs. Stretched an arm across her shoulders to anchor her against his chest. "Yes. Unless you don't want to?"

"Are you kidding? I've always wanted to ride in one of these. I've watched my own brides do it time after time. It's utterly romantic, being snugly in here with you." She bounced again, for the sheer fun of it. Cocoa and a carriage ride with her favorite guy. Gib had more than clawed his way out of the doghouse. Now if only she could get him back on the kissing track, it'd be a perfect night.

"Good. And before you ask, I've never taken a date on a carriage ride before." With a strong jerk, the carriage began to roll. "Well, not here." He paused. "Full disclosure?"

He'd even learned not to just rattle off his sexual history. The man was on his best behavior. "You decide."

"Back home, I borrowed a landau and drove Mary Smythe-Reilly around the estate when we were fourteen. Far less chance for romance, as I had the reins."

Daphne sipped her cocoa. Aside from his expensive suit addiction, Gib didn't flaunt his money. He put in long hours, worked like a demon for his paycheck from the Cavendish. Easy to forget he came from a background of estates and stables. Gib certainly seemed to forget it most of the time. And she liked hearing a rare story from his childhood. "Did you get a kiss?"

"Afterwards. In the stable. Not worth the hour it took

to curry the horse, clean the landau, all while putting up with a steady stream of mocking by my brother."

"Gerald? Your little brother?"

"Yes." He, too, took a slow sip of his drink.

"I can count the times you've mentioned him on one hand." Should she push him? Risk ruining the entire date right from the start? On the other hand, if Gib immediately shut her down, wouldn't that make clear the bar on just how open and honest their relationship would be?

Daphne chugged half her drink. Took a mental video of the snug interior of the carriage, the gentle rocking, the feel of Gib pressed against her from ankle to shoulder. He'd given her a perfect date so far. If she tried to breach the invisible but solid wall he kept around his life in England, it might be over. This perfect date might actually end sooner than his crappy first attempt. No. This was it. Her one big chance to finally get at the truth. Damn it, their relationship had to be more than a sexed-up version of their friendship.

"Would it spoil everything if I asked about him?"

Sharing the story with Daphne of his last carriage ride felt natural. Just popped out. Gib didn't realize it would lead to dredging the entire scum-covered pond of his memories. Daphne already knew more than anyone else. This was exactly the sort of thing Doc Debra had repeated on a weekly basis in therapy. Find someone to open up to—and then follow through. Probably what Ben had alluded to, as well. He gulped at his cocoa. Wished it was a triple shot of Scotch instead.

"It might, but not for the reason you think. If I tell you about Gerald…" He stopped, sighed deeply. Looked deep into her pale blue eyes and hoped they didn't ice over with disdain by the time he finished.

"Gib, you can tell me anything. You know that. You might not exercise that privilege very often, but you know it's true."

"Right. You say that, but you might change your mind." And he didn't think he could bear it. "How about a quick snog instead?" Gib moved his hand in a restless caress on her thigh.

She pushed his hand back onto his own leg. "How about we save that for after?"

"Ah, bribery. Very well." He pulled off his gloves and tossed them onto the opposite bench. Then he removed hers, much more slowly, a finger at a time. Rubbed her hands in between his until the chill dissipated. And tried the whole time to figure out where best to begin. Unzipped both their coats. Took a moment to appreciate the way Daphne filled out the white sweater covered in blue snowflakes. Angora. Resisted the urge to run the backs of his fingers over the soft swell of her breasts. Hopefully, that would still be an option by the time he finished.

"We're all about the heir and the spare in England, even for families as far down the line of succession as mine. My mother suffered three miscarriages after I was born. When Gerald finally came along, there was great rejoicing. They treated him like a miracle child."

Kicked Gib out of his own nursery, so he wouldn't disturb the baby. He remembered that day. The new room was big and cold and the bed so high it had steps. High enough for legions of monsters to hide beneath. Gib had hated his new room. "I thought he was cute. Couldn't wait until he grew enough to play with me."

Daphne tilted her head onto his shoulder. "I feel like you're telling me a fairy tale, and the big bad wolf is about to enter."

He found it easier to talk without Daphne looking at him. "A few years passed. My parents doted on Gerald. Spoiled him rotten, but still, he was my brother, and nothing could be cooler than that. We went on holiday in Majorca. Lots of cliffs about. Gerald fell." Gib would never, ever forget the sound of the screams. First his mother's, when she realized she'd let go of his chubby little hand. Then Gerald's, as the pain and panic set in. "Broke his leg badly. The bone tore through his femoral artery and he almost died. Needed several transfusions."

Daphne gasped. "That's horrible."

"That's the tip of the iceberg. We soon realized that thanks to those transfusions, he'd also picked up hepatitis. Two surgeries for his leg, months of rehabilitation, and then the diagnosis. His liver started failing right away. Gerald was always a sickly little kid, from colic to croup to whooping cough before any of this happened. My mother slept in his nursery more often than her own bed."

"So you two didn't spend days playing together, like you'd hoped?" She put her hand on top of his, fingers interlaced. As though buttressing them against whatever came next. It gave him the strength to keep going.

To remember the hushed, tiptoed, lonely days of his childhood.

"No. No mock sword fights, no racing ponies. But I'd sneak in to act out stories in his room, play with puppets to make him laugh. I was constantly being told off for exciting him."

"You just wanted to spend time with him. You wanted to be a good big brother."

Here's where Gib feared her automatic defense of him might weaken. "The world revolved around Gerald's doctor appointments, treatments, naps. Whatever I accomplished in school, on the soccer pitch, didn't matter. Couldn't compare to anything Gerald was going through." Wait. He sounded like a whinging brat. "I'm not complaining, mind you. As a grown man I don't begrudge him, but as a boy? I felt invisible. I just need you to see the dynamics of my family."

"Oh, I do. I see that your mother abandoned you while she spent every waking minute with Gerald," she said hotly. And she certainly understood now why he'd sought out a therapist. Daphne bolted upright, twisting to look at him. "She punished you for being healthy. Made you feel less important. The one thing a mother is never, ever supposed to do. What about your father?"

"Not around much. When he was, Mother filled his ears with all things Gerald. But that was okay. The thing you have to know, above all else, is that I loved Gerald. The only reason I worked so hard at school was to be a good role model for him. To give him a glimpse of the life he'd have once he got better, got out of bed."

"I'm not sure I want to hear any more. You're already breaking my heart."

Gib didn't want to keep going, either. Keeping the lid on this story would be far easier for both of them. He stared out the window at the brightly lit store windows on Michigan Avenue. Remembered a dark, foggy night in downtown London that changed everything. "One day, when I was twelve, my parents took me to dinner. A fancy restaurant, very grown-up. They informed me I'd be taking some time off from school. Gerald needed a liver transplant. The best plan was to give him a piece of mine. It was my last meal, before going straight to the hospital for the operation the next morning."

"Wait—they *informed* you?" Daphne waved her hands in the air, as if erasing his very words. "They didn't ask? They didn't sit you down with a doctor and a counselor and work through the situation? They didn't give you time to adjust to the idea?"

"No. But I wanted to do it. I'd have done anything to save Gerald. It just would've been nice to have the chance to get used to the idea. Or to at least be asked. So that on that day, instead of being frightened to my core, I could've felt a little brave, too."

"That's child abuse. That's unconscionable. That's… it's…I can't…" she sputtered.

He'd only ever told this story to one person outside his family. His prefect at Eton. Who'd listened quietly, and then called him a selfish bastard. Hearing Daphne's outrage on his behalf made his head swim. And his heart overflow. "It's over and done. I'm like a starfish.

My liver grew back to full size quick enough. Not worth getting yourself worked up over."

"Are you kidding? I want to get on a plane, not even surf for a cheap ticket, fly to London and slap your mother across the face."

"I appreciate it. Really not the best way to spend your money, though." Especially since he hadn't finished the story yet. Daphne might still hop on that selfish bastard bandwagon.

"We'll see. I reserve the right to avenge your childhood." Finishing her cocoa, she set the cup on the floor. "Or did your parents appreciate you saving Gerald's life and turn over a new leaf?"

"Not so much. They didn't have much use for me after that. Gerald was the one who made the miraculous recovery. The one they coddled, even though he's been perfectly healthy ever since."

She wriggled up to her knees, hanging on to his shoulder for balance. "No wonder you left England. The ingratitude!"

"Gerald was grateful. For about six months. And then he caught on that he had a get-out-of-jail-free card. Everyone still treated him with kid gloves. As he got older, his antics got worse." The first time Gerald shoplifted, Gib caught him. Stupid pack of gum slipped in his back pocket. Everyone tries that once. Most people apologize, or get antsy when caught. Gib threatened to tell their parents. And Gerald just laughed.

"Was he making up for all the time he lost while he was sick? Getting a few years' worth of pent-up juvenile idiocy out of his system?"

"That explains the little stuff. The first few years. But the more he got away with, the more he just kept pushing the envelope. Gerald would break a window, and I'd get the blame. He'd come in three hours past curfew, and it would be my fault. Or not do his homework, and tell the teacher that I'd ruined it somehow. I was the straight arrow, the good student…and the scapegoat."

Daphne scooted closer. He waited for her to say something. Instead, she stroked a soft hand through his hair in a slow circle. Gib wasn't so far gone in his story he didn't notice her breasts almost at eye level. He wasn't sure which soothed him more.

"I went off to university, and he spun more out of control. Harder for my parents to cover up with me away. Of course, they used that as an excuse. That Gerald missed me so much, he cut class to come visit me. When in reality, he was smoking pot with the girls from St. Andrew's. Never came within fifty miles of Cambridge."

Gib turned, pillowed his cheek against the padded backing. Listened to the rhythmic clopping of the hooves. Stared at the ornate stone edifice of the Drake Hotel. Not as pretty as Daphne. But he couldn't bear to watch her face fall when he spit out the rest. So much for their romantic date. Listening to Ben had gotten him inches away from a beautiful woman, and yet with absolutely no kissing in his future. Spilling his big, secret story had been a stupid idea. There were other things to share with Daphne. She didn't know the name of his first roommate. Probably hadn't ever mentioned his white-knuckle fear of caves to her, either.

"What happened, Gib?" she asked in a near whisper. "What made you put an entire ocean between you and your family?"

He'd come this far. Daphne wouldn't let him out of the carriage until he finished. Usually, her tenacity tickled him. Tonight it just made him tired. "Right after I graduated university, Gerald crashed a car. So freaking high on cocaine that he didn't even know he'd crashed until the rescue unit pulled him out. He did manage, however, to muster enough caginess to give them my name instead of his own. Created confusion for a few hours. Long enough for my parents to ring me up and ask me to shoulder the blame. I didn't have a job yet, so I suppose they thought I had the time to kill."

Her hand stilled. "That's not funny."

No, it really wasn't. "Gerald was facing jail time. Not a lot, but even a few hours were out of the question. My brother was being groomed for a seat in the House of Lords."

"Not you? Not the eldest son?"

"I didn't want a career in politics. Stood up to my father on that point years earlier." That had been a six-month standoff, alternating between screaming rows and dead silence. "I wanted to work in a business where I could see results. Make people happy. Got my business degree, and interviewed at a dozen different firms before this happened. Testing the waters. Deciding where I fit in the world. A jail sentence would've ruined Gerald's chances." Gib swallowed hard. Even years later, the words still stuck in his throat. "They ordered me to back his lie. To take his place."

Daphne was quiet for quite some time. Long enough

for him to worry about what she'd say. God knows he'd second-guessed himself for years. Wondered if he should've been a better brother. Shouldered the burden long enough for Gerald to grow up and grow out of his self-destructive phase. Made his family proud, instead of making himself happy.

"Your parents—the people who are supposed to have your best interest at heart—they did this? With no regard for how it would ruin your future?"

Gib sucked in a ragged breath. She got it. She got him. That their overprotectiveness blinded them to Gerald's downward spiral. That even if Gib had taken the blame, Gerald would've stayed on the same destructive path, ending up jailed or worse, dead. That if none of them would teach Gerald his actions had consequences, then he would by leaving. Slowly, Gib swiveled back to look at her. "Precisely. It was the last straw. I bolted. Well, after a grandiose speech in which I vowed never to return."

"Good for you." She bounced off her knees back onto the seat. "Did you hop a freighter to America that very day?"

"I'm not that skinny kid from *Titanic*. And this isn't the Industrial Revolution. There are planes now, you know."

"Flying coach for seven hours isn't nearly as dramatic as stowing away near the boiler room. I'm just saying."

He appreciated her effort to tease him out of a very dark place. But it wasn't necessary. Knowing Daphne understood, and supported, the hardest decision of his life was all he needed. Happy to play along, though. Maybe she needed a bit of a boost after the emotional steaming turd he'd dropped on her. "I suppose I lacked the appropriate dramatic flair for turning my back on my family in style. Sorry to disappoint."

"What did you do?"

"Checked into the Cavendish London. Sat in the lobby for hours, staring at the ceiling. Didn't know where to turn. Heard the concierge mention their manager training program to a cluster of bellhops. The only catch was that it involved moving to America. Permanently."

"A fresh start. As far away as possible."

Her understanding rocked him to the core. "Exactly. I interviewed the next day. Trained in Geneva for three months, then Milan for a year, because I spoke Italian."

"Really?" She gave him a sidelong glance that was pure, unabashed flirting. He'd never seen that look on her face before. Good thing, too, since one look at the blue shimmer between those dark lashes hardened him to the point he had to bunch the blanket over his lap. "You're full of surprises tonight. Say something."

"*Grazie per essere stato il mio migliore amico.*"

Daphne clapped. "Next time we go to Vinci for a wine dinner, I want you to speak in Italian and freak out all the waiters."

"Anything for the *bellissima signorina*. I did get a fresh start. And I'd learned an important lesson. Being straitlaced never got me anything. I stopped trying to please other people, and concentrated on making myself happy. Might as well live it up, because I certainly never got a reward for being good. Doc Debra says that's why I'm, in her words, such a playboy."

"Did she call you that before or after you screwed her senseless?"

Ah, there was his call-it-like-she-sees-it friend. "A gentleman never tells."

"You told your therapist this whole thing?"

"No. Just alluded to a few bits and pieces." And that was the point, wasn't it? "I've never told anyone the whole story. Until tonight. Didn't want anyone to know. Why expose my sordid past?"

"Especially when a woman's in and out of your life in less time than it takes to tell the tale."

Daphne didn't pull her punches. Gib couldn't disagree, though. "Didn't really want you to know, truth be told. But I didn't think I could keep such a big secret from you any longer. Not if we're truly going to give this thing a go."

"This thing?" Another glance from beneath tip-tilted lashes. Another jolt of heat straight to his cock.

"You and me. The relationship upgrade."

"Oh, that."

"We are giving it a go, aren't we? Or have I scared you away? Buggered the second chance you gave me? Because there's more to this date." Gib rushed on, before she could turn him down again. Understanding him didn't mean she necessarily wanted to be with him. Or that she forgave his thoughtless behavior of earlier this week. "Thought we'd go for pizza at Giordano's after this. Your favorite. And I've got three pints of Ben &

Jerry's in my freezer with your name on them. Also your favorites."

"Tempting. But I don't feel like ice cream."

Gib's mind raced. He could call Sam to see if the bakery had any leftover brownies, or maybe a slice of cake. Or swing by the Cavendish and get the pastry chef to hand over one of his signature pecan bourbon crème brûlées. "What are you in the mood for, then?"

"Something hot." Daphne threw one leg to the opposite side, straddling his lap. She drew the blanket around her shoulders. Slowly, she lowered her body until her center rested on the part of him already pulsing with need.

"Wait." God, it killed him to say that. Not sure he'd ever said it before to a woman grinding her crotch into his. "I don't want a pity kiss. That's not why I told you my story."

"I know. You told me to share your vulnerability. Like Samson cutting his hair, or when Arwen gives Aragorn her necklace in *Lord of the Rings*."

Both she and Ivy had pestered him for months after every one of those movies. "Damn it, I told you three Halloweens ago. I'm not putting on elf ears and a blond wig just for your amusement."

"Silly, that's Legolas, not Aragorn." Daphne laced her hands behind his neck. "And we agreed earlier that role-playing is down the road a bit. You shared your life with me, Gib. There's nothing more personal. And now I want to share a different kind of intimacy with you."

"I don't need a fucking reward."

Daphne shook her head. "Not out of pity." Her eyes

closed, and she sighed. "I've always admired and respected you as a man. Now that's changed. My admiration's tripled. My respect for the struggles you've overcome, the road you've walked along and the man you've become—well, that's off the charts. I thought I wanted you before." Her eyes opened, gaze forthright and hotter than a blue laser. "Now, I *know* I do. I need you. I need to show you how deep my feelings run."

Well. This night was taking a sharp turn for the better. "Have to admit, I'm a little curious."

Daphne didn't require any more encouragement. Her mouth took his in an absolute frenzy of touching and licking. Gib locked his hands at her waist. Didn't want to take the chance she'd change her mind and slip out of his arms. Not when she was bursting with passion. When he was finally tasting what he'd craved for the six endless days since they last kissed.

She rode him, using the swaying of the carriage to rub against him. Gib couldn't think about how his cock already strained to explode. It took most of his concentration to ignore her heat teasing back and forth in between his thighs. So he ripped his mouth away to use his teeth on her neck. No marks. Hickeys were amateur hour. Gib knew exactly how much pressure to use and not leave behind evidence. Exactly how much to make her sigh, arch her back, thrusting those magnificent breasts right up at him.

"That's…you're…not half-bad," she panted.

"This is just the prelims. Where I learn you. Learn to pleasure you. I'm quite thorough."

He raked his teeth along her taut muscle, nipping

and sucking. Daphne thrust her fingers into his hair. Moaned. Gib growled in response, both in promise and possession. Moved down to trace a path along her collarbone. Lingered on the spot her pulse battered against his lips. Ran his hands up her sides until they bracketed her breasts.

Finally licked an arc across the top of one. The softness was like ice cream melting against his tongue. Gib used his thumb to caress the other stiff peak. Daphne writhed against him in a way that almost made him explode right through the heavy denim of his fly. If she kept doing that, his last shard of control would splinter away. Gib thrust his hands down the back of her jeans. Holding tight, he flipped her onto her back. He put one leg on the floor and braced a knee between her legs.

A glance at the windows showed them to be completely fogged over. Good. One big shrug had his coat on the floor. One quick shove wedged the sweater up beneath her arms. It also revealed a powder-blue bra with tiny white polka dots. A tiny bow nestled in the center of its deep plunge. The contrast of the sweetness with the overflowing sensuality of her breasts kicked his heart up to the same rate as during his weekly wind sprints workout.

"Getting an eyeful?" Daphne asked. "Not entirely fair. When do I get equal time to stare at you?"

"After I get a mouthful." Just to keep her off balance, and despite how much he craved the feel of her nipple against his tongue, Gib put his mouth on her stomach. Traced a damp circle around her belly button. Reveled in the flex of her abs against him. He loved the way she moved with him, offered herself up to him. Considerable practice—which he would *not* mention to Daphne—made him able to undo her jeans with one hand. The other he fanned lightly across her left breast. Peeling back one side past her hip, Gib ran his finger against the edge of a blue ruffle. Dipped his finger beneath the ruffle, toward the heat—

An abrupt jolt to a stop tumbled Gib off the bench entirely. The sharp ache in his elbow was worth it as he looked up at Daphne. Legs splayed open, panties just visible, long, golden locks of hair cascading down her shoulders to brush her ribs, she was a vision of smoldering sex. One he'd never forget. But then she opened her eyes, looked down at him and burst into laughter. He joined a second later.

"I only paid for the half-hour ride. In case you didn't like it."

"Oh, I liked it…fine." She put her clothes to rights and sat up. "You're certainly rounding all the bases on this date." A sudden flush turned her cheeks the color of June strawberries. "I mean, doing everything right. Not *those* bases."

"I'm not as up on baseball as I am on cricket, but I know all about *those* bases. Pretty sure I just scored a triple." He knelt to zip up her jacket. Used the zipper pull to tug her forward. "Care to go for another inning?"

THIRTEEN

A life with love will have some thorns, but a life without love will have no roses

~ *Anonymous*

GIB PUSHED OPEN the glass door to his office suite with his shoulder. Both hands were full of an enormous white box, tied up with the brown Lyons Bakery ribbon.

"Agatha, you look particularly lovely this morning. New dress? New hair?"

His assistant blinked at him. "I bleached my mustache last night. Thanks for noticing."

Now he wished he hadn't asked. But it couldn't dampen his mood. "A subtle but vital change. Stunning." Gib set the box on her desk. Shrugging out of his coat, he tossed it on the tree in the corner.

Agatha pushed her chair back and gripped the edge of the desk. Hard lines grooved around the edge of her mouth. "Are you drunk?"

"Of course not." Punch-drunk, maybe. But that didn't count. "Have you ever known me to come to the office impaired in any way?"

"Sometimes, after you work out with Ben at lunch, you aren't at the top of your game when you come back."

That stung. Gib made a mental note to add an extra

fifteen laps the next time he hit the pool. "It's got nothing to do with Ben. He can barely keep up with me on his best days. I simply like to push myself." Grabbing the scissors, he slit the tape at the sides of the pastry box.

"You're not drunk. And you're definitely not a morning person. But you're acting like you had a gallon of happy juice for breakfast. Did you win the lottery last night?"

"Perhaps I did." She shot out of her chair, eyes wild. Gib roared with laughter. "Sit down. It was a figure of speech, nothing more."

"You shouldn't joke about winning millions of dollars. You'll give me a heart attack."

"Sorry. I can make it better, though." He flung open the lid of the box. The rich scent of cinnamon and sugar steamed out in a cloud. "Did you know it's National Oatmeal Month? My friends at Aisle Bound filled me in on that utterly useless piece of trivia."

"Your friends? Or one in particular?" Agatha tapped her pen against her cheek. "Maybe one with blond hair?"

"There you go, jumping to conclusions again. Or is it listening at doors?"

"A good assistant hears everything, and says nothing."

"You, keeping your opinions to yourself? That'll be the day." And he didn't want her to. Agatha was a vital cog in the hotel's machinery. She knew everyone, knew everything, and best of all, knew how to get things done. He relied on her as much as he relied on his laptop and cell phone. "Besides, I need your wise counsel."

"Don't you forget it." The twinkle in her eyes belied the stern crease between her eyebrows.

Back to the treats. "We should celebrate this ridiculous, honorary day. So I've got cranberry oatmeal muffins, and oatmeal white-chocolate cookies. Get that new kid in the kitchen, Jose, to bring up a stack of napkins. Pitcher of milk and some glasses. We'll do it up right. Be sure he eats his fill, too."

"You do know that Christmas is over? Because you were overly generous to the entire staff for the last month. We all appreciated it. But I have to wonder why you're suddenly celebrating something as lowly as a grain holiday."

Agatha knew Daphne, knew how deep their friendship ran. She popped over all the time to visit him, or to meet before going out to dinner. As he didn't have an older sister to confide in, Gib decided to share the real reason for his great mood.

"I had a date last night."

She sniffed dismissively, swiveled back around to face her computer. "If you brought cookies in every time you had a date, we'd all be as puffy as those balloons in the Macy's Thanksgiving Parade."

Gib grinned. "I had a date with Daphne. Not a one-off, not a hookup. A real date. And we're going to do it again."

"Oh. Oh my." Whipping a tissue out of her sleeve, Agatha dabbed at her eyes. "That is good news."

He circled the desk, sank onto his haunches beside her chair. "Why are you crying?"

With her large, arthritic hands, she patted his fist.

Sniffled again. "You're such a good man. You care about every employee here, from the dishwashers to the bellmen to the executive chef, as if they were family. And you're a good manager. I helped you with the P&L reports to the corporate office. I know our profits are up, even with the past few years of recession."

Flippant praise from naked, grateful women he could take. Sweaty, shoulder-patting praise after beating Ben by a good ten minutes in a five-mile jog along the lake. The gush of praise from Agatha made him uncomfortable in the extreme. His job mattered. He didn't get a paycheck for just showing up every day. Gib had to make everyone, both staff and guests, feel important. Quite simply, because they were. In his mind, that didn't merit any praise. Standing, he backed away from her desk. "A speech like that, are you angling for a raise?"

"You've such a way about you, and so good-looking. But I worried you'd never let your guard down enough to open yourself up to love. Which would just be a tragedy. You deserve love."

"Whoa." Gib held up both hands. "Nobody said anything about love. Don't make this bigger than it is. Yes, I'm happy today. Yeah, I'm going to see Daphne again this week. One step at a time."

She gave him a penetrating look. The kind his nanny used to give him when he snuck his brussels sprouts into his napkin. Damn it, she couldn't make him squirm. *He* was the boss, not the other way around. Gib shot his cuffs, adjusted his already-impeccable Windsor knot. And waited for the standoff to end.

With a sigh, Agatha picked up the phone and called

the kitchen. Right. Gib grabbed a muffin and sauntered into his office. Love. Wasn't it just like a woman to leap ahead like that? Good thing Daphne was more sensible. He sat down, but set the muffin aside. Didn't turn on his computer. Instead, he steepled his fingers, elbows on the desk.

Was she? After all, she did own half of a wedding company with Ivy, the biggest romance addict in the world. Daphne spent all day, every day, putting together flowers to celebrate other people's love. Amid their horror and classic-movie marathons, she did force him to watch a few chick flicks. Kept her parents' wedding photo on the mantel in a burnished gold frame.

Sure, she didn't talk about it much. Over the years, she'd dated casually, hooked up a few times. Didn't seem to have that diamond-ring-focused mind-set. Of course, until last night, he hadn't even known about her secret yen for jewelry. Last night had been perfect. Funny, he'd never thought he'd describe any night that involved talking about his family as perfect. Yet he'd felt a million pounds lighter after finally telling her. Their make-out session in the carriage had been so hot it was amazing the snow on the road hadn't simply evaporated. And they'd laughed for hours over pizza and beers. Followed by more slow, sweet kisses in between bites of ice cream at his apartment. At least, until Milo came home and plopped down on the couch next to them. Did one good date mean she now had expectations? Ones that he was by no means capable of fulfilling?

Fuck. Suddenly he regretted sleeping with Doc Debra. It probably meant that he couldn't go back to her for advice on this. Gib worried he needed advice. Under normal circumstances, he'd turn to Daphne. But that option was off the table. He could only imagine how she'd take an oh-so-casual question about whether or not she realized how huge a step he'd taken, just by committing to *try* a relationship. That love and a fairy-tale ending just weren't in the cards for him. Not now, at least. Would she cut him loose?

He couldn't risk it. Damned if he'd call it love, but damned if he'd lose this woman who was so much a part of him, either. One day at a time. That's how they'd proceed. Daphne would be fine with it. Probably. Hopefully. And maybe he would give Doc Debra a call. See if she wanted to meet for coffee. Someplace public—not his hotel, with all its available rooms—so she wouldn't get the wrong idea. Maybe she'd let him pick her brain one more time.

The phone buzzed. Gib jabbed it to speakerphone. "Gibson Moore. How may I help you?"

"Monsieur Moore, it is a pleasure to hear your voice again." The smooth, French-accented voice belonged to not his North American regional manager, but Philipe Goudreau, the vice president in charge of his division. Gib had worked with the man during his initial training in Geneva. As he rose through the ranks, Goudreau did as well. Once a year, Cavendish Grand flew all their managers in for a weeklong meeting. Depending on your performance, it could also entail a public verbal flogging, or the presentation of a coveted crystal-and-gold-etched award. Gib glanced at the case on his wall, which held three such awards.

Chatting with Goudreau at the annual meeting didn't bother him at all. Receiving an unscheduled call from him, however, raised Gib's hackles.

"Philipe. Hope you enjoyed the holidays." He sped through his mental Rolodex to come up with the name of the man's wife. "Did you get some skiing in at St. Moritz with Eloise and your sons?"

"Some. A blizzard rolled in, confined us to the resort for two days. We stayed at the Kempinski, so it wasn't much of a hardship. Excellent powder after that, though."

"Good to hear." To hell with the small talk. This call couldn't be good news. He'd rather get right to it. Gib couldn't begin to imagine why Goudreau would call. As Agatha had said, his hotel had exceeded its goals for the last eleven straight quarters. They had the usual amount of workers comp claims, and a few outstanding wrongful dismissal suits. One woman who'd been in litigation with them for nine months, claiming their hotel was responsible for her husband's shacking up with stewardesses twice a week. Nothing out of the norm. "I know it's almost the end of your workday in Switzerland, so what can I do for you?"

"This must remain confidential. For the moment."

"Of course."

"The Castellan Compagnie has purchased the Cavendish Grand."

Gib's mind reeled. There hadn't been so much as a hint of an imminent takeover. But Goudreau didn't call just to pass on company gossip. Undoubtedly there'd be a memo circulated to all managers addressing the purchase. Why the personal notification? He braced for the worst. Said in a calm voice, "Quite surprising. Didn't we just change hands ten years ago?"

"*Oui*. Priorities change, cash flow ebbs and flows—and so here we are. We'll describe it as a merger, of course. But the fact remains that they now own a controlling interest. The good news is that they want to keep the Cavendish Grand brand separate, worldwide."

Terrific. Minimal absorption, minimal turnover. Probably nothing more than a change of the company masthead. Maybe a vacation policy or two. The fists Gib didn't realize he'd made relaxed. "That *is* good news."

"Eh, but there is bad news, as well. Castellan is very conscious of the intricacies of doing business on an international level. Being mindful of national pride...how do you say, quirks?"

It would help if Gib could figure out exactly what Goudreau was trying to say. Would they have to fly the flag of every country that boasted a Cavendish Grand? Start providing menus in ten different languages? "Not sure where you're headed with this, Philippe."

"They do not want their American hotel managed by a foreigner. It presents the wrong image. No Frenchmen in London, no Italians in Munich—you get the idea, *non?*"

No. Fuck no. Gib stood, paced to the window and pressed his head against the cold metal of the frame. Stared down at the bumper-to-bumper line of cars barely moving down Michigan Avenue. Couldn't see through the four blocks of buildings between him and the lake, but knew it was there. No matter where he went in Chicago, the presence of Lake Michigan hung over the city, just like the canals in Venice or the Danube River in Budapest. And he loved it. Loved the lake, the city, his whole life here. No bloody way would he give it up without a fight.

"Philippe, you're going to have to spell it out for me. Because my personnel file is bulging with exemplary reviews, early promotions, bonuses. I'm staring at a case full of accolades and trophies, so you need to say exactly what it is you mean."

The sound of shuffling papers. A throat clearing that attested to Philippe's pack a day habit. "Due to your British citizenship, Castellan will no longer permit you to work at any Cavendish in the United States. They are happy, however, to offer you the opportunity to manage the Cavendish Grand London. Once an opening arises. Until such time, there is an assistant manager position open in London."

"I'm not just losing my job here, I'm getting demoted?" Gib couldn't hold back his temper any longer. Not like this was a video conference. He pounded the flat of his hand against the wall. "No. Absolutely not. I'm staying in Chicago."

"You can't."

"Watch me," he growled, equal parts a threat and a promise.

"No, Gibson, you cannot stay in Chicago. You have two weeks to wrap up your affairs and transfer to London. Otherwise Castellan will terminate your employment—which means your American work visa will be revoked. One way or the other, you will have to leave

Chicago in two weeks. My apologies." An aggrieved sigh followed. Gib could picture the Gallic shrug which inevitably accompanied it.

He paced back to the desk. Leaned over to brace his hands on it. Wasn't as satisfying as getting in Goudreau's face, but from four thousand miles away, it would have to suffice. "This is bullshit. I don't display a Union Jack in my office. Keep my mouth shut about politics. Hell, we've hosted the president twice in the last year. If anything, our guests get a kick out of my accent."

"You misunderstand. This isn't a personal vendetta. It is an across-the-board policy being instituted. As black-and-white as our sick leave. Human Resources ran a report for everyone with foreign worker visas. There are multiple employees equally affected by this new policy. It applies to concierges, front desk managers, catering executives…how do you think the assistant manager position just happened to be open? We're shuttling people all around the globe."

If Gib was still manager, he'd care. He'd even offer to help in whatever small way possible. But right now it took all his control not to stalk over to that fucking display case and start lobbing awards through the window.

Silence for a few beats from Philippe. "It pains me to remove you from your position. It is true, you have been *tres magnifique* as manager. If only you were an American, you could continue to head up Cavendish Chicago for years. I wish there were some other way. Let me know what you decide. *Au revoir.*"

The drone of a dial tone filled his office. Gib didn't

move. Couldn't move. Because when a black hole of bu-
reaucracy swallowed up the life you'd worked so hard
to create, what was the point?

How could they do this? How could some faceless
human resources exec who wanted to make his mark at
Castellan so carelessly fuck with people's lives? Years
of training. Years of sixty-, even seventy-hour weeks,
proving himself. Proving his worth to his supervisors.
Once the awards started rolling in, profits edged up,
proving his worth to the company.

All that rendered meaningless. No discussion. No
chance to present his case. Hell, he'd be gone before it
was time to get another haircut. The enormity of this
change felt the same as a sucker punch straight to his
balls. Knocked the breath out of him. Cemented him
to the spot, still hunched over his desk. Erased every
other thought from his mind.

His office door burst open. Pink cheeked and beam-
ing from ear to ear, Daphne said, "Geez, why didn't
you tell me you were going to Lyons? Would've saved
me a trip—" Her voice faded out. Dropping her coat
to the floor, she rushed to him. Threw an arm around
his shoulders. "Gib, what's wrong? Are you hurt? Are
you having a heart attack? Panic attack? Should I call
an ambulance?"

"No."

"No to which?"

"All of it. Everything." Gib let her press him back
into his chair. Knees folded automatically, just like he
kept breathing. Registered the outside chill clinging to
her hair as it swung across his face. The fresh scent of

crushed flowers that clung to her fingers as she stroked his cheek. Daphne must've unloaded an early shipment today. He saw the worry line indented between her eyebrows. None of it mattered. Like Han Solo encased in carbonite, nothing penetrated his layer of icy anger.

Cool lips brushed his. Once. Twice. On the third time, Gib's lips responded involuntarily. No thought, just reaction. The way his heart knew to beat. The way his hand curled around a cricket bat. A soft warmth spread from her lips to radiate through his body. Still working on autopilot, he grabbed, twisted her to land in his lap without breaking their lip-lock. Daphne curled into his embrace with a soft moan.

He speared his hand through her hair. God, it felt like satin and sex rippling through his fingers. Gib opened her lips. Hungrily swept in to lick the sensations straight from her tongue. His other hand slid down to cup that sweet, heart-shaped ass.

Daphne broke away, eyes bright and panting just a little. "Hang on, there. This is nice, don't get me wrong. But we're in your office. With a glass door. With Agatha right outside. Workplace hanky-panky's not very doable. Not here, anyway. My office at least has a supply closet for these sort of shenanigans."

"You're right. Sorry." Gib let her slide off his lap. Part of him couldn't believe he'd acted so unprofessionally. The other part of him, the part with the raging hard-on, pointed out that professionalism hadn't gotten him jack shit. It *had* gotten him demoted and deported. "I needed that. I needed—you," he admitted. She'd managed to pull him back from the brink. "Didn't expect to see you this morning."

"I needed a break from processing a trillion and two tulips. For the party this weekend."

He looked at her blankly. Even with his brain deadened by shock, he knew the event calendar without checking. The Cavendish had three weddings and a bar mitzvah in the next two days, but no party. "What party?"

"Duh. Your party, Gib. The one where *Windy City* magazine honors all its top bachelors. You're the main attraction, remember?" Daphne rested her butt on the edge of his desk. "What's going on? Because you're acting very, very weird. Frankly, you're scaring me right now. Did something bad happen?"

Bad. Catastrophic. Like a fucking stallion kick straight to his balls. "Yes."

"Well, what happened?"

God, where to start? "It's complicated."

Daphne rolled her eyes. "I do have a college degree. Might not be as pretty as the one Cambridge gave you, but I think I can follow along. Unless your current problem involves quantum physics. Just spit it out."

"On second thought, it's simple. I've been notified my services as manager are no longer required here. I've got to ship out to London, and suck up a demotion to assistant manager for who knows how long. And before you suggest that I quit, they'll yank my work visa. One way or the other, I've got to leave Chicago." He'd thought hearing the news was bad enough. But speaking the words stabbed the sword of finality through him once more.

Daphne exhaled, as though his news thumped all the air right out of her. "No."

"In two weeks. That's all the time Goudreau gave me to wrap up my life." He pushed out of his chair. Paced to the far wall, then back again. Did another circuit when Daphne didn't say anything. Wished desperately that there wasn't a foot of snow on the ground. Gib needed to stretch his legs, run along the lakeshore until the cold knifed his chest and his muscles cramped. That would clear his head.

Twisting to face him, Daphne said, "We'll fix it. We'll find a way to make it right."

"You can't fix this." And then, with the weight of a freight train, the truth barreled into him. "In fact, you're the one who caused the problem."

She sucked in a breath. "That's not funny."

"I agree." He cracked his office door. "Agatha, why don't you take those muffins down to the catering office? Chat them up for a good quarter of an hour. Find out if Raquel's having a girl or a boy—I think her sonogram was yesterday." Gib waited until she'd collected her sweater, purse and the bakery box. The woman went nowhere without her purse. Even carried it between the living room and kitchen when he went to her house for their monthly Sunday dinners. Then he locked the outer door behind her. Shut the inner door, too. Couldn't take a chance on any staff member overhearing him lose his shit with Daphne.

Gib advanced on her. His anger hadn't really had a

target before. Hard to yell at a faceless conglomerate. But now he knew where to focus his rage. He knew exactly where the blame should lie. With one finger, he pointed straight at the cause of his ruin. The blonde, blue-eyed living doll with the quivering lip looking as confused as a Bears linebacker would be at the Queen's garden party.

"You cost me my job. You cost me my life here. You cost me *everything*."

"Gib, no." Her voice shook. She slid off the desk, backed away from his tangible anger. "I would never do anything to hurt you."

"But you did. This is all your fault." He stabbed his finger in the air between them.

"How can you say that?"

Gib could barely look at her. "The only reason I'm no longer allowed to work at Cavendish Chicago is because I'm not an American. A detail I tried to remedy five months ago. Got my papers in order. Studied my ass off for the citizenship test. Let Milo stick a tie with the Stars and Stripes on it in my pocket, to put on for the ceremony. Remember what happened next?"

"Oh." Daphne squeezed her eyes shut tight. Bit her lip.

"What's that? Little hard to hear you over the noise of my entire bloody life crashing down around me."

In a near whisper, she said, "I stopped you."

"That's right." Gib crossed his arms over his chest. "You barged into the courtroom. Interrupted the bailiff. Pissed off the judge. And gave me an elaborate song and dance about duty. Birthright. Legacy. Queen and country. How I needed to be constant, honor my heritage."

Her eyes flew back open. "Those things all still hold true."

Christ. How could she be so stubborn as to refuse to shoulder the blame? "Do they? You're in my back pocket most of the time. What part of my daily life involves my title? How often do I speak of my estate holdings? Yearn for anything British other than more soccer on television?"

This time, she advanced into his space. Balled her hands onto her hips and jutted her chin defiantly. "I know you, Gib. You wouldn't have been happy splitting your loyalties. As much as you enjoy America, you're British to your core. I helped you stay true to yourself. I know you made the right choice that day."

Bollocks to that. "Really? Because here's what I know." He splayed his fingers and ticked points off, one by one. "If it wasn't for you, I'd be an American citizen. I wouldn't be sacked. I'd still have a job. I'd still be here in March to throw Ben a bachelor party. I'd still be here to help Sam load up all his chocolates for the Fancy Food Show at the end of the month."

"You can still do all of that." She threw her arms in the air. "Go ahead and quit. We'll find you another job."

All those years of owning her own business must've blinded her to the reality of the job market. "In two weeks? Daphne, positions at my level can take two years for an opening to come around."

"You've got savings. Stick it out until you find one."

Why did people assume money solved everything?

He banged the wall with his fist. It didn't begin to bleed off his tension. "I can't. They don't grant you a work visa to bag groceries in America. It has to be a job that requires a foreign national with special skills. Without a job, I have to leave the country. Period." And, there it was. The simple fact that spun his life into a one-eighty. Saying it out loud again was like opening a valve. Some of his anger drained away, already replaced with crushing defeat. "You know my story now. You know the last thing I want to do is return to England. Don't you think if there was a way out, I'd snatch it with both hands?"

Daphne grabbed his hands. Gib tried to shake her off, but she held firm. "You have to try. Don't just give up."

"I'm not giving up. I'm being realistic."

"Okay, you're entitled to pitch a hissy right now. I get it. And, for what it's worth, I'm sorry."

"It's not worth as much as, say, a bloody American passport would be," he grumbled. Daphne certainly hadn't known how her speech that day would affect him five months down the road. Hadn't torpedoed his career on purpose. Yelling at her wouldn't change his circumstances. Hard to stop, though. Especially with those small, strong hands of hers curled around his. Hard to bundle all those exposed emotions back under wraps. Like a proper British man would do.

"What about that Four Seasons they're building in Milwaukee? Lots of people live on the North Shore and commute to Milwaukee."

Finally, he managed to twist out of her grasp. Sank into his chair and tilted his head back. "It doesn't open until next year."

Daphne braced herself on the arms of his chair. Strad-dling him, she interjected herself into his awesome view of the ceiling. "So look outside Chicago. Find a hotel someplace else for a year, and then come back when they're ready to open. Phoenix, Miami, Los Angeles, anywhere. We're a big country. There's got to be at least one hotel with an opening."

She stared down at him with so much sympathy, so much fucking understanding. Such unquenchable opti-mism. As much as he wanted to keep railing at her, just because she was here and he needed someone to yell at, he couldn't. This wasn't just any convenient woman. This was Daphne, who understood him better than any-one. Who never turned him away, day or night when he needed to talk. Who always, without fail, could coax a smile out of him. Who evidently refused to give up on him, despite the undeniable, unfixable facts.

Beneath the power of her unswerving stare, Gib was helpless. Not that his anger at the situation disappeared with a flutter of her lashes. No, he still seethed at being sacked, and at Daphne for the part she'd played in it. But it simply didn't matter as much as the feelings Daphne stirred in him. The feelings he'd managed to hold at bay all these years. And yet, now that they'd crossed that invisible demarcation from platonic best friends to almost-lovers, every moment he spent with her sucked him deeper into a morass of bloody tender feelings. Feelings that scared the shit out of him. Feelings he couldn't control. Could only marvel at how much he adored the sweet, passionate woman fighting simulta-neously with him and for him.

Gib deliberately softened his grumbling. "Sure. Big, corporate resorts where the hiring process lasts three months and eight rounds of interviews. There's nothing to be done in two weeks but to pack."

"Oh, I don't know. I can think of a few other things to keep you occupied over the next few weeks." She tugged his tie loose with a suggestive smile.

No red-blooded man could resist that smile. Especially not with her hovering an inch above his suddenly very optimistic cock. "Christ, you're relentless. All right. I'll look for a job. I'll scour the web until my eyes bleed. I'll send off a CV to every five-star hotel from sea to shining sea. Is that bloody well good enough for you?"

"It's a start." Daphne sank onto his lap, hands splayed on his chest. "One more thing, though. Do you forgive me?"

Why? The woman was squirming on his lap, and she wanted to be serious? Daphne didn't have her priorities straight. Gib pushed her hair behind her shoulders. He cupped her neck, lightly stroking the back of it. "Do I have to decide right now?"

"Gib, I'm serious."

Damn it. He deserved to be mad for at least five sodding minutes. "If you could go back and change the past, would you still do it? Even knowing it would cost me my job?"

"Yes."

Didn't she understand how forgiveness worked? Daphne had to regret her part in the utter ruination of his life first—then he could forgive her. He dropped his hands to his sides. "Don't you want to think about it for a second?" Gib asked flatly.

"No. I still believe it was the right choice. A choice *you* made, by the way." She stabbed him in the sternum with her index finger. "I didn't hold a gun to your head. Especially considering the twenty-minute wait in line to go through the courtroom metal detectors. You're a grown man, Gib. One who listens to the counsel of his friends, but ultimately makes his own decisions. Something I said that day resonated. You must've been having second thoughts about changing your citizenship already. So don't you dare throw all the blame on me."

"That's your apology?"

"I apologized already. But I'll do it again, if you need a repeat. I'm sorry about what happened today. I'm sorry this big bad news came out of nowhere and crashed into you. Doesn't mean it's the end of the world. You're Gibson Moore. You've got this town wired. You've got connections all across the country. If anyone can find a way out of this mess, it's you." Daphne cocked her head to the side and beamed at him. "Forgive me now?"

Of course he did. But Gib didn't want to let her know how easily he rolled over at one of her smiles. Daphne had his heart wrapped in a bow around her little finger. No reason to give her any more of an upper hand by letting her know that, though. "I'm not finished being angry. Not by a long shot."

"I understand." Dipped her head to the opposite side, with another smile that was like high beams on his heart. "Forgive me now?"

"How about we agree you acted without malice, and leave it at that?"

"Not good enough. Look, you're going to forgive me. And in case you really do only have two weeks here, you might as well stop wasting time and do it now."

"Do I have a choice?"

"Nope."

"Then I suppose so." Gib gave himself up to the distraction of her kisses. While trying not to think about being marooned a bloody ocean away from her.

FOURTEEN

A flower cannot blossom without sunshine, and man cannot live without love

~ Max Muller

"LOVE THE FLOWERS, BOSS," said Milo. "Filling the martini glasses with balls of those white flowers—"

"Chrysanthemums. The official flower of our great city." Daphne didn't bother to look up from the burgundy depths of her Shiraz. It was rare that she both worked an event and attended it as a guest. The novelty of pseudo-drinking on the job, even though she'd finished placing all the flowers an hour ago, made her savor every sip. "Geez, Milo, you signed the invoice for them. Don't you pay attention?"

"They're white and they smell spicy. What else do I need to know? Anyhoo, it plays up the martini bars at each end of the room. Or so I just heard the Style editor from the *Chicago Trib* say. Maybe we'll get a mention in tomorrow's paper. Well done."

This was the perfect time of year for extra good publicity. All the brides who got engaged at Christmas and New Year's were about to start planning. Having Aisle Bound uppermost in their minds couldn't hurt. Frankly, it was the reason they'd taken this gig. Notorious cheapskates, *Windy City* magazine balked at paying their normal rates. They'd compromised by promising Daphne a mention in their multipage spread of the party in the February issue.

"Thanks. This was a tough one." With such a low budget, she'd been tempted to use carnations, the cheapest flower known to man. And only used on homecoming floats. "A party to honor the city's hottest bachelors doesn't really scream out for flowers."

"What did you want to use for centerpieces? Deodorant, and a stick of beef jerky in a beer mug?"

"We are so on the same wavelength. That was totally my first instinct," she mocked. "Or the classic fishbowls full of condoms."

"In the spirit of public safety, those should probably be handed out at the exit." Milo came around the high-top table, hand outstretched. "How bad is the wine? Give me a taste."

Daphne stared at him. Wondered if today was prank-your-boss day. Because there could be no rational excuse for the way Milo looked. "Holy Mother of God, what are you wearing?"

"You like?" He gave a spin. The green plaid kilt flew up, and Daphne quickly averted her eyes. Some things could never, ever be unseen. "It's Scottish Highland Dress. A Prince Charlie jacket, black tie and a kilt."

She didn't care what he called it. Every other man in the room had on pants. Daphne didn't realize that particular dress code choice had apparently been open to interpretation. "You're wearing a skirt."

"Don't you dare get judgy." He waved his hand at the

crowd in the packed brick Museum of Contemporary Art Warehouse. "Look at all these women strutting their stuff. Skintight dresses to show off their waists. Cleavage that'll expose their nipples if somebody sneezes. Airing their attributes for all the hot bachelors to ogle. Well, my best feature happens to be my legs. Why shouldn't I show them off?" He waggled a kneesock-covered calf in the air.

Daphne smothered a giggle. "So you expect to pick up a guy tonight? Wearing that?"

He fig-leafed his hands and gave her a look of pitying condescension. "Sweetie, you don't actually think they're all straight, do you? Percentage wise, I've probably got a far better chance than you of scoring tonight. That is, if you were still single. If you weren't already going home with the hands-down yummiest man in the room."

Trust Milo to pick off the emotional scab, jab a fork in the wound and then squeeze lemon juice over it. "Gib's not what I'd call a slam dunk."

"Why not? I thought you said he'd forgiven you for wrecking his life." He blinked at her, pretending—it could be nothing but sarcastic pretense—the question was wholly innocent.

Daphne glared at him. Milo might be *her* office manager, but evidently he was first and foremost Gib's friend and roommate. "Shut up. I didn't do anything. He assessed the situation and made a reasoned choice, in which I was merely tangentially involved."

"What a mouthful of crap. Did you find a rent-a-lawyer to write up that excuse for you?"

"Of course not." Maybe Ivy's marriage-counselor mother had stopped by to take them to lunch. Just maybe, the whole story had played out over chicken pot pie at the Walnut Room in Macy's. And then, out of love and solidarity for Daphne, Mrs. Rhodes had used her quarter century of experience to squarely lob the guilt ball back into Gib's court. No reason to explain it to Milo. "This has nothing to do with Gib's possible— not at all guaranteed—relocation."

"Then what gives? I'd expect him to be eager to squeeze in as much nooky as possible with you before he's deported." Another look of as much faux innocence as Charles Manson at his parole hearings. "I mean, before he leaves."

There'd be plenty of time for Milo to snipe at her after that black day. For now, she needed his reassurance. "Like you said, look at all these women. You know Gib likes to play the field. Run the board." She'd been watching him for at least half an hour. Since the moment he walked in the door, Gib had been surrounded by a bright bouquet of women. Sure, there were twenty-four of Chicago's other hottest bachelors in the room. But he was the cover boy. The star attraction. The prize everyone wanted to claim.

He'd dressed to play the part, in white tie and tails complete with a silk-fringed scarf. Gib looked debonair. Rakish. Sexy. Doable. Daphne had boutonnieres for all the bachelors. Cute little clusters of white ranunculus with waving loops of beach grass. But her chances of getting within ten feet of Gib were about as good as her shot of tiptoeing through a rugby scrum. And she hated that he'd made her learn enough about rugby to even know that analogy.

"Look again at those women around him." Milo nudged her shoulder when she rolled her eyes. "No, I mean really look."

"At what? Their expensively streaked hair? The sexy dresses that cost more than my rent?"

"Gib's not flirting with them."

Daphne almost snorted her wine right out her nose. "Right. That's about as likely as me sprouting fairy wings. Or you deciding you want to try out women for the night."

"Bite your tongue." Milo shuddered. "I'm serious. He's chatting them up, because that's who he is. But watch him for a minute. Gib isn't touching any of the women."

She hadn't noticed. But now, looking over, Daphne saw him in what she jokingly called his princely stance: both hands tucked behind his back. "So?"

"He's always been about the casual, sneak invasion of a woman's body. A stroke down the arm. Arm around the waist in a teasing hug that stays there. Dancing his fingers across a hand until suddenly they're intertwined. Going in for a cheek peck that ends up as an ear nip."

"You planning to write a how-to manual? The Consummate Flirt, explained?"

"I could never begin to explain the surreal effect he's got on women. Gib's Kryptonite to women's panties. He's like the sexified Pied Piper of babes and bimbos. No offense."

One more crack from him tonight and she'd definitely take offense. Or at least refill her wineglass. And by refill, Daphne meant upgrading to a couple shots of tequila. "As long as I fall into the first category of babes and not bimbos, we're okay."

Milo downed the rest of her Shiraz. "We've lived together for years. Gone out to bars, to parties. Can't help but notice his M.O. You know, the way you notice and blather on about whatever it is that makes the Bears' quarterback special. The touching is a major part of Gib's action. It makes women feel attractive. Appreciated."

Yes. Yes, it did. "Aren't you the armchair shrink?"

"I dabble." His tone was uncharacteristically serious. "I observe people, so I can understand them better. Every problem can be broken down to how two people did or didn't relate. I try to equip myself so that I can relate to anybody."

Every once in a while, the fluorescent-bright exterior candy coating Milo cloaked himself in slipped away. And the genuine, introspective, caring center was a marvel to behold. "I'll take your word that he's dialed back the flirt-o-meter for the night. But he's still surrounded. I've made two trips to the cheese display, scored a handful of stuffed mushrooms from the waiter and demolished the fancy party mix." She nudged the tiny, empty glass bowl in the center of the table. Right next to her carefully placed bud vase with a single tulip spearing out of it.

"Aside from your apparent allergy to good nutrition, what's your point?"

"I've been waiting for him. Gib doesn't seem to be interested in hanging out with me tonight."

"Are you kidding? He's glanced over here half a dozen times since we started talking. Trust me, he wants an out. Why don't you give him an excuse?"

"How?"

Milo tapped the edge of her glass. "Head over to the bar. Slowly." He pointed to the opposite side of the room. "Gib will have you on missile lock before you get halfway. Especially if you put an extra swish in your step. You know, the way I walk."

"You'd better be right," she warned. And then concentrated on putting one foot directly in front of the other. Daphne had a fuzzy memory of Scarlett O'Hara explaining that was how to make a hoop skirt twitch. When Milo grilled her later, she wanted to be able to honestly say she'd given it the old college try.

She skirted around the edge of the runway. Low urns overflowing with white tulips lined both sides of it. Daphne hoped that when the bachelors strutted their stuff down it, none of the urns would end up being accidentally punted across the room.

A warm hand settled at her waist. Gib fell into step with her. "Why's the most beautiful woman in the room walking away from me?"

Milo's utter rightness filled her with relief. And peeved her to no end. "To get you to walk toward me, of course."

"It worked. Gave me an excuse to break free. I must've tried twenty times to come see you, but the magazine's publicist kept me on a tight leash. Frustrated the bloody hell out of me not to be able to talk to the one person I most wanted to." He brushed a light kiss across her cheek. "Fancy a drink?"

"I was just about to get in line."

"Don't be ridiculous. You're with the main attraction." Gib raised his hand in the air, crooked a finger at seemingly nothing more specific than the glass block windows. "I've got someone to do that."

"To do what?"

"Attend to my needs. And my most pressing need is to make sure you're properly taken care of, my sweet." Sure enough, a waiter suddenly appeared at Gib's elbow, carrying two flutes of champagne. "Thanks, Franco."

Daphne smiled as she clinked glasses with him. "You're outrageously spoiled, Viscount Moore."

"You're incredibly stunning, Ms. Lovell."

"Thanks." Self-conscious, Daphne ran her hand down the winter-white angora sweaterdress. Pearled beading created a collar on the high sweetheart neckline, then bordered each side of the deep plunge in the back. It clung to her like soft and fuzzy Saran Wrap. "It was my mom's."

Gib paused, glass halfway to his mouth. "Pardon me?"

Hmm. Would he be weirded out? "When my mother died, Dad kept all her clothes in the cedar closet. He thought—hoped—I might want them someday."

He stared at her for a moment, then ran the backs of his knuckles down her cheek in a soft caress. "That's lovely." Gib clinked his glass against hers in a toast. "And quite brave of you to finally take that step."

"I figured it was time. If I'm going to be seen with you, I needed to step up my game."

His gaze swept down the length of her body to her gold sandals. Then ogled slowly back up to the loose twists of hair gathered over one shoulder. "Trust me when I say it's both not necessary, and very, very much appreciated."

"Are you having a good time tonight?"

"Of course. Great party. Mediocre but limitless wine. Lovely flowers. Interesting people." But his overly bright words didn't ring true.

"How are you really doing?"

"I'd be doing a lot better if I hadn't jammed half my closet into shipping boxes today."

Panic scrabbled through her brain, as insidious as the terrifying Ceti Eel in *Star Trek II: The Wrath of Khan*. She'd just watched the movie with Gib last week, and had nightmares about the stupid creature for three nights running. The thought of him leaving, however, had woken her up in a cold sweat last night. He couldn't go. No way would he let a little thing like corporate guidelines determine his future. They'd find a way around it. They had to. "You can't pack already. There's still time for this situation to work itself out."

"You're right. Frankly, I should've come to you straight off, seeing as how you set this nightmare train on the rails. The solution's right in front of me. Daphne, give me a reason to stay." Gib dropped to one knee. Then he grabbed her hand. "Will you marry me?"

Somehow, in the last few seconds, a giant vacuum must've been installed at the museum doors. Because something sure as heck sucked all the room out of the air. She looked down at her best friend. Her gorgeous, sexalicious, dreamboat of a best friend. And felt all the cheese and wine she'd ingested clawing their way back up her throat in disgust at his words. "Are you fucking kidding me?"

"As a matter of fact, yes." He rose to his feet. "Unless, of course, you're willing to entertain the notion."

"That's not funny." Daphne wasn't as bad as Ivy when it came to dreaming about striding down the aisle under a veil. Especially not since her mom died. She hadn't spent years imagining the color of her wedding dress or picked out her colors. Maybe she'd spared a few thoughts as to what flowers would be nice at her own wedding, but that was purely professional mental meandering. But she had held out a hope—no, a not unreasonable expectation—that her first proposal would be magical. Romantic. Or at least fucking sincere.

Gib brushed off his knee. "I disagree. It's a win-win situation. I become a citizen…or enough of one to satisfy the Cavendish HR department. You become a viscountess. A title for a green card. Fair trade."

He was serious. Mind-bogglingly incredible. Could Gib really not see what an insult he'd just offered? Or did he just not care? They surged forward in line as a sextet of bimbettes lurched away from the bar clutching the signature drink. In honor of the men of the hour, it was blue. Daphne was sure it tasted sweet and nauseating. Worse yet, it probably stained everything it touched bright blue, too.

"I can't believe you'd make light of such a thing. You're talking about marriage. A very real, very serious pledge. A lifelong institution."

"Right. These days, that could mean the life span of a mayfly. Which is a grand total of about thirty minutes."

She shook her head. Wished it would clear away this conversation, like shaking an Etch A Sketch. "Where is this coming from? You really have such disdain for marriage?"

"No. I believe in marriage. I also believe it can be whatever two people need it to be. Right now, my need is for it to be a certified document I can show the INS and the Cavendish."

"You're assuming I'd be willing to throw away a shot at a real marriage? My shot at sharing what my mother and father had?"

"For God's sake, Daphne, this isn't the Middle Ages. Virginity is no longer a requirement to snag a decent guy. In fact, I'll fill you in on a secret. Guys our age? Scared to death of virgins. Too needy. Too much effort."

There, Daphne had to agree with him. Women weren't enthusiastic about breaking in virgins, either. Not that she'd veer off into that entertaining sidebar. "You'd marry any stranger off the street just to stay in America?"

"Of course not. Nobody knows better than me how many messed-up women are roaming the streets of Chicago. So many pretty ones, but so many basket cases, too. Which is why I turned to you. My best friend. The keeper of all my secrets. No unknown dangers there. But if you're going to get in a huff about it, forget I asked."

Fat chance. How was she supposed to forget a botched proposal that essentially pimped her out for a title? She fumed while Gib ordered their drinks from the bartender. Without asking. Because he knew her well enough to know that when the wine sucked, Daphne preferred anything dark and strong on the rocks. And yet evidently he didn't know her, *really* know her, at all.

"Does this whole sham proposal thing mean that you didn't really forgive me the other day? That you still blame me for the actions of some stuffed shirt at Cavendish HQ?"

He shifted from foot to foot. Looked down at the floor. Put his hands in his pockets. "Of course not. Sorry if you thought that. I'm still having trouble processing my life being turned upside down. I forgave you. Though I did mention that I wasn't over being angry. It's only been two days."

But we may only have ten left, she thought. Did he really intend to waste them nursing a grudge?

Gib looked at his watch. "Time for me to take my victory lap on the runway. Stand where I can see you. I'll toss you a secret wink."

"Ooh. I'm all aquiver." The mocking edge to her tone belied the actual, jellylike knees that were inevitable as he strutted his stuff. Because nobody looked as good in a tuxedo as Gibson Moore. And he took her breath away every damn time.

"Don't knock it till you see it."

Half an hour later, the room echoed with applause. Daphne had to admit, it hadn't been a wasted half hour. Whether or not Milo had pegged their sexual preferences didn't matter. The score of men parading down the runway to a throbbing bass Daphne felt in her molars were sheer man candy. Hot, handsome hunks with wide shoulders, long legs and smiles that ignited her hormones from across the room. *Windy City* magazine sure knew how to winnow down a city of four million men to the best and sexiest.

Of course, none of them had the suave animal magnetism of the cover stud. It was like comparing kumquats to grapefruit. Tabby kittens to majestic lions. A fast-food burger to the Kuma's Corner ten-ounce Led Zeppelin burger, topped with pulled pork, bacon, cheddar and pickles. Her perpetually unslaked hunger woke right up. Hmm. This cocktail party shouldn't last much longer. Maybe they could swing by Kuma's afterward.

Gib was just so much more…*everything* than the rest of them. It was why she'd called Adam Miller the morning after her perfect date with Gib. On paper, Adam had it all. Checked off every box on the ideal-man-for-Daphne list. Except for one. The one at the bottom, that counted for more points than all the other boxes combined. The one that simply read Gibson Moore. So she'd apologized profusely to Adam. Showered him with compliments. After all, why cut off a solid connection to Bears tickets? But above all, she'd been honest with him. Instead of the old *it's not you, it's me* speech? Daphne gave him the newly invented *it's not you, it's all about him* version. Being such a nice guy, he seemed to understand. Even with Gib maybe, *maybe*, moving to another country, she didn't regret turning Adam down. He didn't deserve to be a second choice.

Confetti swirled under the pulsing blue-and-white spotlights. Gib took a final bow, tossing his scarf deep into the crowd. Then he was promptly mobbed by a circle of women. More like three-quarters of the room rushed the stage all at once. Those poor bachelors didn't stand a chance. Daphne curled her legs onto the red leather ottoman and wished it had a back. Leaning against the exposed brick wall behind her might snag her dress.

"Finally, someone I recognize." Sam sat down heavily on the coffee table. To be fair, it did look identical to the ottoman, aside from being tan and having one of her mum-ified martini glasses in the middle. On the other hand, Sam was never one to stand on ceremony. Even if it held an entire Russian samovar set, he still probably would've sat without blinking an eye. Daphne adored that about him. Funny, since it made him the polar opposite of Gib.

"Milo's around. And of course, your favorite bachelor is front and center." She pointed at Gib. Or rather, his dark hair jutting out above the tight circle of long, highlighted female tresses. Women who appeared thoroughly comfortable in their slinky cocktail attire. Whereas Daphne felt like her mom's dress was a costume. Completely unnatural.

Sam shoved a hand through the dark hair flopping onto his forehead. "I can't talk to Milo. He's on the prowl. That flannel skirt of his always means business."

"Yes, I've been so warned. Glad he's getting some action tonight."

"And Gib's…occupied." He rolled his eyes.

Daphne rolled hers right back. Gib's dark, full-of-sex laugh rolled atop the chirping women clustered around him. It reached across the room to her like a thumping bass on the car radio and vibrated straight to her core. "No kidding."

"I'm glad. It means we can hang out while I wait for that waitress to bring me a drink."

"The waitresses don't deliver drinks. Except to the bachelors."

"Hey, I'm plenty hot. I could pass for one of those bachelors. The waitress probably thought I dressed down to please the ladies."

She eyed the T-shirt showing at the neck of his blue flannel shirt. "As what, a hot lumberjack?"

"Sure. Maybe I'll suggest that one to Mira. See if she runs with it."

"Ewww. Getting details of your sex life from Mira's okay, but from you it's just weird."

Sam leaned in with a smirk. "Odd—'cause I'd pay good money to hear Gib pass on a few details about what happens when you two hit the sheets." The smirk fell away as he rumbled into a belly laugh, clutching his stomach. "Sorry, I barely got that out with a straight face. And Mira's going to get an earful from me about just how much she's telling you and Ivy."

"Don't worry—you come out really well in every story."

"Good to know. You look terrific, by the way."

"Thanks, Sam."

He narrowed his eyes, gave her a once-over. "The flowers are imaginative and clever enough to be yours. But you're not here to work dressed like that."

"Nailed it." Daphne high-fived him. She did enjoy the unexpected compliments from her friends. "I did the flowers. And Gib asked me to come and watch him strut his stuff. Before…" Her voice trailed off.

"Before you got him thrown out of the country?"

Really? Had all the guys gotten together and pledged to extract their verbal pound of flesh from her? "I'm not doing this again. I already went a round with Milo tonight. I apologized, Gib forgave me—" Or at least he said he did. She thought. His bitterness still floated right at the surface. "Anyway, that's between the two of us. You all need to let me off the hook."

Sam let her stew for a minute. Finally he nodded and said, "Okay."

Damn it to hell. Was Ben on rotation to come after her next? Maybe she could talk to Ivy. Get her to cut him off at the pass. Daphne wished Sam's hypothetical waitress would butt in right about now. Either to change the topic, or to bring a tray of those coconut shrimp within reach.

"What are *you* doing here? This party doesn't seem like your sort of soiree. Especially dressed like that."

"Some women find flannel irresistible." Sam paused, stroked his chin thoughtfully. "Or maybe it's just me they find irresistible. In the flannel. Out of the flannel. Whatever."

"Geez, Mira's inflated your head to the size of the root ball on a redwood. Seriously, you're not here to hit on chicks. I doubt Gib asked you to come watch his standing ovation. What gives?"

He pointed through the doorway to the connecting room. Three event people bent over the registration table, lining up shiny white boxes tied with brown ribbon. "Just dropped off the exit favors. A duo of peanut honey sea salt and cayenne chocolate truffles. Painted like a tuxedo."

A mini mouthgasm trembled over her tongue as she imagined the dark, creamy heat melting onto her taste buds. God, she was lucky to have such talented friends. "Classy and delicious."

Sam gave a playful tweak to the ends of her hair. "Don't worry. I saved the not-quite-perfect ones for you. Drop by the bakery tomorrow and I'll set you up."

Usually it took Daphne two mocha lattes just to make it into the shower. But the promise of those chocolates alone would have her bounding out of bed. "I can always count on you to help me chase the dragon."

"What are friends for?"

She curled her legs underneath her and twisted to stare Sam straight in the eyes. "Can I push my luck and ask you for another favor?"

Sam let out a groan as if she'd just jousted a lance right between his ribs. "Depends. Does it involve you coming to me with another crazy-ass idea for a muffin? Because your idea of peanut butter and pickle was just a waste of good flour."

"I told you, that wasn't my fault. There's a whole series of children's books where the main character, Mrs. Piggle-Wiggle, eats pb and pickle sandwiches. She really sold their deliciousness. I'm just sorry you weren't talented enough to transfer the idea from the printed page."

He glared at her from heavy-lidded eyes. "You've

got a real funny way of buttering a guy up to do you a favor."

Whoops. "Look at the woman with Gib." Daphne pointed to the beautiful blonde draped over him tighter than a bandage. "She seems pretty comfortable with him." Worse yet, he seemed more than okay with having her body plastered against his. So much for Milo's no-touching theory of the night.

Sam squinted across the room. "Which one?"

"God, Sam, are you blind?" Or just blinded by her hotness? Like staring straight into the sun? "The blonde with the boobs in the black dress. If she got any closer, she'd be tattooed on him."

"Oh. Her." He raspberried his lips. "No big deal."

"Um, that's not what it looks like to me. Looks like she's about to close the deal, if you know what I mean."

"Okay, yeah, they know each other. But it's not what you think. That's Doc Debra. She used to be Gib's shrink. Then he sort of passed her on to me."

Daphne almost slid off the ottoman to her knees as she lunged forward for a better look. "How the hell is that supposed to reassure me?"

"Um, that she only messes with his mind, not his body?"

Was he insane? "But they slept together. More than once." The thought of competing on *Flower Power* in only eight days kept her in a constant state of nervousness. But seeing Gib's ex up close and personal jangled her taut nerves two hundred percent more than the fear of being on national television.

"Realllly." He lingered over the word, drawing it out

as though pulling taffy. Then he laughed, slapping his thigh. "That dog. Only Gib would do his own shrink. Good for him." Stopping midchortle, his dark eyebrows drew together into a frown. "You don't think they did it on her couch, do you? I sit on that couch every week."

Daphne didn't remember much of the little she'd learned in biology class. Knew nothing about human genome sequencing—and only remembered that phrase from a cool, futuristic movie where they cloned humans with eagles so people could fly. But she did know that every man's DNA contained a funky twist that turned them both self-centered and clueless at the worst possible times.

"This isn't about you, Sam. And if the thought creeps you out, well, how many times have you been to poker at Gib and Milo's place?"

"I dunno. A lot."

"Think about it—I'm sure Gib's had sex on every flat surface in that condo. Couch, chairs, tables, island, even the sinks."

He scrubbed the heels of his hands against his eyes. "Shit. Just because you're upset doesn't mean you have to mess with me."

"I'm not upset. Just frustrated."

"By Gib?" Sam moved to sit next to her. Laid a comforting hand on her arm. "He hasn't gone a day without flirting since you met him. Didn't mean anything then, and it still doesn't."

"No. I'm frustrated that I'm not a starship."

Sam crossed his arms behind his neck, stretched out his legs. "Oh, this oughta be good. Go on."

"If I were a starship, I could use my tractor beam to pull

him over here to me. Then I'd be able to use my shields to keep all the other women away. Plus, I could turn off my gravity stabilizer. Weightless sex could be fun."

"Are you nuts? It'd be five times the work. I can picture trying to put a condom on. Probably roll into a somersault over and over again until I threw up."

Daphne covered her face with her hands, trying not to picture it but unable to stop. She laughed until it petered out into ugly, hiccup gasping. And when she opened her eyes, there was Gib. Right in front of her.

"Sorry I missed out on the joke. Want to bring me up to speed?"

Swallowing down the last of her giggles, she said, "Not in the least."

Sam stood and engaged in a complicated handshake/backslap ritual with Gib. "Caught the end of the show. Surprised you didn't get pairs of damp panties hurled at you."

Like a magician unfurling an entire deck of cards, Gib fanned out a handful of business cards. "Panties are too obvious for this crowd. Seventeen business cards did find their way into my hands…my pockets…and I think there's one wedged down the back of my pants." He winced. "It'll be embarrassing if one slides out of my cuff in a few steps."

Daphne shook her head. "*That's* what you find embarrassing about all this?"

"No. Most of all, I'm embarrassed by my shocking lack of judgment." He took her hand, and his gaze caressed her cheeks so tenderly, heat rose in them. Heat rose other places, too. Places she couldn't think about with Sam sitting right next to her. "I should've told you at least ten times already how gorgeous you look tonight. I fear I haven't hit the mark yet."

"Night's still young, Moore," she taunted sassily.

"Indeed." He crooked his arm in an offer. "Ready to go?"

Confused, she looked around the packed room. "Now? The party's supposed to last another hour."

"And it will. Just not here. Not with me, at any rate."

"But your public's waiting for you."

He shrugged. "Don't care. Not about any of them. What I want is some privacy, with you. Only you. Say the word. I'll take you anywhere."

So he'd just been playing to the crowd? And was now willing to walk away from all those panting women…in order to make *her* pant? The night was turning around. Maybe she should've rifled through her mom's closet years ago. Confidence coursed through her with the heady zing of a lemon drop martini. Emboldened, she asked, "Back to your place?"

"Absolutely."

"I'll hunt up Milo and tell him to stick to his hunting grounds for a few hours." Sam kissed Daphne on the forehead. "Have fun."

"Not up to me. You'd better warn Gib to bring his A game."

FIFTEEN

Flowers are love's truest language
> ~ *Park Benjamin*

DAPHNE TRIED TO catch her breath. Kinda hard with her heart pounding faster than a long-haul semi with a lead-footed driver. She used the back of her hand to wipe the sweat from her forehead. "I expected more from the great Gibson Moore, lover extraordinaire."

"More of what?" Looking down at her, his brilliant blue eyes twinkled with silent laughter. Silent, probably, because he was panting just as damn hard as she was.

"Not sure. There's a mystique about what you do. People whisper of the results, but never the specifics. Kinda like doing a web search. No idea how the laptop found the answer—you just see it appear. Don't get me wrong. I'm not complaining. I'm just surprised by the venue for tonight."

Gib looked over first one shoulder, then the other. They'd paused for a break at the far end of the Millennium Park ice rink from all the other broomballers. The border of twinkle-lighted trees illuminated only a few families walking by. "Do you want to know the secret?"

"To your success in bed with women?" God, yes. She wanted to hear every single salacious detail. Daphne wanted to know what he did, in what order, and how long she'd wondered. Tried to imagine, and then felt guilty—skeevy—for wondering about her friend.

But now she'd had a taste of his particular brand of bedroom artistry. And she hungered for more. Craved it. Craved him. Would throw him down on the ice in this frigid Chicago night and do him here and now, if he agreed. It had been fourteen days since their first kiss. Five days since the hot and heavy session that steamed up the carriage windows. And two endless days since they'd made out like teenagers on his couch after the magazine party until Milo came home. Still no sex. Even though Daphne knew, from years of stories, that Gib was a sex-right-off-the-bat kind of guy.

So despite the fact that she wanted to drop to her knees and beg for his secret, she didn't. Instead, Daphne batted his broom off the ice with her own. Aimed for a sneer without even the least bit of shameless supplication to indicate how badly she trembled on the brink of desperation. "I shouldn't have to trade magic beans or anything to get it. You've got a smoldering gaze that weakens women's knees, and an accent that all but unhooks their bras."

"That's just the starting point." He balanced the broom against his thighs. Propped his elbows on the rail behind them. The corners of his mouth lifted infinitesimally into a mysterious smile. "There's one thing, in particular, I do when I'm out with a woman."

She'd been head over heels for Gib since they first met. He could read aloud from a calculus textbook and

she'd still want him with the heat of an exploding sun.
But beyond that, they'd all wondered for years how he
did it. How Gib charmed his way so effortlessly into
every single bed he set his sights on. "Tell me," she
demanded.

Gib crooked a finger. Her sneakers slid her across the
ice. She used Gib's body as a brake. Pressed up against
his side and reveled in the feel of his warmth against
her from ankle to shoulder. "Answer me this: are you
having fun?" he asked.

"Best time ever." An evening spent with her best
friend was always fun. A night of take-no-prisoners
broomball against the lazy, weak team Four Seasons
had scrabbled together to try and take down the Cavendish's? In other words, a guaranteed win? Always
good. Daphne loved playing, win or lose. Last time
they'd lost to the Ritz-Carlton's team. Gib was sure
they'd transferred up ringers from Brazil. He thought
he recognized two from a late-night soccer match he'd
caught on cable. She didn't care one way or the other
which hotel won the broomball tournament. It was just
nice to escape the constant prison of four walls in the
middle of a Chicago winter. Stretch her legs. Breathe
some fresh air. Even if the cold did sear her lungs. Get
her blood pumping, and hope that Gib would make it
pump even harder in a few hours.

"That's the secret."

"What?" Had she missed it? The giant silver bean
rising beyond the rink had caught her eye. Squinting,
Daphne had tried to see their reflection in its curved,

shiny surface. Did one second of inattention deprive her of knowing?

His warm breath whispered across the top of her ear. "I help women enjoy themselves."

"Makes you sound like a sex therapist teaching the finer points of masturbation."

"Far from it. The only real magic is in being able to read them. To know exactly what it would be that they most want to do."

Then why weren't they in his bed, right now? Naked? "You thought tonight, more than anything, I wanted to play broomball?"

"Not at all."

"But—"

"What you needed, more than anything, was to release some tension. Trying to stay upright in trainers on ice while whacking a ball with a broom? An easy, quick way to do it. I wanted to see you tonight. A cozy night on the couch ignoring a movie together—" he leered at her with all the subtlety of Groucho Marx, "—sounded like a perfect plan. But it wasn't what *you* needed. You needed the stress relief. So here we are."

"I'm not tense," she protested. Daphne was sure of it. Because she was expending an enormous amount of energy to just enjoy this time with him. To not let it be overshadowed by, yes, the immeasurable stress of the imminent loss of her best friend.

"Please. Stress is like high cholesterol. Denying it doesn't make it go away. You've got a bar mitzvah, a sweet sixteen and a wedding to prep this week. Four meetings with prospective clients. Your competition's in six days. We're running drills for *Flower Power* every day. It's got you nervous, rattled. When Ivy made you a hair appointment, you almost broke out in hives."

"Because it's a waste of money. Who cares if I'm on national television? The important thing is to keep my hair out of my face while I work. I'll just throw it in a ponytail and be done with it."

"No." Gib caught her bundled back hair in his hand. Wrapped it around his palm and tugged her into a soft kiss. "Let Ivy do this for you. It's her contribution to the win that Team Daphne's going to take home."

Oh. She hadn't thought about it like that. And it made sense. She and Ivy were a team. It was weird doing the competition without her. Ivy must feel left on the sidelines. "Aren't you perceptive? Maybe something of Doc Debra's did rub off on you." Daphne couldn't entirely keep the bite out of her voice as she said, "Besides her panties, I mean."

He cocked his head and frowned. "I've told you about most of the women I've dated over the years. Why are you so fixated on that one in particular?"

"It's just weird. You've got to admit that most people don't sleep with their shrinks."

"Ah, but how many want to? Look at Tony Soprano."

"Yeah, he's a stellar role model for you." Daphne bit her lip. They'd promised each other to give a *real* relationship a go. Something deeper, more honest, more intimate than their already-close friendship. Which meant no longer hiding her true feelings behind snark and smiles. Damn it. "She was the last woman you slept with. Right before all…this…started between us." She swirled her hands in a circle.

"So? She certainly wasn't the first. There's no white-washing my past. What difference does it make?"

Female neuroses were not easy to explain. "Pretend you went to dinner at Alinea. Had their sixteen-course, haute cuisine tasting menu."

"I don't need to pretend. I've done it." Gib patted his stomach with a satisfied smile. "Amazing. I could talk for days about how good it was."

"Exactly." Exactly what she was afraid of. "It blew you away. After a dinner like that, would you really want to go to SuperDawg and have a hot dog the next day?"

He shuddered. "That's one Americanism I never adopted. I wouldn't eat a hot dog covered in tomatoes and relish any day." Then Gib dropped his broom to the ice. Tucked an arm around her waist to slide her in be-tween his legs. "Are you saying that Doc Debra is the meal at Alinea? And you're the simple, greasy hot dog?"

"I wouldn't have called it greasy, but yes. I'm the hot dog." Damn it. Now, on top of everything else, Daphne desperately craved one of their pineapple Su-pershakes and an order of Supertamales. "So I'm wor-ried you might need a, um, sexual palate cleanser. Or that I'm just the palate cleanser before you move on to another sixteen-course meal. Or that you would never, ever stoop to sullying your taste buds with a hot dog."

Cupping her cheek, he slowly stroked his thumb down her jaw. "Such a lot of worries in that pretty head of yours. I knew you were stressed. Had no idea I was part of the problem. I'm sorry."

Hmm. Best friend and almost-hope-to-be-lover about to be deported? The thought of Gib's imminent departure definitely stressed her out more than any stupid reality television show. When she allowed herself to think about it. Which wasn't very often, because there were still almost two weeks left, and somebody was bound to snap him up.

"I don't want to disappoint you." There. She'd said it. And didn't feel one iota better for baring her soul.

"Daphne, I've had that sixteen-course feast. If you want to continue with this ridiculous restaurant analogy, I've had the cinnamon rolls at Ann Sather's, and barbecue at Roscoe's. Five-star meals at Charlie Trotter's, and that incredible lobster bisque at Gibsons. Were they all delectable? Yes? Could I go back and revisit them? Yes. But I won't." His other hand rose to frame her face. As if she wasn't already pinned beneath his electric-blue eyes, like a summer sky illuminated by lightning. "I'm choosing you. I'm not comparing you to anyone else. It's impossible. It would be like comparing sand."

It hadn't been that great being a greasy hot dog, but sand kind of sounded worse. "You lost me."

Gib chuckled. Dropped his hands back down to cinch her tight against him. "Well, the restaurant thing was making me hungry. There are millions of grains of sand out there—" he chucked a thumb toward the lakeshore, "—all of which would be easy to grab. Instead, I'm choosing the single, solitary diamond that is you. I don't care about anyone else. I've stopped looking, do you hear me? *You* are the woman I want. The only woman I want."

Good thing he had a strong grip at her hips. Daphne thought her knees might buckle. Gib had been kind to her over the years, thoughtful. Made it clear their friendship was important. But that was the most tender thing he'd ever said to her. That any man had ever said to her. She licked her lips. "I...I prefer the diamond comparison to the greasy hot dog."

"Duly noted."

A whistle blew, indicating the end of break time. Gib plucked his broom off the ice. "Are you ready?"

She'd been ready for years. She'd been ready since their first kiss. She'd been ready since first goggling at his face. "You have no idea."

GIB HUNG UP her coat in the closet next to his. "Good game. Glad we stopped those blighters before they scored."

"Maybe they'll spread word of our epic victory and scare The Peninsula's team so much that they'll forfeit in fear." Daphne looked down the hall toward his always-spotless kitchen. She'd once—only once—left a spoon in the sink. Milo's face had twisted into the same pained grimace as the time he passed three kidney stones. "Milo's not here?"

"Milo's going to an all-night gay comedy rave in Boytown. Starts at midnight, goes till dawn. Some sort of charity thing. He thinks it'll be a great place to find his soul mate."

"He's skipping right past hookup and boyfriend? He wants to nail down his soul mate?"

"Dream big, right? He might get lucky. If it doesn't work, the charity will still get the money for him sitting there all night."

"Good point." Milo gone for the whole night. They were all alone. The possibility of finally, *finally* making love with Gib flashed bright in her head. This was it. Except, for some unknowable reason, Gib wasn't leaping into sex. He was slow rolling it worse than a poker player with a full house. It was up to her.

"Cold one tonight. Shall I make us some cocoa?" He shut the closet, unbuckled his watch and laid it on the console table next to his keys.

"No, thanks."

Gib turned on a lamp, killed the overhead lights. Shut the blinds on the bay window. "I've still got half a pint of mint chocolate chip in the freezer. Want some?"

"Nope." She toed off her sneakers. Kicked them into the corner.

"Movie?" He crossed the length of the room, stopping in front of her with his brows kicked up in a question.

"Nope." What was that old saying? Nothing ventured, nothing gained? Daphne took a deep breath and pulled her sweatshirt off. She stood in front of Gib in only a black satin bra with scalloped edges. "For a man who prides himself on being able to read women? You're kind of falling down on the job."

His Adam's apple bobbed once, twice. "That will be the last time you make a comment like that all night," he promised. With the speed of one of those diamond-shiny vampires, Gib was in front of her. "Are you truly ready to do this?"

"I'm so far past ready I'm already halfway to orgasm."

"Don't. Don't rob me of a moment of giving you bliss." In the space of another single blink, he lifted her into his arms.

Well, she'd have to be dumber than a clump of moss to turn down such a request. Looked like he was on board with her plan. Gib carried her to the back of the apartment. Pushed open the door to his bedroom with his foot. But didn't carry her inside. God, now what? Second-guessing the whole friends-to-actual-lovers thing? Or something as simple as trying to remember if his condom stockpile was current?

"I've thought about this night. Since before New Year's," he admitted. "I always wondered what it would be like to take you to bed." Gib's voice darkened, deepened.

Daphne could only whisper back, "Same here."

"Since New Year's, I started to think about it in more detail. If, for example, I should just grab you the next time you swing by the office. Whisk you up to the penthouse suite at the Cavendish."

"The view's great." And she would've gone. In a heartbeat.

"But, if we do this right, you'll be too distracted to notice the view. Then I thought about lighting the fireplace next time we watch a movie. Seeing your skin painted in the shadow of the dancing flames."

She stared at the rapid thrum of his pulse in his neck. "Sounds hot."

"Then we'll come back to that idea. However, it's not right for tonight."

At this point she would take a quickie in the coat closet. Anything to get him to stop talking and start doing. "How do you know?"

"Because I've learned my lesson. Because you're special, and deserve a night tailored specifically to you." He carried her in and stood her on her feet. Kicked the door shut. In the thick darkness, Daphne scrambled to unbutton her jeans. Gib lunged forward and grabbed her hands. "No. Let me."

It wasn't the eighteenth century. She didn't need help shucking her clothes. Besides, getting naked could be awkward. Bending and twisting and jiggling. Daphne wanted to get between the sheets and get to it. "You're wasting time. Time we could be naked."

"You're half right. I've wasted too many bloody years ignoring what was right in front of me." Gib ran his hands down her arms, leaving a trail of goose bumps in his wake. "And you'll get naked. But please, let me do it. Let me do everything."

Funny how his words completely dried up her mouth—and moistened other parts of her so completely. "You don't have to make this into a big deal, Gib."

"It already is." He took her hand and pressed it to his crotch. "Don't you know what you do to me?"

Daphne didn't. Not for sure. Not until five seconds ago. But now, with her fingers spread around the considerable proof of his arousal, it was clear. As was yet another reason why Gib was legendary throughout Chicago. Lastly, it was clear they'd crossed the big line.

There was no going back to the way things were. Not after squeezing his glorious cock. "I'm getting the picture," she said.

"I hid from you—and from myself—the way you made me feel. But I always noticed. How beautiful you always are." Gib combed his fingers through her hair after he removed the elastic. Pulled it over her shoulders to fan across her breasts. The backs of his knuckles grazed her skin. "Your hair's like sunshine streaming down. Your lips taunt men with their fullness. I'd look into your eyes, and wish I could see them glazed with passion."

Mouth dry, Daphne said, "Maybe stripping my shirt off wasn't obvious enough. I want to do this, Gib. I want to be with you. You don't have to romance me."

"That's why I want to. Why I have to. There's no playbook between you and me. Not anymore. There's just the woman I adore more than I ever thought possible. The woman I crave. Whose breasts," from beneath he lifted, squeezed, "make me want to throw you down on the floor and jam myself into you."

"Sounds good to me." She yanked his fleece over his head. Flattened her palms against his abs. God, they were as hard as the ribs above. Gib's abs put underwear models to shame. In a mad scramble, she alternated between abs and pecs. It was just all so good, so muscled, so damn sexy. Daphne didn't know where she wanted to touch the most. And then she remembered that despite their make-out sessions, she'd never touched his naked ass. That pinged to the top of her priority list. But she barely made it a knuckle south of his waistband before he stepped out of reach.

"You can't touch me," he ordered.

"What fun is that?" She heard him open a drawer. Drop his shoes to the floor. Then—joy—the noisy unzip of his pants. Too dark for her to see much but a tall shape. Oh, how she wanted to see his body. To not have to peek out of the corner of her eye, but to fully stare her fill.

"Look, just because I can barely breathe with how bloody bad I want to fuck you doesn't mean I will." He'd practically snarled. Then immediately shoved her jeans to her ankles.

Obeying his signal, she lifted each foot to allow him to strip her. "Throwing mixed signals here, Gib."

"This is our first time. Not a frenzied bar hookup. This is us. Finally." Daphne jumped as he knelt, skimming the outside of her thighs. "I want to do it right. I want to take care with you. I want to take care *of* you. So you've got to stop driving me crazy with your hands and let me."

"Let you…" She trailed off. Despite his plea, she couldn't resist tangling her fingers in his hair.

"Let me touch you." Another skim, this time down her calf. "Kiss you." A kiss to the back of her kneecap that skittered licks of pleasure up her spine. "Lick you." His tongue swiped a circle around her belly button. This time her knees did buckle a little, against the strong wall of his shoulders. "Show you how I hunger to be inside you. Fill you." One hand cupped her through her panties. Pushed them to the floor.

She tried to remember to breathe. His dark promises tangled her into a sticky web of lust. "If you insist."

"I do." He picked her up. This time it felt different, with him naked and her almost, so many things touching in a new and exciting way. Daphne wasn't sure how long she'd be able to last, either. The panties dropped off her feet. "Like I said before, I thought about how to make tonight special. Just for you."

The words she'd always wanted to hear. Joy speared through her. "You mean I didn't have to strip in your living room? You planned this all along?"

"I hoped. Thought I could bribe you into joining me in here with the ice cream. Nice to know you were just as eager, though."

"Right. The last thing you need is an ego boost in the bedroom."

"Don't. No one else exists in here but you and me. There is no past. Only now, us, together." He gently laid her diagonally across the bed.

Softness enveloped her—and not just his six-hundred-thread-count sheets and pillow-top mattress. Spreading her fingers, Daphne felt…petals? Spread her legs, flexed her toes…the entire bed was covered with a thick blanket of rose petals. "You did this for me?"

"Only for you."

She laughed in delight. Then sucked in a breath when he drew a petal down her abdomen. Stopped breathing entirely when he flicked open her bra with his teeth. Circled her nipple with the edge of a single petal.

Daphne squirmed, reached for his back.

"Uh-uh." Clicking his tongue, Gib circled her wrists with one hand and pinned them above her at the edge of the bed. "Don't make me tie you up. That's something best saved for another night, too."

An entirely different, darker thrill ran through her. She'd fantasized. Had a hushed, 2:00 a.m., giggly conversation with Ivy in a hotel room about the different things they'd be willing to try. With the right guy. Hadn't thought she'd ever find a guy she could trust so completely. To put herself completely at his mercy. And yet, Daphne knew now that she had. That she'd follow Gib down whatever pleasure path he took her. She trusted him. She trusted that he'd never hurt her.

He pressed harder, smashing the softness against her. Swiping it back and forth, around and about. Its scent, and the scent of the rest, surrounded her. Enveloped her. Subsumed her. Gib picked up a fresh petal. Started anew on the other breast. Except this time, while he stroked, his mouth closed around the other nipple.

Daphne shifted, restless, hungering, seeking. Gib moved on top of her. His weight pressed one side of her into velvety, flowery softness. The other side of her body leaped to attention at the rasp of hair on his athletic legs, against her legs. The line of dark hair down his belly had always drawn her attention. Now she discovered feeling it rubbing against her? Even better than seeing it. And pressed at her core was the biggest, thickest, hardest—she had no words. Literally. Daphne tried.

She wanted to tell him how good it all felt. How good *he* made her feel. How each brush of the petal catapulted her into quivers. Each long pull of his mouth on her nipple catapulted her closer to the brink. But all she could do was gasp. Or moan, with a few sighs. The pleasure stripped her words, her thoughts away. Took her to a place where there was only sensation, only Gib.

Finally he let go of her wrists. Sat back on his muscled haunches that she stroked with her own thighs. "Be good," he warned.

Oh, well, if he was going to keep ordering her around, she'd damn sure find her voice again. "You'd better be great," she sassed back.

"No worries." Gib took handfuls of the petals, let them fall one by one onto her legs. Like some exquisite Chinese petal torture. Dropped a huge pile, light as a cloud, ever so slowly, at her hot center. Soon every inch of her body was overstimulated. Daphne thrashed her hips.

"More," she demanded. Begged. Sighed.

"More petals?" Back to a single one, the world's softest, smallest fan. He scraped its edge along the juncture of her legs. How could something so soft create so many sensations? So much, and yet not enough.

"No. More you."

"So…this?" Delicacy abandoned, he wrapped his arms around her thighs. Lifted her ass up and buried his face between her legs. The moment his breath steamed against her overheated flesh, she jerked. That brought her to his lips just as he chuckled. Those vibrations buzzed against her with his first long lick.

"God, yes," she moaned. Her fingers dug into the petals as she tried with all her might not to grab him. Not to do anything that might make him stop. It all felt so wonderful. Gib tasted, explored her as thoroughly as the first time they'd kissed. Took the time to discover what she liked, where, how much. What tensed her muscles. What made her breath hitch. What made her arms sweep restlessly across the bed now redolent with the scent of summer and love.

With one last kiss high on her thigh, he pulled back. Daphne heard the rip of a wrapper. The snap of rubber. And then the welcome weight of his hard body settled against her once more.

"Are you ready?"

She could barely stand the intensity of her feelings—both physical and emotional. So as always, Daphne resorted to snarkiness. "Are you going to shut up and get to it?"

Gib answered by slanting his mouth across hers. Plunged deep within her in a single, slow stroke. Daphne clamped her hands on his ass—as tight and perfect as she'd imagined—locking him against her.

"Hang on," he warned. Gib must've sensed how close she was. Must've been just as crazed and desperate. Because he rode her. He made her his own. Thrust fast and hard, a steady rhythm that almost immediately arched her back and clenched her toes. "Only you," he whispered. Then picked up the pace, arms holding her in an iron grip.

Daphne felt like a live wire jittered up her spine. From her breasts out to her arms, down her legs. Gathering electricity, growing in amplification, sparking through her with jolt after jolt of pure pleasure. Pure Gib. And then it all coalesced, melted into a pool of spreading bliss. As she cried out, a guttural moan tore out of Gib. One final thrust that shimmered an extra ripple of sensation across the top of her pool, and then he stilled.

They both just breathed—or tried to—for a few moments. With Gib collapsed on top of her, Daphne could barely fill half a lung. Didn't matter. Gasping underneath Gib was sooo much better than breathing freely anywhere else. Although when he propped himself up on his elbows, she did grab at the opportunity to reoxygenate her brain.

Once it was back at full capacity, Daphne realized it had been a while, and Gib still hadn't said anything. Not a word. Just hovered above her. Breathing. Staring. Judging? Scoring? No. They were past that. Past her insecurities and his string of ex-lovers longer than the Great Wall of China. Right? God, would she really have to break the silence? Wasn't there a page in the guy's rule book stating they had to speak first after sex?

Leading off with the fact it was the best sex of her life? Sounded too pat, too rote. Sex that made the room spin and the room disappear until Gib consumed her? Tell him that it was better than she'd ever dreamed—and she'd had her fair share of dreams about Gib. While it was all true, he'd probably heard it dozens of other times from every other woman lucky enough to be on the receiving end of his talent. And Daphne certainly couldn't share what threatened to spill right out of her heart. How she'd always loved him as a friend. Tried to ignore being head over heels in lust with him as a man. How having him inside her tipped her over into undeniable, heart-thumping, soul-sharing, forever and ever love.

If she asked what he was thinking, she'd be a cliché. The kind of girl that guys run from. But Daphne really, truly wanted to know. Before the whole relationship and sex thing, she would've known what to do. Whack his arm, tell him to stop breathing so hard like a panting perv, and go get her the ice cream he'd mentioned. Friends before lovers. Friends first and foremost.

"That wasn't weird at all," she whispered.

"Bite your tongue. It was sixteen shades of wonderful."

Whew. "Little weird now, though."

Gib reached over the edge of the bed, grabbed the comforter and covered them as he rolled them over. He nestled Daphne's head onto his shoulder. Kept his legs intertwined with hers. "I disagree. Do you remember our first kiss?"

"New Year's Eve? Of course." When she was eighty and gumming her applesauce she'd still remember that kiss.

"I ran around like a crazy person for two days because it was the best kiss ever. Familiar and exciting and different all at once. As if the woman I'd kissed had been hand-tailored for me."

"In the space of a few hours I've gone from being a greasy hot dog to a diamond to one of your Savile Row suits. I think I'm backsliding."

"Hush." He laid a heavy finger across her lips. "I'm trying to say something important. Daphne, you felt right to me from our first kiss. Being with you like this is the happiest I've ever been. It isn't weird at all. It's perfect. Best friend combined with best sex—oh, and a win at broomball? Equals the best night ever."

Daphne didn't want to jinx anything by agreeing out loud. Perfection was a pretty high bar to set...and keep. But the fact he'd say all that to her unprompted filled her heart to bursting. He'd summed it up, well, perfectly. Their friendship was like a seven-scoop sundae, and sex was just the layer of hot fudge that pulled it all together into something magical. Daphne snuggled closer. "I take it back. Not weird. Should I go with amazing instead?"

"That would be acceptable." Gib lazily caressed her back. "For now."

"What does that mean?"

"It means you, my beautiful girl, got me so worked up that I didn't get a chance to get to know you."

"I'd say you know me pretty well."

"On the surface, perhaps. But you and I, we're both sticklers for attention to detail." He reached over and flicked on the bedside lamp. "I need to see you. To see and touch and taste every inch of you."

Daphne blinked against the suddenly bright light. Sheet clutched to her chin, she was about to protest. Until her eyes locked on to the trail of dark hair at his belly. That line she'd obsessed over since the first time he'd whipped off his shirt after a run. She realized how equally badly she wanted to see all of Gib. "What about the ice cream? Shouldn't we refuel first?"

One jet-black eyebrow shot up. "Excellent point." He shifted her sideways. "I'll start with a dollop here," Gib traced the hollow of her collarbone, "a tiny scoop here," he licked the valley between her breasts, "and then eat my fill here." His hand settled, warm and heavy, between her legs. "We'll both be sticky, so then we'll move round three into the tub."

Daphne gulped. "Sounds like a plan."

SIXTEEN

To be overcome by the fragrance of flowers is a delectable form of defeat

> ~ *Beverley Nichols*

GIB CROSSED HIS ankles, leaning against the metal door to the walk-in. The scent of roses filled the air in this back corner of Aisle Bound. It reminded him of what had happened two nights ago, in his bedroom. Which immediately raised his dick to half-mast. Not that he'd once been completely soft since being with Daphne. They'd knocked off the list doing it in the shower, the tub, in front of the fireplace and on the kitchen island before moving on to her apartment the next night.

Actually, he'd stopped by her office to pick her up for dinner, and they'd moved on to a hot and heavy session on this very table. With her sitting on it, the height accommodated him standing perfectly. Their unquenchable need had been slaked enough to pick up a pizza and make it back to Daphne's. Where the pizza sat by the front door, cold and untouched, for almost two hours.

"That's pretty," he said, pointing at the bouquet she was assembling. Gib always loved to watch Daphne work. It looked like she started from sheer chaos, with the buckets and heaps of flowers around her. And then, with a few intricate twists of wire, she'd produce the most amazing bouquets. Pure works of art. Like watching a painter create a landscape with merely a brush and watercolors.

"Of course it is." Daphne never lacked for confidence when in her workroom. "See how the pitch-black centers of the ruffled white anemones pick up the black hypericum berries? And they fluff out around the tight white roses?"

There were a finite number of correct responses. Gib had hung out back here for years. He still hadn't graduated much beyond thinking all the colors looked pretty together, but he took a shot. "It gives the bouquet depth?"

"Exactly," she said with a satisfied nod. "Tie the stems off with a wide black satin ribbon—" her actions mirrored her words, "—and you've got an elegant winter bouquet. White and black. White and red. White, white and more white." Daphne scrambled the stems in front of her into a messy pile. "God, I'm sick of winter flowers already. Of course, in a few weeks I'll be ranting about how it wouldn't kill people to send something besides red flowers on Valentine's Day."

"We've all got hot-button issues."

"Tell me yours," she pleaded. "Distract me from this field of non-color."

"Gladly." It was, after all, why he'd come over. To bitch about his day to a guaranteed sympathetic ear. To the one person in the world he knew would be able to, amazingly, right his mood in a matter of minutes. And, to be honest, in the hopes of more sex. Gib didn't think it would take much to convince her. His girl matched him in the unflagging lust department. He adored her lack of restraint. The way she threw herself into love-making with a passion that both sapped and invigorated him. And how she laughed with him. It felt so good to not be performing, not be trying his damnedest to impress every time he reached for a condom. Instead, his motivation was first to make Daphne happy, and secondly to just have fun. So different, so natural, so easy. So fucking hot. "My day was crap."

"Really? I thought it started well," she said with a sly smile.

Ah, yes. Daphne had joined him in the shower. They'd gotten far dirtier before they eventually cleaned up. He'd been fifteen minutes late for his first meeting, but it was so worth it. "It did. But when you start the day so well, it's rather bound to go downhill. I spoke to my replacement."

"So soon?"

"There's no time for a leisurely transition. I'm leaving in a week."

"Maybe." She waggled her clippers at him.

Christ. If Gib honestly believed there was any shot at staying, he wouldn't have spent half the morning restarting a life in London. Arranging for a phone. Sifting through Realtor sites for a flat. Booking movers through the Cavendish HR office. "Look, I appreciate your optimism, but you need to balance it with a hefty dose of reality. I've made calls. Nobody is hiring. I know we agreed not to talk about it—"

"Then don't. What's wrong with the new guy?"

"He's a selfish wanker."

Daphne giggled. "That's your professional opinion?"

Professionally? Gib was sure this guy was capable of rotting the Cavendish Grand Chicago from the top down. "Christian's based in Los Angeles right now. He went on and on about moving to the prairie."

"Is he expecting covered wagons? Log cabins?"

"More or less. First he complained about missing all the movie stars. I pointed out that we host famous actors, politicians, titans of industry—he didn't care. Then he asked what he was supposed to eat out here."

"This man's the general manager?"

Of course not. Because thanks to this ridiculous new corporate policy, five managers around the globe were being repositioned. And none of them in countries that did him any good. "Nope. Only an assistant manager. This is a big promotion about two years too early for him. Told him I'd get our concierge to set him up with a list of restaurant recommendations. Turns out he was more interested in the nearest spray tan salon."

She pulled a new fistful of roses out of the bucket of water. "Did you discuss hotel business at all?"

He'd tried. Had asked him to fly out early to spend the day going over transition details with Gib. Christian had laughed. Actually laughed and vowed not to set foot in the "frozen ninth circle of hell" until absolutely necessary. "Not once I mentioned the weather. Christian hung up to go get measured for a tailored parka that wouldn't make him look puffy."

"So he's not excited about moving. Cut the guy some slack. Neither are you, remember? I'm sure he's not all bad. After all, you've got the Cavendish in such good shape, it practically runs itself."

Ben ribbed him about that all the time. It poked at Gib with the nagging fierceness of an impacted wisdom tooth. "Why do you people keep saying that? It looks easy because I work so bloody hard at juggling all the moving pieces."

"Sorry."

He'd poured years of his life into shining the Cavendish into a sparkling star among the luxury hotels. Gib feared it would begin to tarnish in a matter of days under Christian. "My staff is exemplary. But after talking to him for fifteen minutes, I've no doubt Christian will find a way to bring them down."

"Goodness, you are out of sorts. What can we do to cheer you up?"

"That's an easy one." He surged forward. When he lifted her by her waist, Daphne dropped the roses to the floor. Gib walked her back until she was supported by the wall. She wrapped her legs around his hips. "You want to cheer me up? Just follow my lead." Gib slid his hands around to her ass. Her perfect, heart-shaped ass that he loved to nibble on.

"Gib, we're not alone here."

"Yes, we are. Milo left for the day. I locked up behind him. Julianna and Ivy are out at a final walk-through with a bride. Just you, me and the anemones."

"Anemones and roses that need to be turned into bouquets before I can quit for the day. Sorry." With a quick nip at his neck, she slid down his body until her feet touched the floor.

The bloody wedding wasn't for another three days. Couldn't she see that he needed tending to before the blasted flowers? Now that he'd jumped with both feet into an official relationship, Gib wanted to realize some of the perks of that status. "Or, you could take a fifteen-minute break now."

"You say fifteen, but we both know the kind of break you have in mind won't clock in under forty-five minutes."

She had a point. Daphne made him insatiable in a way he'd never experienced before. And not just for the sex. The lying in bed after, talking and laughing had become the favorite part of Gib's day. "Fine. Be a boring, responsible business owner. I'll wait."

"Don't wait. Why don't you go to the gym? Run off your frustration with Christian on a treadmill. By the time you finish and pick up Chinese, I should be finished."

Not a horrible suggestion. "My idea was better."

"By far," she agreed.

"But this will have to do." Maybe he'd call Ben. Hassling his friend into sweating his ass off always put him in a better temper. Ben had a tendency to whine like a little girl during a workout. Always cracked Gib up. "Then dinner? I was thinking Bistrot Zinc. I've a craving for their cassoulet. Plus, you can't show up there in jeans. I'm more than eager to spend the evening ogling you in a dress and stockings. Any chance you've got a garter belt?"

"Perhaps I'll make you wonder all night. Will your night end with me wearing nothing but heels, a garter belt and a pair of pearl earrings?"

"A man can dream."

She touched her fingers to her ear. "Oh, that reminds me. I left my earrings at your place. Hope you didn't think Milo had turned into a cross-dresser."

"Not at all. We had that talk when he moved in," Gib said absently. His mind freeze-framed on the dangly blue earrings he'd seen on his dresser, but not processed. "Told him I didn't want to find bras and slips in our laundry." She'd left her earrings. At his place. Hadn't immediately called him in a panic. Knew she'd be back to get them soon enough.

Christ, but he was in trouble. In over his head. He'd been happier in the last few days than in as long as he could remember. As if tiny soda bubbles buoyed his every step. Or, to reach back to the A levels in English lit that he earned at Cambridge, petals of contentment now cushioned his heart. Part of him had taken for granted the add-on of mind-blowing sex to his best-friend relationship with Daphne. A simple upgrade. Like switching from DVDs to Blu-ray. Assumed nothing would change. Even as his entire world changed with one swipe of the bureaucratic sword.

Now she'd committed the cardinal sin a woman could make. The leave-behind. Classic gambit to force a return to the bedroom. Many women had tried. Gib never stayed in bed as a woman put herself back together. No, he did a full sweep through the apartment, making sure she didn't leave so much as a tissue behind.

With Daphne, he hadn't bothered. They were constantly in and out of each other's places. She had the better television, whereas he had the well-stocked kitchen.

A week didn't pass that one of them wasn't at the other's apartment. It never occurred to him to do a sweep after Daphne. Especially since she spent the entire night— also a first for Gib.

To be fair, he didn't for a second believe she'd done it on purpose. She didn't play those games. Never tried to use her considerable wiles to trick the opposite sex. No doubt the earrings were an honest mistake. But they signified so much more. As bright as neon, the earrings were a sign that she and Gib were morphing from merely a serious relationship to the kind that led somewhere. The kind with a future. And a future here in America was just what Gib didn't have.

"This isn't going to work," he said abruptly. Grabbed the counter for support as his world reeled.

"You don't think we'll be able to get in without a reservation? No big deal. I'm just as happy with grilled cheese sandwiches. As long as we eat them in bed. Naked."

"No. Not naked." Why? Why'd she have to leave behind a stupid pair of earrings? Why did they, of all things, make him realize that he'd fallen in love with her? So swept up in the sheer joy of being closer to her than ever that he'd ignored what a selfish bastard he'd been to take her to bed. As soon as Gib learned he had to leave, he should've stopped all forward momentum with Daphne. Instead, he'd given in to curiosity and need and desire.

He hadn't bothered to worry about what would happen when his plane inevitably took off. Well, hadn't *let* himself worry about it. Hadn't thought about how

fucking much more it would hurt to walk away now
that they'd escalated things. Now that he—God help
him—loved her. The crack beginning to tear his heart
in two threatened to engulf Gib. He'd barely be able to
choke out the words as it was. If she kept nattering on
about sex, he'd lose his resolve.

"Geez, you're really fixated on that garter belt thing,
aren't you? If we stay home, I can put on a lingerie show
for you." Daphne slipped the corner of her shirt down
her shoulder just long enough to tease with a glimpse
of an apple-green bra strap. "How's that for a compro-
mise?"

Gib couldn't beat around the bush. He couldn't ease
into it. He had to put his spanking-new realization out
on the table. "We have to stop seeing each other."

She laughed. "Is this like your whole no-touching
thing from the other night? If you see me in a garter belt, you'll lose all willpower and ravish me on the
floor?"

Yes. Absolutely. "Stop. Listen to me." He guided her
around the worktable to sit on a stool. Time to put his
own wants aside in order to cushion Daphne's heart.
He'd promised her, he'd promised the guys—hell, he'd
even promised himself. Above all else, he wouldn't hurt
Daphne. Yet already they were deep into a real, committed relationship. Gib didn't know how it had happened.
He only knew that he couldn't let it go any further. Not
because he wanted to be apart from her for a single minute. No, not for his sake at all, but for hers.

For the very first time, Gib would be leaving a
woman while still entranced by her. Before he'd had

his fill. So many years of platonic friendship. An utter waste, now that Gib knew how famously they got on in bed. But instead of being an easy add-on, sex had become a catalyst. And he cared for her far too deeply to allow that final transformation to occur.

"This thing between you and me? The being lovers on top of being friends? It has to stop. Immediately."

The laughter in her eyes vanished. "What are you talking about?"

Why did he have to spell it out for her? They usually ran on the same wavelength. But now, Gib's throat choked almost closed with the pain of his sudden realization. At the strength of the love that tightened his lungs and threatened to drown him.

"We have no chance of sharing a future. None. The clock is ticking. In seven days I must return to England. Us not talking about it doesn't change the basic facts. With such short notice, I haven't been able to line up any other jobs. I won't be able to. Period. We're both fooling ourselves if we contemplate any other resolution."

"Such a drama queen." But her voice trembled beneath the sassy sneer. "You're moving to England, not the moon. This doesn't have to be the end."

"Yes, it does." Christ, she was going to make him hammer his point home with a bloody sledgehammer. "We both have demanding work schedules. You can't skip a few weddings in order to visit your boyfriend, who lives a seven-hour flight away. And I've already been almost fired once. I'll have to buckle down like never before, just to claw my way back up to manager."

Bounding off the stool, she paced between the cooler

and her table. "There are such things as long-distance relationships."

Gib wanted to agree. Wanted to cling to the solution she offered. Wanted to snatch at every precious moment she'd grant him. But that would be selfish. Daphne deserved more. She deserved every bit of happiness in the world. She deserved a man who would be her partner, at her side every day, building a life together. And if he had to hurt her a little today to ensure she could find a lifetime of true love, well, so be it. He just couldn't tell her the whole of it. Divulging his newly discovered feelings would be nothing but cruel. Might even make her hang on out of sheer stubbornness, trying to find a way to make it work. Gib loved her enough to not let her put herself through that.

"Those are people fooling themselves. People who don't have the courage to live the lives they deserve. A relationship is built on what we're doing today. Waking up together. Venting to you, then sharing a dinner that erases all the madness of the day. Finding comfort in each other's arms at night. You can't video chat your way through a relationship."

"That's only one side of the possibility coin." She threw her arms out to the sides, voice desperately rising. "You could get a job offer and be back here in a month."

"Or not. Work visas don't grow on trees. Much easier to renew than to get accepted for reapplication. Other companies might follow the example the Cavendish is setting. We have to face facts. I'm as good as gone."

Tears trembled on her lashes. "Don't force me to give up on you."

He couldn't take her tears. Wouldn't be able to keep going if they trailed down her cheeks. Gib all but leaped for the tissue and gently blotted her eyes. "I don't want you to. But we have to do this immediately. A surgical strike, to save ourselves from getting in any deeper. To stop the pain from getting any worse than it is right now."

She snatched the tissue from him. Fisted her hands on her hips. "Is this all a ruse? Now that you've had me, you're ready to dump me? Is this what you see as an easy way to let me down?"

Tempting to let her think that. To let her righteous anger burn away the hurt. But he couldn't lie to her. Gib couldn't let her think she was anything less than amazing. Wanted to tell her those three words engulfing his heart that changed everything. But that would be beyond cruel. A burden he alone would carry. "God, no. There's nothing easy about this. Not spending every last second with you that I possibly can is impossibly hard."

"Then why?" Daphne reached for him, but Gib sidestepped her hands. Much like her tears, the temptation of her touch might derail all his good intentions. "Why miss out on those moments? Embrace what little time we do have left."

"Every touch, every smile, every kiss weaves us closer together. I can't do that to you. Not when each extra second of goodness makes it exponentially more excruciating when I get on that plane."

Those soft, pink lips hardened, and twisted downward. "Cutting me off is a favor?"

"It's a kindness." A kindness that was killing him

with every word. "I'll still come to your competition. I promise. I'll watch you wipe the floor with Sheila Irwin's hackneyed designs. Because you will. I'm so proud of you. For being talented enough to be offered this shot, and being brave enough to take it."

"So this is it? We just go back to being friends? You'll post pithy comments on my Facebook status updates? We'll both pretend that's a way to stay connected?"

"Something like that." Except he wouldn't. Gib couldn't watch her post funny reviews of new restaurants without wishing he'd been there with her. He wouldn't be able to abide, as the months went by, seeing her mention date nights—probably with that Adam fellow. They couldn't be lovers anymore, but they probably couldn't still be friends, either. He loved her too much to take that backward step. He loved her enough to let her go.

It had to start right now. Gib brushed a kiss on her cheek. Swallowed past the pain of a thousand nails flaying his heart to pieces. "Goodbye, Daphne."

SEVENTEEN

Flowers leave some of their fragrance in the hand that bestows them

~ *Chinese proverb*

DAPHNE HAD DONE flowers in every five-star hotel ballroom in the city. Most of the four stars, too, and a good number of the three-star hotels. She'd lugged her dolly stacked with boxes of flowers in and out of service elevators. Crept in when the rooms were quiet and left as the catering staff rose to a harried din as they finished setting the tables for dinner. Put a centerpiece in each hand, and she felt as at home in any of Chicago's famous hotels as a high-class call girl. But today was different. Today, she was the centerpiece.

The Millennium Knickerbocker Hotel had quite a history. Al Capone's brother was reputed to have run a casino and speakeasy in the penthouse. It hosted the Republican National Convention when Nixon became the surprise pick for vice president. The Rolling Stones stayed there. None of these facts intimidated Daphne. Nor did the twenty-five-foot gilded ceiling to the Crystal Ballroom. Not even the illuminated and raised dance floor where she'd be waging war phased her. What scared the spit right out of her mouth were the ten cameras ringing the floor. Were they all going to be pointed right at her?

From beneath an archway outlined in gold paint, her dad raised a hand in greeting. Next to him Marge waved about a hundred times more exuberantly. "How are you doing?" Stuart kissed her on the cheek.

"Contemplating throwing up." Daphne hugged both of them. "Although that would be a waste of the good-luck Belgian waffles Ivy made me."

"You listen to that practical streak of yours," said Marge. A tiny white rosebud nestled over her ear, almost hidden by the crimson tower of curls. "Puking makes you pale, too. Not worth it."

"Thanks for the advice. And thanks for coming. It'll help to have my own personal cheering section."

"This place looks like it holds five hundred people. I'll bet there will be lots of folks cheering for you."

"Closer to seven-fifty," Daphne murmured. She didn't take any pride in knowing the seating capacity. It was just one of those things she learned by osmosis from sharing an office with Ivy. "The balconies hold a lot of people. Since the cameras take up so much space, they're making the general ticket holders sit up there."

Her dad brandished their tickets in his fist. "Good thing I'm related to one of the stars. Marge staked out our chairs already. We're right in front of your station."

The competing florists were set up in a straight line on the wide, white-paneled dance floor. They each got a worktable and a wire rack full of tools. And, in a bit of free publicity that would thrill her whole office to the core, a banner with the company logo draped across the front of the table.

"Great. If you see me freeze, will you do me a favor? Stick out your tongue. Make a funny face. Anything to break me out of my panic coma."

Stuart patted Marge's shoulder. "Marge, why don't you go put your things down to hold seats for the others? Make sure you get enough for everybody."

"Sure thing." She kissed Daphne on the cheek, then scrubbed at the lipstick stain with a tissue she plucked out of her bra. "You're gonna do great."

Daphne watched her sashay the length of the room. "So you brought a date to my big day. Interesting. Did you have to promise Marge she'd get on television to get her to go out with you?"

"This isn't our first date." His always ruddy cheeks reddened to the color of a scarlet azalea blossom. "Just the first one you know about."

"Oh." So now Daphne's sixty-year-old father was having more sex than her. Way to rub salt in the wound. Not that he knew about Gib. Easier to tell him after the competition, when she wasn't using all of her willpower just to hold herself together. "Well, good for you. She's always been like a surrogate aunt to me. You can't do any better than Marge."

He jammed his fingers through his wiry hair. "Can we not talk about my dating?"

Daphne knew that feeling. Her well-meaning friends had all pressed her for details about Gib. They all wanted to commiserate with her. Impossible to keep their three-day-old split a secret from them. Not when

Milo lived with him and Mira was helping him organize his move.

Daphne appreciated their support. Knew she'd need it to make it through the next weeks and months without Gib. But right now, when it was still so raw, talking about him only burned like acid poured straight on her heart. She'd be happy to not discuss the love life of any member of the Lovell family for the foreseeable future. "Sure."

"Actually, I want to talk about your mother." Stuart dug in his pocket to produce a green velvet box. "You've got a lot of her jewelry. But there was one piece she wanted me to hold back. To give you on the most important day of your life. When we talked about it, she meant your wedding day."

Another hit below the proverbial belt—even though her dad didn't know it. "That's going to be a pretty long wait."

"Well, your mother and I didn't sign a blood oath. I don't think she'd mind my using my best judgment. I want you to have this today. To know that she's with you. To make you feel as beautiful as I know you are. As all of America will see you."

She took the box. When it hinged open with a click, Daphne immediately recognized the necklace. It was the one both her mother and grandmother wore in their wedding portraits. A cluster of garnets around a larger solitaire, reminiscent of a flower. Just holding it in her hand after all these years felt like a faint hug from her mother. Eyes welling with tears she refused to shed, Daphne threw her arms around her dad.

"It's wonderful. I'm thrilled to be able to wear it today. Will you put it on for me?" It was easier for both of them in that emotionally charged moment to have him behind her, out of eyeshot.

"Standing up to that Sheila person takes real backbone. I'm very proud of you. No matter what happens today."

"Thanks." She patted the heavy weight of the pendant in the open neckline of her long-sleeved white polo. "But don't worry too hard. I've got a good shot at winning."

Gib hadn't darkened her door—or even her Facebook page—since breaking her heart into a million agonizing shards. But he had given his competition preparation flash cards to Ivy. She'd worked with Daphne, putting her through her paces. Ben pitched in, filming her from every angle so she'd get used to the glare of a camera. Gib had also created a binder of recent work from each of the other competitors. It must've taken hours to pull the pictures from websites. Thanks to his hard work, she had a good sense for what design style they each favored. And knew how to turn that to her advantage.

Daphne had always been driven. One hundred and ten percent committed to creating the most beautiful, eye-catching arrangements in the entire city. With the love of her life soon to be an ocean away, she intended to throw herself even harder into her business. The best way to kick-start that new dedication would be to kick some serious butt tonight.

After another peck on the cheek, her dad wandered off. The room began to fill. Camera and sound techs in jeans and black tees put multiple layers of tape over all the cords snaking across the carpet. Four refrigerators were wheeled in and placed behind each station. They contained the assortment of flowers to be used tonight. Daphne couldn't wait to get her first peek inside. The host and judges huddled in director's chairs, receiving a final spritz of hair spray and powder. Audience members began to fill the seats. The level of energy, excitement and noise amped up with every passing minute. Her level of queasiness, however, remained pretty much the same.

Her friends pushed through the growing crowd to surround Daphne in a tight circle. "We just saw Luther McGraw from Southern Gardens. For a black man, he's surprisingly pale. I think he's nervous," stated Milo. He'd clearly dressed for the minuscule chance a camera might pan his way. A ruffled ascot frilled out of the high neck of a lavender tailcoat. All he needed was a top hat to finish the look, and he could pass for the Mad Hatter.

"He's not the only one," Daphne muttered.

"I've got you covered. Drink this," Ivy ordered. Obediently, Daphne sucked on the straw in front of her. The soothing tickle of ginger ale coated her throat and almost immediately settled her stomach. "You think I really let any of my brides drink champagne? Heck, no. When you're nervous, ginger ale is the only way to go."

"Just what I needed. Thanks."

"If you promise not to upchuck—" palms up, Sam waited to continue until Daphne nodded, "—I'll tell you that we've got a little celebration planned. My mom baked like crazy for you. There's chocolate pecan pie, turtle brownies, amaretto cheesecake and about five kinds of cookies."

The sweetness inherent in their gesture warmed her heart. That is, the teeny tiny speck of it that wasn't a bloody husk from already missing Gib. A party was exactly what she didn't want to do tonight. Daphne couldn't possibly let them know that, though. "Sounds right up my alley. Do I still get the cheesecake if I come in second?"

"Cheesecake, sure." Ben shook his finger at her. "But if you don't walk out of here with the big-ass trophy, then I do get first dibs on the pecan pie."

"Fair enough."

"Especially because you're going to win," said Mira. She smoothed a hand over the top of the perfect, bouffant ponytail that had kept Daphne in a salon chair for more than an hour. "Don't lose sight of that important detail."

"If all it took was sheer faith, you guys would have already earned me the trophy. I'm so glad you're all here." Daphne meant every word. But she couldn't help looking over their shoulders for one more person.

"Gib didn't come with us," Ivy said quietly. Her partner knew her so well. "We all met at the shop and drove over together. He said he'd be there. We waited as long as we could."

Daphne shrugged. But inside she was screaming *he promised* over and over again. "Doesn't matter. The guy's got an entire life to pack up in a few days."

"It does matter. And you matter to him. I'm sure he's

just running late. He promised he'd be here, Daphne. Don't give up on him."

She ground her teeth. Giving up on Gib was exactly what she'd been ordered to do. A detail she'd glossed over during her hiccupping, crying, snotty recitation to Ivy and Mira. She'd fallen apart for no more than ten minutes after he left her shop. Then a clarity descended. Daphne had focused on the competition. Locked away all her heartache and desperation into a thick vault in the deepest recesses of her mind. Once the competition was over, she'd give herself permission to fall to pieces. Even arranged for her part-time helper to come in and cover the shop for her two days next week. Daphne intended to spend both days nailed to the couch, sobbing until she literally ran out of tears. But tonight, she'd give this audience, and the entire nation, one hell of a show.

DAPHNE CLASPED HER hands behind her back. That way she wouldn't leave sweaty splotches on her lavender Aisle Bound apron. Oh, and the camera wouldn't be able to catch the slight tremor in her fingers that developed the moment the buzzer indicated the end of the first round. Go big or go home. That's what had run through her mind as she stared into the flower cooler. Their challenge for round one had been to make an arrangement that used fruits or vegetables along with flowers.

Easy. Do-it-hopping-on-one-leg easy. Many of her brides preferred a natural look. Daphne had made entire centerpieces out of herbs, or fruits. But this was a competition. Doing the expected just wouldn't cut it. Certainly wouldn't earn her the win. So she'd reached past the bucket of lemons and the adorable mini pepper plants for the less predictable. Now it was time to find out if she'd overreached.

Elegant and impeccable in a navy pantsuit, Sheila carried her centerpiece up to the judges. Halved lemons, cut side out, filled a square glass vase. Rising out of the center were branches of bright yellow forsythia. It was very precise. It also looked like two completely different things jammed together—about as cohesive as an alligator head on top of a lion's mane.

Daphne bit her lip to conceal the smug smile threatening to erupt. Thanks to Gib's research, she knew Sheila never used fruits and veggies. Lakeside Florist was known for their perfectly elegant designs. If you wanted an over-the-top, three-foot-high vase sprouting masses of lilies and roses, they'd do it up right. Perfectly classic. And, to Daphne's mind, perfectly boring. Which was, after all, the seed which grew into their long-ago split.

After a cursory glance, the judges beckoned Luther forward. In contrast to Sheila, he'd dressed to actually work in jeans and a logo T-shirt from his shop. His creation bore a similarity to Sheila's—but it was much better executed. A clear vase held whole carrots and skinny peppers in variegated colors. The brilliance to his design was that he'd left on all the leafiness. It frothed out the top of the vase, providing the greenery backdrop for the clutch of yellow-and-orange dahlias. Quirky, natural and fresh.

Maude went a different way, using ornamental cabbages to create a bouquet. They were pretty and looked like purple flowers, but didn't really follow the directive to mix flowers with food. She'd probably be the first finalist sent packing. So Daphne was brimming with confidence when she stepped forward. Her bouquet had three giant, deep-purple artichokes. Despite her recent, self-imposed ban on all Christmasy flowers, she'd spiked evergreens in between them. It was bold and gorgeous.

The three judges put their heads together. Covered their mics. Pushed score sheets back and forth. Mario Ferrante, owner of the swankiest flower shop in Manhattan, clapped his hands to quiet the low buzz of the crowd.

"For this round, we'll just do a best and worst. Best goes to Daphne Lovell's innovative and, yes, audacious presentation."

Applause swelled. The urge to let loose with a fist pump tensed all the muscles in her arm. Instead, Daphne let her smile break free to beam thanks at the judges. Good start. Nobody would question her last-minute inclusion in the final round now that she'd nailed the first design.

Mario continued. "It is not enough to point out the best. We at the judging table hope that all the contestants, throughout this entire season of *Flower Power*, learn from our critiques. The worst arrangement of this round belongs to Sheila Irwin."

Knocked out in the first round? With a tiny gasp, Daphne turned to look at Sheila. The older woman's eyebrows were almost to the ceiling. And her hands were fisted so tight it looked like blood might start leaking out any minute.

"Your centerpiece felt disjointed. There was no cohesion to draw together the elements. Your attempt at this design failed. And if you want to know how you could've fixed it, just look to your left." Mario pointed, with a faint smile. "Luther succeeded with this idea where you did not. Sheila, your flowers simply have no power." An officious wave toward the exit. "Please leave."

Well, that was one way to dispatch her archenemy. A bell dinged, signaling the five-minute break between rounds. Crew members scurried to clean up the stations. One guy rushed over, pulled Sheila's arrangement from her hands and dumped it unceremoniously in the trash. Daphne saw this as her moment to rise above. To be the bigger, better person. Gib would want her to be classy in her victory. There'd be plenty of time to crow over Sheila's downfall later, at the party. She strode over, hand extended.

"Good round. They really put you through the ringer each week on your way to the final round. Congratulations on representing Chicago so well."

Sheila looked her up and down. Stared pointedly at Daphne's chest, then dragged her eyes back up. "I'd still be in it if you hadn't worn a shirt two sizes too small. Everyone knows that Mario's a lecherous old goat."

Suddenly, the cold burn of revenge dissipated. It all seemed so petty. So what if Sheila had tried to blackball her years ago. It hadn't worked. Daphne's career, albeit in a complete juxtaposition to her love life, was thriving. A bitter woman on the downward edge of her own career simply didn't matter. "Sheila, let it go. I didn't ask to be in this competition. I didn't set out to undermine you. There are enough brides to go around in this city of eight million people. Can't we have a truce?"

The host, a peppy local news anchor in a red leather suit, jammed her microphone in front of Sheila. "What's it going to be, Ms. Irwin? Sour grapes or a sweet resolution?"

Sheila batted away the mic. "Why do you care, Mandi? It's not as if you're going to put a former employee stabbing me in the back on the eleven o'clock news."

"America cares." The perfectly coiffed blonde pointed at the cameras ringing them. "This *is* a reality show. We never turn the cameras off. So are you going to bow out gracefully? Congratulate Ms. Lovell on a solid win?"

Daphne kept her hand extended, waiting. Held her breath. She'd had no idea the cameras were still going. Now that she did, she wouldn't budge until Sheila finished this, one way or the other. With a snarl, Sheila grabbed a vase off her station and hurled the water in it at Daphne. It splashed her face and soaked her top. The white shirt did what always happened when wet, and turned see-through. Daphne clapped her hands to her chest. A low buzz of shock ran through the nearest audience members.

"There. I just gave you a leg up on round two. Mario won't even bother to look at your flowers when he hands you the win." Sheila stalked off.

Two techies rushed forward with towels. Daphne

couldn't do anything but laugh. Bad enough looking nearly naked on television. She didn't need two burly union stagehands patting at her boobs like the start to a bad porn flick. "I'm okay, guys. Really."

"Do you want me to ask if you can have an extra few minutes to change?" Mandi asked.

After that, the last thing she needed was any hint of special treatment. "Not necessary." Hunching over, Daphne untied her apron from her waist. Ivy had convinced her to wear it folded halfway down. Something about reducing extra bulk in front of the cameras. Now, it was a quick and easy solution. Daphne shook it out to its full length and fastened it around her neck. She swiped a towel and patted herself down beneath the apron. "Good to go."

Mandi nodded. Didn't bother to hide her relief. "Two minutes, then."

Ivy rushed over. "Are you sure you don't want to change into my shirt?"

"Nope." Calm had descended upon her once more. "You've seen me spill entire buckets of water on myself in the course of a day. Flowers can be messy. So what? I won with a dry shirt, and I can damn well do the same in the next round with a wet shirt."

Ivy glanced at the cameras. Didn't bother to lower her voice. "Sheila's smack talk didn't mean anything."

"I know."

"Nice touch, trying to mend fences with her."

"I thought Gib would approve." Daphne squinted to see past the wall of spotlights. "Did he see it? What did he say?"

This time, Ivy did lower her voice to a whisper. "He's not here."

"Not yet?" Chicago traffic was legendary in its snarliness. She could understand anyone veering a few minutes off schedule. But they were more than half an hour into the competition. Way past the hope-he's-just-gawking-at-a-fender-bender point, and deep into he-broke-up-with-you-and-wants-some-distance territory. It made sense. It also made the back of her throat burn with choked-back tears. "I kind of hoped he'd be, you know, a steadying presence. Unseen but felt."

"Look at you." Ivy lifted Daphne's hands. "You're rock steady. Gib trained you for this. For the actual bearing up under competition stuff. He's already steadied you. Remember that."

Daphne headed back to her station. This moment brought home what it would be like once he was back in England. Out of her life, for all intents and purposes. She didn't like it one bit. So she'd win this competition, and march over to his place so he could share in her triumph. They'd find a way back to being friends whether he liked it or not.

The bell dinged. Mario straightened his chrysanthemum-covered red silk tie. "Round two is about speed. Whoever finishes first will receive an extra ten points. It will give an advantage, but you'll still be judged on creativity, balance and overall beauty."

Fast was no problem. The only thing that might slow her down was indecision over which flowers to pluck from the well-stocked cooler. Without a bride's preferences to guide her. Daphne preferred to take her time when designing. So many options with so many lovely blooms. But they'd used speed rounds on *Flower Power* before. Thanks to Gib's homework, they'd prepared for this eventuality. He'd hammered home the importance of going with her gut. Ivy was right. In the seats or not, Gib was steadying. And she'd be grateful. Right up until she clunked him over the head with the giant trophy for acting like an idiot.

EIGHTEEN

Love is like a beautiful rose, it takes time and patience before it fully blossoms

~ *Anonymous*

GIB SLAMMED THROUGH the condo like a man possessed. He'd changed his tie three times. Changed his suit for a sport coat and slacks. How the hell was he supposed to dress to support the love of his life? Especially as he couldn't let slip that three-little-word detail to Daphne. Since leaving her shop, he'd barely been able to function. As if making the heart-wrenching decision to leave her had sapped him of all mental powers.

He'd completely forgotten the weekly update with the events manager. Told his London Realtor to let two perfectly good properties slide because he couldn't decide between living in Chelsea or Hyde Park. Left his gloves God knows where. Not in his coat pocket. Not in his briefcase. As he upended the sofa cushions, Gib glanced at his watch. Late enough that he'd have to skip meeting everyone at the shop and go straight to the competition.

He patted his breast pocket to be sure Daphne's card, at least, was where it belonged. Writing it had taken four attempts and kept him up until almost dawn. But at least when she read it, she'd know how proud he was. How much faith he had in her creativity and her designs. That to him, she'd always be the best florist in the country, hands down. Gib hoped it would be just the ego boost she needed to power through her fear of the cameras.

A knock sent him sprinting to the door. Milo must've warned them he was running late, and they'd swung by to pick him up. Gib snatched his coat off the rack. "I can't find my blasted gloves," he yelled through the door. Might as well try to fend off his misery by messing with Ben a little. "Ivy, you'll have to sit on my lap. Let me put my hands in your pockets to stay warm." He threw open the door. Not to Ivy. Not even to Ben. But to the little brother he hadn't see in almost ten years.

"Sounds like quite the plan," said Gerald. He looked taller. Finally caught up to stand even with Gib. Filled out from the way his face puffed. Hard to tell much more beneath the layers of winter gear. But it was still like looking in a slightly distorted mirror. One that shaved off a few years and lightened his hair to the color of ash wood.

Gib's mind whirled with a hundred thoughts. A pang of joy rose up at seeing the brother he'd always loved. Almost immediately followed by the remembrance that the same man attempted to send Gib to rot in a jail cell in his place. Love clashed with bitterness, hurt, anger, sadness. How to reconcile those emotions? Of course, if he'd figured that out, Gib wouldn't have set up shop on an entirely separate continent to avoid Gerald. He flailed at the most obvious question. "What are you doing here?"

"In America? Or on your doorstep?"

"Either, I suppose."

"I'm freezing my bum off. Going to invite me in out of the cold?"

Gib hesitated. Just for a moment, but he knew from Gerald's thinned lips that he had noticed. "Of course." As his brother crossed the threshold, Gib clapped an awkward arm around his shoulder. "Good to see you. I'm afraid you caught me off guard. I'm on my way out."

"Gibson. I've flown across the Atlantic to see you after how many years? Surely, whatever pressing engagement to wine and dine your latest bird can wait."

Not really. Nor did Gib think he could quickly sum up the importance of a reality television show competition. And he certainly wasn't going to try and summarize his on-the-rocks relationship with the only woman he'd ever truly loved. Better to sit down for ten minutes, find out what the hell was going on with Gerald and then shove off to the show. Gib took his brother's hat, coat, scarf and gloves. Checked his watch one more time. "Have a seat."

"I'd love a cup of tea. What they served on the airplane was revolting."

Gib headed for the kitchen. "International travel isn't for the faint of heart." Were they really discussing tea? Their big reunion kicking off with a review of the weak, oversteeped plonk served at thirty thousand feet? No. Time to shake off his shock and get down to it. He put on the kettle. Checked his watch again. Turned off the stove. Filled a mug and jammed it into the microwave instead. Gib refused to let Daphne down by not showing up. If he had any hope of making it to the show, he'd have to hustle this along. "What made you decide to pay me a visit?"

"A favor."

Gib froze, one hand in the tea tin. That couldn't be right. After maintaining only sporadic contact, mostly through their grandfather, his brother wouldn't actually have the brass balls to start in with Gib for a fucking favor. Would he? "Pardon?"

"I flew out here to ask you to come home with me."

Coincidence? That his past would chase him down to return to England the same month Cavendish all but deported him? Doubtful. He shoved the tin back into the cupboard. No tea. No more politely meaningless chatter. Gib was about ten seconds from flattening Gerald to the wall with a hand at his throat and demanding answers. He settled for stalking over to his brother, getting an inch from his face.

"Drop the act," Gib demanded. "You tell me everything, right now. Don't bother to sugarcoat it. Don't beat around the bush. Be straight with me or I'll throw you out so fast your balls will bounce up into your throat when you land."

Gerald had the good sense to quake backward a few steps. "All right." He smoothed his thin, navy tie. "I pulled a few strings to get you reassigned to London. You're supposed to be on your way back. Except nobody's received confirmation that you'll be on a plane in two days. So I trekked out here to get it all sorted."

Yet again, Gib was torn. Go with utter shock or mind-searing anger? No. It just wasn't possible. Castellan Compagnie was a huge corporation. They'd implemented a sweeping HR policy. Gerald, a reprobate who considered work beneath his status and partied away his days, couldn't be responsible for that sort of multinational restructuring. "How, exactly, did you get me reassigned?"

"I needed you back at home. But you don't write, you don't call..." He trailed off into a weak laugh.

"Don't," snapped Gib. "Don't joke. Don't fucking presume to toy with me."

"Living here's certainly roughened your edges." Gerald held up his hands when Gib charged forward, pinning him to the refrigerator with a shoulder to the chest. Fear and surprise flickered in his pale blue eyes. "Sorry. I know the wife of one of the Castellan directors."

Gib pulled back a little. "Know? As in you're old school chums? You decided to catch up over a spot of tea and she agreed, as a lark, to redefine employment in a company she doesn't even work for?"

"Fine," he huffed. "I'm sleeping with her."

Classy as ever. "There's so little on your résumé that you're trying to pad it by adding *adulterer* as a title?"

Gerald sneered down his nose. "Like you've never shagged someone else's piece of ass."

"No. I haven't." It was his own personal line in the sand, one he'd never crossed. Marriage might never have been on his to-do list. Not until Daphne, at least. Not that it mattered now, with him an ocean away from the woman he wanted to wake up next to for the rest of his life. But he'd always respected the hell out of people who chose to make that commitment. Sure, he'd been approached by more than one antsy-for-action wife. And politely declined. Gib refused to participate in the breakup of a relationship. He didn't need that on his conscience. And he'd found it to be much less hassle to scoop them up after a divorce. Divorcées tended to be quite desperate.

"Claudette's in an open marriage, anyway. The French are very broad-minded about that sort of thing. She knows I'm in a spot of trouble. It was actually her idea. Her husband's new to Castellan. Needed to take a stand on something to get noticed right from the start. This policy was as good for him as it was for me."

Disgusted, Gib dropped his arm and gave Gerald some breathing room. It certainly explained the out-of-the-blue announcement from Goudreau. On a business level, at least. Not on a how-the-hell-can-you-fuck-with-people's-lives level. "It never occurred to you that I might not appreciate this change in plans? Having my career, my life disrupted without so much as a by your leave? That I might see this as yet another horrible betrayal on your part?"

Gerald shrugged. "It was the only way to guarantee your return home. I knew politely asking you wouldn't do any good."

True. His likely reaction would've been to laugh. Dismiss it as a joke. "Why? Why do you care where I live, after all these years?"

"Father's remarrying."

And the surprises just kept on coming. Gib walked out of the kitchen, right to the antique server in the dining room where they kept all the liquor. Pulled out the first bottle and poured himself two fingers of whatever it was and threw it back in a fast gulp. Wiped the back of his hand across his mouth. "Was anyone going to tell me that he and Mum got divorced?"

"Oh. Sorry." Gerald hovered behind a chair. Probably trying to keep the entire table between himself and Gib. "It all happened rather of a sudden. About six months ago."

"I see." But he didn't. And even though the separation from his family was by his choice, Gib suddenly felt left out. Alone. Saddened more than he thought possible at yet another chasm yawning between him and his parents.

"Father started up with Clare Hastings. Daughter of the Earl of Falmouth. She plays at managing an art gallery in Notting Hill. Everyone knows she was using it to look for a husband. Father discovered he liked having a pretty young thing fawning over him. Left Mum and moved in with her. They're to be married soon."

"I suppose my invitation got lost in the mail," Gib said, hollowly. Wondered if his soon-to-be-stepmother might be young enough to be his sister.

Gerald let out an aggrieved sigh. "He's acting like a complete git. Kicked me out of both the London town house and the castle."

Did he even hear himself? Whining about no longer sponging off the parents in their multiple houses? Definitely what Milo called a first-world problem. "You're his favorite. Why'd he show you the door? Christ, you didn't hit on Clare, did you?"

He drummed his fingers. Flicked them restlessly over the curve at the head of the table. "We had words."

"Obviously." Gib refilled his glass. Decided not to be a complete bastard and filled one for Gerald, too. He slid it across the table and sank into a chair. Hoped that the connection between having his job in Chicago taken away and their father's apparent midlife crisis would reveal itself soon.

"Thanks." Gerald tapped the gold rim of the glass, but didn't take a sip. "He tried for the umpteenth time to get me to gear up for a run for Parliament. According to him, there are so many scandals in politics nowadays, the spots on my record are old enough to be overlooked."

None of this ranked as news. None of it explained anything. Gib was running out of patience. And time. Daphne expected him to be in the audience, cheering her on. It was the last thing he could do for her. "Why don't you? Let Father and his cronies set you up with a nice seat in the House of Lords. They don't make you wear wigs anymore. Buy yourself a nice bowler," he suggested. "You'd fit right in."

Gerald flattened his palms, straightened his elbows as if preparing to launch into a lecture from a podium. "It's not right."

That might be the truly most shocking thing Gerald had said so far. "Since when are you overly burdened by the concepts of right and wrong?"

"You mean because my life is one endless string of house parties and drinking? Well, it was. But not anymore." He pushed the tumbler back across the table toward Gib. "I've been sober for nine months."

Aha. *That* was the most shocking thing to fall from his brother's lips. It had been a long time coming. For just a moment, Gib could overlook all the ugliness between them and be genuinely proud of Gerald's accomplishment. Maybe, with this new leaf, there was hope for them yet. He lifted his glass in a toast. "Good for you."

"Ironic, isn't it, that Father kicked me out *after* I cleaned up my act?" Gerald gave a humorless chuckle. "It takes everything I have to stay on the straight and narrow. I can't bloody well be responsible for an entire constituency."

Not only sober, but also with a more mature outlook, apparently. Gib's respect began to rise. "What made you do it?"

He tipped an imaginary cap. "You did."

Riiiiight. "You mean from when I yelled at you to stop the drugs and the drinking before you killed yourself—that message finally sank in after ten years?"

Gerald shook his head. A shock of hair flopped onto his forehead. "I quit the drugs right away. Well, I didn't really have any choice but to dry out when I was in prison."

"Glad something did the trick." Gib pushed out of his seat. The announcement of his sobriety had earned Gerald a mug of tea. Just one, though. He pulled the still-hot water from the microwave and dunked in a bag of Earl Grey. With a jerk of his head, indicated that Gerald should follow him into the living room.

"Last spring, I took a fancy to fence again. Remember that summer we spent charging the haystacks at the manor with our swords?"

Gib gave merely a curt nod. He didn't want to be dragged down memory lane.

"My sponsor suggested I needed to find a hobby.

Start exercising as a way to do something positive for my body. This felt like killing two birds with one stone. I went up to the attic to find our old épées. Instead, I found a scrapbook. Mum kept it, hidden in a trunk. Full of magazine and newspaper articles from America." Gerald perched on the edge of the detestable white chair.

Gib, on the other hand, sank into the sofa and kicked his legs out onto the coffee table. Folded his arms behind his head. Might as well be comfortable while Gerald droned on with the earnest fervor of the newly reformed. "Of what?"

"Every time a movie star or head of state stayed at the Cavendish Grand Chicago, she'd clip it. Highlight your name if it was mentioned. Write little notes along the margin. Things like *Gibson's first South American president*." He scrubbed his hand through his hair. Pulled on his earlobe. "She always called me her favorite. But deep down, even thousands of miles away, you still mattered so much to her. I figured it was time I mattered."

The joke was on him. Gib didn't matter at all to his parents. They'd chosen Gerald over him from the day they let the doctors go prospecting for a bit of Gib's liver without so much as a by your leave. "Bully for you."

"Father's having another baby. With Clare."

On complete overload now, Gib barely registered that shocker. "Bully for him."

Gerald got up, moved to sit right next to Gib. "I want you to talk him out of marrying her."

This was the reason his life had been upended? Because Gerald didn't like a potential stepmother? Once again, he'd put his own needs above Gib's. And damn the consequences. Guess the introspection inherent in getting on the wagon only went so far. "Who am I to avert the course of true love?"

"Bollocks to that." Gerald slammed his hand on the coffee table. "The only thing he loves are the blow jobs she gives him."

Gib planted his tongue into his cheek. "Must be slightly more to it than that, or she wouldn't be pregnant."

"Very funny." Gerald braced his palms on his thighs, leaned forward. "Gibson, I need you back in London. Back to dining with Father at the club. Popping in to take him to lunch. Work your way back into his good graces."

"Can't go back to something that never existed in the first place."

He waved away Gib's objection. "Rubbish. Father's stubborn. Holds a grudge. But I'm sure he's missed you all this time. You're the eldest. His heir. If you make the first move to reconcile, he'll fall in line."

"All this just to get your bedroom back?"

"While that would certainly be nice, I've a far bigger task for you. If you stop him from marrying that woman, then the new baby won't be in line to inherit any of the family fortune."

Whatever kernel of respect Gerald had gained with that touching story of his journey to sobriety evaporated faster than boiling water on a subzero morning. "Seriously. You have it in for a fetus? For God's sake, I've never heard of anything so wholly self-serving."

"Nonsense." Gerald cuffed him lightly on the shoulder "This affects you, too. We two have to stick together. Protect what's rightfully ours."

Titles and money were the last things Gib cared about getting from his father. Ironically, probably the only things he ever would receive. "Do you think I'm sitting around, hoarding pennies, waiting for Father to die? I've my own revenue from the estate. Bloody sheep and alfalfa and crofters."

"Now that you mention it, could I stay there for a bit?" Gerald's tone was overly casual. As if asking for nothing more than another cup of tea. "At the manor?"

He needed space. To put actual, physical space between he and his brother. Or else Gib might give in to impulse, haul off and smack the supercilious smirk off his face. Was Gerald really that clueless? He expected Gib to say, *sure, bro, you got my visa yanked, let's have a sleepover?*

Gib got up, walked over to the built-in bookcase by the fireplace and stared at the photographs. They'd be the last thing he packed, and the first to unpack back in England. A shot of he and Milo three Halloweens ago, dressed as Batman and the Joker. The whole group at Ivy's family cabin last summer, burned to a crisp but grinning like idiots. A cockeyed picture he'd taken with his phone of him and Daphne at a Chicago Fire game, heads close together. It was his favorite of them all. These people loved him, respected him, understood him. They were his real family. The one he'd put together by choice. As opposed to the wretched excuse for a family tenuously connected to Gib by a random act of DNA.

Turning back to Gerald, he propped his elbows on the mantel. "Forget the manor. Forget the estate. Forget waiting for the Grim Reaper to pay a visit in order to line your pockets. Why don't you give my other income stream a go?"

Gerald frowned. "What else? Do you have a secret trust fund I don't know about? Uncle Charles used to favor you, as I recall. Did the old goat set you up when he died last year?"

So that's how it was. The only way Gerald could imagine supporting himself was by profiting from their relative's death? He shouldn't be too surprised. There'd been a whole cadre of like-minded people at university. Next in line for a big title and an even bigger estate. Content to live off the work of previous generations, rather than creating something of their own. Gib would have none of it. Didn't know how any of them could look in the mirror and see anything but shame.

Overenunciating each word, Gib said, "I. Have. A. Job." When Gerald said nothing, he continued. "It pays a more-than-livable salary. Now that your days are no longer riddled with hangovers, you might even learn to like it."

"Do you, though? Still have a job? Because Castellan doesn't have your transfer paperwork." If Gerald had ever held down a real job, he'd know that human resource departments were notoriously treacle-slow. And they both would've been spared this fact-finding visit. His brother leaned forward, hands outstretched, parallel to each other. As though trying to literally box Gib into an answer. "Are you really coming back to London?"

Tempting to let him twist in the wind. But the answer was simple. Undeniable. He'd been demoted. Said job might very well still be at the mercy of his brother's cheating schemer of a girlfriend. At least one person at his new company was spying on him. Brimming with that knowledge, coupled with how his parents had weathered major upheavals without telling him, and that Gerald was still a selfish bastard, Gib wished there was some other option.

The prospect of his life in England could not be worse—and yet it was the only place he could now go. Was it worse to go someplace where you knew no one? Or to return to where you didn't want to encounter the people that you did? Gib could swallow his pride. Scrabble his way back up the ladder at Cavendish. Suck up a return to his colorless, emotionless world across the Atlantic.

Hunching his shoulders, he picked up the snapshot of Ben, Mira, Ivy, Sam and Daphne. What absolutely gutted him, though, was leaving behind the real family he'd cobbled together here in Chicago. Gib hadn't ever realized he'd been craving love with the thirst of a dying man in the desert. That he'd been seeking the closeness and trust his family never showed him. Or that as soon as he finally experienced it, he'd love enough to sacrifice it. To leave Daphne.

"I haven't any other choice," he said with a shrug.

NINETEEN

*There came a time when the risk to remain tight
in the bud was more painful than the risk it took
to blossom*

~ *Anaïs Nin*

TROPHIES, IN GENERAL, were great. Big trophies, however,
were a pain in the ass. Daphne wrestled her two-tiered
golden cup atop a marble base out of the backseat of her
car. It stood almost four feet tall. Weighed more than
her toddler niece. And it clearly was no more eager to
be in the single-digit wind chill of Chicago than she
was. Reaching from the sidewalk didn't cut it. With a
grimace, she stepped into the gutter to get closer. Wet,
sloppy snow instantly soaked the bottom of her yoga
pants. Dribbled into her sneakers. But she hadn't stra-
tegically planned her wardrobe around being shin-high
in snow.

When the celebration party at the shop had finally
broken up, Ben and Ivy drove her home. Daphne spent
a good half hour sampling the trophy in different display spots around the apartment. Entry hall, dining
room table, even the wide lip of the bathtub. None of
them clicked. It finally hit her that it belonged at Aisle
Bound. Because the victory didn't belong to her alone.

Without Ivy's stint at RealTV, she wouldn't have even been thought of for the show. It was a team effort, so the team deserved to have the trophy displayed.

Gib had been an integral part of that team. He'd taught her how to overcome her camera shyness. How to power past the fear and indecision. His coaching helped keep her focused enough to win. Showing him the trophy, sharing her victory would be the perfect first step toward reestablishing their platonic friendship.

Daphne understood why he hadn't come to *Flower Power*. Or at least, she did once Mira and Ivy came up with an explanation after a bottle and a half of champagne. He must've needed distance to recover from the breakup neither of them wanted. As much as she wanted to see him, to touch him, Daphne certainly knew how much harder that would make saying goodbye. But she loved him too much to not have him in her life in whatever form they could manage. This insight came to her at one in the morning. Not really the time to do anything but jam her feet into the shoes closest to the door and go.

It took a belly-deep grunt, but the damn thing finally slid out of her car. Momentum almost sent her sliding ass-first into a snowbank. But the effort would be worth it when she saw his face light up. 'Cause really, who wouldn't smile at the sight of a trophy taller than Gimli in *Lord of the Rings*?

Daphne hefted the bulky proof of her utter flower-ificness onto her hip. Eyed the block and a half of icy sidewalk she'd have to traverse to reach Gib's place. Her feet were already numb. It'd be safer to just slog through the snow. Barely halfway there, voices traveling through the clear, icy night caught her attention. Her head jerked up. Safety first, in the middle of the night. She sure had one heck of a weapon at hand.

Luckily, the warm yellow glow spilling onto the walkway came from Gib, silhouetted in his doorway. Not just Gib, though. The dark bulk looked big enough to be two people. Sure enough, his arms lifted and a curvy woman stepped out of his embrace. A blonde woman. *The* blonde woman. Daphne was close enough now to recognize her. The one who'd been draped all over him at the *Windy City* magazine party. The one he'd slept with—his therapist, Doc Debra.

She tightened her grip on the trophy. Thought about using it as a weapon after all. Trouble was, Daphne wasn't sure who deserved a good bop on the head more. Gib, for dropping her to go back to his womanizing ways? Or herself, for stupidly falling for his speech about breaking up now to make it hurt less later?

God, it was all so clear. Gib didn't break up with her because he was leaving. Because he thought she deserved more than phone sex and a long-distance relationship. Because he cared so damn deeply. No. Not a word of that rang true. Not anymore. Not when his most recent bed buddy waltzed out of his arms in the middle of the night, only two freaking days after his supposedly heart-wrenching breakup with Daphne.

Oh, and look at that. For some reason her feet kept propelling her forward. The full moon shone down brightly through the leafless branches. It, coupled with the nearby streetlight, provided an almost spotlight on Debra kissing him good-night. Great. Just the visual she needed burned into her brain. It could only mean that Gib ended things because he wanted to play the field again. Go back to his new day/new woman regimen. That he'd given commitment a shot for what, less than a week, and found it not to his liking.

It should hurt. It should devastate her. But since Gib had already decimated her heart into little more than a beating pool of blood, Daphne couldn't really tell. She turned around to slink back to her car before he even shut the door. Chalk up her decision to go on this misguided late-night escapade to a massive sugar overdose from the party. Just go home and pretend he'd already left. After all, in two days there'd be four states, an ocean and, depending on the flight path, one or two countries between them. Out of sight, out of mind. At least, Daphne hoped it'd be that easy.

Then the trophy slipped a little. As did her pants—the drawstring of which she'd been in too much of a rush to bother to tie. Daphne made a wild grab, caught the pants, but dropped the trophy. It landed with a spectacular crack of marble against cement, and then a resounding bong from the metal of the trophy bowl.

The even worse sound was that of Gib's voice. "Daphne? Is that you?"

Shit. Of course he'd heard her. The trophy rang louder than the Sunday mass bells at St. Hyacinth Basilica. And of course he recognized her, due to the whole best-friends-until-two-days-ago thing. No slinking home now. "Um, yeah."

"Are you okay?" He jogged down the sidewalk, no

coat, no gloves. Just fleece pants, a thin cotton Manchester United shirt and a worried expression.

"Yeah. Fine." She tied off her pants.

"What is…" His voice trailed off. Gib looked down at the now cracked but still gleaming marble pedestal broken off at her feet. Over to the wide gold top of it lying half in the street. He picked it up, shook off the snow and carried it over to her. "Oh my God. You won?"

Daphne snatched it from him. "Yeah."

"That's brilliant!" Arms wide open, he rushed forward as if to hug her. Daphne held her broken trophy up like a shield.

"Don't. Don't come any closer. Don't touch me. Just…don't."

"What? Why? What's wrong?"

She'd save the self-recrimination about her questionable judgment for later. Right now, though, she'd be more than happy to tell Gib what was wrong with him. Screw taking the high road. He'd hurt her. Made a fool of her. Tossed her love aside as if it were as disposable as a condom. This could very well be the last conversation they ever had face-to-face. She damn well wouldn't skip the opportunity to give him a piece of her mind. "I'm not blind, Gib. I saw what just happened."

"You mean dropping the trophy?" He squatted in the snow to pick up the hunk of marble. "Looks like a clean break. Come inside. I think we've got some superglue in the junk drawer. It'll fix this right up."

"The trophy doesn't matter. Well it does, but not like you do. Like you did. To me."

"You want to add a few more sentence parts so I can figure out what you're talking about?"

Really? He was going to make her spell it out? Rub her face in it? "I saw you and Doc Debra just now. The hugging. The kissing."

Gib ducked his head. Cleared his throat. His breath hung in the icy air like cartoon thought bubbles. "Ah. Well, what you saw wasn't what it looked like—"

She cut him off by jabbing out her hand, upraised. "Uh-uh. No explanation necessary. Spare me the details. We don't have that kind of a friendship anymore."

"That kind?" he mocked. She could hear the air quotes in his voice. "Have you drawn up a revised friendship agreement? Is that why you came over? Brought me two copies to initial? Is there a notary public waiting in your car?"

"I came over to share this with you." She thrust the top half of the trophy back at him. When he didn't take it, she let it fall back to the ground. "I came over here to thank you. And yes, to make a fresh start. We didn't end things on anything close to a good note. Now I know why." She tapped her head with her index finger. Of course, wearing puffy mittens, it probably looked stupid. Like she was slapping herself.

"Do you?" Gib snapped out the words, obviously pissed. Brows drawn together into a straight line of fury. Of course, he also looked half-frozen. But hey, it was his stupid idea to run out to her without a coat. He could walk back inside any minute. Maybe guilt was keeping him frozen to the spot.

"You promised me no more lines. No more well-used

speeches. No reruns of anything you'd done with your legions of women. But it turns out that what you gave me was nothing more than a variation on that oldie but goodie, it's not you, it's me." Mimicking him, Daphne used her admittedly horrible British accent. "'Break up now, before we care too much for each other.' Can't believe I fell for it. I should've known that you couldn't— no, wouldn't—commit. I should've known you weren't ready." Righteous anger was the only thing that kept her voice from catching on the tears clogging her throat. "I should've known better than to trust you."

Gib thumped his sternum. "I am not your problem. Trusting me was never the problem. The real problem with you, Daphne? It's that you don't trust yourself. You don't believe in yourself. Sound familiar? Because it's the very problem I identified when I started coaching you for the competition."

"What are you saying? That I need to Tinker Bell myself? If only I believed in myself as a sexy, beautiful woman, you wouldn't feel the urge to screw the first bimbette who walks by?"

His mouth quirked into an expression she couldn't decipher. Then he shivered. "Something like that."

Maybe he had an eighth of a percent of a point. Maybe. Something for Daphne to mull as she started the lengthy process of trying to get over the love of her life. But it in no way excused his behavior. "Well, I believed in us, Gib. I thought that would be enough." She spread her arms, palms up. Took one last look at his sharp cheekbones. Meltingly beautiful eyes. The sexiest, most well-shaped lips she'd ever seen on a man. The lips she'd hoped to spend a lifetime kissing. "Guess I was wrong. Good-bye, Gib." Daphne turned and walked away. Hoped the snow crunching underfoot would mask the sound of her breath hitching. And felt the tears freeze on her cheeks as they began to fall.

GIB COULD FEEL Agatha's gaze on him as he lifted his luggage out of her trunk. She'd insisted on driving him to O'Hare. Had filled his ears the entire way on I-94 with complaints about her new boss. But now her silence was even louder.

"Out with it, woman. You've never been shy about expressing your opinion. I can tell you're itching to lay some last bit of wisdom on me before I leave. It had better not be a reminder to wear my raincoat."

She shook her head, making the cream tassel on top of her knit hat bounce. "No advice. I'm just worried about you. The way I'd worry about my own son."

Certainly far more concern than his own mother had ever shared. God, he'd miss Agatha. "No need to worry. After all, I've hit bottom. In one fell swoop, I've lost a job I loved, the true family I forged here, and my best friend." He dropped his suitcase to the curb, crossed his arms over his chest. Grimly continued to recount the cesspool his life had become. "To top it off, I know I'm head over heels in love with Daphne. She is the only woman for me."

"You should know. You've certainly comparison shopped enough for three men."

Gib ignored her jab, just like he had every other dis-approving comment over his dating choices she'd sent his way. "And I love her too much to drag her off to share an uncertain and jobless future. For God's sake, she's a partner in two businesses here. Has family she actually cares about. I'm certainly not enough of a prize to yank her away from all that. My family situation's shit and my job's at the mercy of my brother's mistress. I would give anything to stay with Daphne. The old, selfish Gib would've stuffed her into my suitcase and taken her to England. But I won't ask her to sacrifice her happiness for me."

Matching crinkles of approval bracketed her eyes and lips. "Oh, Gibson, I've said it before, and I'll say it again. You truly are a good man. I'm sorry your current reward for that is life pissing all over you."

He ratcheted his lips into a tight smile. "So if you think about it, I've nowhere to go from here but up."

Agatha enveloped him in a tight hug that strained the seams of her wool coat. "Good luck, Gibson."

"I'll miss you." He waved as she pulled into traffic. Basked in what was probably his last sunny sky for a while, then trudged inside. If anything, the noise level increased. The loudspeaker mumbled loudly almost nonstop. Every line for security stretched out to the check-in counters. Gib couldn't have picked a busier afternoon. Suddenly, exhaustion washed over him. Looked down at the gray-and-white checkerboard tiles, and couldn't summon the energy to go any farther. He sank onto a bench. The bloody endless lines would still be there when he was ready. Gib just needed a moment to regroup.

Shrugging out of his overcoat, he laid it on top of

his pile of suitcases. Rolled his head to stretch the crick in his neck, and saw Sam, of all people. Looking more than a little ridiculous, as he held two tall stalks covered with flowers as bright blue as an Easter egg out in front of him.

"Damn it, I told you I didn't want a big send-off." But he'd grab at any excuse to spend a few more minutes with the guy. As Gib stood, he felt a grin stretch wide across his face. "What's with the mini bouquet? It's a little on the small side to give to Mira. You might want to get Daph to fill it out with some roses or something."

"It's for you." Sam shuffled his feet. Looked up at the skylights while he handed over the flowers. "They're forget-me-nots. In the language of flowers, they mean *true love*."

Gib looked down at the vibrant splotches of yellow at the center of each flower. He'd never been more confused. "Pardon me?" When he looked back up, Mira was only a few steps away. She picked up the pace when she caught his eye, her long legs stretching across the checkerboard tiles. Needle-sharp heels clattered with a distinctive ping.

She handed him a sprig of white flowers. Delicate purple veins spread across the bottom of each petal. "These are white violets. They say *let's take a chance on happiness*."

Gib looked from Mira to Sam, then back again. "I think you're both off your rockers. Definitely the weirdest going-away presents ever. Thanks, though. Nice of you two to come see me off."

"Oh, there's more than just two of us," said Mira. She pointed back toward the entrance.

Panting slightly, Ben jogged through the doors and over to them. "Sorry. Parking was a bitch. Sweet ride, though," he said with a wink.

Panic shot through Gib. He'd left the keys to his precious Moll Davis with Ben. And the first thing he'd done was stick her in rush-hour traffic? "Airport parking lots are a free-for-all. Do you realize how likely it is she'll get dinged?"

"It was an emergency. I didn't have any choice."

"What? What the hell was an emergency?"

"This." From behind his back, Ben produced a clutch of light purple, five-petaled flowers. "It's lungwort. Most hideously named flower ever." He looked at Mira. "I feel like an idiot. Do I really have to say it?"

Before she could answer, Ivy scooted in next to her fiancé. Her cheeks were flushed as if she'd run from the parking lot, too. The ends of the pink ribbon around her ponytail flapped against her neck. "Yes. Romance won't kill you, Ben. We've been over this."

"Fine." He thrust the flowers at Gib. "In the Victorian flower language, these mean *thou art my life*."

Gib was picking up on a theme. He just didn't know what to make of it. "Thanks. I think."

Ivy whipped a long, trailing cutting of ivy out of her shoulder bag. "*Wedded love and fidelity*."

He took it from her. "Same to you?" Was anyone going to explain what the hell was going on? There were two hours to fill before his flight, but this was downright weird. Weirder still when Milo pushed his way out of the stream of travelers along with a tall, older man Gib had never seen before.

"Coral roses signify *desire*." He waggled his eyebrows suggestively and rolled his hips as he handed the long-stemmed blossoms to Gib.

"We slept ten feet away from each other for how many years, and you wait to seduce me in an airport?" Gib heaved an exaggerated sigh. "Bad timing, mate."

"Well, I know a lost cause when I see one. Besides, my unrequited desire's not the issue."

The loose semicircle formed by his friends parted. There stood Daphne. The sight of her stole his breath away. And shattered his heart all over again. She wore the white sweaterdress that she'd worn to the magazine party. The one that clung to her like a sexy second skin. Her hair fell in loose waves down her back. And in her hands was a single yellow flower, its stem wrapped in florist tape as a boutonniere. As she pinned it to his lapel, she said, "This is a jonquil. It translates to *return my affection*."

He grabbed her hand. Drank in the unexpected sight of her before him. Helpless to respond with anything in that moment but the truth, he said, "I do."

Eyes bright, she triple blinked. "A week ago, you jokingly said something to me. At the party. The more I thought about it, the more I realized you were on to something."

What the hell had they talked about at that party? He racked his brain to think, but he couldn't. Gib could only stare at Daphne, grateful for every extra second he got to spend with her. And pretty damn relieved she didn't seem ready to clock him anymore.

"So I'm going to repeat it to you, word for word. With a slight twist. I'm not joking." Daphne rubbed her hands together, then dropped them at her sides. "The solution's right in front of you. Gib, I'm giving you a reason to stay." Awkwardly, she dropped to her knees. Then she grabbed his hand. "Will you marry me?"

He didn't believe her. Half expected a camera crew to pop out from behind a ticket counter. For the life of him, Gib didn't know what to say.

"You see, I was upset when I said all those horrible things to you." She rushed on, her words spurting out faster than a shaken-up soda. "But I heard what you said, too. I should've had more faith in myself. I should've realized you only left me to protect my heart. It doesn't matter that you hooked up with Debra after."

"But I didn't," he protested. The truth might as well come out now. Gib couldn't hold anything back from her. Not anymore. "When we quarreled that night, I thought it would be easier for you to hate me than to pine for me. It was why I let you walk away. Hell, why I goaded you to walk away. That was stupid." He dropped to his knees to look her in the eyes. Laid the flowers on the ground so he could take both her hands. "Please, you have to let me explain."

"It's not necessary."

Yes, it was. He couldn't let any speck of hurt or doubt linger in her heart. "It is if I want a clean slate. Look, I had every intention of going to *Flower Power*. As I was leaving, my brother showed up unannounced."

All his friends gasped. It was almost funny. "Good surprise or bad?" asked Daphne.

"I'd call it the emotional equivalent of the napalm drops back in Vietnam. By the time Gerald left, I was a wreck. I placed an emergency call to Doc Debra so she could help me deal with it. She stepped back into her role as my therapist. All she did was help me—as a professional and as a friend—come to terms with returning home. Aside from saying goodbye, nothing physical happened." Gib gripped her hands even tighter, trying to squeeze the naked truth in his words straight into her. "It couldn't, because I'm so in love with you, Daphne."

Her smile broke across her face with the soft promise of a rainbow. "That's the first time you've said it."

More fool him. "I'll tell you every day, every hour, if you'll let me." He moved her hand onto his chest. "Do you feel that? You're the reason my heart's beating so hard. You're the reason it wants to beat at all. It was a hollow shell when I moved here. And you, you filled it with laughter and life and happiness."

"I want to be your reason to stay—and I want you to choose to stay, with me. Gib, we built such a strong foundation of friendship. Then wove together even tighter as lovers. Now I want us to take the final step. Become husband and wife. Not so you can stay in America. But so you can stay with me."

Without her hand there, his heart might very well fly right out of his chest. "I'm not much of a catch." Gib thought of the behind-the-scenes machinations his brother had already engineered once. Who's to say he wouldn't try again? "There's no guarantee the Cavendish will slot me right back into Chicago. Doc Debra offered to hook me up with a part-time job teaching hotel management at the college where she's on the faculty. It wasn't enough of a job to legally keep me here, but now it could give me a foothold while I continue to search for something more."

"It'll all work out. As long as we're together. I love you so much, Gib."

"I promise to make you proud of me." He shook his head. "No, more importantly, I promise that you are now, and will always be, more than enough woman for me. There's no one in the world better for me."

"And believe me, he's looked," deadpanned Milo.

As of right now, he was closing the book on that chapter of his life. Starting fresh. Starting over as a one-woman man. The only woman for him. He stood, and tugged her up with him. "Call me traditional, but I want to do this right. Your proposal means the world to me. But you have to know how much I want to be with you. You've been brilliant, knocking against my thick skull. Making me fall in love with you just by being yourself."

Daphne swiped at the tear trailing down her cheek. "If I'd known all I had to do was be myself, I'd have kissed you in the dark and set things in motion years ago."

"I've cocked this up so many times. Been a blind, buggered idiot. I need to start fresh with you. Please, let me make the grand gesture. Let me prove to you, for once and for all, that you take precedence over everything and everyone else. That you are my whole life."

More tears sparkled in her eyes. She nodded wordlessly.

Gib dropped back down to one knee. Took her left

hand and cursed the lack of a ring. She deserved the bloody Crown Jewels for putting up with him. But all he could do for now was press his lips to her fourth finger, where he'd soon put a diamond to seal their love.

"I didn't know I could be so full of love. That I could look at you and see a future of happiness reflected back at me. Will you marry me? Promise to always be my best friend and lover? Vow to let me adore you with all that I am for all the days to come? Because nothing would make me happier than to spend the rest of my life with you, Daphne."

Another nod. A sniffle, then a tight squeeze of his hands. "Starting right now, I hope. Right here. We've brought along Judge Henderson to perform the ceremony so you can legally remain in the country."

Looked like Daphne was one step ahead of him, yet again. How'd they manage to scoop up a judge and drag him out to the airport? "You've got a judge on retainer now at Aisle Bound?"

"You aren't the only one in this town with connections," said Ivy. "He's a friend of my father's. There's some paperwork to be cleared up, and you'll have to go a few rounds with the INS. But it's all legal and binding, I assure you."

The gray-haired man stepped forward. "Judge Martin Henderson." Shook his hand. "Daphne convinced me to help with this unusual ceremony by explaining that you've been best friends for years. That should smooth over most any wrinkles that arise."

"She's my very best friend. And always will be." Gib

stood, pulling Daphne up with him. Wanted to sweep her into his arms, but Ivy pulled them apart.

"We'll do the ceremony in a chapel over in Terminal 2. Don't worry, it's outside the security checkpoint." Ivy picked up the flowers and handed them to Daphne. "There's your bridal bouquet."

"I should've known you'd have a plan."

"Yes, you should have," she sassed back.

"I made the same mistake once," said Ben. "Look where that got me." He kissed Ivy's finger, right above her engagement ring.

"We've got you covered for the rings, too." Sam unfolded a handkerchief. Inside were two green rings, plaited out of flower stems. "At least for today. You might want to upgrade to something less biodegradable soon, though."

"They're perfect." He twined his fingers through Daphne's. A simple act he'd done time and time again. This time, it felt like coming home. England hadn't been home for a long time, and neither was America. It was Daphne that was his home.

"Of course, we'll throw you a bigger, better wedding." Mira patted his arm. "Just give us a few months to pull it together."

Gib looked at his friends—no, his family—clustered around him. Looked down at the beautiful woman who'd poked holes in the casing around his empty heart, and cascaded love into it. Knew that he'd never, ever let her go. "This is perfect."

Ivy's ubiquitous schedule would have to wait. A man had priorities, after all. So there, in the middle of the airport teeming with strangers and surrounded by friends, Gib kissed Daphne. Claimed her as his friend. His lover. His bride. His one and only.

* * * * *